One 28th. THE PRIVATEER CAPTAIN HAILS THE BOAT. Frontis.

ONE OF THE 28TH.

A TALE OF WATERLOO.

By G. A. HENTY,

Author of "*Bonnie Prince Charlie,*" "*With Clive in India,*" "*The Dragon and the Raven,*" "*The Young Carthaginian,*" "*The Lion of the North,*"

ILLUSTRATED:

A. L. BURT COMPANY,
PUBLISHERS,   NEW YORK.

PREFACE.

ALTHOUGH in the present story a boy plays the principal part, and encounters many adventures by land and sea, a woman is the real heroine, and the part she played demanded an amount of nerve and courage fully equal to that necessary for those who take part in active warfare. Boys are rather apt to think, mistakenly, that their sex has a monopoly of courage, but I believe that in moments of great peril women are to the full as brave and as collected as men. Indeed, my own somewhat extensive experience leads me to go even further, and to assert that among a civil population, untrained to arms, the average woman is cooler and more courageous than the average man. Women are nervous about little matters; they may be frightened at a mouse or at a spider; but in the presence of real danger, when shells are bursting in the streets, and rifle bullets flying thickly, I have seen them standing kitting at their doors and talking to their friends across the street when not a single man was to be seen.

There is no greater mistake than to think women cowards because they are sometimes nervous over trifles. Were it necessary, innumerable cases could be quoted from history to prove that women can, upon occasion, fight as courageously as men. Cæsar found that the women of the German tribes could fight bravely side by side with the men, and the Amazons of the King of Dahomey are more feared by the neighboring tribes than are his male soldiers. Almost every siege has its female heroines, and in the Dutch War of Independence the female companies at Sluys and Haarlem proved themselves a match for the best soldiers of Spain. Above all, in patient endurance of pain and suffering, women are immeasurably superior to men. I emphasize this point because I know that many boys, simply because they are stronger than girls, are apt to regard them with a sort of contempt, and to fancy themselves without the least justification, not only stronger but braver and more courageous—in fact superior beings in every way.

G. A. HENTY.

CONTENTS.

ONE OF THE 28TH.

CHAPTER I.

UNEXPECTED NEWS.

"I HAVE written to ask Ralph Conway to come and stay
for a time with me." The announcement was a simple
one, but it fell like a bombshell in the midst of the
party at breakfast at Penfold Hall. The party consisted
only of the speaker, Herbert Penfold, and his two sisters.
The latter both exclaimed "Herbert!" in a tone of
shocked surprise. Mr. Penfold was evidently prepared
for disapprobation; he had spoken in a somewhat nervous
tone, but with a decision quite unusual to him. He had
finished his last piece of toast and emptied his last cup of
tea before making the announcement, and he now pushed
back his chair, rose to his feet, and said: "Yes; I have
been thinking of having him here for some time, and I
suppose that as master of this house I am at liberty to ask
whom I like; at any rate I would rather have no discussion on the subject."

So saying, without giving his sisters time to reply, he
walked hastily to the door and went out. Miss Penfold
and Miss Eleanor Penfold gazed at each other in speech-
less astonishment. So accustomed were they to settle
everything that took place at Penfold Hall, that this sudden assumption of authority on the part of their brother
fairly staggered them. Miss Penfold was the first to
speak:

"This is terrible, Eleanor! To think that after all these years Herbert's thoughts should still be turning toward that woman. But it is only what might be expected. The ingratitude of men is terrible. Here we have for the last twenty years been devoting our lives to him—not only keeping his house for him, but seeing that he did not fall a victim to any of the designing women who would have insinuated themselves into his good graces, and preventing him from indulging in all sorts of foolish tastes and bringing himself to ruin; and now you see he turns again to that artful woman, and, without saying a word to us, invites her son to come here. It is monstrous, sister!"

"It is monstrous,"Miss Eleanor Penfold repeated, with tears in her eyes. "It is like flying in the face of Providence, sister."

"It is flying in our faces," Miss Penfold replied sharply; "and just at the present moment that is of more importance. To think that that man must have been brooding over this, and making up his mind to act in this way for weeks perhaps, and never to say a word to us upon the subject. I wonder he didn't ask the woman herself down!"

"He never could have done such a shameless thing, Charlotte," her sister said much shocked. "Of course, we must have left the house instantly."

"I should not have left the house," Miss Penfold said firmly. "If the woman comes—and now he has asked the boy it is quite possible that he may ask the mother —our duty will be to remain here. You know we have been uneasy ever since her husband died. Herbert's infatuation concerning her has been pitiable, and we have always believed it has been that alone which has caused him to refuse so obstinately to enter into our plans, or to pay even decent courtesy to the various excellent young women we have from time to time asked down here, and who were in every way suitable for the position of mistress of this house—women full of sense, and who, with right guidance, would' have made him perfectly happy. And now he flies in our faces and asks the boy down. I have had an idea for some little time that he has had something on his mind; he has been more nervous and fidgety than usual, and several times he has seemed to be on the point of saying something, and then changed his mind. Of course, one can understand it all now. No wonder he was ashamed to look us in the face when he was meditating such a step as this. The duplicity of man is something shocking!"

It was not surprising that Herbert Penfold's sudden assertion of his will was a shock to his sisters. These ladies had so long been accustomed to rule absolutely at Penfold Hall that Mr. Penfold's assertion of his right to act as he pleased in his own house came upon them like an act of absolute rebellion. At their father's death they were women of twenty-seven and twenty-six years old respectively Herbert was a lad of sixteen. He was of a gentle and yielding disposition; and as their father for some years previous to his death had been a confirmed invalid, and they had had the complete management of the house, it was but natural that at his death they should continue in the same position.

Owing to weak health, Herbert had not been sent to school, but had been educated under the care of a tutor. He had wished when he reached the age of nineteen to enter one of the universities; but his sisters had been so opposed to the idea, and had represented so strongly to him his unfitness to take part in the rough sports of the young men, and how completely he would feel out of place in such companionship, that he had abandoned the idea, and had traveled on the Continent for three years with his tutor, his sisters being for most of the time of the party. Soon after his return he had fallen in love with the daughter of Colonel Vernon, an officer living on half-pay at Poole, which was the nearest town to Penfold Hall. The announcement of his engagement came like a thunder-clap upon his sisters, who had agreed that it would be in all respects desirable that Herbert should not marry for some years.

They had, however, been wise enough not to offer any open opposition to the match. Three months later the engagement was broken off. How it came about no one exactly knew. Unpleasant reports were set on foot; there were misunderstandings which should easily have been cleared up, but which grew until they gave rise to serious quarrels. Letters which might have set matters straight somehow failed to come to hand; and so at last things went from bad to worse until there was a final quarrel, a return of letters and presents on both sides, and a final breaking off of the engagement. A year later Mary Vernon married Mr. Conway, an architect, resident in London.

Mr. Penfold had before this become convinced that Mary Vernon had not been to blame in the matter, and that he had in some way or other taken an altogether mistaken view of the subject. He knew by the comments of such friends as were intimate enough to speak, and the coolness of many others, that he was considered to have behaved very badly toward her. And this thought was a most distressing one, for he was deeply attached to Mary; and had he not been convinced that from some reason or other she herself had ceased to care for him, and was anxious to break off the engagement, he would have gone any length towards healing the breach. When it was too late he bitterly regretted his own weakness in submitting to the domination of his sisters, and felt a deep though silent resentment against them for the share that he was convinced they had taken in causing the breach between himself and Mary Vernon; but although he resented, he had neither the will nor firmness to free himself from their domination.

At times he struggled feebly against it; and on two or three occasions had suddenly gone up to town, and thence on to the Continent, and had traveled there for weeks. On one of these occasions he had written to them saying that he thought it would be for the happiness of them all if they were to leave Penfold Hall and set up an establishment of their own. But upon his return he found things going on exactly as before, and Miss Penfold had spoken somewhat severely of the silly letter he had written to them, a letter displaying at once such ingratitude and folly that it had been beneath them to notice it. As Herbert Penfold was in a way really fond of his sisters, who spared no effort in making his home comfortable for him, and who allowed him to have his own way in all minor matters, he could not bring himself to repeat when face to face with them the opinon he had expressed in writing; and so things had gone on for years.

The Miss Penfolds were really anxious to see their brother married. Provided only that it was to a lady who would be, in their estimation, fitted for him, and who would also have a feeling of gratitude towards themselves for their share in instaling her as mistress of the Hall, they were quite prepared to abdicate in her favor, and to retire to some pretty house near a pleasant watering-place, paying visits once or twice a year to the Hall.

The listless life their brother led was a source of grief to them; for they were really attached to him, and believed that they had in every way been working for his happiness.

They had no shadow of regret for the part they had played in breaking off his engagement with Mary Vernon. Having once convinced themselves that she was a frivolous girl, quite unsuited for the position of mistress of Penfold Hall, they had regarded it as an absolute duty to protect Herbert from the consequences of what they considered his infatuation. Consequently, for years they were in the habit of inviting for long visits young ladies whom they considered in every way eligible as their successor, and had been much grieved at their want of success, and at the absolute indifference with which Herbert regarded the presence of these young women. When, four years after his marriage to Mary Vernon, Mr. Conway had died suddenly they had been seized with a vague disquiet; for they believed that the remembrance of his first love was the real cause of Herbert's indifference to others, and considered it probable he might still be sufficiently infatuated with her to attempt to undo the past.

To their gratification Herbert never alluded to the subject, never, so far as they knew, made the slightest effort to renew her acquaintance. In fact, Herbert Penfold was a diffident as well as a weak man. Once convinced that he had acted badly toward Mary Vernon, he was equally convinced that she must despise him and that he was utterly unworthy of her. Had it been otherwise he would have again entered the lists and tried to recover the love he had thrown away

Although he occasionally yielded to the entreaties of his sisters and showed himself with them at county gatherings, gave stately dinner-parties at regular intervals, and accepted the invitations of his neighbors, he lived the life almost of a recluse.

His sole companion and friend was the rector of the parish, who had been his tutor during his Continental tour, and whom he had presented with the living which was in his gift, to the secret dissatisfaction of his sisters, who had always considered that Herbert's tutor had endeavored to set him against them. This had to some extent been the case, in so far, at least, that Mr. Withers, who had left college only a short time before starting with Herbert, had endeavored to give him habits of self-reliance and independence of thought, and had quietly striven against the influence that his sisters had upon his mind. It was not until after the Mary Vernon episode that the living had fallen vacant; had it been otherwise things might have turned out differently, for Herbert would certainly have sought his friend's advice in his troubles.

After that it was too late for his interference. Mr. Withers had watched the state of matters at the Hall, and his young wife had often urged him to try to induce Herbert Penfold to rouse himself and assert himself against his sisters, but the vicar remained neutral. He saw that though at times Herbert was a little impatient at the domination of his sisters, and a chance word showed that he nourished a feeling of resentment toward them, he was actually incapable of nerving himself to the necessary effort required to shake off their influence altogether, and to request them to leave the Hall.

Nothing short of this would suffice to establish his independence; for after a mere temporary assertion of authority he would, if they remained there, assuredly speedily allow affairs to lapse into their present state,

and the vicar thought that harm rather than good would
be caused by his interference, and that, as his influence
would be sure to be suspected, there would be a breach
between the Hall and the Rectory. As it was the connection was an intimate one. Herbert was always glad
to see him when he came in for a talk in the course of his
rounds, or when he and his wife would come up to dine
quietly. The Miss Penfolds were always ready with
their purses to aid him to carry out his schemes for the
good of the parish, and to sympathize with his young
wife in her troubles; for of these she had a large share—
all her children, save one girl, having been carried off
in their infancy.

Mabel Withers was as much at home at the Hall as at
the Rectory She was chief pet and favorite with Mr.
Penfold; and although his sisters considered that the
rector allowed her to run wild, and that under such
license she was growing up a sad tomboy, they could
not withstand the influence of the child's happy and
fearless disposition, and were in their way very kind to
her.

Such was the state of things at Penfold Hall when its
owner's sudden announcement that he had invited young
Ralph Conway to come to stay there had fallen like a
bombshell upon his sisters.

The invitation had caused almost as much surprise to
Mrs. Conway as to the Miss Penfolds. Her father had
died a few months after her marriage, and at the death
of her husband she found herself left with an income of
about a hundred a year—the interest of the sum for
which he had insured his life.

To her surprise she had a month or two later received
an intimation from the lawyer who managed her business
that a friend had arranged to pay the sum of a hundred

pounds every quarter to her account, on condition only that no inquiry whatever should be made as to his or her identity. Mary Conway had thankfully accepted the gift, which had, however, caused her intense wonderment and curiosity. So far as she knew neither her father nor her husband had any relations who could have afforded so handsome a gift. She knew that Colonel Vernon had been most popular with his regiment, and the supposition at which she finally arrived was that some young officer whom he had befriended in difficulties had, on coming into a large property, determined similarly to befriend the daughter of his former colonel.

Had she been alone in the world she would have declined to accept this aid from an unknown benefactor, but for her son's sake she felt that it would be wrong to do so. The idea that the money might come from Herbert Penfold had once or twice occurred to her, only to be at once dismissed, for had she really believed that it came from him she could not, even for Ralph's sake, have accepted it. He had, as she believed, quarreled with her altogether without cause, her letters had been unanswered, and she considered the quarrel to have been simply a pretext upon the part of Herbert to break off an engagement of which he was tired. Words dropped, apparently by accident, by Herbert's sisters had, before the misunderstanding commenced, favored this idea, and although she had really loved him her disposition was too spirited to allow her to take the steps she otherwise might have done to set herself right with him.

At any rate she had no ground whatever for believing that Herbert, after the breach of the engagement, entertained any such feelings toward her as would have led him to come forward to assist her in any way after she had become the wife of another; and so for twelve years she had continued to receive her quarterly income. She had established herself in a pretty little house near Dover, where several old friends of her father resided, and where she had plenty of pleasant society among the officers of the regiments stationed there. Although far from rivaling Portsmouth or Plymouth in life and bustle, Dover was a busy town during the time of the great war. The garrison was a large one, the channel cruisers often anchored under the guns of the castle, and from the top of the hills upon a clear day for months a keen lookout was kept for the appearance from the port of Boulogne of the expedition Napoleon had gathered there for the invasion of England.

The white sails of the English cruisers as they sailed up or down the channel were clearly visible, and occasionally a privateer could be seen making its way westward with a prize it had picked up off Texel. Military and naval matters were the sole topics of conversation, and by the time he was fifteen Ralph had fully determined to follow in his grandfather's footsteps and to become a soldier. Having passed almost all her life among military men Mrs. Conway had offered no objections to his wishes, and as several of her father's old friends had promised to use their influence on his behalf, there was little doubt that he would be enabled to procure a commission as soon as he reached the regulation age.

It was not often that the postman called at Mrs. Conway's with letters; for postage was expensive, and the people in those days only wrote when they had something particular to say. Mrs. Conway had just made breakfast when Ralph came in with a letter in his hand.

"Here is a letter for you, mother; but please don't open it until you have given me my breakfast. · I am very late now, and shall barely have time to get through with it and be there before the gates close."

"Your porridge is quite ready for you, Ralph; so if you are late it will be your own fault not mine. The eggs will be in before you have eaten it. However, I won't open the letter until you have gone, because you will only waste time by asking questions about it."

Ralph began his bread and milk, and Mrs. Conway, stretching out her hand, took the letter he had laid beside his plate, and turning it over glanced at the direction to ascertain from which of her few correspondents it came. For a moment she looked puzzled, then, with a little start, she laid it down by the side of her plate. She had recognized the handwriting once so familiar to her.

"What is it, mother? You look quite startled. Who is it from?"

"It is from no one you know, Ralph. I think it is from a person I have not heard from for some years. At any rate it will keep until you are off to school."

"It's nothing unpleasant, I hope, mother. Your color has quite gone, and you look downright pale."

"What should be the matter, you silly boy?" Mrs. Conway said, with an attempt to smile. "What could there be unpleasant in a letter from a person I have not heard from for years? There, go on with your breakfast. I expect you will hear some news when you get down into the town, for the guns in the castle have been firing, and I suppose there is news of a victory. They said yesterday that a great battle was expected to be fought against Napoleon somewhere near Leipzig."

"Yes; I heard the guns, mother, and I expect there has been a victory. I hope not."

"Why do you hope not, Ralph?"

"Why, of course, mother, I don't want the French to be beaten—not regularly beaten, till I am old enough to have a share in it.   Just fancy what a nuisance it would be if peace was made just as I get my commission.''

"There will be plenty of time for you, Ralph," his mother said smiling.   "Peace has been patched up once or twice, but it never lasts long; and after fighting for the last twenty years it is hardly probable that the world is going to grow peaceful all at once.   But there, it is time for you to be off; it only wants ten minutes to nine and you will have to run fast all the way to be in time.''

When Mrs. Conway was alone she took up the letter, and turned it over several times before opening it.

What could Herbert Penfold have written about after all these years?   Mrs. Conway was but thirty-six years old now, and was still a pretty woman, and a sudden thought sent a flush of color to her face.   "Never!" she said decidedly.   "After the way in which he treated me he cannot suppose that now—" and then she stopped. "I know I did love him once, dearly, and it nearly broke my heart; but that was years and years ago.   Well, let us see what he says for himself," and she broke open the letter.   She glanced through it quickly, and then read it again more carefully.   She was very pale now, and her lips trembled as she laid down the letter.

"So," she said to herself in a low tone, "it is to him after all I owe all this," and she looked round her pretty room; "and I never once really suspected it.   I am glad now," she went on after a pause, "that I did not; for, of course, it would have been impossible to have taken it, and how different the last twelve years of my life would have been.   Poor Herbert! And so he really suffered too, and he has thought of me all this time.''

For fully half an hour she sat without moving, her thoughts busy with the past, then she again took up the letter and reread it several times.   Its contents were as follows:

"DEAR MRS. CONWAY: You will be doubtless suprised at seeing my handwriting, and your first impulse will naturally be to put this letter into the fire. I am not writing to ask you to forgive my conduct in the old days. I am but too well aware how completely I have forfeited all right to your esteem or consideration. Believe me that I have suffered for my fault, and that my life has been a ruined one. I attempt to make no excuses. I am conscious that while others were to blame I was most of all, and that it is to my own weakness of will and lack of energy that the breach between us was due. However, all this is of the past and can now interest you but little. You have had your own sorrows and trials, at which, believe me, I sincerely grieved. And now to my object in writing to you. Although still comparatively a young man, I have not many years to live. When last in London I consulted two of the first physicians, and they agreed that, as I had already suspected, I was suffering from heart disease, or rather, perhaps, from an enfeebled state of my heart, which may at any moment cease to do its work.

"Naturally then, I have turned my thoughts as to whom I should leave my property. My sisters are amply provided for. I have no other near relatives, and therefore consider myself free to leave it as I choose. I have long fixed my thoughts upon the daughter of a dear friend, the rector of Bilston; she is now thirteen years old, and half my property is left her. I have left the other half to your son. The whole subject to an annuity to yourself; which you will not, I trust, refuse to accept. I have never thought of any woman but you, and I hope that you will not allow your just resentment against me to deprive me of the poor satisfaction of making what atonement lies in my power for the cruel wrong I formerly did you.

"Were I strong and in health I can well imagine that you would indignantly refuse to receive any benefits from my hands, but knowing your kindness of heart, I feel sure that you will not sadden the last days of a doomed man by the knowledge that even after his death his hopes of insuring the comfort of the one woman on earth he cared for are to be disappointed.

"I should like to know your son. Would it be too much to ask you to spare him for a while from time to time so long as I live? I have a double motive, I say frankly, in thus asking him to come here. I wish him and my little pet, Mabel Withers, to come to like each other. I wish to divide my property between them, and yet I should be glad if the whole estate could remain intact.

"I should not be so foolish as to make a proviso that two persons who are as yet so young, and who may not in any way be suitable to each other, should marry, but nothing would please me so much as that they should take a fancy to each other; and thrown together as they would be here, for Mabel is constantly at the house, it is just possible that one of those boy and girl affections, which do sometimes, although perhaps rarely, culminate in marriage, might spring up between them. Whether that may be so in the present case I must leave to fate, but I should at any rate like to pave the way for such an arrangement by bringing the young people together. I need not say that it will be best that neither of them should have the slightest idea of what is in my mind, for this would be almost certain to defeat my object.

"If the proposal is agreeable to you, I hope that you will let Ralph come to me at the beginning of his holidays; which must, I fancy, be now near at hand. I think it will be as well that he should not know of my intention as to the disposal of my property, for it is better he should think that he will have to work for his living; but at the same time there would be no harm in his knowing that it is probable I shall help him on in life. This will make him bear better what would otherwise be a dull visit. But I leave this matter entirely in your hands. You know the boy and I do not, and you can therefore better judge what will be best for him to know. And now, dear Mary, if you will pardon my once again calling you so,   "I remain,

"Your affectionate friend,

"HERBERT PENFOLD."

It was characteristic of Mrs. Conway that at the first reading of this letter she thought rather of the writer than of the bright prospects which his offer opened to her son. She thought rather of Herbert Penfold, her first love, now ill, if not dying, of the days of their engagement and its rupture, than of the fact that her son was to inherit half the Penfold estates. She had been sorely hurt at the time; and even after all these years it was a pleasure to her to know that the quarrel was not as she had often thought at the time, a mere pretext for breaking off the engagement, but that Herbert had really loved her, had cared for her all these years, and had been the mysterious friend whose kindness had so lightened her cares.

"I did not throw away my love after all," she said to herself, as with her eyes full of tears she stood at the window and looked out towards the sea. "He cared for me enough to be faithful all this time and to think of me constantly, while I had almost forgotten the past. I ought to have known all the time that he was acting under the influence of others—those sisters of his, of course. I was always certain they hated me—hated the thought of my becoming mistress of Penfold Hall. I knew the influence they had over him. Herbert had no will of his own—it was the only fault I ever saw in him —and they could twist him round their little fingers. And now he is going to make Ralph his heir, or at least his heir with the girl he speaks of. It is a grand thing for Ralph; for the estates were worth, he told papa, eight thousand a year, and if Herbert's little romance comes off Ralph will have all."

Then she thought over the years he had been befriending her, and wondered what she should do about that. Finally, being a sensible woman, she decided to do

nothing. Had she known it before, or learned the truth
by other means, she would have refused absolutely to
touch Herbert Penfold's money; but it would be indeed
a poor return for his kindness were she now, when he
was ill and feeble, and was about to bestow still further
benefits upon her, to refuse to permit him any longer to
aid her. She wished, as she read the letter over again,
that he had expressed some desire to see her. She should
have liked to have thanked him in person, to have told
him how grateful she felt for his care and kindness, to
have taken his hand again if but for a minute.

But he had expressed no wish for a meeting, had never
all these years made an effort to see her. She could read
in the wording of the letter that he had been principally
deterred from making any attempt to see her by the
feeling that he had entirely forfeited her regard, and had
offended her beyond chance of forgiveness. And had she
been asked the day before she would doubtless have replied that she had no wish whatever ever again to meet
Herbert Penfold; whereas now she felt almost aggrieved
that he should express no wish to meet her, should have
stayed away so long without making one effort to bring
about reconciliation.

"Of all faults that a man can have," she said pettishly,
"I do not think there's one so detestable as that of self-
distrust. Why could he not have said ten years ago, 'I
behaved badly, Mary; I treated you abominably; but
forgive me and forget. I was not wholly to blame, except
that I allowed others to come between us?' If he had
come and said that, we could at least have been good
friends. I have no patience with men who cannot stand
up for themselves. Now, how much shall I tell Ralph?"
and she again read the letter through.

"Ralph," she said when he came in to dinner, "you
remember that letter I had this morning?"

"Yes, I know, mother; the one that made you turn so white. You said it was from an old friend, though why a letter from an old friend should upset any one I can't make out. What was it about, mother?"

"Well, my boy, it contains a pleasant piece of news. Mr. Penfold, that is the name of the writer, was a friend of my family. He knew me long ago when we were young people, and at one time it seemed likely that we should be married. However, as you know, that never took place. However, it seems, as he says by his letter, that he has never altogether forgotten me, and he intends to help you on in life if you turn out as he would like to see you. He wishes you to go down to stay with him when your holidays begin."

"That sounds nice," Ralph said; "and if he has got any boys about my own age it will be pleasant."

"He has no children, Ralph. He is what you may call an old bachelor, and lives with his sisters—or, rather, they live with him."

"That does not sound very cheerful, mother. An old gentleman with two old ladies alone in the house can't make much fun."

"He is not an old gentleman, Ralph," Mrs. Conway said almost angrily. "I told you we were young people together. Still it may not be very lively for you, but you must put up with that. He evidently means to be very kind to you, and it will be of great advantage to you going down to stay with him."

"But what are you going to do with yourself, mother, all alone here? I think he might have asked you as well as me."

"I shall do very well, Ralph. I have plenty of friends here."

"Where does Mr. Penfold live, mother?"

"Down in Dorsetshire. It is a very nice place, and only about a mile from the sea. But, as I say, I do not expect you will find it lively; but that you mustn't mind. It will be a very good thing for you, and will be well worth your while puting up with a little dullness for a time. Mr. Penfold is one of the kindest of men, but I do not think you will like his sisters much. Certainly you will not unless they are a good deal changed from what they were as I remember them. Still you must try to get on with them as well as you can, and I dare say you will find some pleasant companions in the neighborhood. I am sure you will do your best when I tell you that I am most anxious for many reasons that Mr. Penfold should like you."

"Of course I will do my best, mother, though I must say that the lookout is not, according to your description, a very cheerful one, and I would a deal rather stop at home with you."

"We can't always do exactly as we like, Ralph; though that is a lesson you have as yet to learn. What day did you say your holidays began?"

"Next Monday week, mother. But I do hope I may have two or three days' sailing with Joe Knight the fisherman before I go."

"Mr. Penfold says he will be glad to see you as soon as your holidays begin, Ralph; still I suppose a day or two will make no difference, so we will settle that you shall go on Friday. As you go down to school this afternoon you had better tell Rogerson the tailor to come up this evening to measure you for a suit of clothes. You must look decent when you go down; and you know except your Sunday suit, you have got nothing fit to wear in such a house as that."

"I am afraid it's going to be a horrible nuisance alto-

gether," Ralph said ruefully. "However, I suppose it's
got to be done as you say so, mother; though it's hard
breaking in on my holidays like that. He might just as
well have asked me in school-time. One could have put
up with it ever so much better if it took one out of old
Harper's clutches for a bit. How long am I to stay there?"

"I expect the greater part of your holidays, Ralph. I
think he wants to get to know all about you."

Ralph groaned loudly. "He may intend very kindly,"
he said; "but I wish he would keep his good intentions
to himself."

"You think so now," Mrs. Conway said with a smile.
"You won't think so when you are in the army, but will
find a little extra allowance or a tip now and then very
welcome."

"I dare say I shall, mother," Ralph said, brightening.
"Anyhow, if the old gentleman—that is to say, the gentleman—takes it into his head to make me an allowance,
it will take me off your hands, and I shall not be always
feeling that I am an awful expense to you. All right,
mother. I think I can promise that I will be on my best
behavior, and will try hard to get on even with his sisters. I wish he had asked Phil Landrey to go down
with me. Two fellows can get on anywhere."

"I should have very little hope of your making a good
impression if you went there with your friend Phil,"
Mrs. Conway said, smiling. "I can believe in your good
conduct while you are alone, but I should have no hopes
whatever of you if you and he were together."

"But how am I to go, mother? It seems such a tremendous way from here down into Dorsetshire."

"I have not thought anything about it yet, Ralph;
but probably Mr. Penfold will give some instructions as
to your journey when he hears from me that you are
coming."

CHAPTER II.

A COUNTRY VISIT.

WHEN Ralph had gone off to school again Mrs. Conway sat down to answer the letter—by no means an easy task —and she sat with the paper before her for a long time before she began. At last, with an air of desperation, she dipped her pen into the ink and began:

"MY DEAR HERBERT PENFOLD: It is difficult to answer such a letter as yours—to say all one feels without saying too much; to express the gratitude with which one is full, but of which one feels that you do not desire the expression. First, a word as to the past. Now that it is irreparable, why should I not speak freely? We were the victims of a mistake! You were misled respecting me. I foolishly resented the line you took, failed to make sufficient allowances for your surroundings, and even doubted a love that seemed to me to be so easily shaken. Thus my pride was, perhaps, as much responsible for what happened as your too easy credence of tales to my disadvantage. At any rate, believe me that I have cherished no such feelings as those with which you credit me toward you. Now that I know the truth, I can only regret that your life has been, as you say, spoiled, by what can but be called a fatal misunderstanding.

"Next, I must thank you, although you make no allusion to it in your letter, for your kindness during past years. Of these, believe me, I never suspected that you were the author; and I need hardly say how deeply I have been touched at finding that the hand to which I and my boy owe so much is that of Herbert Penfold. Of this I will say no more. I leave you to picture my

feelings and my gratitude. Also, most warmly I thank
you for your intentions regarding my boy. He will be
ready to come to you on Friday week. I suppose his
best way will be to go by coach to London and then
down to you, or he could take passage perhaps in a
coaster. He is very fond of the sea.

"We had settled that he should enter the army; but of
course I consider that nothing will be decided on this or
any other point as to his future until I know your wishes
on the matter. Lastly, dear Herbert, believe me that the
news that you have given me concerning your state of
health has caused me deep sorrow, and I earnestly hope
and trust that the doctors may be mistaken in your case,
that you may have a long life before you, and that life
may be happier in the future than it has been in the past.

"I remain,
"Your grateful and affectionate
"MARY CONWAY."

A fortnight later Ralph Conway took his place on the
outside of the coach for London. As to the visit to this
unknown friend of his mother, he anticipated no pleasure
from it whatever; but at the same time the journey itself
was delightful to him. He had never during his remembrance been further away from Dover than Canterbury;
and the trip before him was in those days a more important one than a journey half over Europe would be at
the present time. In his pocket he carried a piece of
paper, on which his mother had carefully written down
the instructions contained in the letter she had received
in answer to her own from Herbert Penfold. Sewn up in
the lining of his waistcoat were five guineas, so that in
case the coach was stopped by highwaymen, or any
other misfortune happened, he would still be provided
with funds for continuing his journey.

Under the seat was a small basket filled with sandwiches, and his head ought to have been equally well

filled with the advice his mother had given him as to his behavior at Penfold Hall. As his place had been booked some days before, he had the advantage of an outside seat. Next to him was a fat woman, who was going up to town, as she speedily informed her fellow-passengers, to meet her husband, who was captain of a whaler.

"I see in the *Gazette* of to-day," she said, "as his ship was signaled off Deal yesterday, and with this ere wind he will be up at the docks to-morrow; so off I goes. He's been away nigh eighteen months; and I know what men is. Why, bless you, if I wasn't there to meet him when he steps ashore, as likely as not he would meet with friends and go on the spree, and I shouldn't hear of him for a week; and a nice hole that would make in his earnings. Young man, you are scrouging me dreadful! Can't you get a little further along."

"It seems to me, ma'am, that it is you who are scrouging me," Ralph replied. "This rail is almost cutting into my side now."

"Well, we must live and let live!" the woman said philosophically. "You may thank your stars nature hasn't made you as big as I am. Little people have their advantages. But we can't have everything our own way. That's what I tells my Jim; he is always a-wanting to have his own way. That comes from being a captain; but, as I tells him, it's only reasonable as he is captain on board his ship I should be captain in my house. I suppose you are going to school?"

"No, I am not. My school is just over."

"Going all the way up to London?"

"Yes."

"That's a mercy," the woman said. "I was afraid you might be only going as far as Canterbury, and then I might have got some big chap up here who would squeeze me as flat as a pancake. Men is so unthoughtful, and seems to think as women can stow themselves away any-wheres. I wish you would feel and get your hand in my pocket, young man. I can't do it nohow, and I ain't sure that I have got my keys with me; and that girl Eliza will be getting at the bottles and a-having men in, and then there will be a nice to-do with the lodgers. Can't you find it? It is in the folds somewhere."

With much difficulty Ralph found the pocket-hole, and thrusting his hand in was able to reassure his neighbor by feeling among a mass of odds and ends a bunch of keys.

"That's a comfort," the woman said. "If one's mind isn't at ease one can't enjoy traveling."

"I wish my body was at ease," Ralph said. "Don't you think you could squeeze them a little on the other side and give me an inch or two more room?"

"I will try," the woman said; "as you seem a civil sort of boy."

Whereupon she gave two or three heaves, which relieved Ralph greatly, but involved her in an altercation with her neighbor on the other side, which lasted till the towers of Canterbury came in sight. Here they changed horses at the Fountain Inn.

"Look here, my boy," the woman said to Ralph. "If you feel underneath my feet you will find a basket, and at the top there is an empty bottle. There will be just time for you to jump down and get it filled for me. A shilling's worth of brandy, and filled up with water. That girl Eliza flustered me so much with her worritting and questions before I started that I had not time to fill it."

Ralph jumped down and procured the desired refreshment, and was just in time to clamber up to his seat again

when the coach started. He enjoyed the rapid motion
and changing scene much, but he was not sorry when—
as evening was coming on—he saw ahead of him a dull
mist, which his fellow-passenger told him was the smoke
of London.

It was nine in the evening when the coach drove into
the courtyard of the Bull Inn. The guard, who had
received instructions from Mrs. Conway, at once gave
Ralph and his box into the charge of one of the porters
awaiting the arrival of the coach, and told him to take
the box to the inn from which the coach for Weymouth
started in the morning. Cramped by his fourteen hours'
journey Ralph had at first some difficulty in following
his conductor through the crowded street, but the stiff-
ness soon wore off, and after ten minutes walking he
arrived at the inn.

The guard had already paid the porter, having received
the money for that purpose from Mrs. Conway; and the
latter setting down the box in the passage at once went
off. Ralph felt a little forlorn, and wondered what he
was to do next. But a minute later the landlady came
out from the bar.

"Do you want a bed?" she asked. "The porter should
have rung the bell. I am afraid we are full, unless it
has been taken beforehand. However, I will see if I can
make shift somehow."

"I should be very much obliged if you can," Ralph
said; "for I don't know anything about London, and I
am going on by the Weymouth coach in the morning."

"Oh, might your name be Conway?"

"Yes, that is my name," Ralph said, surprised.

"Ah, then there is a bedroom taken for you. A
gentleman came three days ago and took it, saying it was
for a young gent who is going through to Weymouth,

Tom," she called, "take this box up to number 12. Supper is ready for you, sir. I dare say you would like a wash first?"

"That I should," Ralph replied, following the boots upstairs.

In a few minutes he returned, and a waiter directed him to the coffee-room. In a short time a supper consisting of fish, a steak, and tea was placed before him. Ralph fell to vigorously, and the care that had been bestowed by Mr. Penfold in securing a bedroom and ordering supper for him greatly raised him in the boy's estimation; and he looked forward with warmer anticipations than he had hitherto done to his visit to him. As soon as he had finished he went off to bed, and in a few minutes was sound asleep. At half-past six he was called, and after a hearty breakfast took his seat on the outside of the Weymouth coach.

Sitting beside him were four sailors, belonging, as he soon learned, to a privateer lying at Weymouth. They had had a long trip, and had been some months at sea; and as their ship was to lie for a fortnight at Weymouth while some repairs were being done to her, they had obtained a week's leave and had run up to London for a spree. Weymouth during the war did a brisk trade, and was a favorite rendezvous of privateers, who preferred it greatly to Portsmouth or Plymouth, where the risk of their men being pressed to make up the quota of some man-of-war just fitted out was very great.

The sailors were rather silent and sulky at first at the cruise on land being nearly over, but after getting off the coach where it changed horses they recovered their spirits, and amused Ralph greatly with their talk about the various prizes they had taken, and one or two sharp brushes with French privateers. Toward evening they became rather hilarious, but for the last two hours dozed quietly; the man sitting next to Ralph lurching against him heavily in his sleep, and swearing loudly when the boy stuck his elbow into his ribs to relieve himself of the weight. Ralph was not sorry, therefore, when at ten o'clock at night the coach arrived at Weymouth. The landlord and servants came out with lanterns to help the passengers to alight, and the former, as Ralph climbed down the side into the circle of light, asked:

"Are you Master Conway?"

"That's my name," Ralph replied.

"A bed has been taken for you, sir, and a trap will be over here at nine o'clock in the morning to take you to Penfold Hall."

Supper was already prepared for such passengers as were going to sleep in the hotel; but Ralph was too sleepy to want to eat, and had made a good meal when the coach stopped at six o'clock for twenty minutes to allow the passengers time for refreshments. At eight o'clock next morning he breakfasted. When he had finished the waiter told him that the trap had arrived a few minutes before, and that the horse had been taken out to have a feed, but would be ready to start by nine. Ralph took a stroll for half an hour by the sea and then returned. The trap was at the door, and his trunk had already been placed in it. The driver, a man of twenty-three or twenty-four, was, as he presently told Ralph, stable-helper at Penfold Hall.

"I generally drive this trap when it is wanted," he said. "The coachman is pretty old now. He has been in the family well-nigh fifty years. He is all right behind the carriage-horses, he says, but he does not like trusting himself in a pair-wheel trap."

"How far is it?"

"A matter of fifteen miles. It would be a lot shorter if you had got off last night at the nearest point the coach goes to; but the master told the coachman that he thought it would be pleasanter for you to come on here than to arrive there tired and sleepy after dark."

"Yes, it will much more pleasant," Ralph said. "The road was very dirty, and I should not like to arrive at a strange house with my clothes all covered with dust, and so sleepy that I could hardly keep my eyes open, especially as I hear that Mr. Penfold's sisters are rather particular."

"Rather isn't the word," the driver said; "they are particular, and no mistake. I don't believe as the master would notice whether the carriage was dirty or clean; but if there is a speck of dirt about they are sure to spot it. Not that they are bad mistresses; but they look after things, I can tell you, pretty sharp. I don't say that it ain't as well as they do, for the master never seems to care one way or the other, and lets things go anyhow. A nice gentleman he is, but I don't see much of him; and he don't drive in the carriage not once a month, and only then when he is going to the board of magistrates. He just walks about the garden morning and evening, and all the rest of the time he is shut up in the library with his books. It's a pity he don't go out more."

"Are there any families about with boys?" Ralph asked.

"Not as I knows of. None of them that ever comes to the Hall, anyhow. It's a pity there ain't some young ones there; it would wake the place up and make it lively. It would give us a lot more work to do, I don't doubt; but we shouldn't mind that. I have heard it used to be different in the old squire's time, but it has always been so as long as I can remember. I don't live at the house, but down at the village. Jones he lives over the stables; and there ain't no occasion to have more than one there, for there's only the two carriage-horses and this."

"How far is the sea from the house?"

"It's about half a mile to the top of the cliff, and a precious long climb down to the water; but going round by Swanage—which is about three miles—you can drive down close to the sea, for there are no cliffs there."

There was little more said during the drive. From time to time the man pointed out the various villages and country seats, and Ralph wondered to himself how he should manage to pass the next three weeks. It seemed that there would be nothing to do and no one to talk to. He had always been accustomed to the companionship of lots of boys of his own age, and during the holidays there was plenty of sailing and fishing, so that time had never hung on his hands; the present prospect therefore almost appalled him. However, he had promised his mother that he would try to make the best of things; and he tried to assure himself that after all three weeks or a month would be over at last. After an hour and a half's drive they passed through a lodge gate into a park, and in a few minutes drew up at the entrance to Penfold Hall. An old servant came out.

"Will you come with me into the library, sir? Mr. Penfold is expecting you. Your box will be taken up into your room."

Ralph felt extremely uncomfortable as he followed his conductor across a noble hall, floored with dark polished oak, and paneled with the same material. A door was opened, and a servant announced "Master Conway." A gentleman rose from his chair and held out his hand.

"I am glad to see you, Ralph Conway; and I hope your

journey has been a pretty comfortable one. It is very good of you to come such a long distance to pay me a visit.''

"Mother wanted me to, sir," Ralph said honestly. "I don't think—" and he stopped.

"You don't think you would have come of your own accord, Ralph? No, that is natural enough, my boy. At your age I am sure I should not have cared to give up my holidays and spend them in a quiet house among strangers. However, I wanted to see you, and I am very glad you have come. I am an old friend of your mother's, you know, and so desired to make the acquaintance of her son. I think you are like her," he said, putting his hand on Ralph's shoulder and taking him to the window and looking steadily at him.

"Other people have said so, sir; but I am sure I can't see how I can be like her a bit. Mother is so pretty, and I am sure I am not the least bit in the world; and I don't think it's nice for a boy to be like a woman."

This was rather a sore point with Ralph, who had a smooth soft face with large eyes and long eyelashes, and who had, in consequence, been nicknamed "Sally" by his schoolfellows. The name had stuck to him in spite of several desperate fights, and the fact that in point of strength and activity he was fully a match for any boy of his own age; but as there was nothing like derision conveyed by it, and it was indeed a term of affection rather than of contempt, Ralph had at last ceased to struggle against it. But he longed for the time when the sprouting of whiskers would obliterate the obnoxious smoothness of his face. Mr. Penfold had smiled at his remark.

"I do not like girlish boys, Ralph; but a boy can have a girlish face and yet be a true boy all over. I fancy that's your case.

"I hope so, sir. I think I can swim or run or fight any of the chaps of my own age in the school; but I know I do look girlish about the face. I have done everything I could to make my face rough. I have sat in the sun, and wetted it with sea-water every five minutes, but it's no use."

"I should not trouble about it. Your face will get manly enough in time, you may be sure; and I like you all the better for it, my boy, because you are certainly very like your mother. And now, Ralph, I want you to enjoy yourself as much as you can while you are here. The house itself is dull, but I suppose you will be a good deal out of doors. I have hired a pony, which will be here to-day from Poole, and I have arranged with Watson, a fisherman at Swanage, that you can go out with him in his fishing-boat whenever you are disposed. It is three miles from here, but you can ride over on your pony and leave it at the little inn there till you come back. I am sorry to say I do not know any boys about here; but Mabel Withers, the daughter of my neighbor and friend the clergyman of Bilston, the village just outside the lodge, has a pony, and is a capital rider, and I am sure she will show you over the country. I suppose you have not had much to do with girls?" he added with a smile at seeing a slight expression of dismay on Ralph's face, which had expressed unmixed satisfaction at the first items of the programme.

"No, sir; not much," Ralph said. "Of course some of my schoolfellows have sisters, but one does not see much of them."

"I think you will get on very well together. She is a year or two younger than you are, and I am afraid she is considered rather a tomboy. She has been caught at the top of a tall tree examining the eggs in a nest, and in many similar ungirl-like positions; so you won't find her a dull companion. She is a great pet of mine, and though she may not be as good a companion as a boy would be for you, I am sure when you once get to know her you will find her a very good substitute. You see, not having had much to do with boys, I am not very good at devising amusement for you. I can only say that if there is anything you would like to do while you are here you have only to tell me, and if it be possible I will put you in the way of it."

"Thank you very much, sir. You are extremely kind," Ralph said heartily; for with a pony and a boat it did seem that his visit would not be nearly so dull as he had anticipated. "I am sure I shall get on capitally."

Just at this moment there was a knock at the door. It opened, and a girl entered.

"You have just come at the right moment, Mabel," Mr. Penfold said as she came in. "This is Ralph Conway, of whom I was speaking to you. Ralph, this is Mabel Withers. I asked her to come in early this morning so as to act as your guide round the place."

The boy and girl shook hands with each other. She was the first to speak.

"So you are Ralph. I have been wondering what you would be like. Uncle has been telling me you were coming. I like your looks, and I think you are nice."

Ralph was taken rather aback. This was not the way in which his schoolfellows' sisters had generally addressed him.

"I think you look jolly," he said; "and that's better than looking nice."

"I think they mean the same thing," she replied; "except that a girl says 'nice' and a boy says 'jolly.' I like the word 'jolly' best, only I get scolded when I use it. Shall we go into the garden?"

Altogether Ralph Conway had a very much pleasanter time than he had anticipated. Except at meals he saw little of the Miss Penfolds. His opinion as to these ladies, expressed confidentially to Mabel Withers, was the reverse of flattering.

"I think," he said, "that they are the two most disagreeable old cats I have ever met. They hardly ever open their lips, and when they do it is only to answer some question of their brother. I remember in a fairy story there was a girl who whenever she spoke let fall pearls and diamonds from her lips; whenever those women open their mouths I expect icicles and daggers to drop out."

"They are not so bad as that," Mabel laughed. "I generally get on with them very well, and they are very kind in the parish; and altogether they are really not bad."

"Then their looks belie them horribly," Ralph said. "I suppose they don't like me; and that would be all well enough if I had done anything to offend them, but it was just as bad the first day I came. I am sure Mr. Penfold does not like it. I can see him fidget on his chair; and he talks away with me pretty well all the time we are at table, so as to make it less awkward, I suppose. Well, I am stopping with him, and not with them, that's one thing; and it doesn't make much difference to me if they do choose to be disagreeable. I like him immensely. He is wonderfully kind; but it would be awfully stupid work if it weren't for you, Mabel. I don't think I could stand it if it were not for our rides together."

The young people had indeed got on capitally from the first. Every day they took long rides together, generally alone, although sometimes Mr. Penfold rode with them. Ralph had already confided to the latter, upon his asking him how he liked Mabel, that she was the jolliest girl that he had ever met.

"She has no nonsensical girl's ways about her, Mr. Penfold; but is almost as good as a boy to be with. The girls I have seen before have been quite different from that. Some of them always giggle when you speak to them, others have not got a word to say for themselves; and it is awfully hard work talking to them even for a single dance. Still, I like them better than the giggling ones."

"You see, Ralph, girls brought up in a town are naturally different to one like Mabel. They go to school, and are taught to sit upright and to behave discreetly, and to be general unnatural. Mabel has been brought up at home, and allowed to do as she liked, and she has consequently grown up what nature intended her to be. Perhaps some day all girls will be allowed the same chance of being natural that boys have, and backboards and other contrivances for stiffening them and turning them into little wooden figures will be unknown. It will be a good thing, in my opinion, when that time arrives."

Ralph was often down at the Rectory, where he was always made welcome, Mr. Withers and his wife being anxious to learn as much of his disposition as they could. They were well satisfied with the result.

"I fancy I know what is in Penfold's mind," the rector had said to his wife a few days after Ralph came down. "I believe he has already quite settled it in his mind that some day Mabel and this lad shall make a match of it."

"How absurd, John. Why, Mabel is only a child."

"Quite so, my dear; but in another three or four years she will be a young woman. I don't mean that Penfold has any idea that they are going to take a fancy to each other at present—only that they will do so in the future.

You know he has said that he intends to leave a slice of his fortune to her, and I have no doubt that this lad will get the main bulk of his property. I have often told you about his engagement to the lad's mother, and how the breaking it off has affected his whole life. It is natural that a lonely man as he is should plan for others. He has no future of his own to look forward to, so he looks forward to some one else's. He has had no interest in life for a great many years, and I think he is making a new one for himself in the future of our girl and this lad.

"As far as I have seen of the boy I like him. He is evidently a straightforward, manly lad. I don't mean to say that he has any exceptional amount of brains, or is likely to set the Thames on fire; but if he comes into the Penfold property that will not be of much importance. He seems bright, good-tempered, and a gentleman. That is quite good enough to begin with. At any rate, there is nothing for us to trouble about. If some day the young people get to like each other the prospect is a good one for the child; if not, there's no harm done. At present there can be no objection to our yielding to Penfold's request and letting them ride about the country together. Mabel is, as you say, little more than a child, and it is evident that the lad regards her rather in the light of a boy companion than as a girl.

"She is a bit of a tomboy, you know, Mary, and has very few girlish notions or ideas. They evidently get on capitally together, and we need not trouble our heads about them but let things go their own way with a clear conscience."

At the end of the time agreed upon Ralph returned home.

"And so, Ralph, you have found it better than you expected?" his mother said to him at the conclusion of his first meal at home

"Much better, mother. Mr. Penfold is awfully kind, and lets one do just what one likes. His sisters are hateful women, and if I had not been staying in the house I should certainly have played them some trick or other just to pay them out. I wonder why they disliked me so much. I could see it directly I arrived; but, after all, it didn't matter much, except just at meals and in the evening. But though Mr. Penfold was so kind, it would have been very stupid if it had not been for Mabel Withers. We used to ride out or go for walks together every day. She was a capital walker, and very jolly—almost as good as a boy. She said several times that she wished she had been a boy, and I wished so too. Still, of course, mother, I am very glad I am back. There is no place like home, you know; and then there are the fellows at school, and the games, and the sea, and all sorts of things; and it's a horrid nuisance to think that I have got to go down there regularly for my holidays. Still, of course, as you wish it, I will do so; and now that I know what it is like it won't be so bad another time. Anyhow, I am glad I have got another ten days before school begins."

The following morning Ralph went down to the beach. "Why, Master Conway," an old fisherman said, "you are a downright stranger. I have missed you rarely."

"I told you I was going away, Joe, and that I shouldn't get back until the holidays were nearly over."

"I know you did," the fisherman replied. "Still it does seem strange without you. Every time as I goes out I says to Bill, 'If Master Conway was at home he would be with us to-day, Bill. It don't seem no ways natural without him.' And there's been good fishing, too, this season, first rate; and the weather has been just what it should be."

' "Well, I am back now, Joe, anyhow; and I have got ten days before school begins again, and I mean to make the most of it. Are you going out to-day?"

"At four o'clock," the fisherman said. "Daylight fishing ain't much good just now; we take twice as many at night."

"No trouble with the Frenchies?"

"Lord bless you I ain't seen a French sail for months. Our cruisers are too sharp for them; though they say a good many privateers run in and out of their ports in spite of all we can do, and a lot of our ships get snapped up. But we don't trouble about them. Why, bless your heart, if one of them was to run across us they would only just take our fish, and as likely as not pay us for them with a cask or two of spirits. Fish is a treat to them Frenchies; for their fishing boats have to keep so close over to their own shores that they can't take much. Besides, all their best fishermen are away in the privateers, and the lads have to go to fight Boney's battles with the Austrians or Russians, or Spanish or our chaps, or else to go on board their ships of war and spend all their time cooped up in harbor, for they scarce show now beyond the range of the guns in their forts. Well, will you come this evening?"

"Yes, I think so, Joe. My mother doesn't much care about my being out at night, you know; but as I have been away all this time to please her, I expect she will let me do what I like for the rest of the holidays."

"Don't you come if your mother don't like it, Master Conway; there is never no good comes of boys vexing their mothers. I have known misfortune to follow it over and over again. Boys think as they know best what's good for them; but they don't, and sooner or later they are sure to own it to themselves."

"I shouldn't do it if I knew she really didn't like it, Joe; but I don't think she does mind my going out with you at any time. She knows she can trust you. Beside, what harm could come of it? You never go out in very rough weather."

"Pretty roughish sometimes, Master Conway."

"Oh, yes, pretty rough; but not in a gale, you know. Beside, the Heartsease could stand a goodish gale. She is not very fast, you know, but she is as safe as a house."

"She is fast enough," the old fisherman said in an injured tone. "But you young gentlemen is never content unless a boat is heeling over, gunnel under, and passing everything she comes across. What's the good of that ere to a fisherman? He goes out to catch fish, not to strain his craft all over by running races against another. Now an hour faster or slower makes no difference, and the Heartsease is fast enough for me, anyhow."

"No, she isn't, Joe. I have heard you use bad language enough when anything overhauls and passes her on the way back to port."

"Ay, that may be," the fisherman admitted; "and on the way home I grant you that a little more speed might be an advantage, for the first comer is sure to get the best market. No, the Heartsease ain't very fast, I own up to that; but she is safe and steady, and she has plenty of storage room and a good roomy cabin as you can stand upright in, and needn't break your back by stooping as you have to do on board some craft I could name."

"That's true enough, Joe," the boy said.

"But what's more, she's a lucky boat; for it's seldom that she goes out without getting a good catch."

"I think that's more judgment than luck, Joe; though there may be some luck in it too."

"I don't know about that, Master Conway. Of course one wants a sharp eye to see where the shoals are moving; but I believes in luck. Well, sir, shall I see you again before the afternoon?"

"I don't much expect so, Joe. I have got to call at some other places, and I don't suppose I shall have time to get down before. If I am coming I shall be sure to be punctual; so if I am not here by four, go off without me."

Mrs. Conway made no objection when Ralph proffered his request. He had sacrificed the greater part of his holidays to carrying out her wishes, and paying a visit to Mr. Penfold; and although she did not like his being out all night fishing, she could not refuse his request; and, indeed, as she knew that Joe Knight was a steady man and not fond of the bottle, there was no good reason why she should object. She, therefore, cheerfully assented, saying at the same time, "I will pack a basket for you before you start, Ralph. There is a nice piece of cold meat in the house, and I will have that and a loaf of bread and some cheese put up for you. I know what these fishing excursions are; you intend to be back at a certain time, and then the wind falls, or the tide turns, or something of that sort, and you can't make the harbor. You know what a fright you gave me the very first time you went out fishing with Joe Knight. You were to have been back at five o'clock in the afternoon, and you did not get in until three o'clock the next morning."

"I remember, mother; and there you were on the quay when we came in. I was awfully sorry about it."

"Well, I have learned better since, Ralph; and I know now that there is not necessarily any danger, even if you don't come back by the time I expect you. And of course each time I have fidgeted and you have come back safe, I have learned a certain amount of sea-knowledge, and have come to know that sailors and fishermen are not accountable for time; and that if the wind drops or tide turns they are helpless in the matter, and have only to wait till a breeze comes up again.''

"I think, mother, you ought to like my going out at night better than in the daytime.''

"Why, Ralph?''

"Because, mother, if I go out in the daytime and don't get back until after dark, you worry yourself, and having no one to talk to, sit here wondering and wondering until you fancy all sorts of things. Now, if I go out in the evening, and I don't come back in the morning at the hour you expect, you see that it is fine and bright, and that there is nothing to make you uneasy; or if you do feel fidgety, you can walk down to the beach and talk to the boatmen and fishermen, and of course they can tell you at once that there's nothing to worry about, and very likely point the boat out to you in the distance.''

"Well, Ralph, perhaps that is so, although I own I never looked at it in that light before.''

CHAPTER III.

RUN DOWN.

"THERE's a nice breeze," Ralph said as he joined the fisherman at the appointed hour.

"Yes, it's just right; neither too light nor too heavy. It's rather thick, and I shouldn't be suprised if we get it thicker; but that again don't matter." For in those days not one ship plowed the waters of our coast for every fifty that now make their way along it. There were no steamers, and the fear of collision was not ever in the minds of those at sea.

"Where's Bill, Joe?"

"The young scamp!" the fisherman said angrily. "Nothing will do for him but to go a-climbing up the cliffs this morning; and just arter you left us, news comes that the young varmint had fallen down and twisted his foot, and doctor says it will be a fortnight afore he can put a boot on. Then the old woman began a-crying over him; while, as I told her, if any one ought to cry it would be me, who's got to hire another boy in his place to do his work. A touch of the strap would be the best thing for him, the young rascal!"

"You are not going to take another boy out to-night are you, Joe?"

"No, Master Conway, I knows you like a-doing things. You have been out enough with me to know as much about it as Bill, and arter all there ain't a very great deal to do. The trawl ain't a heavy one, and as I am accustomed to work it with Bill I can do it with you."

The Heartsease was a good-sized half-decked boat of some twenty-six feet long and eight feet beam. She was very deep, and carried three tons of stone ballast in her bottom. She drew about six feet of water. She had a lot of freeboard, and carried two lug-sails and a small mizzen.

They got in the small boat and rowed off to her.

"There was no call for you to bring that basket, Master Conway. I know you are fond of a fish fried just when it is taken out of the water; and I have got bread and a keg of beer, to say nothing of a mouthful of spirits in case we get wet. Not that it looks likely we shall, for I doubts if there will be any rain to-night. I think there will be more wind perhaps, and that it will get thicker; that's my view of the weather."

They sailed straight out to sea. Joe had fitted his boat to be worked with the aid of a boy only. He had a handy winch, by which he hoisted his heavy lug-sails, and when the weather was rough hauled up his trawls. Of these he carried two, each fourteen feet long, and fished with them one out on each quarter. When he reached the fishing ground six miles out, Joe lowered the mizzen lug and reefed the main, for there was plenty of wind to keep the boat going at the pace required for trawling under the reduced sail. Then the trawls were got overboard, each being fastened to the end of a stout spar lashed across the deck, and projecting some eight feet on either side, by which arrangement the trawls were kept well apart. They were hauled alternately once an hour, two hours being allowed after they were put down before the first was examined.

By the time the first net came up the sun had set.

The wind had freshened a bit since they had started, but there was no sea to speak of, The night had set in thick, and the stars could only occasionally be seen. Joe had picked out two or three fine fish from the first haul, and these he took down and soon had frizzling in a frying-pan over the fire, which he had lighted as soon as the boat was under sail.

"These are for you, Master Conway," he said. "With your permission I shall stick to that ere piece of beef your mother was good enough to send. Fish ain't no treat to me, and I don't often get meat. Keep your eye lifting while I am down below. There ain't many craft about in these days, still we might tumble against one."

"I should not see a light far in this mist, Joe."

"No, you couldn't; and what's worse, many of them don't carry no lights at all."

"It would be a good thing, Joe, if there was a law to make all vessels carry lights."

"Ay, ay, lad; but you see in war times it ain't always convenient. A peaceful merchantman don't want to show her lights to any privateers that may happen to be cruising about, and you may be sure that the privateer don't want to attract the attention of peaceful traders until she is close upon them, or to come under the eye of any of our cruisers. No, no; there ain't many lights shown now, not in these waters. Folks prefer to risk the chance of running into each other rather than that of being caught by a French privateer."

Now that the trawls were out there was no occasion for any one to attend to the helm, consequently when Joe announced that the fish were ready Ralph went down and joined him in the cabin. The first hours of the night passed quietly. Once an hour a trawl was hauled in and got on board, and as the catches were satisfactory Joe was in capital spirit

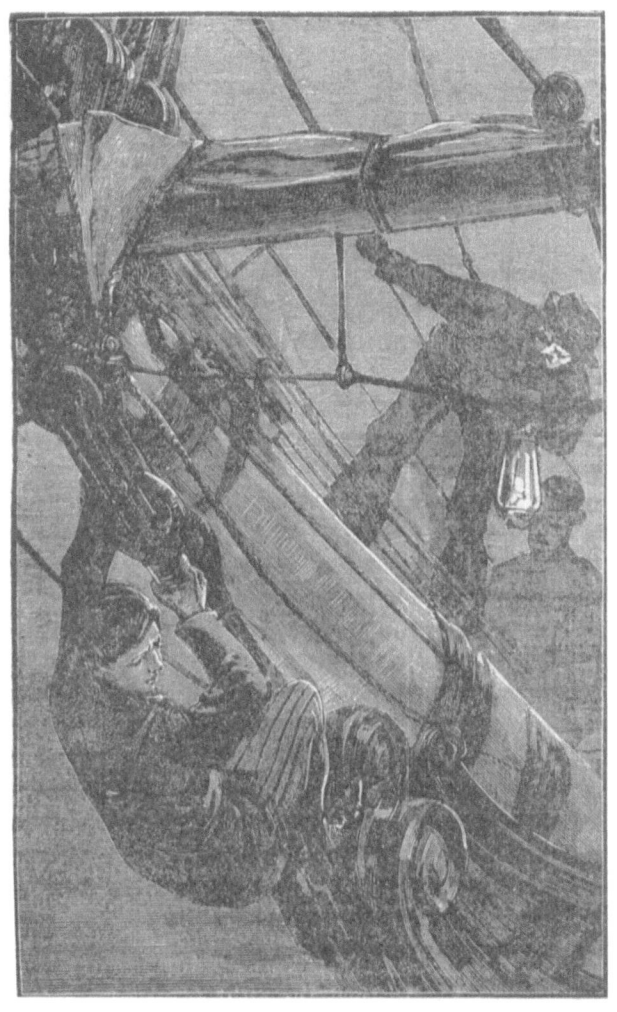

One 28th.   THE BOAT WENT DOWN FROM UNDER HIS FEET.—Page 43.

˙ "You have brought good luck, Master Conway; and I
notices I generally do well when you are out with me. I
am getting more fish to-night than I have any night for
weeks, and if it goes on like this till morning I shall
make a good thing of it. I wants it bad enough, for I
am in arrears a bit with my rent. The war has made
everything so terrible dear that it is as much as a poor
man can do to keep his head above water.

"What time is it now, Joe, do you think?"

"About two o'clock, I reckon. It will begin to get
light in a couple of hours, and at five we will up nets and
make our way back."

He had scarcely spoken when he shouted "Ship ahoy *i*
Look out for yourself, lad! Startled by the suddenness
of the cry Ralph looked round. He saw a crest of white
foam a few yards away in the darkness. A moment later
something dark passed over his head and a rope brushed
his cheek, and as it did so a black mass struck the boat.
There was a crash, a shock, and the Heartsease, after first
heeling deeply over under the pressure, suddenly sank
down like a stone. Ralph had staggered under the force
of the collision, and would have fallen back as the boat
heeled over, but instinctively he threw up his arms and
his hand came in contact with the rope that had an instant before touched his cheek. He seized it with both
hands, and threw his legs round it as the boat went down
from under his feet, the whole thing being so sudden that
it was nearly a minute before he could realize what had
happened. Then he heard voices talking close by and,
as it seemed, above him.

"Hullo!" he shouted. "Help!" A few seconds later
the light of a lantern was flashed down upon him. Then
a figure crawled out on the spar projecting above his
head, seized him by the collar, and lifted him from the

bobstay to which he was clinging on to the bowsprit. A minute later he was standing on the deck.

"Thank you!" he exclaimed. "Have you seen anything of the man who was with me? There were two of us on board. If not, please look for him at once."

"I am afraid it's no use," one of the men said, with a strong foreign accent; "he has gone down and will never come up again. You come along with me to the captain."

An uneasy feeling seized Ralph as he listened. He could see nothing, for the lantern had been placed in a bucket the moment that he touched the deck. At this moment a hail came from the stern of the vessel, and Ralph's fears were at once realized, for it was in French. The reply was in the same tongue, and he was led aft. "Take him down below, Jacques, and let's see what he is like. We have suffered no damage, I hope?"

"Not as far as I could see by the light of the lantern, but the carpenter has gone below to see if she is making water."

The captain led the way down into the cabin. This was comfortably furnished and lighted by a swinging lamp. "Do you come, down Jacques, I shall want you to interpret."

The captain was surprised when he saw by the light of the lamp that the person they had rescued was a lad, well dressed, and evidently above the condition of fishermen.

"Now, young sir, who are you," he asked, "and what have you to say for yourself?" The question was translated by Jacques.

"I like that," the lad said indignantly. "What have I to say for myself! I think it's what have you to say for yourselves? We were quietly fishing when you ran over us and sank the boat and drowned my friend Joe, and haven't even stopped for a moment to see if you could pick him up. I call it shameful and inhuman!''

The French captain laughed as Jacques translated the speech, the purport of which he had, indeed, made out for himself, for although he did not speak English he understood it to some extent.

''Tell him it was his fault as much as ours. We did not see him till we struck him. And as for his companion, what chance was there of finding him on such a dark night as this? Why, by the time we had hove round and got back again we might not have hit it within a quarter of a mile. Besides, if he had been alive he would have shouted.''

Ralph saw, when he understood what the captain said, that there was truth in his words, and that the chances of discovering Joe would indeed have been slight even had the vessel headed round.

''May I ask,'' he said, ''what ship this is, and what you are going to do with me?''

''The ship is La Belle Marie of Dunkirk; as to what we are going to do with you it is not so easy to say. Of course you can jump overboard again if you like, but if not you can stay on board until we have an opportunity of putting you ashore somewhere. How did you come to be on board a fishing smack? For I suppose it was a smack that we run down.''

''I live at Dover,'' Ralph replied, ''and had only come out for a night's fishing.''

''Well, you are out of luck,'' the captain said. ''That will do, Jacques. Take him forward and sling a hammock for him. Hang up his clothes in the cook's galley, they will be dry by the time he wakes.''

Ralph asked no questions, as he was taken forward, as to the character of La Belle Marie. Six guns were ranged along on each side of her decks, and this, and the appearance of the captain's cabin, was sufficient to inform him that he had fallen into the hands of a French privateer. The craft had, indeed, left Dunkirk soon after nightfall, and was making her way down channel with every sail set when she had run down the unfortunate fishing boat.

Jacques, as he hung up the hammock, explained to the sailors who crowded round the character of the passenger who had so unexpectedly come on board.

"Poor lad," one of the sailors said good-naturedly, "he will be some time before he sees his mother again. He hasn't got a very bright lookout before him—a long voyage, and then a prison. I will go and see if the cook has got some water hot. A glass of spirits will do him good."

A few minutes later Ralph was wrapped up in a blanket and the warm glow produced by that and the glass of strong grog soon sufficed to send him soundly to sleep, in spite of the painful uncertainty of his position and of his sorrowful thought of his mother, who would in the morning be inquiring for him in vain. It was nearly midday before he woke. Looking round he saw that he had the forecastle to himself. His clothes were lying on a chest close by, and in a few minutes he was on deck. A sense of disappointment stole over him. He had, while he was dressing, entertained the hope that on going on deck he should see an English cruiser in pursuit; but the wind had dropped and it was still thick, and his vision was confined to a circle a quarter of a mile in diameter. Jacques nodded to him good-temperedly, for all on board the privateer were in high spirits. Their voyage had begun propitiously; the darkness of the preceding night had enabled them to run the gantlet of the British cruisers in the narrow part of the channel, they were now well down the coast of France, and the fog reduced their chances of being seen by an enemy to a minimum.

"Where about are we?" Ralph asked.

"We are somewhere off the mouth of the Seine, and I guess some fifteen miles from land."

"Oh, we are working down the channel then," Ralph said. "And where are we going to?"

"Ah! that question is for the captain to answer if he chooses," Jacques said.

"Are we going to touch at the next French port?" Ralph asked anxiously.

"Not that I know of, unless we have the luck to pick up one of your merchantmen, and we might then escort her into port. But unless we do that we do not touch anywhere, luckily for you; because, after all, it is a good deal pleasanter cruising in the Belle Marie than kicking your heels inside a prison. I know pretty well, for I was for four years a prisoner in your English town of Dorchester. That is how I came to speak your language. It was a weary time of it; though we were not badly treated, not half so bad as I have heard that the men in some other prisons were. So I owe you English no ill-will on that account, and from what I have heard some of our prisons are worse than any of yours. I used to knit stockings and wraps for the neck. My old mother taught me when I was a boy. And as we were allowed to sell the things we made I got on pretty comfortable. Beside, what's the use of making yourself unhappy? I had neither wife nor children to be fretting about me at home, so I kept up my spirits."

"How did you get back?" Ralph asked. "Were you exchanged?"

"No," Jacques answered. "I might have waited long

enough before that. I can't make out myself why the two governments don't agree to exchange prisoners more quickly. I suppose they take about an equal number. Your men-of-war ships capture more prisoners than ours, but we make up for it by the numbers our privateers bring in. At any rate they might exchange as many as they can, say once in six months. One would have thought they would be glad to do so so as to save themselves the trouble and expense of looking after and feeding such a number of useless mouths. Governments always have curious ways."

"But how did you get away from prison?" Ralph asked.

"It was a woman," the man replied. "It is always women who help men out of scrapes. It was the wife of one of the jailers. She used to bring her husband's dinner sometimes when we were exercising in the yard. When I first went there she had a child in her arms—a little thing about a year old. I was always fond of children; for we had a lot at home, brothers and sisters, and I was the eldest. She saw me look at it one day, and I suppose she guessed it reminded me of home. So she stopped and let me pat its cheek and talk to it. Then I knitted it some socks and a little jacket and other things, and that made a sort of friendship between us. You can always win a woman's heart by taking notice of her child. Then she got to letting me carry it about on my shoulder while she took her husband's dinner in to him, if he did not happen to be in the yard. And when the little thing was able to totter it would hold on to my finger, and was always content to stay with me while she was away. So it went on till the child was four years old.

"One day it was running across the court to its mother as she came out from the prison. Two of the men were

what you call skylarking, and running one way while the
child was running the other. One of them knocked it
down heavily. It was an accident, and if he had picked
it up and been sorry, there would have been an end of it;
but instead of that the brute burst into a loud laugh.
By this time I was as fond of the child as if it had been
my own, and I rushed furiously at him and knocked him
down. As he sprang to his feet he drew a knife he used
in wood-carving and came at me. I caught the blow on
my arm and closed with him, and we fell together. The
guard in the yard rushed up and pulled us apart, and we
both got a fortnight's close confinement for fighting.

"The first time I came into the yard again and met the
woman with her child, the little one ran to me; but the
woman, a little to my surprise, said nothing. As she
passed I lifted the child up, and after giving me a hug
and a kiss she said: 'Mammy gave me this to give to
you;' and she put a little note into my hand. I took the
first opportunity to read it in a quiet corner. It was as
follows: 'Dear Jacques—I saw how nobly you stood up
for my Carrie the other day, and how you got wounded
in protecting her. You have always been good to her.
I have often thought I might help you to escape, but was
afraid to try. Now I will do so. It will not be easy, but
I will manage it. Do not be impatient; the child will
give you another note when I have quite arranged things.
I shall not talk much to you in futuie, or else when you
have got away I may be suspected; so do not be surprised
at my seeming cold.'

"After that the woman only brought her child once a
week or so to the prison, and only gave me a nod as she
passed through the yard. Upon the third visit of the
child it gave me a little packet containing two or three
small steel saws and a little bottle of oil. On the paper

which held them was written, 'For the bars. You shall have a rope next time.' Sure enough next time the child had hidden in its frock a hank of very thin cord, which I managed as I was playing with her to slip unobserved into my breast. 'Mammy says more next time.' And next time another hank came. There was a third, and a note, 'Twist the three ropes together and they will be strong enough to bear you. On the third night from this, saw through the bars and lower yourself into the court. There will be no moon. Go to the right-hand corner of the court in the rear of the prison. Fasten a knife to one end of the cord and throw it over the wall. I shall be waiting there with a friend. Directly you feel the cord jerked climb up to the top of the wall. If you can find something to fasten your end of the rope to you can slide down it. If not, you must jump. There will be a boat ready to take you away.'

"It all turned out well. It was a pitch dark night, raining and blowing, and the sentries kept inside their boxes. I got up to the top of the wall all right, and was able to fasten the rope on to the spikes and slide down on the other side. The woman was there with a man, whom she told me was her brother. They took me down to a creek two miles away and there put me on board a boat, and I was rowed out to a smuggling craft which at once set sail, and two days later was landed at Cherbourg. So that's how I came to learn English."

"Did you ever hear whether the woman who helped you was suspected?"

"I saw her brother two months afterward on one of the trips that the craft he belonged to made. He said that of course there were a great many inquiries made, and his sister had been questioned closely. She swore that she had hardly spoken to me for the last two months and that she had given me nothing; which in a way was true enough, for she had not handed them to me herself. The prisoners bore her out about her not coming near me, for it had been noticed that she was not as friendly as she had been. Some had thought her ungrateful, while others had fancied that she was angry at my interfering and making a tumult about the child. Anyhow, whatever suspicions they might have had they could prove nothing. They forbade her entering the prison in future; but she didn't mind that so long as her husband, who had been employed a good many years there, did not lose his situation. He had been kept by her in entire ignorance of the whole affair, and was very indignant at her having been suspected. I sent her a letter of thanks by her brother, and a little present for her and one for the child. The brother was to give them to her as if from himself, so that the husband should not smell a rat, but of course to make her understand who they came from."

"Well, I only hope, Jacques," Ralph said, "that when I get shut up in one of your prisons I shall find some French woman to aid me to escape, just as you found an English woman to help you; only I hope it won't be four years coming about."

"I think we look sharper after our prisoners than you do; still it may be. But it will be some time before you are in prison; and if you play your cards well and learn to speak our language, and make yourself useful, I do not think the captain is likely to hand you over to the authorities when we get back to a French port again."

"I am quite ready to do my best to learn the language and to make myself useful," Ralph said. "It is always a good thing to know French, especially as I am going into the army some day; that is if I get back again in time."

"Oh, I think you will do so," the man said. "You keep up your spirits well, and that is the great thing. There are many boys that would sit down and cry if they found themselves in such a scrape as you have got into."

"Cry!" Ralph repeated indignantly. "You don't suppose a boy of my age is going to cry like a girl! An English boy would be ashamed to cry, especially when Frenchmen were looking on."

Jacques laughed good-temperedly. "There would be nothing to be ashamed of. We are not like you cold English! A Frenchman laughs and sings when he is pleased, and cries when he is sorry. Why shouldn't he?"

"Oh, I can't tell you why," Ralph replied, "only we don't do it. I don't say I shouldn't balloo out if I were hurt very much, though I should try my best not to; but I feel sure I shouldn't cry like a great baby. Why, what would be the good of it?"

Jacques shrugged his shoulders. "People are different," he said. "A man is not a coward because he cries. I have seen two boys fighting and pulling each other's hair and crying all the time, but they fought on. They did not cry because they were afraid."

"Pulling each other's hair!" Ralph repeated contemptuously. "They ought to have been ashamed of themselves, both of them. I don't call that fighting at all. I should call it disgusting. Why, in England even girls would hardly pull each other's hair. I have seen two or three fights between fishwomen in Dover, and even they did not go on like that. If that's the way French boys fight, no wonder our soldiers and sailors—" But here it struck Ralph that the remark he was about to make would be altogether out of place under present circumstances. He was therefore seized with an opportune fit of coughing, and then turned the conversation by asking

Jacques at what rate he thought the vessel was slipping through the water.

A few minutes later the first mate came up and told Jacques to inform Ralph that the captain had ordered him to be supplied with clothes similar to those worn by the rest of the crew, and that he was to be told off to take his post regularly as a boy in the starboard watch. Ralph was well pleased at the news. He felt that his best chance was to make himself useful on board, and to become one of the crew as soon as possible, so that in case an English merchantman was met with and captured he should not be sent with her crew as a prisoner to a French port. As long as he was on board various opportunities of escape might present themselves. He might slip away in port, or the brig might be captured by an English cruiser or privateer; whereas, once lodged in a French prison, the chances of such good fortune as had befallen Jacques were slight indeed. He therefore at once turned to with alacrity.

That he would have a hard time of it for a bit he felt sure; for although in Jacques he had evidently found a friend, he saw by the scowling glances of several of the men as he passed near them that the national feeling told heavily against him. Nor was it surprising that it should be so. The animosity between the two nations had lasted so long that it had extended to individuals. Englishmen despised as well as disliked Frenchmen. They were ready to admit that they might be brave, but considered them as altogether wanting in personal strength. The popular belief was that they were half-starved, and existed chiefly upon frogs and hot water with a few bits of bread and scraps of vegetables in it which they called soup, and that upon the sea especially they were almost contemptible. Certainly the long succession of naval victories that our fleets had won afforded some justification for our sailors' opinion of the enemy. But in fights between detached vessels the French showed many times that in point of courage they were in no way inferior to our own men; and indeed our victories were mainly due to two causes. In the first place, the superior physique and stamina of our men, the result partly of race and partly of feeding; they were consequently able to work their guns faster and longer than could their adversaries. In the second place the British sailor went into battle with an absolute conviction that he was going to be victorious; while the Frenchman, on the other hand, although determined to do his best to win, had from the first doubts whether the British would not be as usual victorious.

It is probable that the French sailors hated us far more than our men did them. We had lowered their national prestige, had defeated them whenever we met them, had blockaded their ports, ruined their trade, inflicted immense damage upon their fisheries, and subsidized other nations against them, and were the heart and center of the coalition against which France was struggling to maintain herself. It was not therefore surprising that among the hundred and ten men on board La Belle Marie there were many who viewed Ralph with hostile eyes, and who only refrained from personal violence owing to the strict order the captain had given that he should be well treated.

Toward midday the fog lifted suddenly and the wind freshened, and lookouts were stationed in the tops. There was little hope indeed of any English merchantmen having come over so far toward the French coast, but British cruisers might be anywhere. A few distant sails could be seen far out on the horizon proceeding up or down channel; but the captain of La Belle Marie had no

idea of commencing operations until very much further
away from the shores of England. All day the vessel
ran down the French coast; and although he was a cap-
tive, and every mile reeled off the log took him further
from home, Ralph could not help admiring the speed at
which the brig slipped through the water, cutting the
waves with her sharp bow and leaving scarcely a ripple
behind her, so fine and clean was her run. Very different
was this smooth, gliding motion from the quick plunge
and shock of the bluff-bowed fishing boat to which he
was accustomed. The sails had been scrubbed until
there was not a speck upon them. The masts were lofty
and tapering, the rigging neat and trim, and every stay
as taut as iron.

We could fight our ships better than the French, but
as far as building and rigging went they were vastly our
superiors; and La Belle Marie looked to Ralph almost like
a gentleman's yacht in its cleanness and order, and in these
respects vied with the men-of-war that he had so often
watched from the heights of Dover. He had, however,
but little time for admiration; for he was kept at work
rubbing and polishing the guns and brass-work, and was
not idle for a minute from the time he came on deck
dressed as a cabin-boy on the morning after he was
picked up until sunset. There were two French boys
about his own age forward, and as soon as his work was
done and the evening watch set they began to torment
him; for, acting as they did as servants to the officers,
they did not take share in the watch.

Fortunately Jacques had gone below at the same time
as Ralph; and when the boys, finding that their taunts
had no effect whatever upon Ralph, began to get bolder,
and one of them snatched off his cap, Jacques interfered
at once. "Look here, youngsters," he said, "this young

English boy is at present one of the crew of this brig, and he has just the same right to fair treatment as any one else, so I warn you if you interfere with him you will have to fight him fairly. I know enough of these English boys to know that with your hands you would not have the least chance with him. He could thrash you both at once; for even little English boys do not wrestle, tear, and kick, but hit straight out just as the men do.

"With swords it would be different, but in a row between you and him it would be just the naked hands. So I advise you to leave him alone, for if you make him fight I will see fair play. All the time I was a prisoner in England I was well treated by his people, and just as I was treated myself and saw other French prisoners treated so I will see him treated. Before this voyage is over it is not impossible the tables will be turned, and that you may find yourselves prisoners in the hands of the English; so I recommend you to behave to him in the same way you would like to be treated yourselves if you were taken prisoners. I can see the lad is good-tempered and willing. He is a stranger here among us all, he can't speak a word of our language, and he has a right to fair treatment. When he gets to know our language he will be able to shift for himself; but until he does I mean to look after him, and any one who plays tricks on him has got to talk to me."

As Jacques Clery was one of the most powerful and active men on board the brig, this assertion was sufficient to put a stop to practical joking with Ralph, and the lad had a much easier time of it than he expected. The men, finding him willing to work and anxious to oblige in every way, soon took to him; and by paying attention to their talk, and asking the French name of every object on board the ship, it was not many days before Ralph found himself able so far to understand that he could obey orders, and pull and haul on any sheet that needed handling.

Upon the second day, the wind having dropped again, more sail was set, and when the word was given to go aloft he went up with the rest; and although he was of little practical use in loosing the gaskets, he soon shook off his first feelings of discomfort and nervousness on seeing how carelessly and unconcernedly the men on each side of him did their work, and before he had been many days at sea was as quick and active aloft as any of the hands on board the brig. After running down nearly as far as Bordeaux the vessel's head was pointed west, and by nightfall the French coast was out of sight. A vigilant lookout was now kept, one man being constantly stationed aloft, and by the increased animation of the crew Ralph judged that they would soon arrive at a point where they should be on the course of homeward bound merchantmen. He had quite made up his mind that, although ready in all other matters to do his duty as one of the crew of La Belle Marie, nothing should induce him to take part in a fight against his own countrymen.

As soon as night fell sail was reduced, and in the morning when at eight bells Ralph came on deck with his watch he found that the whole of the upper sails had been taken off her and the topsails lowered on the cap, and the brig was only moving through the water at the rate of two or three knots an hour. He guessed that she must be just upon the track of ships, and that her object in thus taking off sail was to catch sight of vessels in the distance while she herself would be unobserved by them. During the course of the day several sail were seen passing, but all at a considerable distance. Either the captain did not think that it was safe to commence operations at present, or he did not like the look of some of the passing vessels; but at any rate he made no movement to close with any of them, and it was not until nightfall that sail was again hoisted and the brig proceeded on her course.

Ralph noticed that she carried no light, and that even the binnacle was carefully shaded so that its light could not be seen except by the helmsman. At midnight his watch went on deck, and Ralph perceived that while he had been below the sail had again been greatly reduced, and noticed that from time to time the officer on watch swept the horizon with his night-glass. He apparently observed nothing until about two o'clock, when he stood for some time gazing intently astern. Then he turned, gave an order to a sailor, who went below, and two or three minutes later the captain came on deck. After speaking to the officer he too gazed intently astern. Then the ship's course was suddenly changed, the sheets eased off, and for half an hour she ran at a sharp angle to the course she had before been following, then she was brought up into the eye of the wind and laid to.

Although Ralph strained his eyes in the direction in which the captain had been looking, he could see nothing; but he had no doubt a sail had been seen coming up astern, and that the object of the change of course was to let her pass them without their being seen. He rather wondered that, instead of running off the wind, the captain had not put her about so as to take her position to windward instead of to leeward of the vessel behind; but he soon arrived at the object of the maneuver. There were no stars to be seen, and the bank of clouds overhead stretched away to the east, and the horizon there was entirely obscured; but to the west the sky was lighter, and a vessel would be clearly visible to the eye.

The brig, therefore, in the position she had taken up could not be seen, while she herself would obtain a full view of the other as she passed her.

In an hour the other ship came along. She was a large ship, full rigged, and the French sailors, who had all come on deck, now clustered against the bulwarks and eagerly discussed her. She was about two miles to windward, and opinions differed as to whether she was a man-of-war or an Indiaman. Ralph rather wondered that the privateer had not tried to get alongside in the darkness and take the vessel by surprise, but he understood now that there was a strong probability that the Belle Marie might have caught a tartar and have suddenly run herself under the guns of a British frigate. As soon as the vessel had passed, the braces were manned and the yards swung round, and the brig continued her course. She was brought up almost to the wind's-eye and sailed as closely as possible, so that when morning broke she should have recovered the leeway she had made and should be to windward of the vessel she was pursuing, no matter how much astern.

CHAPTER IV.

THE PRIVATEER'S RENDEZVOUS.

WHEN morning broke the vessel that the privateer had been watching in the night was seen to be three miles directly ahead. She was a large vessel, and for some time opinions differed as to whether she was a frigate or an Indiaman; but when it became quite light a patch or two in the canvas showed that she could not be a man-of-war, and all sail was at once crowded on to the privateer. The other ship at once shook out more canvas, but half an hour sufficed to show that the privateer was much the faster vessel. The stranger took in the extra canvas she had set, and continued her course as if altogether regardless of the privateer.

"They have made up their minds to fight," Jacques said to Ralph. "Now he finds that he can't outsail us he has got on to easy working canvas. She is a big ship, and I expect carries heavier metal than we do. It may be that she has troops on board."

The brig kept eating out to windward until she gained a position about a mile upon the starboard quarter of the Indiaman, then the long pivot-gun was leveled and the first shot fired. The crew had by this time all taken their places by the guns, and Ralph and the other boys brought up powder and shot from the magazine. It was not without a struggle that Ralph brought himself to do this; but he saw that a refusal would probably cost him his life, and as some one else would bring up the cart-

ridges in his place his refusal would not benefit his
countrymen.

He had just come on deck when the gun was fired, and
saw the water thrown up just under the ship's stern, and
the shot was dancing away to leeward. The next shot
struck the merchantman on the quarter. A moment later
the vessel was brought up into the wind and a broadside
of eight guns fired. Two of them struck the hull of the
privateer, another wounded the mainmast, while the rest
cut holes through the sails and struck the water a quarter
of a mile to windward. With an oath the captain of the
privateer brought his vessel up into the wind, and then
payed off on the other tack.

The merchantman carried much heavier metal than he
had given her credit for. As she came round too, some
redcoats were seen on her deck. Apparently well satisfied with the display she had made of her strength, the
ship bore off again and went quietly, on her way, while
the privateer was hove to and preventer stays put to the
mainmast. Ralph remained below for some time; he
heard the men savagely cursing, and thought it was best
for him not to attract attention at present. The sails
were lowered and the brig drifted quietly all day; but
about ten o'clock Ralph heard a creaking of blocks, and
knew that the sails had been hoisted again. Half an
hour later the watch below was ordered to come quietly
on deck. Ralph went up with the rest.

For a quarter of an hour he could see nothing, and then
he made out a dark mass a few hundred yards to leeward; immediately afterward the helm was put up, and
the brig run down toward the stranger. Two minutes
later there was a sharp hail, followed instantly by shouts
and the sound of feet; but before the crew could gain the
deck and prepare for defence the brig was alongside,.

and a moment later her crew sprang upon the decks of
the stranger. A few blows were given; but the resistance offered was slight, and in a very short time the
crew were disarmed or driven below, and the vessel in
the possession of the privateer. She proved to be a
small bark on her way out to the Mediterranean. She
carried only twenty hands and four small guns, and was
laden with hardware.

The privateer's crew at once set to work upon her.
At first Ralph could not understand what they were
about, but he was not long in discovering. The wedges
round the mainmast were knocked out, the topmast
lowered to the deck, the shrouds and stays slacked off,
and then the mast was lifted and carried on board the
brig. As soon as this was done, the second mate of the
brig with eight sailors went on board as a prize crew.
Everything was made taut and trim for them by the brig's
crew. The English prisoners had already been disarmed
and battened down in the hold, and the prize crew then
hoisted sail and prepared to take her under mizzen and
foremast only to a French port. This, if she had luck,
she would reach in safety, but if on the way she fell in
with a British privateer or cruiser she would of course
fall an easy prey.

No sooner was the bark on her way than the priva-
teersmen set to work to lift out their injured mainmast,
and to replace it with that they had brought on board
from the bark. When daylight broke anxious glances
were cast round the horizon; but although a few distant
sails were seen, none of these were following a course
that would bring them near the brig, and the latter without sail and with her foremast alone standing would not
be likely to be noticed. Ralph could not help admiring
the energy with which the crew worked. Ordinarily

they were by no means a smart crew, and did their work in a slow and slovenly manner; but each man now felt the importance of getting everything into order before an enemy appeared, and so well did they work that by midday the new mast was in its place, and before sunset the topmast with all its yards and gear was up and the sails ready for hoisting.

Ralph had been in a state of anxiety in the early part of the night lest he should be sent on board the bark and carried as a prisoner to France. But no one seemed to give a thought to him, and it was not until far on in the morning that the captain happened to notice him hard at work with the rest.

"Ah, are you there?" he said. "If I had thought of it I should have sent you into Best in the bark."

Ralph did not understand the words but he guessed at the meaning, and said, smiling, "I am quite content to remain where I am."

"Tell him, Jacques Clery, that I have noticed that he works willingly, and as long as he behaves well he shall have the same treatment as if he belonged really to the crew; but warn him that if he is caught at any time making a signal, or doing anything to warn a vessel we may be approaching, his brains will be blown out at once."

Jacques translated the warning.

"That's all right," Ralph said. "Of course I should expect nothing else."

As soon as the repairs were completed the sails were hoisted and the brig proceeded on her way. In the days that followed it seemed to Ralph that the tactics of the privateer had changed, and that there was no longer any idea of making prizes. A sharp lookout was indeed kept for any English cruisers, but no attention was paid to any sail in the distance as soon as it was determined that these were not ships of war. Four days later, instead of there being as before five or six sail in sight at one point or other of the horizon, the sea was absolutely deserted. He remarked upon this to his friend Jacques. The latter laughed.

"We are out of their course now, my lad. We passed the latitude of Cape St. Vincent yesterday evening, and we are now pretty well off the coast of Africa. Nine out of ten of the ships we have seen were either bound to the Mediterranean or on their way home. Now that we have passed the mouth of the strait we shall not run across many sail."

"Where are we going to, then?" Ralph said.

"Well, I don't think there is any harm in telling you now, that we are bound south, but how far is more than I know. I expect first we shall go west and try and pick up some prizes among the islands, and after that perhaps go round the cape and lie in wait for Indiamen on their way home. You see, one of those ships is worth a dozen of these Mediterranean traders, and one is not bothered down there as one is between the strait and the channel with your cruisers and privateers; they swarm so there that one can hardly fire a gun without bringing them down on us. I don't suppose the captain would have meddled with that Indiaman if it hadn't been that he thought the owners would be pleased by a prize being sent in so soon. As to the bark, we were obliged to take her to get a new mast. It would never have done to have started on a long cruise with a badly-injured spar."

"But I should think it would be difficult to send home prizes from the West Indies," Ralph said.

"Well, you see, although you have taken most of our islands, there are still two or three ports we can take prizes into. Beside, we can take the best goods out, and if the ship isn't worth the risk of sending to France burn her. Then, too, one can spare hands for prizes better there; because one can always ship a few fresh hands—Spaniards, Mulattos, or blacks—in their place."

"But you can't do that in the case of the Indiamen."

"No; but a single laden Indiaman is enough to pay us well for all our trouble. We can put a crew of thirty hands on board her and send her home. There is little risk of a recapture till we get near France. We have only to hoist the English flag if we do happen to meet anything."

Ralph was glad to hear that the ship was bound for the West Indies, as he thought opportunities for escape would be likely to present themselves among the islands. Madeira was sighted three days later, and after running south for another four or five hundred miles, the brig bore away for the west. By dint of getting Jacques Clery to translate sentences into French, and of hearing nothing but that language spoken round him, Ralph had by this time begun to make considerable progress in the language. Not only was he anxious to learn it for the sake of passing away the time and making himself understood, but his efforts were greatly stimulated by the fact that if any of the crew addressed him in French a cuff on the head was generally the penalty of a failure to comprehend him. The consequence was that when six weeks after sailing the cry of land was shouted by the lookout in the tops, Ralph was able to understand almost everything that was said, and to reply in French with some fluency. As the brig sailed along the wooded shores of the first island they fell in with, Ralph was leaning against the bulwarks watching with deep interest the objects they were passing.

"I can guess what you are thinking about," Jacques Clery said, taking his place quietly by his side. "I have been through it all myself and I can guess your feelings. You are thinking how you can escape. Now, you take my advice and don't you hurry about it. You are doing well where you are. Now you begin to talk French and understand orders it's a good deal easier for you than it was, and the men are beginning to regard you as one of themselves; but you may be sure that you will be watched for a time. You see, they daren't let you go. If you were to get to one of the English ports here we should have five or six of your men-of-war after us in no time.

"If it was not for that I don't suppose the captain would object to put you ashore. He has evidently taken a fancy to you, and is pleased with the way in which you have taken things and with your smartness and willing-ness. Beside, I don't think he considers you altogether as a prisoner. Running you down in the way we did in the channel wasn't like capturing you in a prize, and I think if the captain could see his way to letting you go without risk to himself he would do it. As he can't do that he will have a sharp watch kept on you, and I advise you not to be in any hurry to try to escape. You must remember if you were caught trying it they would shoot you to a certainty."

"I should be in no hurry at all, Jacques, if it were not that the brig is hunting for English vessels. You know what you would feel yourself if you were on board a ship that was capturing French craft."

"Yes, that is hard, no doubt," Jacques agreed; "and I don't say to you don't escape when you get a chance, I only say wait until the chance is a good one. Just at pres-ent we are not specially on the lookout for prizes. We are going to join two other vessels belonging to the same owners. They have been out here some time and have got a snug hiding-place somewhere, though I don't think any one on board except the captain knows where."

For three weeks the brig cruised among the islands. They had picked up no prizes in that time, as the captain did not wish to commence operations until he had joined his consorts and obtained information from them as to the British men-of-war on the station They had overhauled one or two native craft, purchased fish and fruit, and cautiously asked questions as to the cruisers. The answers were not satisfactory. They learned that owing to the numbers of vessels that had been captured by the privateers a very vigilant lookout was being kept; that two or three French craft that had been captured by the cruisers had been bought into the service, and were constantly in search of the headquarters of the privateers. This was bad news; for although the brig with her great spread of canvas could in light winds run away from any of the ships of war, it was by no means certain she would be able to do so from the converted privateers.

One morning two vessels—a schooner and a brig— were seen coming round a headland. The captain and officers examined them with their telescopes, and a flag was run up to the masthead. Almost immediately two answering flags were hoisted by the strangers, and an ' exclamation of satisfaction broke from the captain:

"We are in luck," he said. "If we had not run across them we might have had to search for the rendezvous. I have got the spot marked down on the chart, but they told me before sailing that they understood it was very difficult to find the entrance, and we might pass by within a hundred yards without noticing it."

In half an hour the ships closed up together, and the

captains of the other crafts came on board in their boats.
A hearty greeting was exchanged between them and the
captain of La Belle Marie, and the three then descended
to the cabin. After a time they reappeared, and the
visitors returned to their respective ships. Five minutes
later the schooner got under way, and La Belle Marie
followed her, leaving the other brig to continue her
cruise alone. Toward evening the schooner ran in
toward a precipitous cliff, the biig keeping close in her
wake. Ralph had no doubt that they were now close to
the spot the privateers used as their rendezvous, but he
could detect no opening into the cliff ahead, and it looked
as if the schooner was leading the way to destruction.
Not until within a cable's length of the shore could any
opening be discovered by the keenest eye. Then when
the schooner was within her own length of the cliff her
helm was put about. She came round, and in a moment
later disappeared. An exclamation of surprise broke
from all on board the brig, for they now saw that instead
of the cliff stretching in an unbroken line it projected
out at one point, and the precipitous headway concealed
an extremely narrow passage behind it.

A moment later the brig imitated the maneuver of
the schooner and passed in between two lofty cliffs, so
close that there were but a few yards to spare on either
side of her. Fifty yards ahead the channel made a sharp
turn again, and they entered a basin of tranquil water
three or four hundred yards across. At the further end
the shore sloped gradually up, and here several large
storehouses had been erected, and ways laid down for
the convenience of hauling up and repairing the vessels.

"What do you think of that, youngster?" Jacques said
exultantly. "A grand hiding-place is it not?"

"It is indeed," Ralph replied. "Why, they might

cruise outside for weeks looking for the place and they wouldn't find it, unless a boat happened to row along at the foot of the cliffs."

As soon as the anchor was down the crew were at once given leave to go ashore, and ramble about to stretch their legs after their two months' confinement on board. Ralph was proceeding to take his place in one of the boats when the captain's eye fell upon him.

"Come below with me, young fellow," he said in French. "Jacques Clery, I shall want you too."

"I do not think there is much need of interpreting, captain," the sailor said, as he followed the others into the cabin. "The lad can get on very fairly in French now, and will certainly understand the sense of anything you may say to him."

"Look here, my lad," the captain began, "you have been fairly treated since you came on board this brig."

"I have been very kindly treated," Ralph said. "I have nothing whatever to complain of."

"And we saved your life did we not?"

"Yes, sir, after first nearly taking it," Ralph said with a smile.

"Ah, that was just as much your fault as ours. Little fish ought to get out of the way of great ones, and I don't consider we were in any way to blame in that matter. Still there is the fact in the first place we saved your life, and in the second we treated you kindly."

"I acknowledge that, sir," Ralph said earnestly; "and I feel very grateful. You might have sent me with the crew of that bark to prison had you chosen, and I am thankful to you that you kept me on board and have treated me as one of the crew."

"Now, what I have to say to you is this lad: I know that you are comfortable enough on board, and I have noticed that Jacques here has taken you specially under his wing. You work willingly and well and have the makings of a first-class seaman in you; still I can understand that you would much rather be with your own people, and would be rather aiding them in capturing us than in aiding us to capture them. Consequently you will if you see an opportunity probably try to escape. I shall take as good care as I can to prevent you from doing so, and shall shoot you without hesitation if I catch you at it. Still you may escape, and I cannot run the risk of having this place discovered and our trade knocked on the head. I therefore offer you an alternative. You will either give me your solemn oath not in any case to reveal the existence of this place, or I will put you on shore in charge of the party who remain here, and you will stop with them a prisoner till we sail away from this cruising ground, which may be in three months or may be in a year. What do you say? Don't answer me hastily, and do not take the oath unless you are convinced you can keep it however great the temptation held out to you to betray us."

Ralph needed but a minute to consider the proposal. The oath did not bind him in any way to abstain from making an attempt to escape, but simply to guard the secret of the privateer rendezvous. If he remained here on shore he would have no chance whatever of escape, and might moreover meet with very rough treatment from those left in charge of him. "I am quite ready to take the oath not to reveal the secret of this place, captain," he said. "I do not think that in any case after having been so kindly treated by you I should have been inclined to betray you. However as you offer me the alternative I am ready to take any oath you like of silence, and that oath I will assuredly keep whatever

pressure may be laid upon me, it being understood of
course that the oath in no way prevents my taking any
opportunity that may present itself of making my
escape."

"That is quite understood," the captain said. "That
is a mere matter of business. You try to escape if you
can; I shoot you if I catch you at it But I do not think
you are likely to succeed. But in justice to my employ-
ers and friends I should not be justified in running even
that slight risk unless convinced that if you suceed you
will keep silence as to this. Now, what oath will you
take?"

"No oath can be more binding to me than my promise,
sir; but at the same time I swear upon my word of honor
that I will never give any information or hint that will
lead any one to the discovery of this harbor."

"That will do," the captain said. "I have liked your
face from the moment you came on board, and feel that I
can trust your word."

"I am sure you can do that, captain," Jacques put in;
"from what I have seen of the boy I am certain he will
keep the promise he has made."

"Very well then," the captain said; "that is settled.
You can go on shore in the next boat, and I shall advise
you to take the opportunity, for I warn you that you will
not get the chance of rambling on shore again until we
return here next time. You need not come on board before to-morrow morning."

Half an hour later Ralph went ashore with the last
batch of sailors. He soon found that a general license
had been granted. A barrel of rum and several casks of
wine had been broached, and the men were evidently
bent upon making up for the spell of severe discipline
that they had lately gone through.

Jacques Clery had gone ashore in the same boat with Ralph.

"What are you going to do, lad?"

"I am going for a walk," Ralph said. "In the first place everything is new to me and I want to see the vegetation; and in the second place I can see that in a very short time most of the hands will be drunk, and I dare say quarrelsome, and I don't want either to drink or quarrel. I think I am better away from them."

"You are right boy, and I don't care if I go too. We will take a drink of wine before we start and fill up our pockets with those biscuits. I will get the storekeeper to give us a bottle of wine to take with us, and then we shall be set up for the day. This is my first voyage in these parts; but I have heard from others of their doings, and don't care about getting a stab with a knife in a drunken brawl. I can do my share of fighting when fighting has got to be done, but I do not care for rows of this sort. Still I know the men look forward to what you call a spree on shore, and the captain might find it difficult to preserve discipline if he did not let them have their fling occasionally."

Ralph and the sailor each took a biscuit and a draught of wine, and soon afterward started on their ramble provided with food as arranged. Both were delighted with the luxuriant vegetation, and wandered for hours through the woods admiring the flowers and fruits, abstaining, however, from tasting the latter, as for aught they knew some of the species might be poisonous. Presently, however, they came upon some bananas. Neither of them had ever seen this fruit before, but Ralph had read descriptions of it in books, Jacques had heard of it from sailors who had visited the West Indies before. They therefore cut some bunches. "Now we will bring our-

selves to an anchor and dine. Time must be getting on,
and my appetite tells me that it must have struck eight
bells.'' Jacques sat down on the ground, and was about
to throw himself full length when Ralph observed a
movement among the dead leaves; an instant later the
head of a snake was raised threateningly within striking
distance of Jacques Clery's neck as he sank backward.
Ralph gave a short cry—too late, however, to arrest the
sailor's movements—and at the same moment sprang forward and came down with both feet upon the snake.

"What on earth are you doing?" Jacques asked as he
scrambled to his feet. No answer was made to his question, but he saw at once that Ralph was stamping upon
the writhing folds of a snake. In a minute the motion
ceased.

"That was a close shave, Jacques," Ralph said smiling, though his face was pale with the sudden excitement. "I did not see it until too late to give you warning. It was just the fraction of a second, and even as I
jumped I thought he would strike your neck before my
boot came on him."

"You saved my life, lad," the other said huskily,
trembling from head to foot, as he saw how narrowly indeed he had escaped from death. "I have been in some
hard fights in my time, but I don't know that ever I felt
as I feel now. I feel cold from head to foot, and I believe that a child could knock me down. Give me your
hand, lad. It was splendidly done. If you had stopped
for half a moment to think I should have been a dead
man. Good heavens! what an escape I had."

"I am glad to have been of service for once. You
have been so kind to me since I came aboard the brig
that it is fair that I should do you a good turn for once.
I am not surprised you are shaken, for I feel so myself.

We had better both have a drink of wine, and then we can see about our meal."

"No more lying down on the ground for me," the sailor said. "Once is enough of such a thing as that. However, hand me the bottle. I shall feel better after that."

Ralph looked about and presently discovered an open space, free from fallen leaves or any other shelter for a lurking snake, and persuaded Jacques to sit down and eat his biscuit and bananas in comfort. The sailor did so, but the manner in which his glances kept wandering round him in search of snakes showed that he had not yet recovered his equanimity. When they had finished their meal Ralph proposed that they should climb up to the highest point of ground they could find, and take a view over the island. Two hours' walking took them to the top of a lofty hill. From the summit they were enabled to obtain a distant view. The island was, they judged, some seven or eight miles across, and fully twice that length. Several small islands lay within a few miles distant, and high land rose twenty miles off.

"This must be a large island," Ralph said. "Do you know where we are, Jacques?"

"I have no idea whatever," the sailor said; "and I don't suppose any one on board, except the officers, has, any more than me. The charts are all in the captain's cabin; and I know no more of the geography of these islands than I do of the South Seas, and that's nothing. It's quite right to keep it dark; because, though I don't suppose many fellows on board any of the three craft would split upon us if he were captured, because, you see, we each have a share in the profits of the voyage as well as our regular pay, and, of course, we should lose that if those storehouses, which are pretty well choked

up with goods, were to get taken, there's never any saying what some mean scamp might do if he were offered
a handsome reward. So the fewer as knows the secret
the better.''

"Look Jacques! Look at that full-rigged ship that
has just come out from behind that island. She looks to
me like a frigate.''

"And that she is,'' the sailor replied. "Carries forty
guns, I should say, by her size. English, no doubt.
Well, we had better go down again, lad. I must report
to the captain that this craft is cruising in these waters.
It will be dark before we are back, and I don't want to
be in the woods after dark; there's no saying what one
might tread on. I thought that we would stretch ourselves out under the trees for to-night and go aboard in
the morning, but I feel different now. Bless you, I
should never close an eye. So I propose as we goes
down so as not to be noticed by them chaps up at the
store, and then gets hold of a boat and rows on board
quiet.''

"I am quite willing to do that Jacques. I don't think
I should get much sleep either in the woods.''

"No, I guess not, lad. Come along; the sun is halfway down already, and I would not be left in these
woods after dark, not for six months' pay. The thought
of that snake makes me crawl all over. Who would have
thought now, when I lugged you in over the bowsprit of
La Belle Marie that night in the channel, that you were
going to save my life some day. Well, I don't suppose,
lad, I shall ever get quits with you, but if there is a
chance you can count upon me. You come to me any
night and say I am going to escape, Jacques, and I will
help you to do it, even if they riddle me with bullets five
minutes afterward.''

"I shall never ask that of you, Jacques," Ralph said warmly. "I consider we are quits now, though you may not. Indeed, I can tell you that I don't consider that two months of kindness are wiped out by just taking a jump on to the back of a snake."

There were loud sounds of shouting, singing, and quarreling as they passed near the great fires that were blazing near the storehouse. They reached the water-side without notice, and taking a boat rowed off to the brig. The captain looked over the side:

"Who is that?"

"Jacques Clery and the English lad, captain."

"You got tired of the noise on shore, I suppose?" the captain said.

"Not exactly that, captain, for we have not been near the others at all. We took a long walk through the woods up to the top of the hill in the middle of the island and we came back for two reasons. The first because I have been so badly scared by a snake, who would have bit me had not this young fellow leaped on to its back just as he was about to strike me in the neck, that I would not have slept on the ground for anything; and, in the second place, we came to tell you that from the top of the hill we saw a large frigate—English, I should say, from the cut of her sails—five or six miles off on the other side of the island, and I thought you ought to know about her at once."

"Thank you, Jacques; that is important. I was going to sail in the morning, but we must not stir as long as she is in the neighborhood. So this young fellow saved your life, did he?"

"That he did, captain; and it was the quickest thing you ever saw. I was just lying down at full length when he caught sight of the snake. There was no time to stop me; no time even to cry out. He just jumped on a sudden and came down on the brute as it was on the point of striking. Had he stopped for one quarter of a second I should have been a dead man hours ago.''

"That was a near escape indeed, Jacques. Are they pretty quiet there on shore? I heard them shouting several times.''

"They seem quarreling a bit, captain; but they are sure to do that with all that liquor on hand.''

"They won't come to much harm,'' the captain said. "I gave the strictest orders that all weapons should be left behind before they landed, and that any man carrying even a knife would have his leave stopped during the rest of the cruise. Beside, the first mate is there to look after them. I will go ashore myself at daybreak and take a look round from the top of that hill. If that frigate is still cruising about near the island it must be because they have got some sort of an idea of the whereabouts of our hiding place. We must wait till she moves away. It won't do to risk anything.''

Upon the following morning the captain and Jacques, accompanied by Ralph, landed. They passed close by the storehouse, and saw the men still asleep round the extinguished fires. The captain called out the storekeeper:

"You can serve out one pannikin of wine to each man,'' he said, "but no more. They will want that to pull them together. Tell the first mate to get them on board as soon as possible, and set them to work to tidy up the ship and get everything ready for setting sail at a moment's notice. Tell him an English frigate is reported as close to the island. I am going up to look after her.''

Two hours' steady walking took them to the top of the hill. There were no signs of any vessel as far as they could see. The captain, who had brought his glass with him, carefully examined every island in sight. Presently he uttered an exclamation:

"There are three boats rowing together close under the cliffs there," he said, pointing to the nearest island. "No doubt the frigate is lying behind it. They must be searching for some concealed harbor like ours. *Peste!* this is awkward. What do you think, Jacques?"

"I should say you were right in what you said last night, captain. They must have got an idea that our rendezvous is somewhere hereabouts, though they don't know for certain where, and they are searching all the island round. If they come along here like that we shall be caught in a trap. A vessel might sail close by without suspecting there was an entrance here, however hard they might be looking for it; but if they send boats rowing along the shore they couldn't help finding it. Still, there is nothing to prevent our sailing away now, as the island is between us and them."

"That is so," the captain said. "But if they come while we are away, in the first place they would capture all the booty in the stores, and in the second place they might lie quiet in the harbor and would sink the other ships when they returned. I will go down to the port again, Jacques, and will send up two of the men from the storehouse to keep watch here, turn and turn about. Do you remain here until you are relieved. I will leave my glass with you. If there is anything fresh, leave the boy on watch and come down with the news yourself. I must talk this matter over with the mates. We have no direct interest in the stores, but we must do the best we can for our owners."

Jacques and Ralph watched the distant boats through the glass until they disappeared round the end of the island, then turned the glass seaward. Jacques was using it at the time. "See!" he exclaimed, "there are three sails together there."

"I can see them plainly enough," Ralph said. "What do you make them out to be?"

"A schooner, a brig, and a three-masted vessel. They are lying close together, and I fancy boats are passing between them. However, I couldn't swear to that. They must be fifteen miles away. I expect they are our consorts, and a merchantman they have captured."

"Can they see them from the other side of that island?" Ralph asked excitedly.

"I should say they could," Jacques replied after pausing to calculate the line of sight. "It depends how far round the frigate is lying, and how close in shore. But if they have sent any one up on the hill there, of course they can make them out as plainly as we can." Jacques handed the glass to Ralph.

"Yes, I think I can make out boats, Jacques. What do you suppose they are doing?"

"Most likely they are transferring the valuable part of her cargo on board."

"What will they do with her then?"

"I expect they will let her go; but of course that depends whether she is a new ship and worth taking the risk of carrying her to France."

"They don't burn or sink her, then?"

"No; there would be no good in that; for they wouldn't know what to do with the crew. Of course they don't want the bother of prisoners here, and they wouldn't want to turn them adrift in the boats. They might land on some island near and see us going and coming here, and carry the news to some of your cruisers. No, I expect they will take what is valuable and let them go—that is if the ship isn't worth sending home. I suppose that is so in this case; for if they were going to put a prize crew on board and send it to France, they would not be transferring the cargo. Well, we shall see in another half hour.''

CHAPTER V.

THE BRITISH CRUISERS.

An hour passed. During this time the watchers on the hill saw that the brig had been lying alongside the three-masted vessel, and felt sure that the cargo was being transferred, then the merchantman's sails were hoisted, and she slowly sailed away. For another hour the other two crafts lay motionless, then they hoisted sail and headed for the island. There was a brisk, steady wind blowing, and they came along fast through the water.

"We shall soon see now whether your frigate has made them out," Jacques said; "but I will not wait any longer but will go and tell the captain what is going on. In another hour the others will be up here to relieve you, then you can bring down the latest news."

Left alone, Ralph watched anxiously the progress of the distant vessels, turning the glass frequently toward the other island, beyond the end of which he momentarily expected to see the white sails of the frigate appear. An hour passed. The schooner and the brig were now within about four miles of the nearest point of the island, and still there were no signs of the English ship. Presently he heard voices behind him, and two French sailors came up. Ralph was now free to return, but he thought he had better wait until the brig and schooner reached a point where they would be hidden by the island from the sight of any-one who might be watching on the hill six miles away.

In another half-hour they had reached this point. No signs had been seen of the frigate, and Ralph felt sure that she must have been anchored in some bay whose headland prevented her seeing the approaching craft; for had she noticed them she would assuredly have set out to intercept them before they reached the island, which lay almost dead to windward of them. He was just turning to go when one of the men gave a sudden exclamation. He turned round again and saw the frigate just appearing from behind the other island. She was close-hauled, and it was soon evident by her course that she was beating up for the point round which the other two ships had disappeared.

Ralph was puzzled at this; for if she had made out the brig and schooner, her natural course would have been to have made for the other end of the island, so as to cut them off as they sailed past it; whereas they would now, when they gained the extremity of the island, find themselves five or six miles astern of the other two craft. The French sailors were equally puzzled, and there was a hot argument between them; but they finally concluded that her appearance at that moment must be accidental, and she could not have made out the privateers. They had just told Ralph to run down with the news to the harbor when a light was thrown upon the mystery; for from the other end of the island from which the frigate had emerged a large schooner appeared. Every sail was set, and her course was directed toward this other end of the island upon which the watchers were standing. The two French sailors burst out into a torrent of oaths, expressive of surprise and alarm; for it was evident that from the course the schooner was taking she intended to intercept the two privateers, and engage them until the frigate came to her assistance.

"Run, boy! run for your life!" one of them exclaimed,
"and tell the captain. But no; wait a moment," and he
directed the glass upon the schooner. "A thousand
curses!" he exclaimed. "It is the Cerf schooner the
English captured from us six months ago. She is the
fastest craft in these waters. Tell the captain that I am
coming after you, but your legs will beat mine."

Ralph dashed off at full speed, but as soon as he had
fairly distanced the French sailor he began to run more
slowly. For the moment he had so entered into the feelings of his companions that he had identified himself
with them, but now he had time to think, his sympathies
swung round to the English ship. He did not particularly want La Belle Marie to be captured; for he had
been so well treated on board her that he felt no ill-will
toward her. But her capture meant his deliverance.

He thought over the matter as he ran, and wondered
first why the frigate did not take the line to cut the
privateers off, instead of going round by the other end
of the island. He could only suppose that it was because the schooner was the fastest vessel, and was more
likely to arrive in time at the point. Beside, if she
showed there before the privateers reached the point they
might double back again, and the frigate would make the
other end of the island before they were halfway back.
It might be, too, that the captain has suspected the
truth, knowing that the privateers had a rendezvous
somewhere in that neighborhood, and that his object in
remaining so long behind the island was to give them
time to enter their port in ignorance of his being in the
neighborhood. At any rate, the great thing was, that
the schooner and brig should enter the little harbor before knowing that they were pursued. Once in, it would
be impossible for them to get out again and beat off

shore with the wind blowing dead on the land, before both the schooner and frigate had rounded their respective ends of the island.

Therefore, although Ralph ran fast enough to keep well ahead of the sailor, he made no effort to keep up a greater rate of speed than was necessary for this. As soon as he reached the shore a boat rowed off from the brig to fetch him. He saw with satisfaction that although the men were all on board, no preparations were made for getting under way at once; and, indeed, the captain would have no anxiety for his own ship, as he would know that the privateers, if they saw the frigate coming out to meet them, would sail right away from the island, and the frigate would be sure to pursue until out of sight of land.

"What news, boy?" the captain asked as the boat came close alongside. "Is the frigate in chase of the others?"

"Yes, sir," Ralph replied; "the frigate and a schooner are both in chase."

"Which way are they bearing?"

"The privateers do not know they are chased sir. The frigate did not show round the island over there until the schooner and brig were hidden behind the end of this island. She made toward the western end, and the schooner is making for the eastern end. The sailors who came up told me to tell you that the schooner is the Cerf, one of the fastest vessels out here."

The captain uttered an exclamation of dismay, which was echoed by those standing round him.

"Row out through the entrance," he shouted to the coxswain of the boat, "and warn the others of the danger! Tell them to make straight out If they come in here, we shall all be caught in a trap together!"

The oars dipped in the water, but before the boat was fairly in motion there was an exclamation, for the head sail of the schooner glided in past the projecting cliff. A moment later the whole vessel came into view.

"Bring the boat back alongside!" the captain shouted. "I will go on board her at once. She may get out in time yet!"

As the schooner rounded up her sails came down, and she headed straight toward the brig. The captain of the Belle Marie stood up in the stern-sheet of the boat, shouting and waving his hands and gesticulating to them to get up sail again. Those on board the schooner looked on in surprise, unable to guess his meaning.

"There are two English cruisers, one coming round each end of the island!" he shouted as he approached the schooner. "Get out again if you can, otherwise they must catch us all in here!"

The captain in the schooner at once saw the emergency, and roared out orders. The boats were all lowered at once, and the men tumbled on board. Hawsers were lowered from the bows, and they began at once to tow her head round, for there was not a breath of wind in the land-locked harbor.

"How much time have we got?" the captain asked as the schooner's head came slowly round.

"I don't know," the other captain replied. "It's a question of minutes, anyhow. Ah, here is the brig!" and the boat dashed forward and he gave similar orders to those that had been given to the schooner.

"Get them both round!" the captain shouted. "I will row out through the entrance and give you warning if these accursed cruisers are in sight."

The boat dashed through the narrow entrance, and at once felt the full force of the breeze. "Dead on shore," the captain muttered bitterly. "They will have to work right out into the arms of one or other of them."

They rowed a hundred yards out, when, beyond the furthermost point they could see to the east, the sails of the schooner were perceived.

"Take her round," the captain said sharply. "It's too late now, we have got to fight for it."

They rowed back through the entrance. The schooner slowly towed by her boats was approaching.

"It is no use," the captain said, "you are too late. The schooner has rounded the end of the island, and with this breeze will be here in half an hour. You never can work out in time. Beside, they would see you come out; and even if you got away, which you couldn't do, they would come back and capture the depot. We have got to fight for it, that's evident; and the boats of a fleet could hardly make their way in here. We had best get the three craft moored with their broadsides to the entrance. We will blow the boats to tinder if they try to come in, and then we can load up with all the most valuable goods and slip out at night-time. That is our only chance."

The captain of the schooner jumped into the boat, and they again rowed out into the entrance. He saw at once that the other's advice was the only one to be followed. It would be impossible to beat off the shore before the schooner came up and while they were talking the frigate appeared round the other end of the island. They therefore returned into the harbor. The Belle Marie's anchor was raised, and the three vessels moored head and stern across the harbor, a hundred yards from the entrance. As soon as this was done strong parties were sent ashore from each of the vessels, and six heavy ship's guns that had been landed from some captured vessel were dragged from their place near the storehouse and planted on the heights, so as to sweep the narrow channel.

It was late in the evening before this was finished, and an earthwork thrown up to shelter the men working the guns from musketry fire. In the meantime the two ships of war had met outside, and again separating cruised several times from end to end of the rocky wall, evidently searching for the entrance through which the privateers they had been pursuing had so suddenly disappeared. In the morning the French sailors were at work early, and two or three strong chains were fastened across the mouth of the passage.

"Now," the captain of the Belle Marie said exultantly, as he regained the deck of his ship, "we are ready to give them a warm reception. The boats of all the British cruisers on the station would never force their way through that gap."

Ralph had not been called upon to assist in the work of preparation, he and Jacques having done their day's work on the journey to the top of the hill and back. He saw from the exultation in the faces of the Frenchmen that they considered their position was impregnable, and he shuddered at the thought of the terrible carnage that would ensue if the boats of the English vessels should try to force an entrance. The following morning a lookout on the cliffs reported that two boats had left the ships and were rowing toward the shore. On reaching the foot of the cliffs they rowed along abreast at a distance of thirty or forty yards of the shores. They stopped rowing at the mouth of the entrance, and were suddenly hailed by the captain of the schooner, who was standing on the cliff above.

"If you try to enter," he said, "you will be destroyed at once. We don't want to harm you if you will leave us alone; but we have guns enough to blow a whole fleet out of water, and will use them if we are driven to it."

"Thank you for your warning," a voice shouted back from the boats, and then an order was given, and they rowed back to the ships.

"Well, have you found the place, Lieutenant Pearson?" the captain of the frigate asked as the young lieutenant stepped on deck.

"Yes, sir, we have found it. It is just where the boat turned and came out again."

"I can see no signs of it now," the captain said, examining the shore with his telescope.

"No, sir; you wouldn't until you were within a hundred yards of it. But rowing close in as we were we saw it some time before we got there. The rocks overlap each other, and there is a narrow channel some fifty yards long between them. Apparently this makes a sharp turn at the other end and opens out. We saw nothing of the vessels we were chasing yesterday, but on high ground facing the channel there is a battery of six guns planted so as to rake anything coming in. There are some chains across the end. While we were lying on our oars there we were hailed." And he then repeated the warning that had been given.

"Nasty place to get into—eh?" the captain said thoughtfully.

"Very nasty, sir. You see, the guns would play right down into the channel; then there are the chains to break down, and perhaps more batteries, and certainly the ships to tackle when we get inside."

"Is there width for the frigate to enter?" the captain asked.

"Just width, I should say, and no more, sir. We should certainly have to get the yards braced fore and

aft, but the ship herself would go through with something to spare, I should say.''

"What depth of water is there close in shore?''

"Plenty of depth sir, right up to the foot of the cliffs;
but of course I can say nothing as to the depth in the
channel.''

"No, of course not,'' the captain said. "Well, it's
something that we have run these pests to earth at last,
but I see it is going to be no easy matter to get at them.''

The captain now signaled to the captain of the
schooner to come on board, and when he did so the two
officers retired to the cabin together and had a long
consultation. The young officer on coming on deck got
into his boat, and taking Lieutenant Pearson with him
rowed for the cliffs, a few hundred yards to the west of
the inlet. Here they could obtain a view of the channel
and its surroundings. Not a man was to be seen. The
muzzles of the six guns pointed menacingly down into
the passage, and the chains could be seen just above the
water's edge.

"I think we will go back now, Mr. Pearson. I really
think we ought to be very much obliged to those fellows
for not sinking us. I wonder what was their motive in
letting us off so easily?''

"I suppose they feel pretty confident that our report
is not likely to encourage an attack, and they think that
if they were to blow us to pieces it would only make Captain Wilson the more determined to destroy them. At
least that is the conclusion I came to as I rowed back
last time.''

"Yes, I should think that is it,'' the young captain
said. "It is certainly as awkward a looking place to
attack in boats as I ever saw. Of course were it not for
the chains my vessel could get in, and I dare say she has

been in there many a time before we captured her, but it would be a very risky thing to take the frigate in without knowing anything of the depth of water either in the channel or inside."

Both returned to the frigate. "Mr. Pearson's report is fully borne out, Captain Wilson. It would be a most desperate enterprise to attack with our boats. Half of them would be sunk before they got to the chains; and even if they got past them, which I doubt, there is no saying what difficulties and obstacles may be inside."

"And now about the frigate, Captain Chambers."

"Well, sir, that is for you to decide. I am quite ready to take the schooner in; though with the plunging power of that battery raking her fore and aft I say fairly that it would be a desperate enterprise, and if she had not sufficient way upon her to carry away the chains nothing could save her. As to the frigate, it seems to me that she would run an equal risk with the schooner, with the additional danger that there may not be water enough for her."

"Well, it certainly doesn't seem to be an easy nut to crack," Captain Wilson said. "As we agreed before you started, we should not be justified in risking both our vessels in assaulting a place which is certainly extremely formidable, and where there may not be water enough for the frigate to float. Still the question remains, what is to be done? It is no use anchoring here and trying to starve them out; they may have provisions enough to last them for years, for anything we know. If the weather were to turn bad we should have to make off at once; it would never do to be caught in a hurricane with such a coast as that on our lee. I might send you to Port Royal with a letter to the admiral, asking him to send us two or three more ships; but I don't like

doing that when it is a mere question of capturing two
rascally privateers.''

"I think the admiral would be glad to send them,"
the younger captain said; "for these two vessels have
done a tremendous lot of damage during the last year.
I believe that upward of twenty ships have reported
being boarded and stripped by them.''

"But if they came what could they do?" Captain Wilson asked. "You see we consider it is not worth the
risk of throwing away two ships two force this passage,
still less would it be to risk four.''

"That is so, no doubt," Captain Chambers agreed.
"I should suggest that however many of us there may be
we should all draw off and keep a watch at a distance.
Of course it would be necessary to approach at night,
and to lie behind the island somewhere in the daytime
just as we did yesterday, for from the top of that hill
they can see any distance round."

"Yes, and as soon as it is dusk they will have two or
three hours to get away before we can come round here.
Beside, with their night-glasses from the top of the
cliffs they will be sure to be able to make us out. There
is only one other way that I can see of getting at them,
that is to find a landing-place and attack them from on
shore.''

"Ah! that's much more hopeful business. As far as I
saw yesterday there are cliffs all round the island; but it
is hard indeed if we cannot find some place where we
can manage to effect a landing.

"This is the plan we must follow out. This afternoon
an hour before it gets dark you get up sail and make
away as if you were bound for Port Royal. I shall keep
my station here. They will think you have gone off to
get some more ships. As soon as it is thoroughly **dark**

bear round and come back to the island; bring the schooner in close to the cliffs on the other side and get into a bay if you can find one. You will then be out of sight altogether unless somebody happens to look down from the edge of the cliffs above you.

"Then search the whole of the back of the island with boats, keeping at oar's length from the cliffs. There must be some places where a man can climb up, probably gulleys worn by streams. Then to-morrow night sail round and join n e again. I will be waiting for you about two miles off the land, and will show a light to seaward so that you will know where to find me. Then we can talk matters over, and you can get back to the other side again before morning."

While the captains of the two English vessels were holding consultations a similar talk was going on between the three captains of the privateers, and the conclusion they arrived at was precisely similar to that of the English officers. It was agreed that no attack was likely to be made by the ships, as they would almost certainly be sunk by the plunging fire of the battery as they came along the channel; while an assault by the boats would be sheer madness.

"We have only to wait and tire them out," the captain of the schooner said, rubbing his hands. "The first gale from the north they must run for shelter, and before they can come back to their station again we shall be gone. Of course we will load well up beforehand with all that is really worth taking away, and can let them have the pleasure of destroying the rest after we have gone."

"They will know all that as well as we do," the captain of La Belle Marie said. "They will never be fools enough to try and starve us out, but you are quite mistaken if you think we are out of danger."

"Why, what danger can there be?" the others asked.
"We have agreed they cannot attack us by the channel."

"No, they cannot attack us from the channel, but they can attack us from somewhere else now they know we are here. They will find some place where they can land and take us in rear."

An exclamation of dismay broke from the other captains.

"*Sapriste!* I never thought of that. Of course they can. I have never examined the coast on the other side, but there must be places where they could land."

"No doubt there are; and you may be quite sure that is the course they will adopt. These English are slow, but they are not fools; and I will bet ten to one that is the next move they will be up to. If you like I will take a score of my men and cross the island this afternoon, and to-morrow will examine the whole line of shore. If there are only one or two places they can land at we may be able to defend them; but if there are four or five places far apart our force won't be sufficient to hold them all, for they could land two hundred and fifty men from those two ships, perhaps a hundred more."

"That is the best thing to be done, Vipon. Of course you will send us word across directly you see how the land lies. If we find that they can land in a good many places, there will be nothing for us to do but try and make a bolt for it. Keeping close in under the cliffs at night we may manage to give them the slip, or in any case one if not two of us may get away. Better that than to run the risk of being all caught like rats in a trap here."

An hour afterward the captain of the Belle Marie started for the other side of the island with twenty picked men, carrying with them their arms, axes, and two days' provisions. The rest of the crews were employed during the day in filling up the three vessels with the most valuable portion of the booty in the storehouses, care being taken not to fill the vessels so deeply as would interfere seriously with their sailing powers. An arrangement had been made between the captains that the Belle Marie should transfer her cargo to the first vessel worth sending to France that she captured, receiving as her share one-third of its value if it reached port safely.

The captain of the Belle Marie was well content with this arrangement, for the storehouses contained the spoils of upward of twenty ships, and his share would therefore be a considerable one, and he would only have to carry the cargo till he fell in with an English merchantman. All speculation as to the British schooner's whereabouts was put an end to the next morning, by a message from Captain Vipon saying she had been discovered lying close in under the cliffs at the back of the island, and that her boats were already examining the shore. An hour later the captain himself arrived.

"It is as I feared," he said when he joined the other captains; "there are three bays about two miles apart and at all of these a landing could be easily effected. The land slopes gradually down to the edge of the sea. They might land at any of them, and of course the guns of the schooner would cover the landing if we opposed it."

"Still we might beat them back," one of the others said. "We can muster about three hundred men between us, and they are not likely to land more than that."

"I don't think that would be a good plan," Captain Vipon said. "To begin with, we can't tell which of the

three places they may choose for landing at. We certainly cannot hurry through the woods anything like so
fast as they can row along the shore, so that would place
us at a disadvantage. In the second place, you know
very well that we can't rely upon our men defeating an
equal number of these John Bulls; and in the last place,
we should not gain much if we did. We should lose a
tremendous lot of our men, and the schooner would go
off and fetch two or three more ships of war here, so that
in the end they must beat us. I think that there is no
question that it will be better for us to take our chances
of escape now.''

"Either the schooner will come back to-night and tow
the boats of the frigate round the other side of the island,
or she will send a boat with the news that she has found
a landing-place, and then the frigate will send all her
boats. I don't think the attack will take place to-night;
but it may be made. It certainly won't if the schooner
comes round, for the wind is very light. She will not
leave her anchorage until it is quite dark; and by the
time she has got round to the frigate, and the boat's
crews are ready to start, and they all get to the back of
the island, it will be morning. If they send a boat it
would reach the frigate after three hours' rowing; give
them an hour to get ready and start, and three hours to
row back, so that brings it to nearly the same thing.
Beside, I don't suppose in any case they would land before morning, for they would run the risk of losing their
way in the woods. So my proposal is that at about two
o'clock in the morning we make a start, separate as soon
as we get out of the harbor, and each shift for himself.
The frigate will have more than half her crew away, and
being so short-handed will not be so smart with her sails,
and will not be able to work half her guns; so that at

the outside two out of the three of us ought to get safely off.''

"But suppose that the schooner happens to be round here, and they make up their minds to wait a day before attacking, we should have two of them after us then; and that schooner sails like a witch."

"I have thought of that," Captain Vipon said. "My idea is to put a man on the top of the cliff just above where the schooner is anchored. If she is lying there he is to light a fire a short distance back from the edge of the cliff. There should be another man on the top of the hill. When he sees the fire he shall show a lantern three times. We will return the signal to let him know that we see it. If the schooner goes away early in the evening the lookout is not to light the fire until he sees her returning, at whatever hour it may be. The moment we see the light we will set sail."

"But how about the two signallers?" one of the other captains said. "They would be left behind and might not get the chance of rejoining us again."

"I have thought of that too," Captain Vipon, said. "I have an English lad on board whom I picked up in the channel. He is a smart lad, and has been working as one of the crew. He would of course be glad to stay behind, because it will give him the chance of rejoining his friends."

"That would do capitally. But how about the other man? You see, if he showed himself he would be made prisoner and sent to England; if he didn't show himself he might be on this island for years before he got a chance of joining a French ship. It would need a high bribe to induce anybody to run such a risk as that."

This was so evident that there was silence for two or three minutes, then Captain Vipon spoke again. "I have a man who would be more likely to do it than any one else I think, because he has taken a strong fancy to this young English boy. He is a good hand, and I don't like losing him; still the thing is so important that I should not hesitate at that. Still we must offer him something good to run the risk, or rather the certainty of imprisonment. I propose that his name shall be put down on the books of all three ships, so that if he ever gets back to France again he will have a fair certainty of a good lot of prize money, for it will be hard luck if two out of the three of us do not manage to get back safely.'' The other captains agreed to this.

"He will be here in half an hour,'' Captain Vipon said. "The men were sitting down to a meal when I came away, and I ordered them to make their way back as soon as they had done. If he refuses, the only other way I can see will be for all the men to cast lots, when, of course, whoever stays would get his three shares as we agreed.''

Half an hour later the twenty men arrived from the other side of the island. As soon as they came on board Captain Vipon called Jacques into the cabin and told him that it would be necessary to leave two men behind, explaining the duties they would have to perform.

"Now Jacques,'' he said when he had finished, "I thought that perhaps you would be more likely than any other man on board the three ships to volunteer for this work.''

"I volunteer!'' Jacques said in astonishment. "What should make you think of such a thing, captain?''

"For this reason, Jacques: I have settled to leave the English lad here as one of the signallers. Of course he will gladly undertake the job, as it will enable him to join his friends when they land; and as you like him

and he likes you, he might be able to make things easy
for you. In the second place we have determined that
the name of whoever stops shall be borne on the ship
books of all three vessels to the end of their cruise, so
that there would be a good bit of money coming even if
only one out of the three ships gets back, and enough to
set you up for life if all three get back safely. Of course
you may have a spell of imprisonment; but it is likely
that one at least of the ships may be caught going out
to-night, and if it happened to be ours you would get
the prison without the prize-money.''

"That is so," Jacques agreed. "If you give me half
an hour to think it over I will give you an answer. It's
come upon me sudden-like. I will talk it over with the
boy. I suppose I can tell him, captain?"

On regaining the deck Jacques looked about for Ralph.

"Come and sit along with me out on the bowsprit, lad.
I want to have a private talk with you."

Somewhat surprised Ralph followed his friend out on
to the bowsprit.

"Now, boy," he said, "I have got a bit of news to tell
you that will be pleasant to you. That's the first thing;
and the next is, I want your advice. You are a sensible
young chap, you are, although you are but a lad, and I
should like to know what you think about it."

"Well, what's the good news, Jacques?"

"The good news is this; you 'are likely, before this
time to-morrow, to be with your friends." Ralph gave
such a start of delight that he nearly slipped off the
bowsprit.

"How is that Jacques? It seems too good to be true.''

"This is the way of it," Jacques said. "The three
vessels are all going to cut and run to-night. That
schooner of yours is round the other side of the island,

and we want to be sure she is stopping there, then there will only be the frigate to deal with, and in these light winds and dark nights we ought to be able to give her the slip; but the only way to be sure the schooner keeps the other side is to watch her. So one man is to be placed on the cliff above her, and at two o'clock in the morning, if she is still there, he is to light a fire well back from the cliff, so that the light will not be seen by her. Another man is to be on the top of the hill, where we were together with a lantern. You see, we can just see the top of the hill from here. When he sees the fire he is to show a light three times. If he sees it answered here he will know it's all right, and his work is done; if not, of course he shows the lights again until it's answered. Now, they are going to leave you as one of the two signallers, and of course all you will have to do will be to wait for a bit, and then come down and join your friends."

"That is capital," Ralph said. "Nothing could be better. Now, what is the other matter that you want my advice about, Jacques?"

"Well, you see, it will be awkward for the other man, for he will either have the choice of coming down and giving himself up and being carried off as a prisoner, or of stopping on this island perhaps for years till a French ship happens to come along; for once off the Marie will continue her cruise to the Indian seas, and the other two will make straight for France. Of course there is another course which might be taken. A boat might be hidden away for him, and he might go for a cruise on his own account and take the chance of being picked up.

"Well, they have offered to the man as stops to put his name down on the books of all the three craft. That means, of course, that he will get a share in the prize-

money of all three ships if they get back. That's a
pretty good offer, you know. You see, a fellow on board
may get captured or killed in battle or wrecked, and in
that case there would not be a penny of prize-money.
The man who stops here is sure of prize-money if only
one of the three craft get back to France. Now, they
ask me if I will undertake it. I should be better off
than the others; because in the first place I shall have
you to talk with till I get to prison, and in the next
place as I can talk English I can get on a good deal better in prison than other fellows would do. Now, what's
your advice, lad?"

"I should say certainly accept the offer, Jacques.
You see, I can tell them all what a good friend you have
been to me, and it maybe they will let you go free; but
even if they don't I could make it pleasant for you with
the men, and you may be sure that if they take you to
an English prison I will do all I can to get you out of
it. You see, when you get back to France you would
have really a good sum coming to you from these three
ships. The two that have been out here have collected
a tremendous lot of valuable plunder, and the Bell Marie
is likely to get quite as much if, as you say, she is
going to spend two years out in the Indian seas. So I
really think you would be wise to take the offer. Another thing, if you like I will not show myself at all, but
will stop here with you, and we will take a boat together
and make for some port, where we can give out that we
are shipwrecked sailors."

"No, lad, that wouldn't do; though I thank you for
your offer. You might get a ship back to England, but
I should have very little chance of getting one for
France."

"No; but we might get one together for America, and
from there you might get to France easily enough."

Jacques thought for some minutes. "No, lad; I will give myself up with you. We might get lost in a boat, seeing that neither of us know the geography of these seas; we might get short of water, or caught in a hurricane. No, I will give myself up. I know the worst that way, anyhow. Another spell in an English prison; but from that I may either get exchanged, or escape, or the war come to an end. So that's the best thing for me to do."

CHAPTER VI.

HOME AGAIN.

HAVING decided to stay as one of the signallers, Jacques proceeded at once to the captain's cabin.

"I am glad you have decided so, Jacques. It would have been a troublesome business to cast lots, and some of the men might have absolutely refused doing so; so I am glad it's settled. I have arranged with the other captains that you shall have an advance of twenty napoleons. You had best hide them about you; you may find them come in useful. The boy is to have ten. Of course he is glad of the chance; but at the same time he is doing us good service, and he has worked well since he came on board. It will help him to get a passage home."

"Thank you, captain. That twenty napoleons may help me to get out of an English prison. I will manage a hiding place for them. And now I think, captain, we will be off at once—at least as soon as we have had our dinner. It's a good long way across the island to where that schooner was lying, and I shall have to choose a place for my fire so that it can be seen from the top of the hill."

At dinner Jacques told his comrades that he was going to remain behind and act as signalman for them. A good deal of regret was expressed by his shipmates, many of whom came like himself from Dunkirk, and had known him from a boy. Before starting he went to the sailmaker and got him to open the soles of his shoes; he then inserted ten napoleons in each, and the sailmaker sewed them up again. Then making his clothes into a kit and getting a couple of bottles of wine from the steward, he shook hands with his messmates, and was with Ralph rowed ashore.

On landing they cut two sticks and hung their kits upon these, Ralph taking charge of the lantern, while both were provided with tinder and steel.

They walked for half a mile together, and then Jacques said:

"Here our paths separate, lad; you can't miss your way to the top of the hill. I go almost the other way, for the schooner lies but a short distance from the end of the island. If I were you I should lie up for a sleep as soon as I get there. Remember you will not see my fire till two o'clock. If you do not see it then you must keep watch till morning, for there's no saying when it may be lit. As soon as you see it you show a light three times in the direction of the creek. If you see it answered you will have nothing more to do; if not you must keep on showing the light till you do get an answer. In the morning you wait till the sun has been up an hour, then come to this spot and wait for me. I shall start at daybreak, but I have a lot further to walk than you have, so I shan't be there before you. If we find your people haven't come into the harbor we will wait till they do so; then when they find that there is no one there we can show ourselves quietly; but if we got there first they might begin to shoot directly they saw us without stopping to ask any questions."

Ralph made his way up to the top of the hill, threw himself down under some trees near the summit, and was soon fast asleep. When he awoke it was already dark.

He lit his lantern, covered it up in his jacket, and took his station at the highest point. He had plenty to think about. Another twelve hours and he would be with friends! He had no reason to complain of the treatment he had received on board the privateer, but had he remained with her he might not have returned to France for a couple of years, and would then have had difficulty in crossing to England; beside, it was painful to him to be with men fighting against his country, and each prize taken instead of causing delight to him as to his comrades, would have been a source of pain.

But most of all he thought of his mother, of how she must have grieved for him as dead, and of the joy there would be at their reunion. The hours therefore passed quickly, and he could scarcely believe it to be two o'clock when he suddenly saw the light of a fire far way toward the end of the island. A glance at the stars showed him that the time was correct. He rose to his feet, and taking the lantern held it aloft, then he lowered it behind a bush and twice raised it again. He knew exactly the direction in which the harbor lay, and no sooner had he put down the lantern for the third time than three flashes of light followed in close succession.

He knew that everything would be prepared in the afternoon for the start. Orders had been issued before he left that the oars of the boats were to be muffled, that the chains at the entrance of the channel were to be removed, and the ships got in a position, with shortened cables, for a start. He could picture to himself, as he stood there gazing into the darkness, that the men would be already in the boats awaiting his signal, and as soon as it was seen they would begin to tow the vessels out of the harbor.

During the daytime the frigate cruised backward and

forward under easy sail some two miles off the entrance; but the sailors believed that at night she came very much closer to the shore, the lookout with night-glasses having reported that she had been seen once or twice within a quarter of a mile of the entrance to the channel.

Half an hour passed without any sign that the frigate was aware that the ships were leaving the harbor; then Ralph heard the sound of a distant musket-shot, followed by several others, and had no doubt that one of the frigate's boats on watch near the channel had discovered them.

A few minutes later there was a flash some distance out at sea, followed after an interval by the deep boom of a gun; then came a broadside, followed by a steady fire of heavy guns. These were evidently fired on board the frigate, no answering sounds from the French ships meeting his ear. He could see by the direction of the flashes that the frigate was under way. The firing continued for two hours, becoming more and more distant, and then it ceased altogether.

When the sun rose he saw the frigate some twenty miles away. There was a smaller craft two or three miles further off, and two others were visible ten or twelve miles further away to the west. Two of the privateers had evidently made their escape, and the third seemed to be leaving her pursuer behind, for the wind was exceedingly light. Some miles nearer to the island than the frigate a schooner was visible. She was heading for the two vessels that had gone toward the west, but as these were fully fifteen miles to windward her chance of overtaking them appeared to be slight. Ralph waited an hour, and then proceeded at a leisurely pace toward the spot where he was to meet Jacques. He was but five minutes at the spot agreed upon when he saw him coming through the trees.

"I heard nothing of the landing-parties," he said as the French sailor approached.

"The reason is not far to search for," he replied. "They did not land at all, and I did not much expect that they would. The boats from the frigate arrived a few minutes before I lighted my fire. I was lying down at the edge of the cliff, looking right down upon her deck. They came up in a body, rowing with muffled oars. I could just hear the sound of their talking when they came on deck. As soon as I had the fire fairly alight I saw your signal and then went back to watch them. Everything was quiet till I heard the boom of the first gun; then I heard 'Silence!' ordered on the schooner. I suppose some one had said that he heard a gun, and other's didn't. Of course the sound did not come to them under the shelter of the cliff as it did to me. Then came the sound of another gun, and then three or four close together; then orders were given sharply, the capstan was manned and the anchor run up, and they were not a minute getting her sails set. But under the shelter of the cliff there was not enough wind to fill them, and so the boats were manned, and she went gliding away until I could no longer make her out. They guessed, of course, that our craft were making off, and went to help the frigate."

"They were too late to be of any use, Jacques."

"Ah! you have seen them from the top of the hill. I did not think of that. What is the news?"

"The frigate was in chase of ono of them. It was too far for me to see which. I should say he was two or three miles ahead, certainly well out of gunshot, and as far as I could see during the hour I was watching them, was increasing her lead. Unless the wind freshens I think she is safe. The other two were on the opposite tack, ten or twelve miles away to the west. The schooner was heading after them, but was at least fifteen miles from them."

"She is very fast in a light wind like this, they say."

"Well, if she should catch them, they ought to be able to beat her off, Jacques, as they are two to one. So far I think your chance of getting your three shares is a good one."

"Maybe, lad. I have not had much luck so far. I began on the sea when I was eleven. At twenty-one I had to go into the navy, and it was seven years later when I got back to Dunkirk after that spell in the prison. I did not report myself, for I had no wish to do any more man-of-wars' work; and now I have had six years privateers' work, and have not made much by it. If I get back this time and get those three shares I will buy a fine fishing smack for myself and a snug little house on shore. There is some one I promised—if the voyage turned out well—she should have a nice little house of her own, and she promised to wait for me. After that, no more long voyages for me. I suppose we may as well go down to the harbor now, lad. They are sure to come back sooner or later, whether they catch any of the privateers or not."

"Oh, yes! we shall be all safe now. We will be on the beach when they come in. When they see that we are alone and unarmed there's no chance of their firing. We can go up occasionally to the cliffs and watch for them."

It was not until the following evening that the frigate was seen approaching the island.

"She will take another four or five hours to work in," Jacques said, "and they are not not likely to try to land till to-morrow morning. All their boats and half their men are away in the schooner. I should think she would be back to-morrow morning. Either she caught them before it got dark last night—which I don't think likely —or they will have given her the slip in the night. In that case she might look about for another day and then make sail to rejoin.''

As Jacques predicted the schooner was seen by daylight eight or ten miles away.

"We may as well hoist a white flag, Jacques. The captain of the frigate will be savage that all the privateers have escaped him, but it may put him into a good temper if he takes possession here before the schooner arrives.''

Ralph ran down to the storehouse, got hold of a sheet and an oar, and a white flag was soon hoisted on the top of the cliff. Five minutes later two gigs were seen rowing off from the frigate. Ralph and Jacques took their places on the battery. When the boats reached the mouth of the narrow entrance the order was given for the men to lay on their oars. Ralph shouted at the top of his voice:

"You can come on, sir! We are the only two here!''

The order was given to row on, and Ralph and his companion at once went down to meet them at the end of the harbor. The captain himself was in the stern of his own gig, while a young lieutenant held the lines in the other boat.

"Who are you? the captain asked, as he stepped ashore on the little wharf. You are English by your speech.''

"I am English, sir. I was on board a fishing boat in the channel when we were run down by one of those privateers in the dark. I believe the fisherman with me was drowned, but I clung to the bobstay and was got on board. She was on her way out here and had no opportunity of landing me. She only arrived here two days before you came up.''

"You are not a fisherman?" the captain said abuptly.

"No, sir; my mother is living at Dover, and I was at school there. I lost my father, who was an architect, some years ago."

"And who is this who is with you?"

"He is a sailor in the brig I came out in, and has been extremely kind to me during the voyage, and kept the others from persecuting me."

"How is it he is left behind?" the captain asked.

"He was round the other side of the island watching the schooner," Ralph replied, "and the others sailed away without him;" for Ralph had agreed with Jacques that it was better to say nothing about the signalling.

"Have you done any fighting since you were on board the privateer?" the captain asked sternly.

"No, sir. We have only exchanged shots with one ship since we sailed. She fired one broadside and the privateer drew off a good deal damaged. Another was surprised by night, but I took no part in it. I don't know what she was laden with or what was her name."

"Well, lad, your story sounds truthful, and will, of course, be inquired into when we get to England. As to this man, he is of course a prisoner."

"I hope not, sir," Ralph pleaded. He has not been taken with arms in his hands, and is, in fact, a castaway mariner."

The captain's face relaxed into a smile. "I see you are a sort of sea lawyer. Well, we shall see about it. What is there in these storehouses?"

"A quantity of things, sir. They took away a great many with them, but there must be ten times as much left. I heard them say they had the cargoes of more than twenty ships here."

"That is satisfactory at any rate," the captain said.

"Mr. Wylde, will you just take a look round these store-houses and see what there is worth taking away. You had better take my boat's crew as well as your own to help you to turn things over. Are you quite sure, lad, that there is no one beside yourselves on the island?"

"I can't say that, sir. The orders were for all hands to embark last night, and so far as I know none of them were left behind except Jacques Clery. We have been here for two days now and have seen no one, so I do not think any one else can have been left."

"How did you get on on board the brig?" the captain asked. "I suppose you cannot speak French?"

"I couldn't speak any French when I first was got on board, sir, but I picked up a great deal on the voyage out. Jacques speaks English very well. He was a prisoner in England for three years, and learned it there, and it was that which caused him to speak to me directly he had got me on board, for no one else understood me. So he set to work at once to help me in my French, so that I could get along. The captain was very kind too. He said that as I had been picked up in that way he should not treat me as a prisoner; but he expected me to make myself useful, and, of course, I did so. It was the only way of having a comfortable life."

"Is this the only place the privateers had on shore here? the captain asked, looking round. "I only see one or two huts."

"The storekeepers lived in them, sir. They stopped behind to look after things when the privateers were away. The men slept on board their vessels, only landing to disembark the cargoes they had captured, and for a drunken spree when they first returned. I am sure they have no other place."

"So your brig only arrived here four days ago? I was

puzzled in the morning when I saw there were two brigs
and a schooner when we had only expected one brig.
Of course your arrival accounts for that. What was her
name, and how many guns and men did she carry?"

"She was La Belle Marie of Dunkirk," Ralph replied.
"She carried fourteen guns, mostly eighteen-pounders,
and a thirty-two-pounder on a pivot. She had eighty
hands at first, but eight of them went away in the prize."

"Do you know whether she has gone off straight for
France or whether she is going to remain here?"

"From what I gathered from the men, sir, I believe
the other two privateers are going straight home. They
loaded up from the storehouses, taking, of course, the
most valuable stuff. There was a great deal of copper,
but what the rest was I do not know. Our brig was
loaded up too, but I believe her intention was to transfer
her cargo into the first prize she took and send it to
France. I do not know whether she was going to cruise
about here for a time, but I should rather think that now
that her consorts have gone and this place been discovered she will not stay here, for she never intended to
cruise in these waters long. I know that her destination
was the Indian Ocean, and she intended to capture Indiamen on their way out or home."

"In that case our expedition has been more satisfactory than I expected," the captain said. "We shall
have discovered and destroyed their depot here, captured
anyhow some valuable stuff, and caused the two privateers that we have been hunting for so long to leave the
islands, to say nothing of this brig of yours, of which
we had not heard. Well, Mr. Wylde, what is your
report?"

"It will take a long time to go through the whole sir;
but I should say that we have taken a most valuable

prize. Part of the goods consist of produce of these parts—puncheons of rum and hogsheads of sugar in any number. Then I see they have left a good many tons of copper behind them; overlooked them, I suppose, in the hurry of loading. A considerable portion of the stores consist of home produce—cottons, cloths, silks, furniture, musical instruments, mirrors, and, in fact, goods of all kinds.''

"That is most satisfactory, Mr. Wylde, and we sha'n't have had our trouble for nothing. Ah! here come the other boats.''

As he spoke the pinnaces, long-boats, and cutters of the two ships of war dashed into the harbor, and in a minute or two reached the landing-place.

"So they gave you the slip as well as me, Chambers?'' Captain Wilson said.

"Confound them, yes. I was within about four miles of them at sunset, but they both gave me the slip in the dark.''

"Mine fairly outsailed me,'' Captain Wilson said. "I am afraid we have made rather a mess of the affair; though we acted for the best, and I don't see how we could have done otherwise. However. I have learned that the brig and the schooner we have been chasing so long have made straight for France, so that we shall have no more trouble with them. The other brig, which only arrived two days before we chased the others in here, has, it is believed, also gone off. So we shan't have done so badly; for we can report that we have found out and destroyed their nest here, and I fancy from what my lieutenant says we have made a very valuable capture, enough to give us all a round sum in prize-money.''

"That will be some consolation,'' the other laughed; "but I would give my share of it if I could but have come up with and engaged those rascally craft I have been hunting all over the islands for these last two years. Whom have we got here—two prisoners?"

"Well, I hardly know whether they can be called prisoners. One is an English lad who was in a boat they run down in the channel, and who, I dare say, they were glad to get rid of. It seems that he is a gentleman's son, and his story is clear enough. The other belongs to the brig I chased, which it seems only arrived here two days ago. The young fellow says that he has been particularly kind to him, and has begged me to regard him in the light of a castaway sailor, seeing that he was found here unarmed and away from his ship. I think there is something in his plea; and as there is no credit or glory to be obtained from handing over one prisoner, I consider that under the circumstances we shall be justified in letting him go ashore quietly and in saying nothing about it. At one time the man was a prisoner of war in England and has picked up our language, so I dare say he will be able to manage to find his way home without difficulty."

"What are you thinking of doing with all this stuff?" Captain Chambers asked, pointing to the storehouses.

"I think we had better take it away with us. I don't like turning the Alert into a storeship; but it would be better to do that than to have the expense of chartering two or three ships to come here to fetch it away. Beside, if I did that, you would have to stop here until it is all carried away, and to burn the storehouses afterward."

"Then by all means let us load up," Captain Chambers said. "I certainly have no wish to be kept here for six weeks or a couple of months. I will go out and bring the Seagull in at once."

"The sooner the better, Chambers. I will set a couple of boats at work at once to take soundings here and in the channel. If I can get the Alert in I will; it would save a lot of trouble and time."

It was found that the channel and the harbor inside contained an abundance of water for the frigate. The width between the rocks was, however, only just sufficient to let her through; and, therefore, while the schooner sailed boldly in, the frigate was towed in by her boats. The next morning the work of shipping the contents of the storehouses commenced, but so large was the quantity of goods stored up that it took six days of hard work before all was safely on board. The sailors, however, did not grudge the trouble, for they knew that every box and bale meant so much prize-money.

"I hope we shall meet nothing we ought to chase on our way to Port Royal," Captain Wilson said, looking with some disgust at the two vessels. "It has brought the Alert nearly two feet lower in the water; while as to the Seagull she is laden down like a collier."

"Yes, her wings are clipped for the present," Captain Chambers replied. "Of course those rascals carried off the pick of their booty with them; but we may be well content with what they left behind. It will be the best haul that we have made for some years. As a rule, the most we have to hope for is the money fetched by the sale of any privateer we may catch, and they generally go for next to nothing. I retract what I said—that I would give my share of the prize-money to come up with the privateers. I certainly never calculated on such a haul as this. I suppose they intend to have gone on storing away their booty till the war came to an end, and then to have chartered a dozen ships to carry it away."

Captain Wilson had introduced Ralph to the midshipmen, telling them he would be in their mess till he reached port. He was soon at home among them, and his clothes were replaced by some they lent him. Jacques made himself equally at home among the crew. Captain Wilson had intimated to the first lieutenant that the man was not to be considered as a prisoner, but as a castaway, picked up on the island; and from his cheery temper, his willingness to lend a hand and make himself useful in any way, and his knowledge of their language, he was soon a favorite with them.

When all the goods were on board fire was applied to the storehouses and huts. The two vessels were then towed out of the harbor, and hoisting sail made for Port Royal. The winds were light, and it was six days before they entered the harbor. A signal was at once hoisted from the flagship there for the captain to come on board.

"I have no doubt he is in a towering rage at our appearance," Captain Wilson said to the first lieutenant; "but I fancy he will change his tone pretty quickly when he learns what we have got on board. His share of the prize money will come to a pretty penny."

The next morning a number of lighters came alongside the ships, and the work of discharging the cargo commenced. After breakfast Ralph and Jacques were rowed ashore.

"You will want some money to pay for your passage, young gentleman." Captain Wilson said to Ralph before leaving the ship. "I will authorize you to tell an agent that I will be security for the payment of your passage-money."

"I am very much obliged to you, sir," Ralph replied; "but I shall work my way home if I can. I have learned to be pretty handy on board the privateer, and I would

as lief be working forward as dawdling about aft all the
way home. Beside, I don't want to inconvenience my
mother by her being called upon suddenly to pay thirty
or forty pounds directly I get home. I have caused her
trouble enough as it is."

"That's right, my lad," the captain said. "I like
your spirit. Have you money enough to pay for your
hotel expenses while you are waiting for a ship?"

"Yes, thank you, sir. The French captain said I had
fairly earned wages, and gave me ten napoleons when he
started."

"He must have been a good sort of fellow," the captain said; "though I wish we had caught him for all
that. Well, good-by, and a pleasant voyage home."

Ralph put up at a quiet boarding-house, kept by a
Mulatto woman. He and Jacques got a fresh rig-out of
clothes at once, and went down to the port to inquire
about ships. Ralph was greatly amused at the aspect
of the streets crowded with chattering negroes and
negresses, in gaudy colors. The outlay of a few pence
purchased an almost unlimited supply of fruit, and Ralph
and his companion sat down on a log of wood by the
wharves and enjoyed a feast of pine apples, bananas, and
custard apples. Then they set about their work. In an
hour both were suited. Jacques Clery shipped as a
foremast hand on board an American trading schooner,
which was about to return to New York; while Ralph
obtained a berth before the mast in a fine bark that
would sail for England in a few days.

Next morning they said good-by to each other, for
Jacques had to go on board after breakfast. They made
many promises to see each other again when the war
came to an end.

"I shall never forget your kindness, Jacques; and if I

am still at Dover when peace is proclaimed I will run over to Dunkirk by the very first vessel that sails."

"As for the kindness, it is nothing," Jacques replied; "and beside that, you saved my life from that snake. I dream sometimes of the beast still. And it was really owing to you that I am here now, and that I shall get a round sum coming to me when I return home. If it hadn't been for you I should not have been chosen to stop behind and get three shares instead of one of the prize money. And in the next place it is your doing that I am free to start at once, and to make my way back as soon as I can, instead of spending four or five years, it may be, in an English prison. Why, my Louise will be ready to jump for joy when she sees me arrive, instead of having to wait another two years for me, with the chance of my never coming back at all; and she will hardly believe me when I tell her that I shall be able to afford to buy that fishing boat and set up in a house of our own at once; and she will be most surprised of all when I tell her that it is all owing to an English boy I fished on board on a dark night in the channel."

"Well, Jacques, we won't dispute as to which owes the other most. Anyhow, except for my mother, I am not sorry I have made the trip in the Belle Maire. I have seen a lot of life, and have had a rare adventure; and I have learned so much of sailor's work, that if I am ever driven to it I can work my way anywhere before the mast in future."

Ralph went on board his own ship as soon as he had seen Jacques off, and was soon hard at work assisting to hoist on board hogsheads of sugar and other produce. He was startled by the sound of a heavy gun. It was answered presently by all the ships of war in the harbor and by the forts on shore, and for five minutes the heavy

cannonade continued. The captain, who had been on
shore, crossed the gangway on to the ship as the crew
were gazing in surprise at the cannonade, exchanging
guesses as to its cause.

"I have great news, lads," he said. "Peace is proclaimed, and Napoleon has surrendered, and is to be shut
up in the Isle of Elba in the Mediterranean. No more
fear of privateers or French prisons."

The crew burst into a hearty cheer. This was indeed
surprising news. It was known that Wellington was
gradually driving back the French marshals in the south
of France, and that the allies were marching toward
Paris. But Napoleon had been so long regarded as in-
vincible, that no one had really believed that his downfall was imminent.

Four days later the cargo was all on board, and the
Fanny sailed for England. The voyage was accomplished
without adventure. As soon as the vessel entered dock
and the crew were discharged Ralph landed, and having
purchased a suit of landsman clothes, presented his kit
to a lad of about his own age, who had been his special
chum on board the Fanny, and then made his way to the
inn from which the coaches for Dover started. Having
secured a place for next day, dined, and ordered a bed,
he passed the evening strolling about the streets of London, and next morning at six o'clock took his place on
the coach.

"Going back from school, I suppose, young gentleman?" a military-looking man seated next to him on the
coach remarked as soon as they had left the streets behind them, and were rattling along the Old Kent Road.

"No, I am not going home from school," Ralph said
with a smile. "At least not from the sort of school you
mean; though I have been learning a good deal too. I
arrived yesterday from the West Indies."

"Indeed!" the gentleman said, scrutinizing him closely. "I see you look sunburned and weather-beaten now that I look at you; but somehow I should not have put you down as a sailor."

"Well, I am not exactly a sailor; though I may say I have worked as one before the mast both out and home. That was my first experience; and I suppose one takes longer than that to get the regular nautical manner."

"Before the mast, were you? Then I suppose you have been getting into some scrape at home, young sir, and run away; for, from your appearance, you would hardly have been before the mast otherwise. Boys never know what is good for them. But I suppose after your experience you will be inclined to put up with any disagreeables you may have at home rather than try running away again?"

"You are mistaken!" Ralph said with a laugh. "I did not run away. I was run away with!"

"Kidnapped!" the gentleman said in surprise. "I know that merchantmen have often difficulty in getting hands owing to the need of men for the navy, but I did not know that they had taken to press-gangs on their own account."

"No, I don't know that they have come to that," Ralph replied. "The fact is, sir, I was out fishing a few miles off Dover, when the smack I was in was run down in the dark by a French privateer. I was hauled on board, and as she was bound for the West Indies I had to make the voyage whether I liked it or not."

"How long ago is it that you were run down?"

"About five months," Ralph replied.

"Why, you are not the son of Mrs. Conway of Dover, are you?"

"Yes, I am, sir. Do you know her, and can you tell me how she is?" Ralph asked eagerly.

"I believe that she is well, although of course she must have suffered very greatly at your disappearance. I haven't the pleasure of knowing her personally, but several friends of mine are acquainted with her. I heard the matter talked about at the time the boat was missing. Some portions of her were picked up by other fishing boats, and by the shattered state of some of the planks they said that she had been run down; beside, there had been no wind about the time she disappeared, so that there was little doubt some vessel or other had cut her down. I happened to hear of it from Colonel Bryant, who is a friend of your mother."

"Yes, I know him," Ralph put in.

"I have heard Colonel Bryant say that she has not altogether abandoned hope, and still clings to the idea that you may have been run down by some outward-bound ship and that you had been saved and carried away, and that she declares that she shall not give up all hope until ample time has elapsed for a ship to make the voyage to India and return."

"I am very glad of that," Ralph said. "It has been a great trouble to me that she would be thinking all this time that I was dead. I should not have minded having been carried away so much if I had had a chance of writing to her to tell her about it; but I never did have a chance, for I came home by the very first ship that left Port Royal after I arrived there."

"But how did you get away from the French privateer —was she captured?"

"Well, it is rather a long story, sir," Ralph said modestly.

"All the better, the gentleman replied. "We have got fourteen hours journey before us, and your story will help pass the time; so don't try to cut it short, but let me have it in full. Ralph thereupon told the story, which lasted until the coach reached Tunbridge, where it stopped for the passengers to dine.

"Well, that is an adventure worth going through," the officer, who had already mentioned that his name was Major Barlow, said; "and it was well for you, lad, that you possessed good spirits and courage. A man who is cheerful and willing under difficulties will always make his way in the world, while one who repines and kicks against his fate only makes it harder for him. I have no doubt that if, instead of taking matters coolly when you found yourself on board the privateer you had fretted and grumbled, you would have been made a drudge and kicked and cuffed by everyone on board. You would not have had a chance of landing at that island or of being chosen to make the signal when they went away, and you would now be leading the life of a dog on board that brig. Cheerful and willing are two of the great watchwords of success in life, and certainly you have found it so."

It was eight o'clock when the coach rattled up the streets of Dover. Major Barlow had already offered Ralph to take him to Colonel Bryant's quarters, and to ask the colonel to go with him to call on Mrs. Conway and prepare her for Ralph's coming.

CHAPTER VII

A COMMISSION.

COLONEL BRYANT was just rising from dinner at the mess when Major Barlow and Ralph arrived at the barracks, and after congratulating the lad on his return he willingly agreed to accompany them to Mrs. Conway. A quarter of an hour's walk took them to her house. Ralph remained outside when the two officers entered. Colonel Bryant lost no time in opening the subject.

"I have brought my friend Major Barlow to introduce to you, Mrs. Conway, because he has happened to hear some news that may, I think, bear upon the subject that you have most at heart."

"Ralph!" Mrs. Conway exclaimed, clasping her hands.

"We think it may refer to your son, Mrs. Conway," Major Barlow said. "I have just returned from town, and happened to hear that a vessel had been spoken with that reported having picked up a lad from a smack run down in the channel some five months ago, which corresponds pretty well, I think, with the time your son was missing."

"Just the time," Mrs. Conway said. "Did they not say the name?"

"Well, yes. The name, as far as I heard it, for as I had not the pleasure of knowing you I was not of course so interested in the matter, was the same as yours."

"I think that there is no doubt about it, Mrs. Conway," Colonel Bryant said kindly. "I consider you may quite set your mind at ease, for I have no doubt whatever it is your son who has been picked up." Mrs. Conway was so much overcome that she sank into a chair and sat for a short time with her face in her hand, crying happy tears and thanking God for his mercy. Then with a great effort she aroused herself.

"You will excuse my emotion, gentlemen, and I am sure you can understand my feelings. I am thankful indeed for the news you have brought me. I have never ceased for a moment to hope that my boy would be restored to me; but the knowledge that it is so, and that God has spared him to me, is for the moment overpowering. And where was the ship met with, Major Barlow, and where was she bound for? How long do you think it is likely to be before Ralph comes home?"

"Well, Mrs. Conway," Major Barlow said, hesitating a little, "the ship was bound for India; but I understood from what was said that the vessel, that is the vessel that brought the news, had also brought home the lad who had been carried away."

"Then, in that case," Mrs. Conway cried, "he may be home in a day or two. Perhaps—perhaps—and she paused and looked from one to the other.

"Perhaps he is here already, Colonel Bryant said gently. "Yes, Mrs. Conway, if you feel equal to it you may see him at once. No word was needed. Major Barlow opened the door, went through the hall, and called Ralph, and in another moment the lad was clasped in his mother's arms, and the two officers without another word went quietly out and left them to themselves. It was some time before a coherent word could be spoken by mother or son, and it was not until they had knelt down together and returned thanks to God for Ralph's restoration that they were able to talk quietly of what had passed. Then Mrs. Conway poured out question after question, but Ralph refused to enter upon a narrative of his adventures.

"It's a long story, mother, and will keep very well till to-morrow. It is past nine o'clock now, and I am sure that you want a night's rest after this excitement; and after fourteen hours on a coach, I sha'n't be sorry to be in bed myself. Beside, I want you to tell me first how you have been getting on while I have been away, and all the news about everyone; but even that will keep. I think, mother, a cup of tea first and then bed will be best for us both."

The next morning Ralph related all his adventures to his mother, who was surprised indeed at his story.

"I suppose poor old Joe was never heard of, mother?"

"No, Ralph. His son has been up here a good many times to inquire if we had any news of you. He has gone into another fishing boat now, and his sister has gone out to service. Their mother died years ago, you know."

"I was afraid that he had gone straight down, mother. Nobody on board the brig heard any cry or shout for help. He must have been injured in the collision."

"I must write to-day to Mr. Penfold. He has written to me several times, and has been most kind. He has all along said that he believed you would turn up one of these days, for as the weather was fine and the sea fairly calm when you were run down, the probabilities in favor of your being picked up were great, especially as you were such a good swimmer. I am sure he will be delighted to hear of your return."

"I hope he will not be wanting me to go straight off down there again," Ralph said ruefully. "I was only back with you one day, mother, after my visit to them,

and now I have been five months away it will be very
hard if I am to be dragged off again."

"I am sure Mr. Penfold will not be so unreasonable as
to want to take you away from me," Mrs. Conway said.

"And am I to go back to school again, mother?"

"Not now, certainly, Ralph. The holidays will be
beginning in a fortnight again; beside, you know, we
were talking anyhow of your leaving at the end of this
half year."

"That's right, mother. It's high time I was doing
something for myself. Beside, after doing a man's work
for the last five months I shouldn't like to settle down to
lessons again."

"Well, we must think about it, Ralph. You know I
consented greatly against my will to your choosing the
army for your profession, and I am not going to draw
back from that. You are just sixteen now, and although
that is rather young I believe that a good many lads do
get their commissions somewhere about that age. In
one of his letters Mr. Penfold said that as soon as you
came back he would take the matter in hand, and though
I have good interest in other quarters and could probably
manage it, Mr. Penfold has a great deal more than I have,
and as he has expressed his willingness to arrange it I
shall be grateful to him for doing so."

"That will be first rate, mother," Ralph said in delight. "I thought in another year I might get my commission; but of course it would be ever so much better
to get it a year earlier."

For the next few days Ralph was a hero among his boy
friends, and had to tell his story so often that at last he
told his mother that if it wasn't for leaving her so soon
he should be quite ready to go off again for another visit
to Mr. Penfold.

"You won't be called upon to do that," she said smiling; "for this letter that I have just opened is from him, and he tells me he is coming here at once to see you, for he thinks it would be too hard to ask me to spare you again so soon."

"You don't mean to say that he is coming all that way?" Ralph said in surprise. "Well, I am very glad."

"He asks me in his letter," Mrs. Conway said with a passing smile of amusement, "if I can take in a young friend of his, Miss Mabel Withers. He says she has never been from home before, and that it would be a treat for her to get away and see a little of the world. He is going to stop a few days in London, and show her the sights on his way back."

"That will be very jolly, mother. You know I told you what a nice sort of girl she was, and how well we got on together. I don't know how I should have got through my visit there if it hadn't been for her. Her father and mother were very kind too, and I was often over at their house."

Mr. Penfold had not succeeded in inducing Mr. and Mrs. Withers to allow Mabel to accompany him without much argument. "You know what I have set my mind on, Mrs. Withers," he said. "But of course such an idea doesn't enter the young people's heads, it would be very undesirable that it should do. But now Ralph has returned he will be wanting to get his commission at once, and then he may be away on foreign service for years, and I do think it would be a good thing for the young people to see as much of each other as possible before he goes. If anything happens to me before he comes back, and you know how probable it is that this will be the case, they would meet almost as strangers, and I do want to see my pet scheme at least on the way

.

to be carried out before I go. It would be a treat for
Mabel, and I am sure that Mrs. Conway will look after
her well.''

"How long are you thinking of stopping there, Mr.
Penfold?"

"Oh, ten days or a fortnight. I shall be a day or two
in town as I go through, for I want to arrange about
Ralph's commission. Then, perhaps, I shall persuade
Mrs. Conway to come up with Ralph to town with us,
and to go about with the young people to see the sights.
Now, if you and Mrs. Withers would join us there, that
would complete my happiness.''

The clergyman and his wife both said that this was
impossible. But Mr. Penfold urged his request with so
much earnestness, that at last they agreed to come up to
town and stay with him at a hotel. And, indeed, when
they recovered from the first surprise at the proposal,
both of them thought that the trip would be an extremely
pleasant one; for in those days it was quite an event in
the lives of people residing at a distance from a town to
pay a visit to the metropolis.

"Then everything is arranged delightfully," Mr. Penfold said. "This will be a holiday indeed for me; and
however much you may all enjoy yourselves I shall enjoy
myself a great deal more. Now, I suppose I may tell
Mabel of our arrangement?"

"But you don't know that Mrs. Conway will take her
in yet. Surely you are going to wait to hear from her?"

"Indeed I am not, Mrs. Withers. I am as impatient
as a schoolboy to be off. And I am perfectly certain that
Mrs. Conway will be very glad to receive her. She
knows Mabel, for I have given her an idea of my fancy
about that matter; and of course she will be glad to learn
something of your girl.''

"But she may not have a spare room," Mrs. Withers urged feebly.

"It is not likely," Mr. Penfold said decisively; "and if there should be any difficulty on that score it will be very easily managed, as Ralph can give up his room to Mabel, and come and stay at the hotel with me."

Mr. Withers laughed. "I see that it is of no use raising objections, Penfold; you. are armed at all points. I scarcely know you, and have certainly never seen you possessed of such a spirit of determination."

Mr. Penfold smiled. "It would have been better for me, perhaps, if I had always been so determined, Withers. At any rate I mean to have my own way in this matter. I have not had a real holiday for years."

So Mr. Penfold had his own way, and carried off Mabel wild with delight and excitement upon the day after he had received Mrs. Conway's letter. There was no shade of embarrassment in the meeting between Mrs. Conway and the man who had once been her lover. It was like two old and dear friends who had long been separated and now come together again. Mr. Penfold's first words after introducing Mabel had reference to Ralph.

"Your boy has grown quite a man, Mary, in the last six months. I scarcely recognized the bronzed young fellow who met us at the coach office as the lad who was down with me in the summer. Don't you see the change, Mabel?"

"Yes, he is quite different," the girl said. "Why, the first time I saw him he was as shy as shy could be. It was quite hard work getting on with him. Now he seems quite a man."

"Nothing like that yet, Mabel," Ralph protested.

"Not a man!" Mr. Penfold exclaimed. "What! after

wandering about as a pirate, capturing ships, and cutting men's throats for anything I know, and taking part
in all sorts of atrocities? I think he's entitled to think
himself very much a man."

Ralph laughed.

"Not as bad as that, Mr. Penfold. They did take one
ship, but I had nothing to do with it; and there were
no throats cut. I simply made a voyage out and back as
a boy before the mast; and, as far as I have been concerned, the ship might have been a peaceful trader instead of a French privateer."

"Well, Mary, you have not changed much all these
years," Mr. Penfold said turning to Mrs. Conway, while
the two young people began to talk to each other. "I
had thought you would be much more changed; but
time has treated you much more kindly than it has me.
You are thirty-seven, if I remember right, and you don't
look thirty. I am forty, and look at the very least ten
years older."

Mrs. Conway did not contradict him, for she could
not have done so with truth.

"You are changed, Herbert; a great deal changed,"
she said sadly, "although I should have know you anywhere. You are so much thinner than when I saw you
last; but your eyes have not changed, nor your smile.
Of course your hair having got gray makes a difference,
and—and—" and she stopped.

"I am changed altogether, Mary. I was a headstrong,
impetuous young fellow then. I am a fragile and broken
man now. But I am happy to meet you again. Very
happy in the thought that I can benefit your son. I
have an interest in life now that I wanted before; and in
spite of my being anxious about Ralph while he was
away, have been happier for the last six months than I

have been for seventeen years past." Mrs. Conway turned away to conceal the tears that stood in her eyes, and a moment later said:

"I am a most forgetful hostess, Mabel. I have not even asked you to take off your things. Please come along and let me show you your room. Supper will be ready in a minute or two, and here are we stopping and forgetting that you and Mr. Penfold must be almost famished."

As soon as they had sat down to supper, Mr. Penfold said, "By the way, Ralph, I have a piece of news for you. We stopped a couple of days, you know, in town, and I saw my friend at the Horse Guards, and had a chat about you. He seemed to think that you would be better if you were a few months older; but as he acknowledged that many commissions had been given to lads under sixteen, and as you had just arrived at that age, and as I told him you have had no end of experience with pirates and bucaneers, and all that sort of thing, he was silenced, and your commission will appear in the next *Gazette.*"

"Oh, Mr. Penfold!" Ralph exclaimed as he leaped from his seat in delight. "I am obliged to you. That is glorious. I hardly even hoped I could get a commission for some months to come. Don't look sad, mother," he said, running round and kissing her. "I shan't be going out of England yet, you know; and now the war is over you need have no fear of my getting killed, and a few months sooner or later cannot make much difference."

"I shall bear it in time, Ralph," his mother said, trying to smile through her tears. "But it comes as a shock just at first."

The sight of his mother's tears sobered Ralph for a time, and during supper the conversation was chiefly supported by Mr. Penfold, who joked Ralph about his coming back in a few years a general without arms or legs; and was, indeed, so cheerful and lively that Mabel could scarcely believe her ears, so wholly unlike was he to the quiet friend she had known as long as she could remember. The next fortnight was a delightful one to Mabel, and indeed to all the party. Every day they went driving-excursions through the country round. Ramsgate and Deal and Folkestone were visited, and they drove over to Canterbury and spent a night there visiting the grand cathedral and the old walls.

The weather was too cold for the water, for Christmas was close at hand; but everthing that could be done was done to make the time pass happily. Mrs. Conway exerted herself to lay aside her regrets at Ralph's approaching departure, and to enter into the happiness which Mr. Penfold so evidently felt. The day before their departure for town an official letter arrived for Ralph, announcing that he was gazetted into his majesty's 28th Regiment of foot, and that he was in one month's date from that of his appointment to join his regiment at Cork.

"Now, Miss Mabel," Mr. Penfold said gayly, after the first talk over the commission was concluded, "you will have for the future to treat Mr. Ralph Conway with the respect due to an officer in his majesty's service."

"I don't see any change in him at present," the girl said, examining Ralph gravely.

The boy burst into a laugh.

"Wait till you see him in uniform, Mabel," Mr. Penfold went on. "I am afraid that respect is one of the moral qualities in which you are deficient. Still I think that when you see Ralph in his uniform, you will be struck with awe."

"I don't think so," Mabel said, shaking her head. "I don't think he will frighten me, and I feel almost sure that he won't frighten the Frenchmen."

"My dear child," Mr. Penfold said gravely, "you don't know what Ralph is going to turn out yet. When you see him come back from the wars seven or eight inches taller than he is now, with great whiskers, and perhaps three or four ornamental scars on his face, you will be quite shocked when you reflect that you once treated this warrior as a playfellow."

Upon the following day the party went up to London, and were joined next morning by Mr. and Mrs. Withers. Mabel declared that she did not think any people ever could have enjoyed themselves so much as they all did. They went to Exeter 'Change to see the animals and to the theater at Drury Lane, to the Tower and Ranelagh Gardens, to Westminster Abbey and St. Paul's, and they went down by coach to Hampton Court and to Greenwich, and they saw his majesty the king review the Guards in Hyde Park. Altogether it was a glorious fortnight. Mr. Penfold was the life and soul of the party, and had he had his way they would have seen far more than they did. But Mr. and Mrs. Withers and Mrs. Conway all said that they wanted to enjoy themselves and not to be worn out, and several times they stayed at home when Mr. Penfold and the two young people went to see sights, or to wander about the streets and look at the shops, which was as great a treat as anything. Mr. Penfold went with Ralph to a military tailor and ordered his outfit, and to other shops, where he purchased such a stock of other garments that Mrs. Conway declared Ralph would require nothing for years. On the last day of the fortnight the uniforms and trunks and clothes all arrived at the hotel, and of course Ralph

One 28th. MABEL IS SEIZED WITH A FIT OF SHYNESS.—Page 133.

had to dress up and buckle on his sword for the first time. Mrs. Conway shed a few tears, and would have shed more had not Mr. Penfold made every one laugh so; and Mabel was seized with a fit of shyness for the first time in her life when Mr. Penfold insisted that the ladies should all kiss the young officer in honor of the occasion. And the next morning the whole party went down to the wharf below London Bridge to see Ralph on board the packet for Cork. Before leaving the hotel Mr. Penfold slipped an envelope with ten crisp five pound notes in it into Ralph's hand.

"I have paid in, my boy, two hundred pounds to the regimental agents, and in future shall make you an allowance of the same amount every year. You will see what other officers spend. My advice to you is: do not spend more than others, and do not spend less. Money will keep very well, you know, and a little reserve may always come in useful. When you once go on foreign service you will not find much occasion for money. I want you just to hold your own with others. I consider that it is quite as unfortunate for a young man to spend more than those around him as it is for him to be unable to spend as much. No, I don't want any thanks at all. I told your mother I should look after you, and I am going to, and it has given a vast pleasure to me to have such an interest. Write to me occasionally, my boy; your letters will give me great pleasure. And should you get into any scrape, tell me frankly all about it."

The evening before Mrs. Conway had had a long talk wit Ralph. "I do not think I need to give you much advice, my boy. You have already been out in the world on your own account, and have shown that you can make your way. You are going into a life, Ralph, that has many temptations. Do not give way to them, my boy.

Above all, set your face against what is the curse of our times: over-indulgence in wine. It is the ruin of thousands. Do not think it is manly to be vicious because you see others are. Always live, if you can, so that if you kept a true diary you could hand it to me to read without a blush on your cheek; and always bear in mind, that though I shall not be there to see you, a higher and purer eye will be upon you. You will try; won't you, Ralph?"

"I will indeed, mother."

Mr. Penfold did his best to keep up the spirits of all of the party when they parted on board the packet; but Mrs. Conway quite broke down at last. Mabel cried unrestrainedly, and his own eyes had a suspicious moisture in them as he shook hands with Ralph. Fortunately they had arrived a little late at the wharf, and the partings were consequently cut short. The bell rang, and all the visitors were hurried ashore; then the hawsers were thrown off and the sails hoisted. As long as the party remained in sight Ralph stood on the stern waving his handkerchief to them; then, having removed the traces of tears from his cheeks, he turned to look at what was going on around him.

The packet was a brig of about two hundred tons, and she carried about twenty passengers, of whom fully half Ralph judged by their appearance to be military men. Before they had reached the mouth of the river he found that one among them Captain O'Connor, belonged to his own regiment, as did another young fellow about his own age named Stapleton, who had been gazetted on the same day as himself. Captain O'Connor, who was a cheery Irishman, full of life and spirits, at once took Ralph in hand, and was not long in drawing from him the story of his adventures with the privateers.

"You will do, my lad. I can see you have got the roughness rubbed off you already, and will get on capitally with the regiment. I can't say as much for that young fellow Stapleton. He seems to be completely puffed up with the sense of his own importance, and to be an unlicked sort of cub altogether. However, I have known more unlikely subjects than he is turn out decent fellows after a course of instruction from the boys; but he will have rather a rough time of it at first I expect. You will be doing him a kindness if you take an opportunity to tell him that a newly-joined ensign is not regarded in the same light as a commander-in-chief. It is like a new boy going to school, you know. If fellows find out he is a decent sort of boy, they soon let him alone; but if he is an ass, especially a conceited ass, he has rather a rough time of it. As you are in the same cabin with him, and have had the advantage of having knocked about the world a bit, you might gently hint this to him."

"I have been chatting with him a bit," Ralph said. "He has never been to school, but has been brought up at home, and I think from what he said he is the heir to an estate. He seemed rather to look down upon schools."

"So much the worse for him," Captain O'Connor said. "There is nothing like a school for bringing a fellow to his level, unless it is a regiment; and the earlier in life the process takes place the less painful it is."

"I don't think he will turn out a bad sort of fellow," Ralph said. "He is, as you say, rather an ass at present. I will do what I can to give him a hint; but as I should say he is at least a year older than I am, I do not suppose it will be of much use."

The voyage was a pleasant one, and Ralph was quite sorry when they entered the Cove of Cork and dropped anchor. The next morning the ship sailed up the river, and the following day the party disembarked. Captain O'Connor's servant came on board as soon as the vessel reached the quay, and his master charged him to pick out his luggage and that of the two young officers; he then at once proceeded with them to the barracks. Ralph felt extremely pleased that Captain O'Connor was with them, as he felt none of the shyness and unpleasantness he would otherwise have experienced in joining a set of entire strangers.

Captain O'Connor was evidently a favorite in the regiment, for his arrival was heartily greeted. He at once introduced the two lads to their future comrades, took them to the colonel, looked after their quarters, and made them at home. In their absence he spoke warmly in favor of Ralph. "You will find Conway a first-rate young fellow. He has seen something of the world, has been carried out to the West Indies by a French privateersman, and has gone through a lot of adventures. He is a bright, pleasant, good-tempered fellow. The other is as green as grass, and has never been away from his mother's apron-string. However, I do not think you will find him a bad sort of fellow when he has got rid of his rawness. Don't be too hard upon him, you boys. Remember easy does it, and don't be pushing your jokes too far. He is not a fool and will come round in time."

CHAPTER VIII.

STARTLING NEWS.

THREE weeks after Ralph's departure to join his regiment Mrs. Conway received a letter which gave her a great shock. It was from Mrs. Withers, and was as follows:

"MY DEAR MRS. CONWAY: I have very sad news to tell you. An event has happened which will, I know, be as afflicting to you as it has been to us. Our dear friend Mr. Penfold, who but three weeks ago was so bright and happy with us in London, has passed away suddenly. Up to the day before yesterday he seemed in his usual health; but yesterday morning he did not appear at breakfast, and the servant on going up to his room, found him sitting in a chair by his bedside dead. The bed had not been slept in, and it appears as if before commencing to undress he had been seized with a sudden faintness and had sunk into the chair and died without being able to summon assistance.

"His death is a terrible shock to us, as it will be to you. My husband and myself have long been aware that our dear friend suffered from disease of the heart, and that the doctor he consulted in London had told him that his death might take place at any moment. At the same time, he had been so bright and cheerful in London, as indeed with us he was at all times, that his death comes almost with as great a surprise to us as if we had not known that he was in danger. Mr. Tallboys, the solicitor of Weymouth who managed Mr. Penfold's affairs, called here last night. The funeral is to take place on Thursday, and had Ralph been in England he

said that he should have written to him to come down to
it, which he could have done in time had he started immediately he received the letter announcing the event;
but as he is over in Ireland, of course nothing can be
done.

"He said that had Ralph come he should have sug-
gested that you also should be present at the reading of
the will, but that as matters stand he did not think there
was any occasion to trouble you. I should tell you that
Mr. Tallboys appeared a good deal worried, and one of
his reasons for calling was to ask my husband whether
he knew where Mr. Penfold was in the habit of keeping
his papers. It seems that upon the day after his return
from London Mr. Penfold called upon him and took away
his will, saying that he wanted to look over it, as he had
two or three slight alterations that he wanted to make,
and he would bring it back in the course of a day or two
and get him to make the changes required. From that
time Mr. Penfold had not been in Weymouth, and, indeed, had scarcely left the house except to come down
here; for, as he said to my husband, he did not feel quite
himself, and supposed it was a reaction after his late dis-
sipations.

"Mr. Tallboys, who is one of the executors named in
the will, had searched for it in the afternoon among Mr.
Penfold's papers; but found that it and several other
documents—leases and so on—of importance were all
missing. He had asked Miss Penfold if she knew where
her brother was in the habit of keeping important papers;
but she replied shortly that she knew nothing whatever
of her brother's business matters. He had, therefore,
driven over to ask my husband, knowing how intimate
he had been with poor Herbert. He knew, it seems, that
Mr. Penfold had some secure place for such papers, because he had one day spoken to him upon the subject,
saying it would be more prudent for him to leave the
leases in the strong-box in his office at Weymouth. But
Herbert replied that they were stowed away in a far safer
place, and that he had not the least fear in the world of
their being stolen.

"Now, this is just what my husband knew also. Once

when they were chatting together Herbert mentioned that the house like many other old mansions contained a secret chamber. He said: 'I can't tell you where it is, Withers; for although it is never likely to be used again, the knowledge of this hiding-place has been passed down from generation to generation as a family secret. I gave a solemn promise never to reveal it when I was first informed of its existence; and although in these days there is no occasion to hide priests or conspirators, I do not consider myself released from the promise I gave. Possibly some day the hiding-place may prove of value again. There may be a price set on the head of a Penfold, who can tell? Anyhow it is likely to remain a secret as long as the old house stands; and in the meantime I find it a useful place for keeping things that I do not want lying about.' Mr. Tallboys appeared very vexed at hearing what my husband said.

" 'It is very strange,' he said, 'that sensible men will do such foolish things. It is probable enough that Herbert Penfold has placed this will in the hiding-place you speak of, and in that case I foresee that we shall have no end of trouble. I know you are both aware of the nature of Mr. Penfold's will, and you may be sure that if those sisters of his also know of it—whether they do or not I can't say—they will bitterly resent it. I know enough of the family history to know that. It was evident by Miss Penfold's answer to me to-day that either she does not know the secret of this hiding-place—which is of course possible—or that if she does know she does not mean to say. I should imagine myself that she does know.

" 'Had Herbert Penfold been of age when his father died it is likely enough that he only as head of the family would have been told by his father of its existence; but you see he was but a lad at that time, while the Miss Penfolds were women, and were therefore probably informed of the secret. It is very awkward, extremely awkward. Of course the will may turn up between this and the funeral; but if not I hardly know what steps had best be taken. If those Penfold women have made up their minds that this will shall not see the

light they are likely to carry it through to the end.'
My husband quite agreed with Mr. Tallboys about that,
and so do I. I have never been able to abide them,
though, as my husband says, they are good women in
many respects, and always ready to help in parish matters. Still I can't abide them, nor I am sure have you
any reason to do so; for when I and my husband first
came here we learned a good deal of the part they had
played in a certain matter, and that of course set me altogether against them.

"Of course, my dear Mrs. Conway, I do not wish to
alarm you about the will; still you ought to know how
things stand, and my husband this morning asked me to
tell you all there was to tell. I hope in a few days to be
able to write and give you better news. Things may not
be as they fear."

Mrs. Conway sat for a long time with this letter before
her. She had not read it straight through, but after
glancing at the first few lines that told of the death of
Herbert Penfold she had laid it aside, and it was a long
time before she took it up again. He had been the love
of her youth; and although he had seemingly gone for
so many years out of her life, she knew that when she
had found how he had all this time watched over her and
so delicately aided her, and that for her sake he was
going to make Ralph his heir, her old feeling had been
revived. Not that she had any thought that the past
would ever return. His letters indeed had shown that
he regarded his life as approaching its end; but since
the receipt of that letter she had always thought of him
with a tender affection as one who might have been her
husband had not either evil fate or malice stepped in to
prevent it.

The fortnight they had spent in London had brought
them very close together. He had assumed the footing
of a brother, but she had felt that pleasant and kind as

he was to all the rest of the party it was for her sake
alone that this festivity had been arranged. They had
had but one talk together alone, and she had then said that
she hoped the expressions he had used in his letter to
her with reference to his health were not altogether justified, for he seemed so bright and well. He had shaken
his head quietly and said:

"It is just as well that you should know, Mary. I
have seen my physician since I came up to town, and I
don't think it will last much longer. A little time ago I
did not wish it to last, now I should be glad to go on
until I can see my little scheme realized; but I am quite
sure that it is not to be. Anyhow I am ready to go when
I am summoned, and am happy in the thought that the
few people I care for are all in a fair way to be happy.
Don't cry, dear. I don't want a single cloud to hang
over our memories of this time. I am happier than I
have ever been in my life, and I want you and all of
them to be very happy too. I have set my mind upon
that, and if I see a cloud on your face it will spoil it all."

Still in spite of this she had hoped the doctor might
have taken too gloomy a view of the case, and that Herbert Penfold's death might yet be a distant event.

And now it was all over. Herbert Penfold was dead.
The heart that had beat so kindly for her was silenced
forever. It was then a long time before Mrs. Conway
recovered sufficiently from her emotion to take up the
letter again. She did so with an air almost of indifference. She had learned the news, and doubtless all this
long epistle contained many details of comparatively little
interest. But as she read her air of languid grief gave
way to an expression of keen interest, and she skimmed
through the last page or two with anxious haste. Then
she reread it more slowly and carefully, and then throw-

ing it on the table stood up and walked up and down the little room.

So these women, who had as she believed ruined her life and Herbert's, were now going to attack her son and rob him of his rights. They should not do it if she could help it. Never! Mary Vernon had been a high-spirited girl, and, although those who had only known her through her widowhood would have taken her for a gentle and quiet woman, whose thoughts were entirely wrapped up in her boy, the old spirit was alive yet, as with head thrown back, and an angry flush on her cheeks, she declared to herself that she would defend Ralph's rights to the last. How or in what manner she did not ask; she 'only knew that those who would defraud him were her old enemies.

Had it been otherwise the fact that they were Herbert's sisters would have softened her toward them; now that fact only added to the hostility she bore them. They, his nearest relations of blood, had ruined his life; now they would defeat his dying wishes. It should not be if she could help it. She would fight against it to the last day of her life. There was of course nothing to be done yet. Nothing until she heard again. Nothing until she knew that the discovery of the will was given up as hopeless. Then it would be time for her to do something.

The thought barely occurred to her that the loss of this will might make material difference in her own circum-stances, and that the allowance Herbert Penfold had made her, and which he had doubtless intended she should continue to receive, would cease. That was so secondary a consideration that it at present gave her no trouble. It was of Ralph she thought. Of Ralph and Herbert. Were the plans that the latter had made—the plans that had given happiness to the last year of the life of him who had known so little happiness—to be shattered? This to her mind was even more than the loss that Ralph would suffer.

"They may have destroyed the will," she said at last; "but if not I will find it, if it takes me all my life to do so."

A week later two letters arrived. The one was from Mrs. Withers. The will had not been found. Mr. Tallboys had searched in vain. Every cabinet and drawer in the house had been ransacked. No signs whatever had been found of the will.

"Mr. Tallboys is perfectly convinced that it must be hidden in some altogether exceptional place. The will was not a bulky document, and might have been stowed away in a comparatively small hiding-place, such as a secret drawer in a cabinet; but the leases that are also missing are bulky, and would take up so large a space that he is convinced that had a secret hiding-place sufficiently large to hold them existed in any of the articles of furniture he has searched he should have discovered it.

"Of course, my dear Mrs. Conway, we feel this matter personally, as our Mabel was as you know made joint-heiress with your Ralph of Herbert's property. We cannot but feel, however, that the loss is greater in your case than in ours. Mabel was never informed of Herbert's intentions toward her, and although we should of course have been glad to know that our child had such brilliant prospects, the loss of them will not we may hope in any way affect her happiness. In the case of your son it is different, and his prospects in life will of course be seriously affected by the loss, and my husband begs me to express to you his very deep regret at this.

"We have talked over your letter together, and while

fully sharing your indignation at the conduct of the Misses Penfold, hardly see that anything can be done to discover the will. However, should you be able to point out any manner in which a search for it can be carried on, we shall be happy to do what we can to aid in the matter, as it is clearly our duty to endeavor to obtain for Mabel the fortune Herbert Penfold willed to her. Mr. Tallboys tells us that it is clear the Misses Penfold have quite determined upon their line of conduct. Whatever they may know they have declined altogether to aid him in his search for the will, Miss Penfold saying, in reply to his request that they would do so, that they had every reason to believe from what their brother had let fall that the will was an unjust and inquitous one; that if Providence intended it should see the light it would see it; but they at least would do nothing in the matter.

"He asked them plainly if they were aware of the existence of any place in which it was likely that their brother had placed it. To this Miss Penfold, who is, as she has always been, the spokesman of the two sisters, said shortly, that she had never seen the will, that she didn't want to see it, and that she did not know where her brother had placed it; indeed, for aught she knew, he might have torn it up. As to hiding-places, she knew of no hiding-place whose existence she could, in accordance with the dictates of her conscience divulge. So that is where we are at present, Mrs. Conway. I believe that Mr. Tallboys is going to try and get a copy of the will that he has in his possession admitted under the circumstances as proof of Herbert Penfold's intentions. But he owned to us that he thought it was very doubtful whether he should be able to do so, especially as Herbert had stated to him that he intended to make alterations; and it would be quite possible that a court might take the view that in the first place the alterations might have been so extensive as to affect the whole purport of the will, and in the second place that he might have come to the conclusion that it would be easier to make the whole will afresh, and so had destroyed the one he had by him.''

Mrs. Conway laid down the letter, and after thinking for a time opened the other, which was in a handwriting unknown to her. It began:

"DEAR MADAM. : Mrs. Withers tells me that she has informed you of the singular disappearance of the will of my late client, Mr. Herbert Penfold. I beg to inform you that we shall not let this matter rest, but shall apply to the court to allow the copy of the will to be put in for probate; if that is refused, for authorization to make a closer search of the Hall than we have hitherto been able to do, supporting our demand with affidavits made by the Rev. Mr. Withers and ourselves of our knowledge that the late Mr. Penfold was accustomed to keep documents in some secret receptacle. In the second place, we are glad to inform you that the annual sum paid by us into the Kentish bank to your credit will not be affected by the loss of the will; for at the time when that payment first commenced, Mr. Penfold signed a deed making this payment a first charge on the rents of two of his farms during your lifetime. This assignment was of a binding character, and of course continues to hold good. We shall consider it our duty to acquaint you from time to time with the course of proceedings in the matter of the late Mr. Penfold's will.''

Little as Mrs. Conway had thought of herself from the time when she first heard that the will was missing, the news that her income would remain unchanged delighted her. She had formed no plans for herself, but had vaguely contemplated the necessity of giving up her house as soon as it was decided that the will could not be found, selling her furniture, and for the present taking a small lodging. She was glad that there would be no occasion for this; but very much more glad that she should be able now to make Ralph an allowance of seventy or eighty pounds a year, which would make all the difference between his living comfortably and being obliged to pinch himself in every way to subsist upon his pay. It would also enable her to carry out without difficulty any plans she might determine upon.

Upon the receipt of the letter announcing Mr. Penfold's death, she had written to Ralph telling him of it, but saying nothing about Mr. Tallboys' visit to the Withers, or his report that he was unable to find the will. She now wrote to him relating the whole circumstances. He had not previously known Mr. Penfold's intention to make him his heir, being only told that he intended to push his way in life, and had considered that the promise was carried out by his obtaining him a commission and arranging some allowance. His mother was glad of this now.

"Of course the loss of Mr. Penfold's will, my boy, will make a difference to you, as there can be no doubt that he had made some provisions in it for the regular payment of the allowance he had so kindly promised you. This, unless the will is found, you will of course lose. Having been a soldier's daughter, I know that to live comfortably in the army it is necessary to have something beyond your pay; but fortunately I can assist you a little. I have now one less to feed and clothe, and no schooling expenses; and I have been calculating things up, and find that I can allow you seventy-five pounds a year without making any difference in the manner of my living. You will be able to see that for yourself. You need, therefore, feel no hesitation in accepting this allowance.

"It is not a large one; but I know it will make a very great difference in your comfort, and it will be a great pleasure to me to know that you will be able to enter into what amusements are going on and not to look at every penny. It makes all the difference in the world whether one has four and sixpence or nine shillings a day to live upon. You wrote and told me of the handsome present Mr. Penfold made you at parting. This, my boy, I should keep if I were you as a reserve, only to be touched in case of unexpected difficulties or needs. No one can ever say when such needs may occur. I hope you will not pain me by writing to say you don't want this allowance, because nothing you can say will alter my determination to pay that allowance regularly every quarter into your agent's hands; and it will be, of course, very much more pleasant to me to know that it is as much a pleasure to you to be helped by me as it is to me to help you. I have heard several times from Mrs. Withers; they are all well, and she asked me to send their remembrances to you when I write. I do not give up all hope that the will may be found one of these days, but it is just as well that we should not build in the slightest upon it."

Ralph's reply came in due time, that is in about a fortnight afterward; for Mrs. Conway's letter had first to go by coach to London, and then a two days' journey by the mail to Liverpool, then by the sailing packet across to Dublin, and then down to Cork by coach. He had already written expressing his regret at the news of Mr. Penfold's death.

"My dear mother," he began. "It is awfully good of you to talk about making an allowance to me. After what you say, of course I cannot think of refusing it, though I would do so if I thought the payment would in the slightest way inconvenience you. But as you say that now I am away it will make something like that sum difference in your expenses, I must of course let you do as you like, and can only thank you very heartily for it. But I could really have got on very well without it. I fancy that a good many men in the regiment have nothing but their pay, and as they manage very well there is no reason I could not manage too.

"Of course in war times things are not kept up so expensively as they were before, and lots of men get commissions who would not have done so when the army was only half its present size, and was considered as a gentlemanly profession instead of a real fighting machine. However, as you say, it is a great deal more pleasant having nine shilling a day to live on instead of four and sixpence.

"I am getting on capitally here. Of course there is a lot of drill, and it is as much as I can do not to laugh sometimes, the sergeant, who is a fierce little man, gets into such wild rages over our blunders.

"I say our blunders, for of course Stapleton and I are drilled with the recruits. However, I think that in another week I shall be over that, and shall then begin to learn my work as an officer. They are a jolly set of fellows here, always up to some fun or other. I always thought when fellows got to be men they were rather serious, but it seems to me that there is ever so much more fun here among them than there was at school. Of course newcomers get worried a little just as they do at school. I got off very well; because, you see, what with school and the privateer I have learned to take things good temperedly, and when fellows see that you are as ready for fun as they are they soon give up bothering you,

"Stapleton has had a lot more trouble; because, you see, he will look at things seriously. I think he is getting a little better now; but he used to get quite mad at first, and of course that made fellows ever so much worse. He would find his door screwed up when he went back after mess; and as soon as they found that he was awfully particular about his boots, they filled them all full of water one night. Then some one got a ladder and threw a lot of crackers into his bedroom in the middle of the night, and Stapleton came rushing down in his nightshirt with his sword drawn, swearing he would kill somebody.

"Of course I have done all I can to get them to leave him alone, for he is really a good fellow, and explained to them that he had never been to school, or had a chance of learning to keep his temper. But he is getting on now, and will, I think, soon be left alone. This has been an awfully long letter, and there is only just enough candle left for me to get into bed by. Anyhow mother, I am not a bit upset about losing Mr. Penfold's allowance; so don't you worry yourself at all about that."

Some weeks passed on. Mr. Tallboys wrote that he had failed to induce the court to accept the copy of the will, the admission he was forced to make that Mr. Penfold had intended to make an alteration in it being fatal. He had, however, obtained an order authorizing him thoroughly to search the house, and to take down any wainscotting, and to pull up any floors that might appear likely to conceal a hiding-place. A fortnight later he wrote again to announce his failure.

"The Miss Penfolds," he said, "were so indignant that they left the house altogether, and you may believe that we ransacked it from top to bottom. I had four carpenters and two masons with me, and I think we tapped every square foot of wall in the house, took down the wainscotting wherever there was the slightest hollow sound, lifted lots of the flooring, and even wrenched up several of the hearthstones, but could find nothing whatever, except that there was a staircase leading from behind the wainscotting in Mr. Penfold's room to a door covered with ivy, and concealed from view by bushes to the left of the house; but the ivy had evidently been undisturbed for fifty years or so, this passage, even if known to Mr. Penfold, had certainly not been used in his time.

"I truly regret, my dear madam, that the search should have been so unsuccessful, and can only say, that all that could be done has been done. That the will is concealed somewhere I have not a shadow of doubt, unless, of course, it has been torn up before this. As to that I give no opinion; and, indeed, as it is a matter in which women are concerned, your judgment as to the probabilities is much more likely to be correct than mine. As I expected, my business connection with the family has come to an end. The Miss Penfolds have appointed another agent, who has written to me requesting me to hand over all papers connected with the property. This, of course, I shall do. I need hardly say that in no case could I have consented to act for those whom I consider to be unlawful possessors of the property. In conclusion, I can only say that my services will at all times be at your disposal."

Mrs. Conway was scarcely disappointed at the receipt of this letter, for she had quite made up her mind that the will would not be found. These women had clearly made up their minds to deprive Ralph and Mabel of their rights, and unless they had felt perfectly satisfied that no search would discover the hiding-place of the will, they would not improbably have taken it, and either

destroyed it or concealed it in some fresh place where
the searchers would never be likely to look for it. She
did not think it likely, therefore, that the hiding-place
would be discovered, and she felt assured that were it
discovered it would be found empty.

"Very well," she said, in a quiet, determined voice,
as she laid down the letter. "Mr. Tallboys has failed.
Now, I shall take up the matter. I dare say you think
that you have won, Miss Penfold; that you are now mistress beyond dispute of Herbert's property. You will
see the battle has only just begun. It will last, I can
tell you, all your lives or mine."

A week later an altogether unexpected event took
place. When Mr. and Mrs. Withers were at breakfast a
letter arrived from Mr. Littleton, now solicitor to the
Miss Penfolds. Upon opening it it was found to contain
an offer upon the part of the Miss Penfolds to settle the
sum of a hundred a year for life upon Mabel, upon the
condition only that the allowance would be stopped upon
her marriage, unless that marriage received the approval,
in writing, of the Miss Penfolds. The letter was addressed to Mr. Withers, and after reading it through he
passed it to his wife without a word. She was too surprised to say anything for a moment, especially as Mabel
was in the room, and she laid the letter beside her until
breakfast was over and Mabel had gone out.

"Well, James, what do you think of it?" she asked.

"What do you think of it yourself?" he replied.

Mrs. Withers hesitated, and then said: "Well, James,
it is a sort of thing that requires so much thinking about
that I have scarcely had time to turn it over in my mind
yet, especially with Mabel there eating her breakfast
opposite, and having no idea that this letter contained
anything of such importance to her. I would really

rather hear what you think about it." Mr. Withers remained silent, and she went on: "Of course it would be a very nice thing for Mabel to have such a provision for life."

A slight smile passed across Mr. Withers' face, and his wife saw that that was not at all the way in which he looked at it.

"That is just like you men, James," she said a little pettishly. "You ask us what we think about things when you have perfectly made up your minds what you mean to do, whether we agree with you or not."

"I don't think that's often the case with us. Still I did want to see whether the matter would have struck you at once in the same light in which I see it, and I perceive that it has not."

"Well, James, let me hear your view of the matter. I dare say I shall agree with you when you tell me what it is."

"Well, then, Amy," Mr. Withers said seriously, "it appears to me that we cannot accept this offer for Mabel."

Mrs. Withers looked a little blank. The living was not a rich one, and assured as they had been by Mr. Penfold that he intended to provide for Mabel, they had not endeavored to lay by anything for her, and had freely dispensed their surplus income among the sick and needy of the parish. The disappearance of the will had disappointed their hopes, and raised many anxious thoughts in Mrs. Withers' mind respecting Mabel's future, and the offer contained in the letter had therefore filled her with pleasure. But she greatly valued her husband's judgment, and therefore only replied:

"Why, dear?"

"Well, you see, wife, we are both thoroughly agreed that these ladies are depriving Mabel of the fortune Herbert Penfold left her. They are concealing or have destroyed his will, and are at present in what we may call fraudulent possession of his property. Now, I do not think that under these circumstances we can accept a favor at their hands. To do so would be practically to acquiesce in what we consider the robbery of our child, and the acceptance would of course involve a renewal of friendly relations with them; a thing which, believing as we do that they are acting wickedly would be distasteful in the extreme, not to say impossible."

"Of course you are right, dear," Mrs. Withers said, rising from her seat and going over and kissing her husband tenderly. "I had not thought of it in that light at all. In fact I had hardly thought about it at all, except that it would be nice to see Mabel provided for."

"It would be nice, my dear. But we surely need not be anxious about her. We may hope that she will make a happy marriage. We may hope too that we may be spared long enough to make some provision for her, for, of course, we must now curtail our expenses and lay by as much as we can for her. Lastly, dear, we need not be anxious; because we trust that God will provide for her should we not be enabled to do so. But even were I sure that we should both be taken together, I would rather leave her in His hands than accept money wrongfully obtained and condone an abominable action. There is, too, another point from which the matter should be looked at. You see this curious condition that they propose, that the annuity shall be forfeited unless she marry with their sanction. Why should they propose such a condition?"

"I am sure I don't know, James; for of course, we should never give our sanction to her marriage unless we approved of her choice, and surely the Miss Penfolds would not disapprove of a choice that we approved of?"

"Well, they might, my dear. You know how bitterly they disliked Ralph Conway, and how they resented his being at the Hall. It is quite possible they may have had some idea of Herbert's views about him and Mabel, and are determined that he shall not benefit through Mabel by one penny of their brother's property; and this clause is specially designed so that in case the two young people ever should come together they may be able if not to stop it—at any rate to stop the annuity. That is the only interpretation I can give to this condition."

"Very likely that is so James. Really these women seem to get more detestable every day."

Mr. Withers smiled at his wife's vehemence. "There is still another reason why we cannot take the money. Ralph Conway has been as much defrauded as Mabel, and his mother, as you see by her letters, is determined not to sit down quietly under the wrong. What she means to do I have not the slightest idea, nor do I think that there is the most remote probability she will ever succeed in finding the will. Tallboys appears to have made a most thorough search of the house, and do what she will she cannot have any opportunity of searching as he has done. Still she clearly has something on her mind. She intends to make some attempt or other to discover the will, which, if found, will benefit Mabel equally with her son. Therefore we cannot but regard her as our friend and ally. Now, were we to accept the money for Mabel we should in fact be acquiescing, not only in the wrong done to her but in that done to Ralph. We should, in fact, be going over to the enemy. We could not take their money and even tacitly connive in her efforts to find the will."

"I agree with you entirely, James. It would be im-

possible; only I do wish you had said all this before letting me be so foolish as to say that I thought we ought
to take it."

"You didn't say so, dear," Mr. Withers said smiling.
"You only gave expression to the first natural thought of
a mother that it would be a nice thing for Mabel. You
had given the matter no further consideration than that,
and I was quite sure that as soon as you thought the
matter over you would see it in the same light that I do.
But I think that before we send off our reply we should
put the matter before Mabel herself. I have no doubt
whatever what her answer will be, but at the same time
she ought to know of the offer which has been made to
her."

CHAPTER IX.

MR. TALLBOYS' VISITOR.

MR. WITHERS was fully justified in his conviction that there need be no doubt as to the view Mabel would take of the Miss Penfold's offer. The girl had hitherto been in entire ignorance both as to the will being missing, and of the interest she had in it. She was now called in from the garden, and was much surprised when her father told her to sit down, as he and her mother wished to have a serious talk with her.

"Do you know, my little Mabel," he began, "that you have had a narrow escape of being an heiress?"

"An heiress, papa! Do you mean of having a lot of money?"

"Yes, of coming in some day to a fortune. Mr. Penfold some time ago confided to your mother and me his intention of dividing his property equally between Ralph Conway and yourself."

"What! all the Penfold estates, papa, and the house and everything?"

"Yes, my dear. Everything, including the large sum of money that has accumulated during the years Mr. Penfold has not been spending a third of his income."

"Then if he meant that, papa, how is it that I am not going to be an heiress?"

"Simply, my dear, because the will by which Mr. Penfold left the property to you and Ralph is missing."

Mr. Withers then told the whole story of the loss of

the will, the search that had been made for it, and the strong grounds there were for believing in the existence of some secret place in the Hall, and that this place of concealment was known to Mr. Penfold's sisters.

"But they surely could never be so wicked as that, papa. They have always seemed to like me—not very much, you know, because they thought I wasn't quiet and ladylike enough. Still I don't think they really disliked me."

"No, I think in their way they liked you, Mabel; and perhaps if Mr. Penfold had half left his property to you, divided the other half between them the will would have been found. But they certainly did not like Ralph Conway. They disliked him partly no doubt for himself, but principally on account of a wrong which I believe they once did to his mother. Now, it is in human nature, Mabel, that you may forgive a wrong done to you, but it is very hard to forgive a person you have wronged. Anyhow, I am convinced that it was more to prevent Mrs. Conway's son from getting this money than to get it themselves that they have concealed this will, or rather that they refuse to point out its place of concealment."

"But it does seem hard, papa, that Mr. Penfold should have left everything to Ralph and me and nothing to his sisters."

"The Miss Penfolds have a very comfortable income of their own, Mabel, and their brother might very well have thought there was no occasion for them to have more; beside, although they lived in his house, and indeed managed it and him, Mr. Penfold had, I know, strong reason to believe that they had ruined his life. But this is a matter into which we need not go. Well, Mabel, the Miss Penfolds have just given a proof that they do not dislike you. Now I will read you this letter, because I think you ought to know it has been written, and I will then tell you the reasons why your mother and I think that the offer cannot be accepted."

Mabel listened in silence until her father had finished the arguments he had used with his wife, with the exception only of that relating to the Miss Penfolds' motives in putting in the condition concerning Mabel's marriage. When he ceased speaking she exclaimed indignantly

"Of course, papa, we could not take the money, not if it were ten times as much! Why, we could not look Mrs. Conway and Ralph in the face again! Beside, how could we speak to people one believes to have done such a wicked thing?"

"Very well, Mabel. I was quite sure that you would agree with us, but at the same time I thought it was right before we refused the offer you should know that it was made. Whatever our sentiments on the subject might be, we should not have been justified in refusing without your knowledge an offer that might, from a worldly point of view, be your interest to accept."

"Why, papa," Mabel said, "I would rather go out and weed turnips or watch sheep, like some of the girls in the village, than touch a penny of the Miss Penfolds' money."

A short time after this Mr. Tallboys' clerk brought a letter into his private office.

"A lady asked me to give you this, sir." The solicitor opened it. It contained only a card.

"Show the lady in. How are you, madam? I am glad to have the pleasure of making your acquaintance. I suppose you are staying with Mr. Withers?"

"No, Mr. Tallboys, I am at the hotel here. I only arrived an hour since by the packet from Dover."

"Dear me. I am afraid you have had a very unpleasant voyage."

"It has not been pleasant," Mrs. Conway said quietly. "But I preferred it to the long journey by coach up to London, and down here again. We were five days on the way, as the vessel put in at so many ports. Still that was quite a minor question with me. I wanted to see you and have a talk with you personally. There is no saying into whose hands letters may fall, and one talk face to face does more good than a score of letters."

Mr. Tallboys looked rather surprised, and the idea flashed across his mind that the only business Mrs. Conway could want to see him about must be some proposal for raising money upon the security of her annuity.

"I presume, Mr. Tallboys, from what I hear, that you are as thoroughly convinced as I am myself that this will of Mr. Penfold's is in existence, and is hidden somewhere about the Hall?"

"Yes, I think so, Mrs. Conway. That is, supposing it has not been destroyed."

"Do you think it likely that it has been destroyed, Mr. Tallboys?"

"Well, that I cannot say," the solicitor said gravely. "I have, of course, thought much over this matter. It is one that naturally vexed me much for several reasons. In the first place, Mr. Withers and you yourself had been good enough to place the matter in my hands, and to authorize me to act for you, and it is always a sort of vexation to a professional man when his clients lose their cause, especially when he is convinced that they are in the right. In the second place, I am much disturbed that the wishes of my late client, Mr. Penfold, should not have been carried out. Thirdly, I feel now that I myself am somewhat to blame in the matter, in that I did not represent to Mr. Penfold the imprudence of his placing valuable papers in a place where, should anything happen to him suddenly, they might not be found. Of course I could not have anticipated this hostile action on the part of the Miss Penfolds. Still, I blame myself that I did not warn Mr. Penfold of the possibility of what has in fact happened taking place. Lastly,'' and he smiled, ''I have a personal feeling in the matter. I have lost a business that added somewhat considerably to my income.''

''I don't think any of us have thought of blaming you in the matter, Mr. Tallboys. I am sure that I have not. You could not possibly have foreseen that Mr. Penfold's sisters were likely to turn out thieves.''

''Well, that is rather a strong expression, Mrs. Conway; though natural enough I must admit in your position as Mr. Ralph Conway's mother. You see, there is a difference between concealing and not disclosing. Mr. Penfold himself concealed the will. The Miss Penfolds simply refuse to assist us in our search for it.''

''And as the nearest heirs take possession of the property.''

''Quite so, Mrs. Conway. I am not defending their conduct, which morally is dishonest in the extreme, but I doubt whether any court of law would find it to be a punishable offense.''

''Well, now, Mr. Tallboys, I want you to let me know whether you suspect that they have destroyed the will; which, I suppose, would be a punishable offense.''

Certainly the destruction of the will, in order that those who destroyed might get possession of property, would be criminal. Well, I don't know; I have thought it over in every sense, and think the balance of probability is against their having destroyed it. In the first

place the Miss Penfolds doubtless consider that the will
is so securely hidden there is little, if any, chance of its
being discovered. That this is so we know, from the fact
that although I ransacked the house from top to bottom,
pulled down wainscoting, lifted floors, and tried every
imaginable point which either I or the men who were
working with me suspected to be a likely spot for a hiding-place, we did not succeed in finding it.

"Now, I have noticed that ladies have at times somewhat peculiar ideas as to morality, and are apt to steer
very close to the wind. The Miss Penfolds may consider
themselves perfectly justified in declining to give us any
assistance in finding the will, soothing their consciences
by the reflection that by such refusal they are committing no offense of which the law takes cognizance; but
while doing this they might shrink from the absolutely
criminal offense of destroying the will. I do not say
that now they have entered upon the path they have that
they would not destroy the will if they thought there
was a chance of its being discovered. I only say that,
thinking it to be absolutely safe, they are unlikely to
perform an act which, if discovered, would bring them
under the power of the law.

They may consider themselves free to believe, or if not
actually to believe, to try and convince themselves, that
for aught they know-their brother may have destroyed
the will, and that it is not for them to prove whether he
did so or not. Upon these grounds, therefore, it seems
to me probable that the will is still in existence; but I
acknowledge that so far as its utility is concerned it
might as well have been destroyed by Mr. Penfold himself or by his sisters."

"Well, Mr. Tallboys, no doubt you are thinking that
you might as well have expressed this opinion to me on

paper, and that I have troubled myself very unnecessarily in making this journey to have it from your own lips."

"Well, yes, Mrs. Conway, I do not deny that this was in my mind."

"It would have been useless for me to make the journey had this been all, Mr. Tallboys. I am very glad to have heard your opinion, which agrees exactly with that which I myself have formed, but it was scarcely with the object of eliciting it that I have made this journey. We will now proceed to that part of the subject. We agree that the will is probably still in existence, and that it is hidden somewhere about the Hall. The next question is, how is it to be found?"

"Ah! that is a very difficult question indeed, Mrs. Conway."

"Yes, it is difficult, but not, I think, impossible. You have done your best, Mr. Tallboys, and have failed. You have no further suggestion to offer, no plan that occurs to you by which you might discover it?"

"None whatever," Mr. Tallboys said decidedly. "I have done all that I could do; and have, in fact, dismissed the question altogether from my mind. I had the authority of the court to search, and I have searched very fully, and have reported my failure to the court. The power to search would certainly not be renewed unless upon some very strong grounds indeed."

"I suppose not, Mr. Tallboys; that is what I expected. Well, it seems to me that you having done all in your power for us, your clients, and having now relinquished your search, it is time for us, or some of us, to take the matter in hand.'"

Mr. Tallboys looked surprised.

"I do not quite understand, Mrs. Conway, how you can take it in hand."

"No? Well, I can tell you, Mr. Tallboys, that I am going to do so. I am not going to sit down quietly and see my son robbed of his inheritance. I have quite made up my mind to devote my life to this matter, and I have come, not to ask your advice—for I dare say you would try to dissuade me, and my resolution is unalterable—but to ask you to give me what aid you can in the matter."

"I shall be glad to give you aid in any way, Mrs. Conway, if you will point out to me the direction in which my assistance can be of use. I suppose you have formed some sort of plan, for I own that I can see no direction whatever in which you can set about the matter."

"My intention is, Mr. Tallboys, to search for this hiding-place myself."

Mr. Tallboys raised his eyebrows in surprise.

"To search yourself, Mrs. Conway! But how do you propose to gain admittance to the Hall, and how, even supposing that you gain admittance, do you propose to do more than we have done, or even so much; because any fresh disturbance of the fabric of the house would be out of the question?"

"That I quite admit. Still we know there is the hiding-place, and it is morally certain that that hiding-place is opened or approached by the touching of some secret spring. It is not by pulling down wainscoting or by pulling up floors, or by force used in any way, that it is to be found. Mr. Penfold, it would seem, used it habitually as a depository for papers of value. He certainly, therefore, had not to break down or to pull up anything. He opened it as he would open any other cabinet or cupboard, by means of a key or by touching a spring. You agree with me so far, Mr. Tallboys?"

"Certainly, Mrs. Conway. There can be no doubt in

my mind that this hiding-place, whether a chamber or a small closet, is opened in the way you speak of.''

"Very well then; all that has to be looked for is a spring. No force is requisite; all that is to be done is to find the spring.''

"Yes, but how is it to be found? I believe we tried every square foot of the building.''

"I have no doubt you did, but it will be necessary to try every square inch, I will not say of the whole building, but of certain rooms and passages. I think we may assume that it is not in the upper rooms or servants' quarters. Such a hiding-place would be contrived where it could be used by the owners of the house without observation from their dependants, and would therefore be either in the drawing-room, dining-room, the principal bed-chambers, or the passages, corridors, or stairs between or adjoining these.''

"I quite follow you in your reasoning, Mrs. Conway, and agree with you. Doubtless the place is so situated as to be what I may call handy to the owners of the Hall, but I still do not see how you are going to set about finding it.''

"I am going to set about it by going to live at the Hall.''

"Going to live at the Hall, Mrs. Conway! But how is that possible under the circumstances? You are, I should say, the last person whom the Miss Penfolds would at present invite to take up her residence there.''

"I agree with you, if they had any idea of my identity; but that is just what I intend they shall not have. My plan is to go there in the capacity of a servant. Once there I shall examine, as I say, every square inch of the rooms and places where this hiding-place is likely to exist. Every knob, knot, or inequality of any kind in the wood-work and stone-work shall be pressed, pulled, and twisted, until I find it. I am aware that the task may occupy months or even years, for, of course, my opportunities will be limited. Still, whether months or years, I intend to undertake it and to carry it through, if my life is spared until I have had time thoroughly and completely to carry it out."

Mr. Tallboys was silent from sheer astonishment.

"Do you really mean that you think of going there as a servant, Mrs. Conway?"

"Certainly I do," she replied calmly. "I suppose the work will be no harder for me than for other women; and whereas they do it for some ten or twelve pounds a year I shall do it for a fortune. I see not the slightest difficulty or objection in that part of the business. I shall, of course, let my house at Dover, making arrangements for my son's letters there being forwarded, and for my letters to him being posted in Dover. I shall have the satisfaction that while engaged upon this work my income will be accumulating for his benefit. I own that I can see no difficulty whatever in my plan being carried out.

"Now, as to the assistance that I wish you to give me. It could, perhaps, have been more readily given by Mr. Withers, for naturally he would know personally most of the servants of the Hall, as the majority of them doubtless belong to the village. But Mr. Withers, as a clergyman, might have conscientious scruples against taking any part in a scheme which, however righteous its ends, must be conducted by what he would consider underground methods, and involving a certain amount of deceit. At any rate, I think it better that neither he nor Mrs. Withers should have any complicity whatever in my plans. I therefore come to you. What I want, in the first place, is to find out when a vacancy is likely to be caused by some servant leaving; secondly, if no such vacancy is likely to occur, for a vacancy to be manufactured by inducing some servant to leave—a present of a year's wages would probably accomplish that; thirdly, the vacancy must occur in the case of some servant whose work would naturally lie in the part of the building I have to examine; finally, it must be arranged that I can be so recommended as to insure my getting the place.''

Mr. Tallboys was silent for some time.

''Certainly your plan does appear feasible, Mrs. Conway,'' he said at length. ''It does seem to me that if once installed in the way you propose at the Hall, and prepared to spend, as you say, months or even years in the search, it is possible and even probable that in the end you may light upon the spring that will open this mystery. You must be prepared to face much unpleasantness. You will have for all this time to associate with servants, to do menial work, to relinquish all the luxuries and appliances to which you have all your life been accustomed, and possibly to fail at last. Still, if you are prepared to face all this, there does appear to me to be a possibility of your enterprise being crowned with success.''

''I have thought it all over, Mr. Tallboys, and am quite prepared to submit to all the sacrifices you mention, which, however, will scacrely be felt by me to be sacrifices, working, as I shall be, for the future of my son. And now, can I rely upon your assistance?''

''You shall have any assistance I can give, assuredly, Mrs. Conway. The matter is by no means a simple one, still I can see no reason why it should not be successfully carried out.''

''It must take time, that I quite anticipate, Mr. Tallboys. Time, fortunately, is of no consequence.''

"Well, Mrs. Conway," Mr. Tallboys said, after sitting for some minutes in thought, "it is a matter that will require careful thinking over. How long do you intend staying here?"

"Just as long as it is necessary," Mrs. Conway said, "a day or a month. I have not given my own name at the 'George,' but shall be known there as Mrs. Brown. As you saw, I sent my card in in an envelope, so that even your clerk should not be aware that Mrs. Conway was in Weymouth."

"But," the solicitor said suddenly, "surely the Miss Penfolds knew you in the old time?"

"Certainly, they did. But, to begin with, that is nearly twenty years ago; and, of course, I have changed very much since then."

"Not very much, Mrs. Conway," the lawyer said; "for I once had the pleasure of seeing you when I went to the Hall to see Mr. Penfold on business. I do not say that I should have known you anywhere, but having had your card I remembered you at once when you came into the room; and, indeed, if you will excuse my saying so, you might pass anywhere as thirty."

"So much the better for my purpose at present," Mrs. Conway replied. "Thirty will do very well for the age of a housemaid at the Hall. I should imagine the Miss Penfolds would prefer a woman of that age to a young girl; beside, you see, I must be an upper housemaid in order to have charge of the part of the house I want to examine. As to knowing me, in the first place the Miss Penfolds will not have the advantage of receiving my card, and, in the second place, it is not very difficult for a woman to alter her appearance so as to be unrecognizable by another who has not seen her for twenty years. My hair is a good deal darker now than it was then, and

I wore it altogether differently. A little black dye on that and my eyebrows, a servant's cap and gown, will so alter me that you who see me now would hardly know me; certainly they will not do so. You need not trouble about that, Mr. Tallboys; I will answer for it that they shall not know me. It is possible, just possible, that Mr. and Mrs. Withers might know me if they saw me in church; but I shall, without letting them know my plans, guard against any indiscretion. Now, as we have quite settled the matter, Mr. Tallboys, I shall go back to the inn, and when you have thought the matter over and decided upon the best plan for carrying out my wishes, you will send a note to Mrs. Brown at the 'George,' making an appointment for me to meet you here.''

Mr. Tallboys sat for some time in thought after Mrs. Conway had left him. It was certainly a daring scheme, requiring no little courage, resolution, and self-possession to carry out, but his client evidently possessed all these qualities. She had a clear head, and seemed to have grasped every point in the matter. There was really no reason why she should not succeed. There must be a spring somewhere, and if she was as patient as she declared herself to be, she would surely find it sooner or later; that is, if she could carry out her search without exciting suspicion.

The first difficulty was to get her settled at the Hall. What was the best way to set about that? It certainly was not as easy as she seemed to think, still there must be some way of managing it. At any rate he must act cautiously in the matter, and must not appear in it in any way personally. And so he sat thinking, until at last the clerk, who had been a good deal surprised at receiving no instruction from him as to several matters he had in hand, knocked at the door, and came in with a number of papers, and Mr. Tallboys was obliged to dismiss the matter from his mind for a time, and to attend to present business. The very next morning Mrs. Conway received the note, and again went to the office.

"Do you know, Mrs. Conway," he began, as soon as his client entered, "the more I think over the matter, the more I feel that it is extremely difficult to manage it from here. I should have to engage some one to go over in the first place. He would have to stay in the village some time before he could make the acquaintance of the servants at the Hall. He would have to get very intimate with them before he could venture to broach such a thing for if he made a mistake, and the woman told her mistress that some one had been trying to persuade her to leave in order to introduce another into the place, their suspicions would be so aroused that the scheme would become hopeless."

"Yes, I see the difficulty, Mr. Tallboys; for I thought it over in every way before I came to you. Beside I don't like the thought of this intermediate. No doubt you would choose a trustworthy man. Still I don't like the thought of any one knowing the secret, especially as the plan may take so long working out."

"What I have been thinking, Mrs. Conway is this. No doubt the servants at the Hall have taken sides on this matter. Of course from our searches there they know that Mr. Penfold's will is missing, and that it is because it is missing that the Miss Penfolds are now mistresses there. Without knowing anything myself about the feelings of the servants there, beyond what would probably be the case from the difference of character between Mr. Penfold and his sisters, I should imagine that they were fond of him, for he was the kindest and most easy-going of masters, and not very fond of his sisters, who are, as I have always observed in the course of my professional visits there, the reverse of agreeable.

"If this is the case, not improbably there may be one or other of these women with whom you might open direct negotiations. What has struck me is this. The men who were over there with me of course slept and took their meals in the village; still, going about as they did in the house, no doubt they talked with the servants. The Miss Penfolds were away, and I dare say the women had plenty of time to gossip; and it is probable the men gathered from their talk something of their sentiments toward the Miss Penfolds and their brother, and which side they would be likely to go with. I might ask the foreman about it."

"I think the idea is a capital one, Mr. Tallboys; but there is one detail I think might be improved. I imagine that if instead of asking the foreman you choose the youngest and best-looking of the men, provided he is unmarried, you are more likely to get at the women's sentiments."

Mr. Tallboys laughed. "No doubt you are right, Mrs. Conway. That shall be done. I must get the foreman first, though, for I don't know the names or addresses of the other men. I shall tell him frankly that I want to find out the opinions of the servants at the Hall about the missing will, ask him which of his men was the most given to gossip with them, and tell him to send him here to me at ten o'clock to-morrow morning; then when you see him and hear what he has to say, you can judge for yourself how far you care to trust him in the matter, or whether to trust him at all. Perhaps you will come here a few minutes before ten, and then I can tell you what the foreman has said first."

Accordingly at a quarter to ten the next day Mrs. Conway was again at the office.

"I think, Mrs. Conway, that things are going even better than we hoped. The foreman said that from what little talk he had with the servants, he thought they had all been attached to Mr. Penfold, and that his sisters were by no means popular among them. He said very often one or other of them would come into the room where they were working and make suggestions, and hunt about themselves to see if they could find anything. But the best part of it is that one of the carpenters, a steady fellow of twenty-five, took up, as he calls it, with the upper housemaid, and he believes there is a talk about their being married some day. If this is so it would be the very thing for you. You could help him to get married, and the girl could help you to get her place."

"The very thing," Mrs. Conway said. "Nothing could have turned out better."

In a few minutes the young carpenter arrived. He was a pleasant-looking young fellow, and Mrs. Conway was not surprised at the impression he had made upon the housemaid at the Hall.

"Sit down, Johnson," Mr. Tallboys began. "You know what I asked you to come here for?"

"Mr. Peters told me that it was something to do with that job we had at the Miss Penfolds', sir."

"Yes, that is it, Johnson. You know we were looking for a missing will there?"

"Yes, sir; so I understood."

"Now, what we wanted to ask you specially, Johnson, was whether you can tell us what the servants at the Hall thought about it?"

The young carpenter turned rather red in the face, and twisted his cap about in his fingers.

"Well, sir, I don't know that I can say much about

that. I don't think most of them was overfond of the Miss Penfolds, and wouldn't have been sorry if the will had been found that would have given them another master or mistress.''

"Just so, Johnson, that is what I thought was likely. Now, the point I want to know, Johnson, and this lady here is, I may tell you, interested in the matter of this will being found, is as to whether there is in your opinion any one of the maids at the Hall who could be trusted to aid us in this business? Of course we should make it worth her while to do so.''

Again the young carpenter colored, and fidgeted on his chair, examining his cap intently.

"I suppose it would depend on what you wanted her to do,'' he said at last. "The Hall is a good service, though they don't like the mistresses, and of course none of them would like to do anything that might risk their place.''

"That's natural enough, Johnson. But, you see, we could perhaps more than make up to her for that risk.''

"Well, I don't know, sir,'' the man said after another pause. "It isn't only the place; but, you see, a young woman wouldn't like to risk getting into a row like and being turned away in disgrace, or perhaps even worse. I don't know what you want, you see, sir?''

Mr. Tallboys looked at Mrs. Conway, and his eyes expressed the question, How far shall we go? She replied by taking the matter in her own hands.

"We can trust you, can't we, whether you agree to help us or not?''

"Yes, ma'am,'' he said more decidedly than he had hitherto spoken. "You can trust me. If you tell me what you want, I will tell you straight whether I can do anything. If I don't like it, the matter shan't go beyond me.''

"Very well, then, I will tell you exactly what we want. We believe that the will is still there, and we believe that if some one in the house were to make a thorough search it might be found. It is right that it should be found, and that the property should go to those to whom Mr. Penfold left it, and who are now being kept out of it by the Miss Penfolds. I am very much interested in the matter, because it is my son who is being cheated out of his rights; and I have made up my mind to find the will. Now, what I want to know is, do you think that one of the housemaids would be willing to give up her place and introduce me as her successor, if I gave her twenty-five pounds? That would be a nice little sum, you know, to begin housekeeping with."

Mrs. Conway saw at once by the expression of the young carpenter's face that she had secured him as an ally.

"I think that might be managed, ma'am," he said in a tone that showed her he was endeavoring to hide his gladness. "Yes, I think that could be managed. There is certainly a young woman at the Hall—" and he stopped.

Mrs. Conway helped him. "I may tell you, Mr. Johnson, that the foreman hinted to Mr. Tallboys that he thought you and the upper housemaid were likely one of these days to come together, and that is principally why we spoke to you instead of to one of the others who were there. We thought, you see, that she might probably be leaving her place one of these days, and that perhaps this twenty-five pounds might enable you and her to marry earlier than you otherwise would have done. In that case, you see, it would suit us all. You and she would, moreover, have the satisfaction of knowing that you were aiding to right a great wrong, and to restore to those who

have been defrauded the property Mr. Penfold intended
for them. What do you say?"

"Well, ma'am, I think that, as you say, it would be
doing the right thing; and I don't deny that Martha and
I have agreed to wait a year or two, till we could save up
enough between us for me to start on my own account;
for as long as I am a journeyman, and liable to lose my
work any day, I would not ask her to come to me. But
what with what we have laid by, and this money you
offer, I think we might very well venture," and his
radiant face showed the happiness the prospect caused
him.

"Very well, then. We may consider that as settled,"
Mrs. Conway said. "What I want is for you to tell your
Martha that she is to give notice to leave at once, and
that if she has an opportunity she is to mention to Miss
Penfold that she has a friend who is out of place at
present, and whom she is sure will suit. Of course as
she will say that she is going to leave to be married,
Miss Penfold cannot be vexed with her, as she might be
otherwise, and may take her friend on her recommenda-
tion."

"But suppose she shouldn't, ma'am," and the young
carpenter's face fell considerably at the thought, "where
would Martha be then?"

"I shall pay the money, of course," Mrs. Conway said,
"whether I get the place through her or not. I should
think that Miss Penfold will very likely be glad to be
saved the trouble of looking for another servant. But,
if not, I must try some other way to get the place."

"What name am I to say her friend has?"

"Let me think. Ann Sibthrope."

"But suppose she asks about where her friend has been
in service, ma'am, and about her character?"

"We will settle that afterward. The first thing to do is for you to go over and see her, and ask her if she is willing to leave and do this."

"I think I can answer for that, ma'am," the young carpenter said with a quiet smile.

"Very well. Still, we had better have it settled. Will you go over to-day and see her? and then by to-morrow Mr. Tallboys and I will have talked the matter over and settled about the other points. Of course you will tell her not to give notice until she has heard from you as to what she is to say about me."

"Very well, ma'am. I will start at once."

"I can arrange about the character," Mr. Tallboys said when they were alone. "I have a cousin in London, to whom I shall write and explain the matter, and who will, I am sure, oblige me by writing to say that Ann Sibthorpe is all that can be desired as a servant: steady, quiet, industrious and capable. Well, I really congratulate you, Mrs. Conway. At first I thought your project a hopeless one; now I think you have every chance of success."

CHAPTER X.

ON DETACHMENT.

RALPH was soon at home in the regiment. He found his comrades a cheery and pleasant set of men, ready to assist the newly-joined young officers as far as they could. A few rough practical jokes were played; but Ralph took them with such perfect good temper that they were soon abandoned.

He applied himself very earnestly to mastering the mystery of drill, and it was not long before he was pronounced to be efficient, and he was then at Captain O'Connor's request appointed to his company, in which there happened to be a vacancy for an ensign. He had had the good luck to have an excellent servant assigned to him. Denis Mulligan was a thoroughly handy fellow, could turn his hand to anything, and was always good tempered and cheery.

"The fellow is rather free and easy in his ways," Captain O'Connor told Ralph when he allotted the man to him; "but you will get accustomed to that. Keep your whisky locked up, and I think you will be safe in all other respects with him. He was servant to Captain Daly, who was killed at Toulouse, and I know Daly wouldn't have parted with him on any account. His master's death almost broke Denis' heart, and I have no doubt he will get just as much attached to you in time. These fellows have their faults, and want a little humoring; but, take them as a whole, I would rather have an

Irish soldier servant than one of any other nationality, provided always that he is not too fond of the bottle. About once in three months I consider reasonable, and I don't think you will find Mulligan break out more frequently than that."

Ralph never regretted the choice O'Connor had made for him, and found Denis an excellent servant; and his eccentricities and the opinions which he freely expressed afforded him a constant source of amusement.

A few days later Captain O'Connor came into his room. "Pack up your kit. The company is ordered on detached duty, and there is an end to your dancing and flirting."

"I don't know about flirting," Ralph laughed. "As far as I can see you do enough for the whole company in that way. But where are we going to?"

"We are ordered to Ballyporrit. An out of the way hole as a man could wish to be buried in. It seems that there are a lot of stills at work in the neighborhood. The gauger has applied for military aid. A nice job we have got before us. I have had my turn at it before, and know what it means. Starting at nightfall, tramping ten or fifteen miles over the hills and through bogs, and arriving at last at some wretched hut only to find a wretched old woman sittting by a peat fire, and divil a sign of still or mash tubs or anything else. We start the first thing to-morrow morning; so you had better get your kit packed and your flask filled to-night. We have nineteen miles march before us, and a pretty bad road to travel. I have just been in to Desmond's quarters, and he is tearing his hair at the thought of having to leave the gayeties of Cork."

"I think it is a nice change," Ralph said, "and shall be very glad to have done with all these parties and balls. Ballyporrit is near the sea, isn't it?"

"Yes. About a mile away, I believe. Nearly forty miles from here."

The detachment marched next morning. Ralph enjoyed the novelty of the march, but was not sorry when at the end of the second day's tramp they reached the village. The men were quartered in the houses of the villagers, and the officers took rooms at the inn. Except when engaged in expeditions to capture stills—of which they succeeded in finding nearly a score—there was not much to do at Ballyporrit. All the gentry resident within a wide circle called upon them, and invitations to dinners and dances flowed in rapidly. As one officer was obliged to remain always in the village with the detachment, Ralph seldom availed himself of these invitations. O'Connor and Lieutenant Desmond were both fond of society; and, as Ralph very much preferred staying quietly in his quarters, he was always ready to volunteer to take duty upon these occasions.

Ballyporrit lay within a mile of the sea, and Ralph, when he had nothing else to do, frequently walked to the edge of the cliffs, and sat there hour after hour watching the sea breaking among the rocks three or four hundred feet below him, and the sea-birds flying here and there over the water, and occasionally dashing down to its surface. A few fishing boats could be seen, but it was seldom that a distant sail was visible across the water; for not one vessel in those days sailed for the west to every fifty that now cross the Atlantic. The rocks upon which he sat rose in most places almost sheer up from the edge of the sea; but occasionally they fell away, and a good climber could make his way over the rough rocks and bowlders down to the water's edge. As, however, there was nothing to be gained by it, Ralph never made the attempt.

Looking back over the land the view was a dreary one. There was not a human habitation within sight, the hills were covered with brown heather, while in the bottoms lay bogs, deep and treacherous to those who knew not the way across. It was rarely that a human figure was visible. Once or twice a day a revenue man came along the edge of the cliff, and would generally stop for a talk with Ralph.

"There was," he said, "a good deal of smuggling carried on along that part of the coast during the war; but there is not so much of it now, though no doubt a cargo is run now and then. It does not pay as it did when the French ports were all closed, and there was not a drop of brandy to be had save that which was run by the smugglers. Now that trade is open again there is only the duty to save, and I fancy a good many of the boats have gone out of the business. You see, the revenue has got its agents in the French ports, and gets news from them what craft are over there loading, and what part of the coast they come from. Along the English coast there is still a good deal of it. There lace pays well; but there is not much sale for lace in Ireland, and not much sale for brandy either, excepting in the towns. The peasants and farmers would not thank you for it when they can get home-made whisky for next to nothing."

"I suppose that there is a good deal of that going on."

"Any amount of it, sir. For every still that is captured I reckon there must be a hundred at work that no one dreams of, and will be as long as barley grows and there are bogs and hills all over the country, and safe hiding-places where no one not in the secret would dream of searching. The boys know that we are not in their line of business, and mind our own affairs. If it were not for that, I can tell you, I wouldn't go along these cliffs at night for any pay the king would give me; for I know that before a week would be out my body would be found some morning down there on the rocks, and the coroner's jury would bring in a verdict of tumbled over by accident, although there wouldn't be a man of them but would know better."

"Well, I am sure I don't want to find out anything about them. I belong to the detachment in Ballyporrit, and of course if the gauger calls upon us we must march out and aid him in seizing a still. But beyond that it's no affair of ours."

And yet although he so seldom saw any one to speak to, Ralph had sometimes a sort of uncomfortable feeling that he was being watched. Once or twice he had caught a glimpse of what he thought was a man's head among some rocks; but on walking carelessly to the spot he could see no signs of any one. Another time, looking suddenly round, he saw a boy standing at the edge of some boggy ground where the land dipped suddenly away some two hundred yards from the edge of the cliff; but directly he saw that he was observed he took to his heels, and speedily disappeared down the valley.

Ralph did not trouble himself about these matters, nor did he see any reason why any one should interest himself in his movements. Had he wandered about among the hills inland he might be taken for a spy trying to find out some of the hidden stills; but sitting here at the edge of the cliff watching the sea, surely no such absurd suspicion could fall upon him. Had he been there at night the smugglers might have suspected him of keeping watch for them; but smugglers never attempted to run their cargoes in broad daylight, and he never came down there after dark. One day a peasant came strolling along. He was a powerful-looking man and carried a heavy stick. Ralph was lying on his back looking up at the clouds and did not hear the man approach till he was close to him, then with a quick movement he sprang to his feet.

"I did not hear you coming," he said. "You have given me quite a start."

"It's a fine day, yer honor, for sleeping on the turf here," the man said civilly.

"I was not asleep," Ralph said; "though I own that I was getting on for it."

"Is yer honor expecting to meet any one here?" the man asked. "Sure, it's a mighty lonesome sort of place."

"No, I am not expecting any one. I have only come out for a look at the sea. I am never tired of looking at that."

"It's a big lot of water, surely," the man replied, looking over the sea with an air of interest as if the sight were altogether novel to him. "A powerful lot of water. And I have heard them say that you often come out here?"

"Yes, I often come out," Ralph assented.

"Don't you think now it is dangerous so near the edge of the cliff, yer honor? Just one step and over you would go, and it would be ten chances to one that the next tide would drift your body away, and divil a one know what had become of you."

"But I don't mean to take a false step," Ralph said.

"Sure, there is many a one takes a false step when he isn't dreaming about it; and if ye didn't tumble over by yourself, just a push would do it."

"Yes, but there is no one to give one a push," Ralph said.

"Maybe and maybe not," the man replied. "I don't say if I was a gentleman, and could spind me time as I liked, that I would be sitting here on the edge of these cliffs, where you might come to harm any minute."

"I have no fear of coming to harm," Ralph answered; "and I should be sorry for any one who tried. I always carry a pistol. Not that I think there is any chance of having to use it but it's always as well to be prepared."

"It is that,yer honor, always as well; but I don't think I should be always coming out here if I was you."

"Why not, my good fellow? I harm no one, and inter- fere with no one. Surely it is open to me to come here and look at the sea without any one taking offense at it."

"That's as it may be, yer honor. Anyhow I have told you what I think of it. Good-morning to you."

"I wonder what that fellow meant," Ralph said, look- ing after him. "He meant something, I feel certain, though what it is I can't imagine. I thought it was as well to let him know that I had a pistol handy, though he didn't look as if he intended mischief. I suppose after this I had better not come here so often, though I have not the remotest idea in the world why I should annoy any one more by standing here than if I was standing on the cliff in front of Dover Castle. However, it certainly is a lonely place, and I should have precious little chance if two or three men took it into their heads to attack me here."

"They are queer people these Irish peasants of yours, O'Connor," Ralph said as they sat at dinner that evening.

"What's the matter with them now, Conway?"

"One can't even go and look at the sea from their cliffs without their taking it amiss," and Ralph related the conversation he had had with the peasant, adding that he was convinced he had been watched whenever he went there.

"It is curious, certainly," the captain said when he

had finished. "No doubt they think you are spying after something; but that would not trouble them unless there was something they were afraid of your finding out. Either there has been something going on, or there is some hiding-place down there on the face of the cliff, where maybe they have a still at work Anyhow, I don't think I should neglect the warning, Conway. You might be killed and thrown over the cliff, and no one be the wiser for it. I should certainly advise you to give up mooning about."

"But there is nothing to do in this wretched village," Ralph said discontentedly.

"Not if you stop in the village, I grant; but you might do as Desmond and I do when we are off duty; go over and take lunch at the Ryans', or Burkes', or any of the other families where we have a standing invitation. They are always glad to see one, and there's plenty of fun to be had."

"That's all very well for you, O'Connor. You are a captain and a single man, and one of their countrymen, with lots to say for yourself; but it is a different thing with me altogether. I can't drop in and make myself at home as you do."

"Why, you are not shy, Conway?" O'Connor said in affected horror. "Surely such a disgrace has not fallen on his majesty's Twenty-eighth Regiment that one of its officers is shy? Such a thing is not recorded in its annals."

"I am afraid it will have to be recorded now," laughed Ralph. "For I own that I am shy; if you call shy, feeling awkward and uncomfortable with a lot of strange people, especially ladies."

"Do not let it be whispered outside," O'Connor said, "or the reputation of the regiment is gone forever among

Irish girls. Desmond, this is a sad business. What are we to do with this man? You and I must consult together how this thing is to be cured."

"No, no, O'Connor," Ralph said earnestly, knowing how fond O'Connor was of practical jokes, and dreading that he and the lieutenant would be putting him in some ridiculous position or other. "You will never cure me if you set about it. I shall get over it in time; but it's the sort of thing that becomes ten times worse if you attempt to cure it."

" We must think it over, my lad," O'Connor said seriously. "This is a serious defect in your character; and as your commanding officer I consider it my bounden duty, both for your sake and that of the regiment, to take it into serious consideration and see what is to be done. You may never have such a chance again of being cured as you have here; for if a man goes away from Ireland without being cured of shyness his case is an absolutely hopeless one. Desmond, you must turn this matter seriously over in your mind, and I will do the same. And now it is time for us to be starting for the dance at the Regans'. I am sorry you can't go with us, Desmond, as you are on duty."

"I shall be very glad to take your duty, Desmond," Ralph said eagerly. "I told you so this morning, and I thought you agreed."

"As your commanding officer," O'Connor said gravely, "I cannot permit the exchange to be made, Mr. Conway. You have your duty to perform to the regiment as well as Mr. Desmond, and your duty clearly is to go out and make yourself agreeable. I am surprised after what I have just been saying that you should think of staying at home."

"Well, of course, if you want me to go I will go,"

Ralph said reluctantly. "But I don't know the Regans, and don't want to."

"That is very ungracious, Conway. Mr. Regan is a retired pork merchant of Cork He has given up his business and bought an estate here, and settled down as a country gentleman. They say his father was a pig-driver in Waterford. That's why he has bought a place on this side of the county. But people have been rather shy of them; because, though he could buy three-fourths of them up, his money smells of pork. Still, as the election is coming on, they have relaxed a bit. He's got the militia band, and there will be lashings of everything; and his girls are nice girls, whether their father sold pork or not. And it would be nothing short of cruel if we, the representatives of his majesty's army, did not put in an appearance; especially as we have doubtless eaten many a barrel of his salt pork at sea. So put on your number one coatee and let's be off."

With a sign Ralph rose to carry out his orders, and he would have been still more reluctant to go had he observed the sly wink that passed between his captain and lieutenant.

"He is quite refreshing, that boy," O'Connor said as the door closed behind Ralph. "That adventure in the West Indies showed he has plenty of pluck and presence of mind; but he is as shy as a girl. Though I don't know why I should say that, for it's mighty few of them have any shyness about them. He will grow out of it. I was just the same myself when I was his age."

Lieutenant Desmond burst into a roar of laughter.

"I should have liked to have known you then, O'Connor."

O'Connor joined in the laugh.

"It's true though, Desmond. I was brought up by

two maiden aunts in the town of Dundalk, and they were always bothering me about my manners; so that though I could hold my own in a slanging match down by the riverside, I was as awkward as a young bear when in genteel company. They used to have what they called tea-parties—and a fearful infliction they were—and I was expected to hand round the tea and cakes, and make myself useful. I think I might have managed well enough if the old women would have let me alone; but they were always expecting me to do something wrong, and I was conscious that whatever they were doing they had an eye upon me.

"It's trying, you know, when you hear exclamations like this: 'Thé saints prosarve us! if he hasn't nearly poked his elbow into Mrs. Fitzgerald's eye!' or, 'See now, if he isn't standing on Miss Macrae's train!' One day I let a cup of coffee fall on to old Mrs. O'Toole's new crimson silk dress. It was the first she had had for nine years to my knowledge, and would have lasted her for the rest of her natural life. And if you could have heard the squall she made, and the exclamations of my aunts, and the general excitement over that wretched cup of coffee, you would never have forgotten it.

"It had one good result, I was never asked to hand things round again and was indeed never expected to put in an appearance until the tea-things were taken away. I suffered for months for that silk dress. My aunts got two yards of material and presented them to Mrs. O'Toole; and for weeks and weeks I got short allowance of butter to my bread and no sugar in my tea, and had to hear remarks as to the necessity for being economical. As for Mrs. O'Toole she never forgave me, and was always saying spiteful things. But I got even with her once. One evening the doctor, who was her partner at whist, was called out, and I was ordered to take his place. Now, I played a pretty good game at whist, better than the doctor did by a long chalk I flattered myself; but I didn't often play at home unless I was wanted to make up a table, and very glad I was to get out of it, for the ill-temper of those old harridans when they lost was something fearful.

"It was only penny points, but if they had been playing for five pounds they couldn't have taken it more to heart; and of course if I had the misfortune of being their partner they put it down entirely to my bad play. Well, we held good cards, and at last we only wanted the odd trick to win. I held the last trump. Mrs. O'Toole was beaming as she led the best spade, and felt that the game was won. I could not resist the temptation, but put my trump on her spade, led my small card, and the game was lost. Mrs. O'Toole gave a scream and sank back in her chair almost fainting, and when she recovered her breath and her voice went on like a maniac, and had a desperate quarrel with my aunts. I made my escape, and three days later, to my huge delight, was sent off to Dublin and entered the university. I only stayed there about six months, when a friend of my father's got me a commission; but that six months cured me of my shyness."

"I am not surprised," Desmond laughed; "it can only have been skin deep, I fancy, O'Connor."

"I will give Conway his first lesson to-night," the captain said.

Dancing had already begun when Captain O'Connor and Ralph drove up in a dog-cart to the Regans', who lived some four miles from Ballyporrit. O'Connor introduced Ralph to his host, and then hurried away. In a short time he was deep in conversation with Miss

Tabitha Regan, who was some years younger than her brother, and still believed herself to be quite a girl. She was gorgeously arrayed with a plume of nodding feathers in her headdress.

"You are looking splendid to-night, Miss Regan," O'Connor said in a tone of deep admiration. "You do not give your nieces a chance."

"Ah! you are flattering me, Captain O'Connor."

"Not at all, Miss Regan; it's quite a sensation you make. My young friend Conway was tremendously struck with your appearance, and asked me who that splendid woman was." Which was true enough, except for the word "splendid;" for as they had walked through the room Ralph's eyes had fallen upon her, and he had exclaimed in astonishment, "Who on earth is that woman, O'Connor?"

"He is dying to be introduced to you. He is a little young, you know; but of good family, and may come into a lot of money one of these days. Only son, and all that. May I introduce him?"

"How you do go on, Captain O'Connor," Miss Tabitha said, much flattered. "By all means introduce him."

O'Connor made his way back to Ralph.

"Come along, Ralph; I will introduce you to our host's sister, Miss Regan. Charming creature, and lots of money. Awfully struck with your appearance. Come on, man; don't be foolish," and, hooking his arm in Ralph's, he led him across the room to the lady Ralph had before noticed.

"Miss Regan, this is my brother-officer, Mr. Conway. Ralph, this is Miss Regan, our host's sister, although you would take her for his daughter. Miss Regan, Mr. Conway is most anxious to have the pleasure of the next dance with you if you are not engaged."

One 28th.   RALPH HAS AN UNDESIRABLE PARTNER.—Page 189.

Ralph murmured something in confirmation, and Miss Regan at once stood up and placed her hand in his arm. Ralph gave a reproachful glance at his captain as he moved away. Fortunately, he was not called upon to say much, for Miss Regan burst out:

"It is too bad of you not having been here before, Mr. Conway—quite rude of you. Captain O'Connor has spoken of you frequently, and we girls have been quite curious to see you. There is the music striking up. I think we had better take our places. I suppose as I am at the head of my brother's house we had better take the place at the top."

Ralph never forgot that dance. Miss Regan danced with amazing sprightliness, performing wonderful steps. Her ostrich plumes seemed to whirl round and round him, he had a painful feeling that every one was grinning, and a mad desire to rush out of the house and make straight for his quarters.

"Your aunt is going it," Captain O'Connor remarked to one of the daughters of the house with whom he was dancing. "She sets quite an example to us young people."

The girl laughed. "She is very peculiar, Captain O'Connor; but it is cruel of you to laugh at her. I do wish she wouldn't wear such wonderful headdresses; but she once went to court a good many years ago at Dublin, and somebody told her that her headdress became her, and she has worn plumes ever since."

"I am not laughing at her, Miss Regan," O'Connor said gravely; "I am admiring her. Conway is doing nobly too."

"I think he looks almost bewildered," the girl laughed. "It's a shame, Captain O'Connor. I was standing quite close by when you introduced him, and I could see by your face that you were playing a joke upon him."

"I was performing a kindly action, Miss Regan. The lad's young and a little bashful, and I ventured to insinuate to your aunt that he admired her."

"Well, you shall introduce him to me next," the girl said. "I like his looks."

"Shall I tell him that, Miss Regan?"

"If you do I will never speak to you again."

As soon as the dance was over Captain O'Connor strolled up with his partner to the spot where Miss Tabitha was fanning herself violently, Ralph standing helplessly alongside.

"That was a charming dance, Miss Regan. You surpassed yourself. Let me recommend a slight refreshment; will you allow me to offer you my arm? Miss Regan, allow me to introduce my brother-officer, Mr. Conway."

Ralph, who had not caught the name, bowed to the girl thus left suddenly beside him and offered her his arm.

"Why, you look warm already, Mr. Conway," she began.

"Warm is no word for it," Ralph said bluntly. "Did you see that wonderful old lady I have been dancing with?"

"That is my aunt, Mr. Conway; but she is rather wonderful all the same."

Ralph had thought before that he was as hot as it was possible for a man to be; but he found now that he was mistaken.

"I beg your pardon," he stammered. "I did not catch your name; but of course I oughtn't to have said anything."

"I wonder you didn't see the likeness," the girl said demurely. "My aunt considers there is a great likeness between us."

"I am sure I cannot see it the least bit in the world,"
Ralph said emphatically; not the smallest. But I hope
you forgive me for that unfortunate remark; but the fact
is, I felt a little bewildered at the time. I am not much
of a dancer, and your aunt is really so energetic that I
had to exert myself to the utmost to keep up with her."

"I think you did admirably, Mr. Conway. We quite
admired you both. There," she said laughing at Ralph's
confusion, "you need not be afraid about my not forgiv-
ing you for the remark. Everyone knows that Aunt
Tabitha and we girls never get on very well together;
and she does make herself dreadfully ridiculous, and I
think it was too bad of Captain O'Connor putting you
up with her."

"Thank you, Miss Regan," Ralph said earnestly.
"The fact is I haven't joined long, and I don't care
much for parties. You see, I have only left school a few
months, and haven't got accustomed to talk to ladies yet;
and O'Connor—who is always up to some fun or other—
did it just to cure what he calls my shyness. However,
I can quite forgive him now."

"I don't think you are so very shy, Mr. Conway,"
Miss Regan said with a smile. "That last sentence was
very pretty, and if I had not hold of your arm I should
make you a courtesy."

"No, please don't do that," Ralph said, coloring
hotly. "I didn't mean anything, you know."

"Now, don't spoil it. You meant I suppose, what was
quite proper you should mean, that Captain O'Connor
by introducing me to you had made up for his last
delinquency."

"Yes, that is what I did mean," Ralph agreed.

"Captain O'Connor tells me that you have been
through all sorts of adventures, Mr. Conway—been car-

ried off by a French privateer, and taken to a pirate island, and done all sorts of things."

"The 'all sorts of things' did not amount to much, Miss Regan. I made myself as useful as I could, and picked up French; and at last when the privateer sailed away I walked down to the shore and met our sailors when they landed. There was, I can assure you, nothing in any way heroic about the part I had to play."

"Still it was an adventure."

"Oh! yes, it was that; and upon the whole I think I liked it, except when there was a chance of having a fight with our own people."

"That would have been dreadful. What would you have done?"

"Well, I certainly wouldn't have fought; but what I should have done would, I suppose, have depended upon circumstances. I suppose I should have jumped overboard if I had the chance."

"And is it true what Captain O'Connor was saying, that you had to do like the other pirates on the island?"

"I don't know that there was anything particular they did, except to get drunk, and I didn't do that."

"He hinted that the rule was that each man had to take a wife from the people they captured."

"What nonsense!" Ralph exclaimed indignantly. "The idea of my taking a wife. You mustn't believe what Captain O'Connor says, Miss Regan; except, of course," he added slyly, "when he is saying pretty things to you."

"I think you will do, Mr. Conway," the girl laughed. "Six months in Ireland and you will be able to give Captain O'Connor points if you go on as well as you are doing. You have paid two very nicely-turned compliments in ten minutes. But there, our dance is finished."

"May I have another later on, Miss Regan?"

"Yes. Let me see; I am engaged for the next five. You can have the sixth if you like, if you haven't secured my aunt for that."

"You are getting on, Conway," Captain O'Connor said as they drove away from the Regans. "I have had my eye upon you. Three dances with Polly Regan, beside taking her down to supper."

"It was too bad of you putting me on to her aunt in that way."

O'Connor laughed. "It was a capital thing for you, youngster, and paved the way for you with Polly; who, by the way, is not such a respectful niece as she might be. But she is a very nice little girl. I had thought of making up in that quarter myself, but I see it's no use now."

"None at all," Ralph said seriously. "We are not actually engaged, you, know, but I think we understand each other."

"What!" Captain O'Connor exclaimed in a changed voice. "You are not such a young ass as to get engaged before you have joined three months?"

Ralph burst into a laugh. "That's good," he said. It is not often I get a rise out of you, O'Connor."

"Well, you did there fairly," the captain admitted, joining in the laugh. "I thought for a moment you were serious."

"No," Ralph said. "I may make a fool of myself in other directions; but I don't think I am likely to in that sort of way."

"Prior attachment—eh?" Captain O'Connor asked quizzically.

"Ah, that's a secret, O'Connor," Ralph laughed. "I am not going to lay my heart bare to such a mocker as you are."

When they reached the village they found a body of twenty men drawn up opposite their quarters.

"Is that you, O'Connor?" the lieutenant asked as the trap stopped. "Just after you had gone the gauger came in and requested that a party might accompany him at three o'clock this morning to hunt up a still among the hills. I am glad you are back in time, as I did not like going away without there being any one in charge here. It's a nuisance; for it is just beginning to rain. However, it can't be helped."

"I will go if you like Desmond," Ralph said, jumping down. "I should like a good tramp this morning after that hot room."

"Are you quite sure you would like it?" the lieutenant asked.

"Quite sure. Beside, it's my turn for duty this morning; so that really it's my place to go with them, if Captain O'Connor has no objection."

"Not the least in the world, Conway. I don't suppose Desmond has any fancy for tramping among the hills, and if you have, there is no reason in the world why you should not go."

A couple of minutes sufficed to exchange the full-dress regimentals for undress uniform, covered by military greatcoat, then Ralph hurried out just as the excise officer came up.

"We are going to have a damp march of it, Mr. Fitzgibbon," Ralph said.

"All the better, sir. There will be a thick mist on the hills that will hide us better even than night. There is a moon at present, and as likely as not they will have a boy on watch. Are you ready, sir?"

"Quite ready. Attention! Form fours! March!" and the little party started.

"How far are we going?" Ralph asked the revenue officer.

"About seven miles, sir. It's about half-past three now; we shall be there somewhere about six. It does not begin to be light until seven, so there is no particular hurry."

"I hope you know the way, Mr. Fitzgibbon? It is so dark here I can scarcely see my hand. And if we get into the fog you talk about it will be as black as ink."

"Oh, I know the way," the officer said confidently. "We keep along the road for two miles, then turn up a track leading up a valley, follow that for three miles; then branch to the right, cross over one or two slight rises, and then follow another slight depression till we are within a hundred yards of the place. I could find my way there with my eyes shut."

"That sounds easy enough," Ralph said; "but I know how difficult it is finding one's way in a fog. However, we must hope we shall get there all right. Sergeant, have the men got anything in their haversacks?"

"Yes, sir. Captain O'Connor ordered them to take their breakfast ration of bread, and he told me to see that their water bottles were filled; and—" (and here he moved closer up to Ralph, so that he should not be heard by the men) "he gave me a couple of bottles of whisky to mix with the water, and told me to fill the bottles myself, so that the men shouldn't know what was in them till they had their breakfast; otherwise there would be none left by the time they wanted to eat their bread. He is always thoughtful the captain is."

"That's a very good plan, sergeant. I shall bear it in mind myself for the future. They will want something before they get back after a fourteen-mile march."

The fine mist continued steadily as they tramped

along; but the night seemed to grow darker and darker. They turned off from the road; and as they began to ascend the track along the valley the cloud seemed to settle round them. The excise officer walked ahead, keeping upon the path. Ralph followed as closely as he could in his footsteps; but although almost touching him he could not make out his figure in the darkness.

"Tell the men to follow in single file, sergeant," he said; "keeping touch with each other. As long as we are on the beaten track we know we are right, but there may be bowlders or anything else close by on one side or the other."

Marching as closely as they could to each other the party proceeded.

"How on earth are you going to find the place where we turn off, Mr. Fitzgibbon?" Ralph asked.

"We shall find it easy enough sir. The path regularly forks, and there is a pile of stones at the junction, which makes as good a guide as you can want on a dark night. We can't miss that even on a night like this."

Ralph had struck a light with his flint and steel, and looked at his watch at the point where they turned off from the road, and he did the same thing two or three times as they went along.

"It's an hour and twenty minutes since we turned off, Mr. Fitzgibbon. Even allowing for our stoppages when we have got off the path, we ought to be near the turning now."

"Yes, I fancy we are not far off now, sir. I can feel that we are rising more sharply, and there is a rise in the last hundred yards or so before we reach the place where the road forks. We had better go a little more slowly now, sir."

Another five minutes there was a stumble and a fall in front of Ralph.

"Halt!" he exclaimed sharply. "What is it, Mr. Fitzgibbon?"

"I have fallen over the pile of stones," the officer said, "and hurt myself confoundedly."

"Don't you think we had better halt till daylight?"

"I think we can keep on sir. The nearer we get there the better; and if we should miss the path we can halt then and wait till daybreak."

"Well, we can do that," Ralph agreed.

"I will go on ahead, sir, twenty or thirty yards at a time and then speak, and you can bring the men on to me, then I will go on again. It will be slow work, but I can keep the path better if I go at my own pace."

Ralph agreed, and they proceeded in this manner for some time.

"I don't think we are on the track now," Ralph said at last.

"Oh, yes, we are," the officer replied confidently.

Ralph stooped and felt the ground. "The grass is very short," he observed, "but it is grass."

The officer followed his example.

"Oh, it is only a track now," he said. "Just a foot-path, and the grass is not worn off. I am convinced we are right."

"Well," Ralph said, "just go a little way to the right and left, and see if the grass gets longer. It seems to me all the same."

The officer did so, and was obliged to own that he could not perceive any difference. Ralph now spread his men out in a line and directed them to feel on the ground to see if they could discover the track. They failed to do so, and Ralph then ordered them together again.

"We will halt here, sergeant, till daylight. It's no

use groping about in the dark. For anything we know we may be going exactly in the wrong direction. The men can of course sit down if they like; and they may as well eat a piece of bread and try their water-bottles. But tell them not to eat more than half their ration. We may be longer before we get out of this than we expect."

The order was given, the men piled their arms and seated themselves on the short turf. Presently Ralph heard a sudden exclamation of surprise and satisfaction as one of the men tasted the contents of his water-bottle, and in a minute there was a buzz of talk. Before scarce a word had been spoken; the men had been marching in a sort of sulky silence, disgusted at being taken from their beds for work they disliked, and at their long march through the damp night air; but their satisfaction at this unexpected comfort loosened their tongues.

Pipes were produced and lighted, and the discomfort of the situation altogether forgotten. Desmond had handed to Ralph the flask and packet of sandwiches he had prepared for himself, and he, too, felt less strongly the chilling effects of the damp and darkness after partaking of them. The excise officer had also made his preparations.

"We should be more certain as to our whereabouts if we had stopped at that heap of stones as I proposed, Mr. Fitzgibbon."

"I don't deny, sir, you were right as it has turned out; only I wouldn't have believed that I could have missed the path, and I did want to get close to the place before we were observed. I knew that we couldn't actually surprise them till morning; for the hut lies some distance in a bog, and there would be no crossing it unless we could see. Still if we could have got to the edge without the alarm being given, they would not have time to hide the things before we reached them. I have ridden across this place many a time after dark, and never missed my way."

"That was the sagacity of your horse more than your own, I expect," Ralph said. "A horse can find his way along a path he has once traveled better than any man can do. In the first place, I think he can see better in the night; and in the second, he has some sort of instinct to guide him. However, I don't suppose it much matters; we shall find the path easily enough in the morning. And, as you said, the mist will hide our movements quite as effectually as the darkness would do."

At last the morning began to break in a dim misty light, and as it grew stronger they were able to perceive how dense was the fog that surrounded them. At three paces distant they were invisible to each other.

"It does not seem to me that we are much better off than we were before, so far as finding the path lies. What do you think?"

"It looks bad, certainly," the officer admitted reluctantly. "I am awfully sorry I have led you into this mess."

"It can't be helped," Ralph said. "We must make the best of matters. At any rate it's better than it was, and the mist is not nearly as heavy as when we were marching up that valley."

CHAPTER XL

STILL-HUNTING.

"Now, sergeant, the men may as well fall in," Ralph said cheerfully, "and then we will set about finding this path. On which side do you think it is most likely to lie, Mr. Fitzgibbon?"

"I really can't give an opinion, sir. You see there is not a breath of wind to help us, and in this sort of light there is no telling where the sun is, so I don't know at the present moment which way we are facing."

"Well, we will try to the right first, sergeant," Ralph said. "I will lead the way. Let the men follow at a distance of about ten paces apart. I will keep on speaking. Do you stand at the left of the file, and when the last man has gone ten paces from you pass the word along. By that time I shall be about two hundred yards away. If I have not found the path then we will come back to you and do the same thing on the left. If we don't light upon the path itself we may come upon some rise or bog or something that will enable Mr. Fitzgibbon to form an idea as to where we are."

This was done, but beyond finding that the ground on the right was higher than that on the left no index as to their position was discovered.

"You see, Mr. Fitzgibbon, we are on sloping ground rising to the right. Now, does that help you at all?"

"Not much sir. The country here is all undulating."

"Very well, then, we must try a march forward. Now,

sergeant, place the men five paces apart. Do you put yourself in the center. I will move on three yards ahead of you. I shall go as straight forward as I can, but if you think I am inclining either to the right or left you say so. The fact that the ground is sloping ought to be a help to us to keep straight. I wish it sloped a little more, then one would be able to tell directly whether one was keeping straight. Let the men speak to each other every few paces so as to keep the right distances apart."

Mr. Fitzgibbon placed himself by Ralph's side, and they started. For half an hour they kept on, then Ralph cried, "Halt. I am certain I am going downhill, it may be because I have changed my direction, or it may be because there is a change in the lay of the ground. What do you think?"

"It's impossible to say," Mr. Fitzgibbon replied. "It seems to me that we have been going straight, but when one can't see a yard before one one may have turned any direction."

"How long do you think that this rascally fog is likely to last?"

"It may clear up as the sun gets high, sir, but I must acknowledge that it may last for days. There is never any saying among these hills."

"Well, at any rate you must give up all idea of making a raid on this still, Mr. Fitzgibbon. That has become a secondary object altogether now. What we have to do is to find our way out of this. Hitherto I have tried what we could do in silence. Now I shall give that up. Now, sergeant, get the men together again. I will go ahead, and shall, if I can, keep on descending. If one does that one must get out of these hills at last. When I get about fifty yards I will shout. Then you

send a man on to me. When he reaches me I will shout
again and go on another fifty yards. When I shout send
another man forward. When he gets to the first man
the first man is to shout and then come on to me, and
you send off another. In that way we shall make a regular line fifty yards apart, and I don't think any one can
get lost. Should any one get confused and stray, which
he can't do if he keeps his head, he must shout till he
hears his shouts answered. After a time if he doesn't
hear any answer he must fire his gun, and we must
answer till he rejoins us. But if my orders are observed
I do not see how any one can miss their way, as there
will be posts stationed every fifty yards. You remain
till the last and see them all before you. You quite
understand? When each man comes up to the one in
front of him he is to stop until the next man joins him,
and then move on to the man ahead."

"I understand, sir."

"They must not be in a hurry, sergeant; because moving ahead as I shall, I shall have to move to the right or
left sometimes so as to make as sure as I can that I am
still going down. Now, Mr. Fitzgibbon, if you keep
with me, between us we ought to find the road."

The plan seemed a good one, but it was difficult to
follow. The fall of the ground was so slight that Ralph
and the officer often differed as to whether they were
going up or down, and it was only by separating and
taking short runs right and left, forward or backward,
that they arrived at any conclusion, and even then often
doubted whether they were right. The shouting as the
long line proceeded was prodigious, and must have
astonished any stray animals that might have been graz-
ing among the hills. So bewildering was the fog that
the men sometimes went back to the men behind them

instead of forward to the men in front, and long pauses were necessitated before they got right again. Ralph, finding the cause of the delays, passed the word down for the first man to keep on shouting "number one," the second "number two," and so on, and this facilitated matters. The line of shouting men had at least the advantage that it enabled Ralph to keep a fairly straight course, as the sound of voices told him if he was deviating much to the right or left.

"We may not be going right," he said to his companion, "but at least we have the satisfaction of knowing that we are not moving in a circle."

After some hours' marching Ralph, to his great delight, came upon a hill rill of water.

"Thank goodness," he said, "we have got a guide at last. If we follow this we must get somewhere. We need not go on in this tedious way, but will halt here till all the men come up."

It was half an hour before the sergeant arrived.

"We have got a guide now, sergeant, and can push on. I suppose you have no idea what stream this is, Mr. Fitzgibbon?"

"Not at present," the officer admitted. "There are scores of these little rills about. They make their way down from the bogs at the top of the hills, and there is nothing to distinguish one from the other."

They now tramped on briskly, keeping close to the little stream. Sometimes the ground became soft and marshy, and it was difficult to follow its course; but they went straight on and after three more hours' marching came upon a road that crossed the stream over a little culvert. There was a cheer from the tired men as they stood on hard ground again.

"Now, the question is shall we turn to the right or the

left, for we have not the faintest idea as to the points of the compass. What do you say, Mr. Fitzgibbon?"

"I should say that it is an even chance; but at any rate whichever way we go we are sure to come in time upon a hut or village, and be able to find out where we are."

"Very well, then; we will take the right," Ralph said. "Form fours, sergeant. We shall get on better by keeping in step. Now, sergeant, if any of the men can sing let him strike up a tune with a chorus. That will help us along."

There was a little hesitation, and then one of the men struck up a song, and with renewed life and energy they all marched along. It was nearly an hour before they heard the welcome sound of voices close by. Ralph halted his men and proceeded toward this sound, and then discovered what the fog had prevented them from seeing before, that they were passing through a village, the voices being those of some women who were brought to their doors by the sound of music, and who were somewhat puzzled at the, to them, mysterious sounds."

"What place is this?" Ralph asked.

"It is Kilmaknocket."

"Bless me!" Mr. Fitzgibbon exclaimed, "we are twenty miles away from Ballyporrit if we are an inch."

"Then it's evident we can't get there to-day," Ralph said. "We must have come more than that distance since we halted in the night. Now, my good woman, I have a party of twenty men here, and we have lost our way in the hills, and must stop here for the night. How many houses are there in the village?"

"There are ten or twelve, sir."

"That is all right, then. We must quarter two men on each. I will pay every one for the trouble it will

give, and for something to eat, which we want badly
enough, for we have come at least twenty-five or twenty-
six miles, and probably ten more than that, and have had
nothing but a bit of bread since we started."

"It's heartily welcome you will be, sir," the woman
said, "and we will all do the best we can for you."

The men were now ordered to fall out. The sergeant
proceeded with them through the village, quartering two
men on each house, while Ralph went round to see what
provisions were obtainable. Potatoes and black bread
were to be had everywhere, and he also was able to buy
a good-sized pig, which, in a very few minutes, was
killed and cut up.

"We have reason to consider ourselves lucky indeed,"
Ralph said, as he sat down with the excise officer half an
hour later to a meal of boiled potatoes and pork chops
roasted over a peat fire. "It's half-past four now, and
will be pitch dark in another half-hour. If we had not
struck upon that stream we should have had another
night out among the hills."

Ralph's first measure after seeing his men quartered in
the village was to inquire for a boy who would carry a
message to Ballyporrit, and the offer of half a crown produced four or five lads willing to undertake it. Ralph
chose one of them, an active-looking lad of about fifteen,
tore out a leaf from his pocketbook, and wrote an
account of what had happened, and said that the detachment would be in by two o'clock on the following day.
Then directing it to Captain O'Connor or Lieutenant
Desmond, whichever might be in the village, he gave it
to the lad, who at once started at a trot along the road in
the direction from which they had come.

"He will be there in four hours," Mr. Fitzgibbon said.
"It's a regular road all the way, and he can't miss it

even in the dark. It's lucky we turned the way we did, for although it was taking us further from home it was but two miles along the road here, while, if we had gone the right way, it would have been six or seven before we arrived at the next village."

"I think we are lucky all round," Ralph said. "An hour ago if any one told us we were going to sit down at half-past four to a hot dinner of pork and potatoes we should have slain him as a scoffer. It would have seemed altogether too good to be true."

Ralph had no difficulty in purchasing whisky, and he ordered the sergeant to serve out a tot to each man with his dinner and another half an hour later, and by seven o'clock there was scarcely one of the tired men who was not already asleep. The next morning they started at eight o'clock, having had a breakfast of potatoes before they fell in. Ralph rewarded the peasants generously for their hospitality, and the men set off in high spirits for their tramp, and reached Ballyporrit at half-past two in the afternoon.

"You gave us a nice scare yesterday, Conway," was Captain O'Connor's greeting as they marched in. "When twelve o'clock came and you didn't come back I began to think you must have lost yourselves; and a nice time we had of it till your messenger arrived at eight. It was no use sending out to look for you on the hills. But I went out with a party, with two or three men to guide us, to the end of a valley, up which a path went; beyond that there was no going, for one couldn't see one's hand. I stayed there an hour, firing off guns once a minute, and as there was no reply was sure that you must be a good distance off, wherever you were; so there was nothing to do but to come back and hope you had found shelter somewhere. Come in, lad; I have got

some hot lunch waiting for you. Come in, Mr. Fitzgibbon. It's lucky I didn't catch you yesterday, or I should
have considered it my duty to have hung you forthwith
for decoying his majesty's troops among the hills.''

"Well, Conway, you didn't bargain for all this when
you offered to change places with me,'' Lieutenant Desmond said when they were seated at table.

"No; but now it's all over I am glad I did change, in
spite of the tramp we had. It has been an adventure,
and beside, it was a good thing to learn how best to get
out of a fog.''

"How did you manage, Conway?'' Captain O'Connor
asked; "for once lost in such a fog as that on those hills
there really does not seem anything to be done.''

Ralph related the various steps he had taken, and how,
eventually, they had come upon running water and followed it down to a road.

"Well, I really think you have done remarkably well,
youngster. I shouldn't be surprised if we have some
more tramps before us, for I had a letter this morning
from the colonel saying that the fellow known as the Red
Captain, a notorious scoundrel who has been with his
gang committing all sorts of atrocities in Galway, has
made the place too hot for him at last, and is reported to
have made his way down to the south coast, somewhere
in this direction; and we are ordered to keep a sharp
lookout for him. He is an unmitigated ruffian, and a
deperate one. He has shot several constables who have
tried to capture him, and as he has three or four men
with him nearly as bad as himself I expect we shall have
some trouble with him. There has been a reward of a
hundred pounds for his capture for a long time, but so
far without success. One man, whom he suspected
rightly or wrongly of intending to betray him, he killed

by fastening the door of his cottage and then setting the thatch alight; and the man, his wife, and four children were burned to death."

That evening, just as dinner was over, the sergeant came in and said that a woman wished to speak to the captain.

"What does she want, sergeant?"

"She won't say what she wants, sir; only that she wishes to speak to you privately."

"Show her in then, sergeant."

The sergeant brought in the woman and then retired. As soon as the door closed behind him the woman threw back the shawl which had hitherto almost covered her face. She was about twenty-five years old, and strikingly pretty.

"What can I do for you?" Captain O'Connor asked. "The sergeant says you wish to speak to me on some particular business."

"Yes, sir; sure, and it is very particular business."

"You don't wish to speak to me quite alone, I suppose?" O Connor asked, seeing that she hesitated.

"No, your honor; seeing that these gentlemen are all officers there is no reason in life why they should not hear what I have to say. But, sure, sir, it's little my life would be worth if it were known outside these walls that I had been here. My name is Bridget Moore, sir, and I belong to County Galway. Well, your honor, there was a desperate villain, they call the Red Captain, there. He was hiding in the hills for some time near the little farm my husband holds. We did not know who he was—how should we? but thought he was hiding because the revenue officers were after him on account of a bit of a still or something of that kind; but we found out one day, when he had been taking too much of the

cratur and was talking big like, that he was the Red
Captain.

"My Denis was troubled in his mind over it. Av
coorse he was not one to inform, but he had heard so
much of the Red Captain and his doings that he was
onaisy at the thought of having him as a neighbor. He
wasn't one to pretind to be frindly when he wasn't, and
the captain noticed it and took offince, and there were
mighty high words between them. One night, your
honor, he and his gang came down and broke in the
door, and tould Denis he was a black-hearted informer.
Denis said it was a lie, and they were nigh shooting him,
but at last they said he should have the choice either of
joining them or of being shot; and Denis, being druv to
it, and seeing no other way to save his life, was forced
to agree. Then the villains made him kneel down and
take a great oath to be faithful and secret.

"I was away off; for I had caught up the child and
run out by the back door when they came in, but I crept
round to a broken window there was, so that I could hear
what was said. When they took him away wid them
and went off, I followed at a distance, for I wasn't sure
whether after all they didn't mean to murther him. But
they went up to the hut where they lived at the edge of
the bog, and as they seemed more friendly like I went
back to see after the child, who was left all alone. The
next morning I took it over to a neighbor and asked her
to keep it till I came back. Then I went up to the hut
again and found it was empty.

"A day or two after that I found out from a man who
run a still, and knew the Red Captain well, that he had
made up his mind to lave Galway and come down south,
where he had some friends; so I just shut up the house
and walked down here. Now you know, your honor,

that I don't come here for the sake of the reward. Not a penny of it would I touch if I were dying of hunger, and sooner than be pointed at as an informer I would throw myself over them big rocks. But they have got Denis, and either they will make him as bad as themselves— which I don't think—or they will shoot him; and if they don't shoot him he will be shot one of these days by the soldiers. What I want you to promise, your honor, is, that if I point out where you can lay your hands on the villains, you won't say who tould you, and that you will tell your soldiers not to shoot Denis.

"You will know him aisy enough, your honor, for he is a dacent-looking boy; and when the time comes you will find he will do what he can to help you. I found out who the people were that the Red Captain had come down to, and I watched and watched their place, till one day I saw him come there. Then I followed him and found out whereabout they were hiding. I kept about till, that evening, I had a chance of spaking to Denis for a minute. He is broken-hearted, your honor, but he daren't lave them. He said they had sworn if he ever tried to run away they would hunt him down; and the Red Captain said that he would send information to the poliss that it was Denis who helped him fire the hut when those poor cratures were burned, and would say he had been in the thick of it all along; and how could he prove the differ? So he daren't for the life of him move, your honor; and tould me to keep away and go home, for I could do him no good, and if they caught me spaking to him they would kill the two of us."

"I promise you willingly," Captain O'Connor said, "I will not say who pointed out their hiding-place, and if your husband does not join in the resistance he certainly shall receive no hurt. If he is caught with them I am

afraid that I shall be exceeding my duty in letting him
go; but surely he would have no difficulty in proving that
he had only accompanied them in consequence of their
threats.''

"That's what he couldn't prove, sir. That's just
what they tould him: if they were caught themselves
they knew there was no chance for them, and they would
all swear together that he had been with them all along;
and how could the boy prove that he wasn't?''

"Well, Mrs. Moore, I will try and strain a point,''
Captain O'Connor said. "You see, people sometimes
escape after they are taken, and I think we shall be able
to manage somehow that Denis shan't appear at the bar
with the others; and if it should turn out that cannot be
managed I will engage to make such representations to
the authorities that your husband shall get off free.''

"Very well, sir; then I will tell you where they are to
be found. I can't take you there, your honor, but I can
tell you whereabout it is. There is a footpath turns off
from the road at the end of the village, and goes straight
down to the top of them big rocks that come out of the
sea. Well, sir, a few hundred yards to the right of that
there is a sort of break in the rocks, and there is a track
goes down there. You won't see it onless you look close
for it, and it gets lost a little way down, becase the
rocks are all broken about and heaped on each other.
It's down there they go. There's always a man on watch
not far from the top; and there is generally a gossoon
from their friends here somewhere at the edge of the bog
behind, who would run forward and tell the man on
watch if he saw any soldiers coming from here. So you
will have to be mighty careful; but they are down there,
sure enough, somewhere.

"Denis tould me there was no chance of their being

taken, for they have got a little boat hid away down among the rocks by the water, and if the alarm was given they would make off in that. I can't tell you any more than that, you honor; but I should think that may be enough to help you to find them.''

"I should think so too, Mrs. Moore. And what do you propose doing yourself?''

"I shall go off, sir, at once. Folk have been wondering at me, and asking where I came from and what I was doing here, and I want to get away. If it came to the Red Captain's ears there was a woman about he might guess it was me, and if he did he would like enough shoot Denis and make away. I can't see as I can do any good by stopping, and I may do harm; so I will go over to Dunmanway and stop there till I hear what your honor has done. If I find Denis has got hurted I shall come back, if not I shall go home to the farm. Maybe your honor will tell him I shall be expecting him there.''

Captain O'Connor accompanied her outside to see that no one spoke to her, and when he saw her disappear in the darkness he returned to the room.

"I think you have had a lucky escape, Conway," he said as he entered. "The matter is explained now about your being watched and questioned, and it is very lucky that they did not quite make up their minds you were a spy; for if they had you may be sure they would have had no more hesitation in putting an ounce of lead into you, and throwing you over the cliff, than they would in shooting a sparrow. Well, this is an important piece of news. The authorities have for a long time been trying to lay their hands on this scoundrel and his gang, and if we can catch him it will be a feather in our caps, for he has defied all their efforts for the last three years. Now, we must arrange the line of battle, how it is to come off, and when.

"In the first place we must arrange with the coast-guard to have a well-manned boat somewhere along the coast to cut the scoundrels off if they try to escape by sea. The attack must be made by daylight, that is evident, for half the men would break either their legs or their necks if they tried to get down in the dark. I think it will be best to place half the company along the top of the cliffs, posting two or three men at every point where it looks possible that they may ascend, then with the other half we will go down on this track she speaks of and search the whole place thoroughly. If they are there we must find them sooner or later; and find them we will, if the search takes us a week."

"Who is this Red Captain?"

"I believe his real name is Dan Egan. He was mixed up in some brutal outrage on an inoffensive farmer, had to leave the county, went to Dublin, and enlisted. He went out to Spain with his regiment, was flogged twice for thieving, then he shot an officer who came upon him when he was ill-treating a Portuguese peasant; he got away at the time, and it was months before he was heard of again. It was thought that he had deserted to the French, but I suppose he got down to a port somewhere in disguise and shipped on board a vessel for England. The next thing heard of him was that he was back again at his native place. The police here were of course ignorant as to what had become of him from the time he disappeared; but the fellow made no secret of what he had been doing, and boasted of having shot the officer.

"The regiment was communicated with, and by a comparison of the date of enlistment and the personal description there was no doubt that the man who had enlisted as Mark Kelly was Dan Egan. Of course every effort was made to capture him, but in vain. I believe the peasants would have informed against him, for he was hated for his violence and overbearing way, but he soon established a sort of terror in the district. He was joined by three or four of the greatest ruffians in County Galway, and unless the whole of these had been captured at one swoop, vengeance would be sure to fall upon whoever had betrayed him.

"He has killed four or five police officers at various times, and I should say twice as many peasants who have ventured to offend him. He and his band levied a sort of blackmail in the district, and woe betide the small farmer who refused to send in a sheep or a bag of meal once a month. Their cattle were killed and their ricks set on fire; and so in a short time he had the whole neighborhood under his thumb. Whenever a party went in pursuit of him he was sure to obtain early information. Not from love, but from fear; for it was a well understood thing that any one seeing a body of police and failing to send instant word would suffer for it.

"Just as we left I heard that a company of foot and a troop of cavalry were to be sent from Galway to search every hut and hiding-place in the district, and I suppose that it was this that drove him down here. He has red hair and beard; and it is this partly, and partly no doubt the fellow's murderous character, that has gained him the name of the Red Captain. He is a prize worth taking, and if we can lay hands on him and his band together we shall have done better work than if we had unearthed a hundred illicit stills. At any rate we will lose no time. I will write a letter at once to the revenue officer at the coast-guard station. I shall mention no names, but say that we hope to make an important capture to-morrow morning on the cliffs here, and asking him to send a well-armed boat at daylight, with instructions to stop and arrest any boat that may put out from the shore. If the revenue cutter happens to be lying off his station, or within reach of a messenger, I will tell him to have her off the shore if possible.''

Captain O'Connor at once wrote the letter. ''Sergeant Morris,'' he said, when the non-commissioned officer came in, ''I want you to take this letter yourself to Lieutenant Adcock at the coast-guard station in the cove three miles along to the east. It is of the highest importance. I want you to see the officer yourself and obtain an answer from him. Take a man with you, and carry your side-arms. Don't go along the cliff, but keep to the road till you come to the lane that leads direct to the village in the cove. Just tell the landlord to come here, will you?''

''Landlord,'' he said, when the host appeared, ''I want you to lend a couple of long greatcoats and two hats or caps of any kind. I am sending two of my men off on a mission, and I don't want them to be noticed. It does not matter how old the coats are so that they are long.''

''I will get them your honor. I have one that will do, and will borrow the other for you in no time.''

''You see, sergeant, I don't want your presence in the village to be noticed. You know how these fellows hang together. The sight of two soldiers in uniform there would be sure to attract attention. Choose a man you can rely on to play his part cleverly. I tell you to take your side-arms, because I happen to know that there are men about who, if they suspected your mission, would not have the least hesitation in knocking you on the head. This is no question of finding a still, sergeant, but of making the capture of one of the most desperate bands in the country; and it is well worth taking the utmost pains and precaution to insure everything going well.''

"I understand, sir. I will take Pat Hogan with me; he has plenty of the brogue, and can talk the language too. So if any one should speak to us as we go along he can do the talking, and no one will suspect that we are not a couple of countrymen."

"That will do very well, sergeant. It is just seven o'clock now. If Lieutenant Adcock is in when you get there you ought to be back, well, before ten. It's about four miles by road. I would borrow a couple of heavy sticks if I were you. I don't think it at all likely there will be any occasion to use them, but it is just as well to be prepared. If, when you get near the village, or on your way back, you come across any one who questions you inquisitively, and seems to you to be a suspicious character, I authorize you to make him prisoner and bring him over with you. Knock him down if he attempt resistance. You may as well take a pair of handcuffs with you and a short coil of rope. The object of the rope is, that if you capture any one on your way to the village you had better handcuff him, gag him, and tie him up securely to a tree or some other object at a distance from the road, and pick him up as you come back. I need hardly say that you are not to go into any house in the village, not to speak to any one beyond what is absolutely necessary."

"I understand, sir, and you can rely upon me to carry out your orders."

"You had better fetch Hogan in here, sergeant. Tell him what he has to do before you bring him in, then we can see the disguises on you both; and it's better for you to start from an inn, where people are going in and out, than from one of the houses where you are quartered."

The landlord returned with the disguises almost immediately after the sergeant had gone out, and in a few minutes the latter came in with Hogan. The greatcoats were put on, the hats substituted for military caps, and with the collars of the coats turned up and the addition of two heavy sticks, the disguise was complete, and the two smart soldiers would pass anywhere as peasants.

"You had better take your gaiters off, sergeant. You look too neat about the feet; although that would not be noticed unless you went into the light. Here is the letter, put it carefully inside your jacket. There, now, I think you will do."

It was nearly ten when the two soldiers returned. "Here's a letter sir, from the revenue officer. He quite understands what is wanted, and will have a boat off the cliffs at daybreak with a well-armed crew. He does not know where the cutter is at present. She touched there two days ago, sailing west."

"You met no suspicious characters, sergeant?"

"No, sir. We spoke to no one until we got to the village, beyond asking a woman which was the turning from the main road. There didn't seem to be a soul about in the village, and we had to wait about some time before I could get hold of a boy to tell me which was the revenue officer's cottage. I left Hogan outside when I went in; but he saw no one, nor did any one speak to us on our return beyond one or two men we met passing the time of night, which Hogan answered."

"All the better, sergeant. The great object is secrecy. Now, leave these things here and put on your caps again. If you go to the bar the landlord has orders to give you a glass of grog each. Don't say a word as to where you have been, Hogan, but get back to your quarters. When you have had your grog, sergeant, look in again before you go."

When the men had gone out Captain O'Connor opened the letter, which merely confirmed what the sergeant said. When Sergeant Morris returned Captain O'Connor told him that the company were to parade an hour before daylight.

"Don't give the order to-night, sergeant; but go round from house to house yourself in the morning, rouse the men, and tell them to fall in quietly without beat of drum.

"Everything is going on well, boys," he said when the sergeant had left, "and I think we have a good chance of laying these scoundrels by the heels to-morrow. However, we must insure that word is not sent from the village, when the troops begin to get up. A stir an hour before the usual time is sure to excite remark, and as it is certain these fellows will have arranged with some one in the village for early news of any unusual movement, we must take steps to prevent a messenger passing. I propose that you two shall be astir half an hour before the troops; and that you shall, before any one else is moving, go along the path leading to the cliffs, stop a couple of hundred yards beyond the village, and arrest any one who may come along."

"Yes, I think that will be a very good plan," Lieutenant Desmond said. "No one shall pass us, I warrant."

"Don't forget to take your pistols; it is likely enough you may have to use them before the day is over. These scoundrels know they fight with ropes round their necks, and are almost sure to resist desperately. Now we will have one glass more, and then be off to bed. The day will begin to break about seven, and I will impress upon the landlord the urgent necessity of calling you both by five."

"I suppose we are to stay where we take up our station

till you come along with the company, O'Connor, whether we take any prisoners or not?"

"Yes, that will be the best way, Desmond. If you have caught any one I will send them back with a guard to the village. No, it would not do for you to move before we come up, for there is no saying what time a messenger will go along. They may not take the alarm until just as we are starting, or even until they see which road we are taking. By the way, you may as well take that pair of handcuffs the sergeant has left on the table with you, otherwise if you do get a prisoner you would have to keep your hands on his collar, or he might make a bolt any moment. There is nothing like being on the safe side.

"You had better take up your post at some place where your figures will not be seen by any one coming along the road till he is close to you, or instead of coming straight along he might make a bolt round; and some of these fellows can run like hares. We must not let the smallest chance escape us. If we succeed in the affair we shall get no end of credit, beside the satisfaction of freeing the country of as desperate a band of ruffians as any that infest it, and that's saying a good deal. Now, here's success to our work to-morrow." O'Connor drained his glass and placed it on the table, and then rising and taking up his sword made his way to his room, his companions at once following his example.

CHAPTER XII.

THE CAVE AMONG THE ROCKS.

AT five o'clock on the following morning Ralph was
roused by the landlord, who brought him a candle; he
lost no time in dressing, buckled on his sword, looked to
the priming of the double-barreled pistols Mr. Penfold
had given him, and placed them in his belt. Then he
went downstairs and put the handcuffs into the pocket
of his great coat. He then went to the bar, where the
landlord was kindling a fire.

"I want a bottle of whisky, landlord, a loaf of bread,
and a big lump of cheese." As he was waiting for these,
Lieutenant Desmond joined him.

"That's right, Conway, there is nothing like laying in
a stock of creature comforts when you have the chance.
Look here, landlord, get an empty bottle and put half
the whisky in, and then fill them both up with water.
Cut that loaf of bread in halves; in that way we can get
it in our pockets. That's right; now do the same with
the cheese. You and I may not be together, Conway, so
it's just as well to divide the commissariat; to say nothing of the convenience of carriage. Now, have you got
the handcuffs? That's right, we will be off at once."

The landlord went to the door with them and looked
after them, somewhat surprised at seeing no soldiers
about.

"What can they be up to by themselves at this hour of
the morning?" he said to himself. "Well, they are two

nice young fellows anyway, and I hope that they are not going to get into mischief. Now I will just make up the fire, and then sit down for an hour's snooze in my armchair. The captain said he was to be called at six. I suppose they are going out still-hunting somewhere. Well, I wish them luck; for when the boys can get their whisky for next to nothing they don't care about coming here, and small blame to them, for I shouldn't myself.''

Not a soul was astir in the village as the two young officers passed along. They turned off at the lane leading to the sea, and after proceeding a quarter of a mile came to a point where the roadway ended, the path beyond this being merely a track. Here there was a gate across the lane, and a wall running right and left.

''We can't find a better spot than this, Conway,'' Lieutenant Desmond said. ''If we sit down one on each side against the wall, a hundred men might pass along without noticing us.''

''Which side shall we sit, Desmond?''

''We will sit this side,'' the lieutenant replied. ''If we were the other side a man might possibly wrench himself way from our grasp, and might outrun us, but on this side of the gate he couldn't do so; for even if he did break away he would have to run back toward the village, the gate would stop his going the other way.''

Accordingly the young officers took their posts against the wall, one on either side of the gate, and with their swords drawn awaited the coming of a messenger to the Red Captain.

''There is no chance of any one being here for another twenty minutes,'' Desmond said. ''The sergeant will not rouse the men up till a quarter to six, therefore no one is likely to come along until within a few minutes of the hour. It's precious cold here, though the wall does shelter us from the wind a bit; still it's not a lively job having to wait here half an hour, with the thermometer somewhere below freezing point."

The time passed slowly. Occasionally they exchanged a few words in low tones, but as the time approached when they knew that the sergeant would be going his rounds to call the men they spoke less.

"It must be nearly six o'clock now," Desmond said at last. "The men would be called at a quarter to, so if any one is coming he will most likely be here in a few minutes. Hush! I think I can hear footsteps."

A few seconds later they dimly saw a figure running toward them at full speed. As it dashed up to the gate they sprang out and seized it. There was a sharp frightened cry.

"Don't make a noise," Desmond said sternly, "or it will be the worse for you. Where were you going?"

It was a girl of about twelve years old whom they had captured. She was silent a moment.

"Sure, your honor," she said in a whimper, "I was doing no harm. I was only running to tell Mike Brenan that his ould mother is taken bad with the cramps, and wanted to see him bad."

"Where do you expect to go to, you little liar?" Desmond asked. "We know what you are up to. You were running to tell some one that the soldiers were getting up. Now, if you are quiet and keep still no harm will come to you; but if you try to scream or to get away we shall hand you over to the police, and there's no saying whether they may not make it a hanging matter for aiding the king's enemies."

"I suppose we needn't fasten her?" Ralph said.

"Not fasten her! Why, she is as slippery as a young eel, and if you take your hand off her for a moment she would be off like a hare. No, no, we must make her safe. Beside," he whispered in Ralph's ear, "she would scream to a certainty if she saw any one else coming, then they might strike off and get round us. No, no, we can't run any risks; there is too much depends on it. Now just sit down there, young woman, by the wall. We are not going to hurt you, but you have got to keep quiet. Now put your feet together." Desmond took out his pocket handkerchief and folded it, and tied the girl's ankles firmly together. "Now then, Ralph, do the same with her wrists. That's right now. Wrap that shawl of hers three or four times tightly round her mouth. That's it; let her breathe through her nose. Now you keep a sharp watch over her, and see she doesn't wriggle out of these things. If you see any one coming clap your hand over her mouth, and see she doesn't make a sound. When he comes up you can let go and help me if necessary; it won't matter her giving a bit of a scream then."

"Now," he went on, this time speaking aloud, "if that girl makes the least noise, run her through with your sword at once. Don't hesitate a moment."

"Very well," Ralph said in the same tones. "I will silence her, never fear."

Ralph sat down close to the girl and watched her sharply. They had fixed the shawl as well as they could, but he felt sure that by a sudden effort she could free her mouth sufficiently to scream. She sat perfectly still; but in about three minutes he saw her suddenly throw her head back, and in an instant he clapped his hand over her mouth. She struggled violently in spite of her bonds, and tried to bite; but with the other arm he held her head firmly, and succeeded in preventing the slightest sound escaping her. Then he glanced up the path.

As he had expected the girl's quick ear had heard approaching footsteps that were inaudible to him. A figure was bounding rapidly toward them. As it reached the gate Desmond sprang upon it. There was a sharp scuffle for a moment.

"All right, Conway. I have got him."

It was a lad of some fifteen years old this time. He struggled furiously till Desmond placed a pistol against his head, and told him that he would blow his brains out if he was not quiet, and taking out the handcuffs fastened them on to his ankles.

"There is no fear of his doing any running now. Just come and sit down by this wall, my lad, and remember if you make the slightest sound I will run my sword through your body."

The lad shuffled to the wall and sat down. Ralph released his grasp of the girl.

"This is a regular young wildcat, Desmond. She very nearly got my hand in her mouth, and if she had she would have bitten a piece out. Well, I shouldn't think there will be any more of them."

"No, I should think not. They would scarcely send off more than two messengers. However, we must still keep a sharp lookout."

But no one else came along, and in a quarter of an hour they heard the deep tramp of a body of men approaching, and Captain O'Connor soon came up at the head of the company.

"Well, any news, gentlemen?" he asked as the two young officers stepped out.

"Yes, Captain O'Connor. We have two prisoners—a girl and a boy. They came along about ten minutes apart, both running at full speed and evidently going with messages. We put the handcuffs on the boy's ankles, and tied the girl's with our handkerchiefs."

"Sergeant, tell off two men and let them take these prisoners back to the village, and guard them carefully till we return. They may as well keep the handcuffs on the boy's ankles, and untie the girl's; but let one of them keep a tight hold of her arm, and be sure that she doesn't slip away."

Two men were told off for the duty, and the march was then resumed. Daylight was faintly breaking when they reached the edge of the cliff. Ralph, with ten men, was posted at the spot where a slight track was visible going down into a sort of gulley. Captain O'Connor then proceeded with half the company to the right, Desmond taking the remainder to the left; each posting men at intervals along the edge of the cliff, and placing parties of four at every point where there appeared the smallest probability of an ascent being practicable.

All were ordered to load at once. They were to make prisoner any one coming up the cliff, and in case of resistance to fire without hesitation. The two officers then returned to the spot where they had left Ralph. It was now nearly broad daylight. Leaving the soldiers they went a short distance to a point where the rocks fell away precipitately, and from here had a clear view of the face of the cliffs.

"We had better wait here for a time," the captain said. "The chances are that before long one of them will look out from their hiding-place, and perhaps make his way up to the top to look round. If he does, that will give us an index as to the direction at any rate of their hiding-place. Now, I will take the ground in front; do you watch to the left, Conway, and you to the right, Desmond. We had better lie down, or on this jutting point we may catch the eye of any one down there before we can see him. Keep a sharp lookout lads; it will save us a world of trouble if we can see one of them."

For half an hour they lay quiet, then Desmond suddenly exclaimed:

"There is a man among those fallen rocks halfway up the side. There! he is gone. Perhaps we shall see him again in a moment."

For five minutes they lay with their eyes fixed on the rocks that Desmond pointed out, but there were no signs of life.

"Are you sure you were not mistaken, Desmond?" O'Connor asked.

"Quite certain. He suddenly appeared by the side of that gray bowlder, stood there for a moment, and sunk down again. I expect he must have got a view of one of the men somewhere along the top."

"We will wait another ten minutes," O'Connor said, "and then we will take a party to the spot and search it thoroughly. There is the coast-guard boat, so there is no fear of their getting away by water."

Another quarter of an hour passed.

"It is no use waiting any longer. Go along the line, one each way, and bring ten men from points where they can be spared. We will leave them at the top of the path and take the party there down with us. There are only four or five of them, and ten men beside ourselves are ample for the business."

The arrangements were soon made. Before starting on the descent O'Connor said to the men: "We wish to take the fellows who are hiding down there alive if possible. They are the gang of the fellow known as the 'Red Captain,' and have committed a score of murders; but if it is absolutely necessary you will of course fire. There is one man among them who is there on compulsion, and is less guilty than the rest. He is a fair-haired man, and I should think you would notice the difference between him and the rest. Whatever resistance they make it is not probable that he will join in it. At any rate, do not fire at him unless it is absolutely necessary to save life. Now see to your priming before we start, and fix bayonets. Mind how you climb over these rocks, because if any of you fall your muskets may go off and shoot some one in front of you. Wherever it is possible scatter out abreast of each other, so as to prevent the possibility of accident. Now, then, march!"

Leading the way, Captain O'Connor descended the little track. It extended but a short distance. Beyond that a chaos of fallen rocks—the remains of a landslip many years previously—stretched away to the shore.

"There is no working along these sideways, Desmond," Captain O'Connor said after they had climbed along for some little distance. "We had better make straight down to the shore, follow that for a bit, and then mount again to the spot where you saw the man."

It was difficult work, but at last the party reached the shore. Lieutenant Adcock, who was himself in command of the boat, had watched the party making their way down the rocks, and now rowed in to within a few yards.

"Good-morning, lieutenant," Captain O'Connor said. "I think we have got them fairly trapped; but doubtless they would have made off if they hadn't seen you on the watch outside. It's that notorious scoundrel the Red Captain of Galway who is, I hear, hiding here with his gang."

"Indeed!" the revenue officer said; "that will be a capture worth making. Shall I come ashore with four of my men? I expect they are more accustomed to climbing about among the rocks than yours are, and I should like to lend a hand."

"Do, by all means," Captain O'Connor replied. "I see you have got ten, and six will be quite enough in the boat, even if they do manage to get down and embark, which I don't think they will. Your men are all armed, I suppose?"

"Yes; they have all carbines and cutlasses. Now, coxswain, I leave you in charge. Row out a quarter of a mile, and if any boat pushes off you are to stop it and arrest all on board. They will almost certainly resist, and in that case you must use your arms. Now, the four bow oars get out and step ashore."

When the lieutenant and his four men had landed, the boat again pushed off, and the party on shore made their way along over the rocks at the edge of the water until they were opposite the rock where Lieutenant Desmond had seen the man appear. Then the ascent was commenced. The four officers went first, the men following in a line.

"Bear a little to the left," Captain O'Connor said; "it is likely to lie somewhere in that direction. The man we saw would have been making toward the path and not from it. Keep a sharp lookout between these great rocks; there is no saying where the entrance to their hiding-place may be."

Almost as he spoke there was a sharp crack of a rifle, and the bullet struck the rock on which he was standing.

"Come on, lads!" he shouted, "the sooner we are there the less time they have got to fire;" and with a cheer the men hurried forward, scrambling recklessly over the rocks. Again and again puffs of smoke darted out from the rocks in front; and one of the soldiers fell, shot through the heart.

"Don't stop to fire!" Captain O'Connor shouted as a yell of rage broke from the men; "you will do no good, and it will only give them more time."

A dozen more shots were fired. One of the coast-guard men was shot through the shoulder; but this was the only casualty, for the quick movements of the men as they scrambled over the bowlders disconcerted the aim of those above. Breathless and panting the four officers gained the spot from which the shots had been fired, the men close up behind them; but not a soul was to be seen.

"Wait a moment till you get breath, lads," their leader said. "They can't be far from here. We will find their hiding-place presently, never fear."

As they stood panting there was a shout from above. The soldiers were standing along the edge of the cliff, looking down upon the fight. Sergeant Morris waved his arm.

"They have made away to your left, sir!" he shouted at the top of his voice. "We have just caught sight of them among the rocks!"

In two or three minutes Captain O'Connor led the way in that direction.

"Keep your eyes sharply about, lads. No doubt the place is cunningly hidden. Search among every clump of bushes between the rocks."

Presently the sergeant shouted down again from above:

"I think you are far enough now, sir! We did not catch sight of them beyond that!"

For an hour the search continued, but without avail.

"They must be here somewhere, lads!" Captain O'Connor said. "We will find them if we have to stop here a week, and have provisions brought down from the village. It's pretty evident there is no opening between the great rocks or we must have found it. We must ex-amine the smaller bowlders. They may have one so placed that it can be dropped down over the entrance.

That flat slab is a likely-looking place, for instance. Three or four of you get hold of it and heave it up.''

The men gathered round to lift it. Ralph stooped down and peeped under as they did so.

"Hurrah!" he shouted, "there is an opening here."

Several of the others now got hold of the stone. It was up-ended and thrown backward, and the entrance to a passage some three feet high and two feet wide was revealed.

"I can smell a peat fire!" one of the men exclaimed.

"This is the entrance, no doubt," Captain O'Connor said. "See, the bottom is evidently worn by feet. The passage must have been used for a long time; but it's an awkward place to follow desperate men into."

"It is, indeed," Lieutenant Adcock agreed. "They could shoot us down one after one as we go in. They would see us against the light, while we should be able to make out nothing."

"Surrender in there!" Captain O'Connor shouted. "You can't get away; and I promise you all a fair trial."

His summons was followed by a taunting laugh; and a moment later there was a sharp sound within, and a rifle bullet struck the side of the entrance and flew out.

"It would be throwing away one's life to go in there," Captain O'Connor said. "At any rate we have got them secure, and they must come out in time. But it would be madness to crawl in there on one's hands and feet to be picked off by those scoundrels at their ease. Now, lads, two of you stand by this entrance. Keep out of the line of fire, and be ready with your bayonets to run any one through who comes out. Let the rest scatter and search round this place. They may have another entrance. If so, we must find it. In the first place, it may be easier of entry; in the second they might escape from it after dark."

Again the search began.

"Do you think it is likely to be higher up or lower down, O'Connor?" Lieutenant Desmond asked.

"There is no saying, Desmond; the passage seems to go straight in. I should fancy above rather than below."

For a long time they searched without success; then Ralph, who had gone higher up the rocks than the rest, came upon a clump of low bushes growing between some large bowlders. There was nothing suspicious about them, and he was just turning away when he perceived a slight odor of peat smoke.

Silently he made his way down to the captain.

"I have found another entrance," he said. "At any rate I think so; for I certainly smelled smoke. If we go quietly we may take them unawares."

Captain O'Connor passed the word along for the men to gather silently, and Ralph then led the way up to the clump of bushes.

"Yes, I can smell the peat plainly enough. Now, Conway, do you search among the bushes. Carefully, lad, we don't know what the place is like."

Cautiously Ralph pushed the bushes aside. He saw at once that these had been carefully trained to cover a large hole. This was about three feet wide; and descended at a sharp angle, forming a sloping passage of sufficient height for a man to stand upright. Captain O'Connor knelt down and looked in.

"This looks more possible," he said; "but it's very steep. I should say it is not used by them, but acts as a sort of chimney to ventilate the cavern and let the smoke out. At any rate we will try it; but we must take our boots off so as to get a better hold on the rocks, beside we shall make less noise. Blunt and Jervis, do you go down to the other entrance again. It is likely enough that they may try to make a bolt that way if they hear us coming. Keep a sharp lookout down there, and be sure no one escapes.''

"Don't you think, Captain O'Connor, that it will be a good thing to enter from there also the moment a row is heard going on within. Their attention will be taken up with your attack, and we may get in without being noticed.''

"That's a very good idea, Conway; and you shall carry it out. Take two more men with you, and make your way in as soon as you hear us engaged. But remember that it is quite possible we may not be able to get down. This passage may get almost perpendicular presently; and though I mean to go if possible, even if I have a straight drop for it, it may close up and be altogether impracticable. So don't you try to enter till you are quite sure they are engaged with us, otherwise you will be only throwing away your life.''

"I understand, sir," Ralph said as he turned to go off. "If you get in you can reckon on our assistance immediately; if not, we shall make no move.''

Ralph now took up his station at the mouth of the cavern with his six men, and lay down just in front of the opening listening attentively. He could hear a continued murmur as of many voices.

"Get ready, lads, to follow me the instant you see me dive in," he said. "I am sure by the sound there are more than four men in there, and Captain O'Connor may want help badly.''

Grasping a pistol in his left hand, and his sword in his right, Ralph listened attentively. Suddenly he heard a shout, followed by a volley of imprecations, and then the discharge of a gun or a pistol.

In an instant he threw himself forward along the low

narrow passage. He had not gone more than three or four yards when he found that it heightened, and he was able to stand upright. He rushed on, keeping his head low in case the roof should lower again, and after a few paces entered a large cabin. It was dimly illuminated by two torches stuck against the wall. In a moment a number of figures rushed toward him with loud shouts; but before they reached him two of the soldiers stood by his side.

"Fire!" he shouted as he discharged his pistol, and at the same moment the soldiers beside him discharged their muskets.

A moment later he was engaged in a fierce hand-to-hand conflict. Several firearms had flashed off almost in his face. One of the soldiers fell with a sharp cry, but those who were following rushed forward. Ralph narrowly escaped having his brains dashed out by a clubbed rifle, but springing back just in time he ran his opponent through before he could recover his guard.

Just at this moment a big man with a shock of red hair and a huge beard leveled a blunderbuss at him. It flashed across him that his last moment had come, when a man behind leaped suddenly upon the ruffian's back and they fell to the ground together, the blunderbuss going off in the fall and riddling a soldier standing next to Ralph with slugs.

For two or three minutes a desperate struggle went on between Ralph and his six men and those who attempted to break through them. Sturdily as the soldiers fought they had been driven back toward the entrance by the assailants, armed with pikes and clubbed guns. There was no sound of conflict at the other end of the cave, and Ralph felt that the attack there had for some reason failed.

"Shoulder to shoulder, lads!" he shouted. "We shall have help in a minute or two."

He had emptied both his double-barrelled pistols. His sword had just broken short in his hand while guarding his head from a heavy blow. He himself had been almost struck to the ground, when there was a rush of men from behind, and the rest of the soldiers poured in.

"Give them a volley, lads!" he shouted; "and then charged them with the bayonets!"

The muskets rang out, and then there was a shout of "We surrender! we surrender!"

A minute later the men were disarmed. There was still a desperate struggle going on on the ground.

"Here, lads," Ralph said to two of his men. "Secure this red fellow, he is their leader. One of you bring a torch here."

The light was brought. It was seen that the man who had sprung upon the Red Captain's back had pinioned his arms to his sides, and held them there in spite of the efforts of the ruffian to free himself. Two of the soldiers took off their belts and fastened them together, passed them between the back of the man and his captor, and then strapped his arms firmly to his side. The man who held them then released his grip.

"Stand over him with fixed bayonets, and if he moves run him through. Now, where's Captain O'Connor?"

"I don't know, sir. He and Mr. Desmond and the naval officer went down the hole in front of us. We were following when the naval officer shouted up to us to run round to this entrance and make our way in there, for he could go no further."

"I am here, Conway," a faint voice said from the other end of the cabin; "but I have broken my leg I think, and Desmond has knocked all the wind out of my body."

Ralph hastened to the spot whence the voice came and found Captain O'Connor lying on the ground, and Lieutenant Desmond insensible beside him.

"What has happened?" Ralph exclaimed. "Have they shot you?"

"No. Hold the torch up and you will see the way we came."

The soldier did so, and Ralph looking up saw a hole in the top of the cave twenty feet above.

"You don't mean to say you came through there, O'Connor?"

"I did, worse luck to it!" O'Connor said. "The passage got steeper and steeper, and at last my foot slipped, and I shot down and came plump into the middle of a peat fire; and a moment later Desmond shot down on to the top of me. We scattered the fire all over the place, as you can imagine; but I burned my hands and face, and I believe the leg of my breeches is on fire —something is hurting me confoundedly."

"Yes, it is all smoldering!" Ralph exclaimed, putting it out with his hands.

"Have you got them all?" Captain O'Connor asked.

"Everyone; not one has made his escape. It would have fared badly with us, though, if Lieutenant Adcock had not sent down the men to our assistance. Where is your leg broken, O'Connor?"

"Above the knee," the captain said.

"Here is some whisky and water," Ralph said, handing him his bottle. "Now, I will see what has happened to Desmond," and he stooped over the insensible officer.

"He has got a nasty gash on his forehead, and I think his right arm is broken," he said. "I will pour a little spirits between his lips, and then he had better be carried out into the air."

This was done; and then Ralph went outside, and shouted to Sergeant Morris to bring down another twenty men.

"If you please, sir," one of the coast-guard men said, touching his hat, "I don't see any signs of our officer. Have you seen him?"

"No," Ralph said. "Perhaps he is still in that passage. You had better run up to the top and see."

Two minutes later the man returned:

"He's down there, sir; but he says he can't get up or down."

"You had better run down to the boat at once," Ralph said. "I see she is close inshore. Bring a couple more . of your men up with you and a rope. If you tie that round your body you can go down and bring him up."

Ralph then returned to the cavern, where the men were still guarding the prisoners.

"You can march them outside now," he said. "Then make them sit down, and stand over them with fixed bayonets till Sergeant Morris arrives. Now let us look to the wounded."

An examination showed that two of the soldiers were dead, and three others badly wounded. Seven of the party in the cave lay on the ground. One only was alive; the rest had fallen either from bullet or bayonet wounds. Seeing that nothing could be done here Ralph looked round the cavern. He soon saw that just where Captain O'Connor had fallen there was an entrance into another cave. He reloaded his pistols before he entered this, but found it deserted.

It contained two large stills, with mash tubs and every appliance, two or three hundred kegs of whisky, and some thirty sacks of barley. This at once accounted for the cave being known, and for the number of men found

in it; for in addition to the seven that had fallen six
prisoners had been taken. The walls of the cave were
deeply smoke-stained, showing that it had been used as
a distillery for a great number of years.

"That is satisfactory," Captain O'Connor said when
Ralph reported to him the discovery he had made.
"That place where I came down is of course the chimney.
Peat does not give much smoke, and making its way out
through that screen of bushes it would be so light that it
would not be noticed by any one on the cliffs. Well, it's
been a good morning's work—a band of notorious scoundrels captured and an illicit still discovered in full
work. It was a cleverly contrived place. Of course it
is a natural cavern, and was likely enough known before
the fall of rocks from above so completely concealed the
entrance. I wish those fellows would come, though, for
my leg is hurting me amazingly, and these burns on my
hands and face are smarting horribly. Shout out to
them on the cliff, Conway, and tell them to send at once
to fetch Dr. Doran from the village. The wounded
ought to be seen to as soon as possible, and it is likely
enough that some of them cannot be taken up over the
rocks to the top of the cliff. I dread the business
myself."

In a quarter of an hour Sergeant Morris arrived with
his party. By this time Lieutenant Desmond had recovered consciousness, and although in great pain from his
broken arm was consoled upon hearing of the complete
success of the expedition. The soldiers were furious on
hearing that three of their comrades had been killed,
and two of their officers badly injured.

"Sergeant," Ralph said, "bring four of your men into
the cave with me. Now," he continued when they
entered, "there is a pile of blankets in that corner; take

one of them and fasten it across two of the men's muskets, so as to make a litter. Then we must lift Captain O'Connor carefully and put him on it and get him outside. It will be a difficult business getting him through the narrow entrance, but we must manage it as well as we can. But first let us thoroughly examine the caves; there may be another entrance somewhere."

Searching carefully they found a passage behind the stack of kegs. It was some eight feet high and as much wide. They followed it for a short distance, and then saw daylight. Their way was, however, speedily blocked by a number of rocks piled over the entrance.

"This was evidently the original entrance to these caves," Ralph said, "but it was covered up when the rocks came down from above. That would account for the place not being known to the coast-guards. I thought the passage we came in by looked as if it had been enlarged by the hand of man. No doubt it was originally a small hole, and when the entrance was blocked the men who made up their minds to establish a still here thought that it would be the best way to enlarge that and to leave the original entrance blocked.

"Well, it's evident we must take Captain O'Connor and the wounded out by the small entrance. It would be a tremendous business to clear those great rocks away."

Captain O'Connor and the two wounded men were with great difficulty taken through the narrow passage. The soldier who was alive was the one who had received the charge of the blunderbuss in his legs; he was terribly injured below the knee, and Ralph had little doubt that amputation would be necessary. The other man lived but a short time after being brought into the air.

Ralph now turned to the peasant who had saved his

life by grappling with the Red Captain at the moment he was about to discharge his blunderbuss, and who had by his orders been left unbound. He was sitting a short distance from the other prisoners.

"Your name is Denis Moore?" he said.

"It is, your honor," the man replied in surprise; "though how you came to know it beats me entirely."

"I heard it from your wife last night," Ralph said.

"From Bridget?" the man exclaimed. "Why, I thought she was a hundred miles away!"

"She came down here like a brave woman to try and save you," Ralph said, "and gave us information that brought us to this hiding-place; but her name is not to appear, and no one will know how we heard of it. We promised her that no harm should come to you if we could help it, and, thanks to the act by which you saved my life, you have escaped, for being down on the ground you were out of the line of the fire of our bullets. Of course at present we shall treat you as a prisoner, as you were captured with the others; but I think we shall manage to let you slip away. Your wife is to remain at Dunmanway till she hears the news of this affair and that you are safe, and she bade me tell you that you would find her at home, so no one will dream that either she or you had any hand in this affair. Now, point me out which are the four men that belong to this gang that brought you down here."

"The man who has just died was one of them," Denis replied. None of the other three are here, so I expect they fell in the cabin. They were in the front of the fight. I saw one go down just as I grappled with our captain."

"So much the better," Ralph said. "As to their leader, there will be no difficulty in getting evidence about him. The regiment he belonged to is in Dublin, and they can prove the shooting of his officer; beside, they can get any amount of evidence from Galway."

"Ay; they will be ready enough to speak out now the whole gang are down," Denis Moore said. "They would not have dared to open their lips otherwise. The other prisoners all belong about here. One of their party is the captain's brother. That's how it is they came to take us in. But I think they would have been glad to get rid of us, for the Red Captain's lot were too bad for anything; and it isn't because men are ready to cheat the king's revenue that they are fond of such villains and murderers as these."

In a short time the doctor arrived. He had brought a case of instruments with him.

"There's nothing for it but amputation here," he said when he examined the wounded soldier. "His legs are just splintered. The sooner I do it the better."

Sergeant Morris and three of the men held the poor fellow while the operation was performed. As soon as it was over the doctor applied splints and bandages to Captain O'Connor's leg and Lieutenant Desmond's arm, and dressed the wounds of three of the other men, who had suffered more or less severely.

CHAPTER XIII.

STARTLING NEWS.

"WHAT do you think is the best thing to be done now, doctor?" Ralph asked.

"I don't know," he replied. "I don't see how on earth we are going to get them over these rocks and up to the top. A slip or a fall would cost either of your friends their limbs, and that poor fellow his life. I don't see how it is to be managed. It's hard work for a man to climb those rocks, and how a litter is to be carried I can't see. If it were anywhere else I should say build a hut for them; but it would be a tremendous business getting the materials down, and I don't think it could possibly be managed by night."

"I am sure it couldn't," Ralph said, shaking his head. "I think, though, if we got two long poles and slung a piece of canvas like a hammock between them we may possibly get them down to the shore. You see we have plenty of strength to get them over rough places."

"We could manage that easy enough," Lieutenant Adcock, who had some time before joined the party, said. "There are some sixteen-feet oars in the boat and some sails. We could easily rig up the hammock. I suppose you mean to take them off in the boat, Mr. Conway?"

"Yes; that's what I meant," Ralph said. "Then you can land them in your cove, and they might stop in the village till they are fit to be moved."

"That would be an excellent plan," the doctor said. "Let us set about it at once."

In half an hour the sailors brought up the hammock.

"I will go first," Captain O'Connor said, "as I am the heaviest. You will see how you manage to get me down. If it's done pretty easily you can bring down the two others; if not, they had better stop in the cave for to-night, and we will get a hut for them to-morrow. By the way, Conway, you had better get the dead carried out and taken down to the seashore. Have them laid down out of reach of the tide. Some of them belong about here, and their friends will wish to give them a decent burial. Our own dead had better be put in the boat, if Mr. Adcock will allow it, and taken to the village with us. Then they can be carried over to Ballyporrit for burial. A corporal with four men must be left for to-night in charge of the caves."

"I shall want my men to row the boat," Lieutenant Adcock said. "In the morning I will send over a warrant officer and four men to take charge of the cave till I can take its contents round to our stores."

Captain O'Connor was now lifted into the hammock, and six sailors carried him down to the water. They managed it excellently, easing him down with the greatest care over the rocks, and succeeded in getting him down to the sea without a single jerk. Lieutenant Desmond and the wounded soldiers were then taken down in the same way, while the men carried down the dead bodies of their three comrades and of the peasants who had fallen.

"I will take charge of the wounded," Lieutenant Adcock said, "and see them comfortably housed and cared for. I suppose Dr. Doran will go with us."

"Certainly," the doctor said, stepping into the boat.

I shall not give up charge of them until I see them all safely in bed."

"I shall come over and see you O'Connor," Ralph said, "as soon as I get the company back to the village. Shall I write a report of this business, or do you feel equal to doing so?"

"I will manage it, Conway. I can dictate it if I don't feel up to writing it. But you had better not come over to-day. There will be a good deal of excitement over this capture, and no doubt several of the killed and prisoners belong to Ballyporrit; so it wouldn't do for you to leave the detachment without an officer. Be sure you have a strict guard put over the prisoners, and keep an eye upon them yourself. You can send over to inquire about us, but till you have got them off your hands you had better not leave the village. If a party are wanted for still-hunting send Sergeant Morris with them. I shall dispatch my report to-night, and no doubt the colonel will send an officer out to help you as soon as he gets it."

The boat now pushed off. A corporal and four men were told off to occupy the cave until relieved by the revenue men, and then, with the prisoners in their center, the party climbed the cliff, and again, having been joined at the top by the rest of the company, marched to Ballyporrit. They found the village in a state of excitement. The soldier who had gone to fetch the doctor had brought the news that a fight had take place down on the face of the cliff, but he could not say whether any had been killed. As soon as the detachment returned with the prisoners in their midst many women flocked round with cries and lamentations, and exchanged greetings with the prisoners.

Ralph at once took possession of the stables at the inn,

and saw that the prisoners were all handcuffed, the Red ruffian's legs being also securely bound. Then he placed two sentries inside and two out. The news that some of the men had been killed soon spread, and many of the villagers who did not see their relations among the prisoners hurried off toward the scene of action. Ralph informed the landlord that the dead had all been placed together on the seashore, and that their friends were at liberty to remove and bury them without any questions being asked. He then sent a corporal over to bring back news how the wounded men had borne the journey, and how they were disposed. But before his return the doctor drove up in a trap that he had borrowed.

"Adcock has put up the two officers in his own house," he said, "and his wife will look after them, so you need not worry about them. The other poor fellows are in the cottage next door. It belongs to the coxswain of the boat, who is also a married man. So you need be under no uneasiness about any of them. As far as I can see, they are all likely to do well. I shall go over the first thing in the morning, and will bring you news of them as soon as I get back."

Ralph had given orders that Denis Moore was not to be treated as a prisoner; and he now told the sergeant to send him in to him.

"I have been thinking it over, Moore," he said; "and it seems to me the best plan will be to allow you to go quietly away. Your conduct in the fight in the cave in itself showed that you were not voluntarily with the others; and I do not think, therefore, that it is necessary to report you among the prisoners. I suppose the Red Captain's gang have not done any unlawful act beyond taking part in the still business since they took you away from home?"

"No, your honor. We just came straight down here, traveling at night and hiding away by day."

"Very well. In that case you can give no special evidence against them. It is probable that at the trial evidence may be required from Galway as to the deeds that that red-bearded scoundrel committed there; and it is possible that you may be summoned with others, but I should think that the evidence of the constabulary will be sufficient. So, if you will give me your address there I will take it upon my self to let you go at once. In that case you can join your wife this evening and travel back with her."

"Thank you, sir," Denis replied. "I have no objection at all to give evidence as to what I know, so that it does not come out it was Bridget who tould you where they were hiding."

"You need not be afraid of that, Denis. Captain O'Connor gave her his word that her name should not be mentioned. At the same time I have no doubt he will claim for her the hundred pounds reward that was offered; and if he obtains it he will send it to you, so that nobody will be any the wiser."

"I should not like to take informer's money," Denis said.

"Not in ordinary cases," Ralph replied. "But you see she spoke out, not for the sake of money, but to get you out of their hands. And considering how much mischief those fellows have done, and how much more they would have done had we not laid hands on them, it is a very different case from that of an ordinary informer. None of your neighbors will know that she has had anything to do with the capture of these men, therefore no one will be any the wiser, and no doubt a hundred pounds will be very useful to you. I am sure you deserve some sort of compensation for being dragged away from home, and for the risk you ran in that fight; for a bullet might just as well have struck you as any of the others. I know that if I were in your place I should accept it without the least hesitation. And now, as I don't suppose they have left any money on you, and as your wife is not likely to be very well provided, I will give you five pounds on account; and remember that I shall always feel your debtor for the manner in which you saved my life by springing upon that ruffian just at the critical moment."

"You will deduct it from the other money, your honor?" Denis said, hesitating.

"Certainly I will, Denis. I should not think of offering you money for such a service as you rendered me. Now, if you will just give me your address in Galway I will make a note of it; though I don't think it at all likely you will be wanted at the trial. They will most likely proceed against him on the charge of shooting his officer and deserting; for they will have no difficulty in proving that, as the regiment he belonged to is in Dublin."

Denis started at once to rejoin his wife, highly pleased to have got away so quickly. Two days later Captain Morrison and Mr. Stapleton arrived from headquarters.

"I congratulate you, Conway," the latter said heartily. "We all pitied your being ordered away to this dreary place; and now you have been getting no end of honor and credit. O'Connor's report speaks in the strongest terms of you, and says it was entirely owing to your promptness and courage that the band was captured, and his life and that of Desmond saved. The Cork papers are full of the affair; and the capture of that notorious scoundrel, the Red Captain, created quite an excitement,

I can tell you. The only bad part of the affair is that we have had to come out here, for I am afraid there is no chance whatever of another adventure like yours.''

''Oh, I fancy there are plenty more stills to be captured, Stapleton; and that's good fun in its way, though it involves a good deal of marching and hard work.''

''And how are O'Connor and Desmond getting on?'' Captain Morrison asked.

''I had a very good report of them this morning from the doctor, and now that you have come I shall take a trap and drive over and see them at once. I had O'Connor's orders not to leave here till you arrived.''

''You are to go back yourself to-morrow morning, Conway,'' Captain Morrison said. ''You are to take the prisoners in with an escort of a corporal and ten men, and to hand them over to the civil authorities; which means, I suppose, that you are to take them to the prison.''

''I suppose I shall come straight out again?'' Ralph asked.

''I should think so; for with all this still-hunting business three officers are wanted here. But of course you will report yourself to the colonel and get orders. Here are the orders he gave me to give you. You are to start early, make a twenty-mile march, halt for the night, and go on again the first thing in the morning. You are to hire a cart for the wounded prisoners, and to exercise the utmost vigilance on the way. The men are to carry loaded muskets. It is not likely there will be any attempt at a rescue; but such things have happened before now. If anything of the sort should take place, and you find that you are likely to get worsted, your orders are that you are not to let the Red Captain be carried off alive. Put a man specially over him, with instructions to shoot him rather than let him be taken away from

him. The colonel will hold you harmless. The scoundrel has committed too many murders to be allowed to
go free.''

"I understand," Ralph said, "and will carry out the
orders; and now I will be off at once, for it will be dark
in an hour."

Ralph was glad to find that the two officers were going
on better than he had expected. Lieutenant Desmond
was already up, with his arm in splints and a great patch
of plaster across his forehead. O'Connor was still in
bed, and was likely to remain so for some time. The
regimental surgeon was with him, having left the other
two officers at the turn of the road leading to the village.

"I am glad to see you, Conway," Captain O'Connor
said cheerfully. "I was expecting you. The doctor
said Morrison and Stapleton had gone on to Ballyporrit.
None the worse for your brush, I hope?"

"Not a bit," Ralph said. "The bump on my head
caused by that musket blow hurt me a bit the first day
or two, but it's going down now. I am glad to see you
and Desmond looking so well."

"Oh, we shall soon be all right; though I am afraid I
shall be kept on my back for some little time. Desmond
is rather in despair, because he is afraid his beauty is
spoiled; for the doctor says that cut on his forehead is
likely to leave a nasty scar. He would not have minded
it if it had been done by a French dragoon saber; but
to have got it from tumbling down a chimney troubles
him sorely. It will be very painful to him when a partner at a ball asks him sympathizingly in what battle he
was wounded, to have to explain that he tumbled head
foremost into a peat fire."

Desmond laughed. "Well, it is rather a nuisance;
and you see Conway, the ashes have got so ground up in

the place that the doctor is afraid it will be a black scar. O'Connor chaffs me about it, but I am sure he wouldn't like it himself.''

"Why, my dear fellow, it's a most honorable wound. You will be able to dilate upon the desperate capture of the noted ruffian the Red Captain, and how you and that noble officer Captain O'Connor dashed alone into the cavern, tenanted by thirteen notorious desperadoes. Why, properly worked up, man, there is no end of capital to be made out of it. I foresee that I shall be quite a hero at tea-fights. A battle is nothing to such an affair as this. Of course it will not be necessary to say that you shot down into the middle of them like a sack of wheat because you could not help it. - You must speak of your reckless spring of twenty feet from that upper passage into the middle of them. Why, properly told, the dangers of the breach at Badajos would pale before it.''

"I am glad to see that you are in such high spirits," Ralph said when the laugh had subsided. "There's no fear of your being lame after it, I hope?''

"No, Dr. Doran says it is a clean snap of the bone, and it will, he thinks, mend all right; and as Macpherson, who has been examining it, says the same, I hope it is all right. It is very good of the colonel sending the doctor over to us; but I think Doran understands his business well, and has made a capital job of both of us.''

"How is Rawlinson going on?''

"Oh, I think he will do very well," the surgeon said. "Of course he's a little down in the mouth about himself. It is not a pleasant prospect for a man to have to go about on two wooden legs all his life. Still it's been done in the service; and as the fight was a sharp one, and such an important capture was made, he will get his full pension, and I shall strongly recommend him for Chelsea Hospital if he likes to take it. But he tells me he was by trade a carpenter before he enlisted, and I expect he would rather go down to live among his own people. His wooden legs won't prevent him earning a living at his trade; and as he is rather a good-looking fellow I dare say he won't have much difficulty in getting a wife. Maimed heroes are irresistible to the female mind.''

"That's a comfort for you, Desmond, anyhow,'' O'Connor laughed. "That black patch on your forehead ought to add a thousand a year to your marketable value.''

The next morning Ralph marched with his detachment, and arrived at Cork without adventure. Here he handed his prisoners over to the civil authorities of the jail, and then marched up to the barracks. He at once reported himself to the colonel, who congratulated him warmly upon the success that had attended the capture, and upon his own conduct in the affair.

"I will not keep you now,'' the colonel said, "for the mess-bugle sounded five minutes ago. I shall see you again in the morning.''

As Ralph entered the messroom the officers had just taken their seats. He was greeted with a boisterous outburst of welcome. His comrades got up and shook his hand warmly, and he had to answer many inquiries as to how O'Connor and Desmond were going on.

"Sit down, gentlemen!'' the major who was president of the mess shouted. "Conway has had a twenty-mile march, and is, I have no doubt, as hungry as a hunter. Let him eat his dinner in peace, and then when the wine is on the table he shall relate his adventures in detail. By the way, Conway, I hope you have lodged that ruffian safely in jail?''

"Yes, sir, I have handed him over, and glad I was to

get him off my hands; for though I had him handcuffed and his feet tied, and brought him along in a cart, I never felt comfortable all the way. The fellow is as strong as a bull, and as he knows what is before him he was capable of anything desperate to effect his escape."

"I remember the man well," one of the officers said; "for, as you know, I was in his regiment before I exchanged into the Twenty-eighth. He was a notorious character. He had the strength of two ordinary men, and once or twice when he was drunk it took eight men to bring him into barracks. I am heartily glad he is caught, for the poor fellow he killed was one of the most popular men in the regiment—with the soldiers as well as with us—and if they could have laid hands on this fellow I believe they would have hung him up without a trial. I shall have real pleasure in giving evidence against the scoundrel for I was present at the time he shot poor Forrest. I wasn't five yards away, but it was all over and the villain was off before I had time to lift a hand."

After dinner was over Ralph gave the full history of the capture in the cavern, of which Captain O'Connor had sent but an outline.

"It was a sharp fight indeed," the major said when he had finished; "for, for a time you were greatly outnumbered, and in the dark discipline is not of much avail. I think on the whole you got very well out of it, and O'Connor and Desmond were lucky in having got off with a broken limb each."

Ralph was detained some days in Cork, as he had to be present at the courthouse when the prisoners were brought up before the magistrates. After giving his evidence as to the capture, his attendance was no further required. All with the exception of the Red Captain were committed at once upon the charges of working an illicit still, and of offering a forcible resistance with arms to the authority of the king's officers. The Red Captain was charged with several murders, and was remanded in order that evidence might be obtained from the regiment to which he belonged in Dublin, and of the constabulary and other people in County Galway. Ralph then returned to Ballyporrit.

A fortnight later the detachment was recalled, the colonel having received the news that the regiment would be shortly under orders for America. Lieutenant Desmond was able to travel to Cork at once, although still unfit for duty; and the surgeon reported that in another fortnight Captain O'Connor would be also fit to be removed.

Ten days later definite orders were received for the regiment to be ready for embarkation, as soon as the two transports which had been ordered round from Plymouth arrived. Soldiers are always fond of change; and although there were few more pleasant quarters than Cork, there was a general feeling of animation and excitement at the thought of service at the other side of the Atlantic. All officers and men on furlough were at once recalled. The friends of many of the officers came across from England, to be with them till they sailed upon what was then considered a long and perilous voyage. Balls and dinners were given to and by the regiment. Officers overhauled their kits and belongings, getting what new things were required, bargaining with brokers for their furniture, and making all preparations for a prolonged absence from England.

"Ah, Stapleton," Ralph said, as the young ensign came into his quarters one day in high spirits, "there will be a sad change come over you before long. You almost wished you might die on your way round here from London. What will be your feelings when you have to face the waves of the Atlantic?"

"Don't talk about it, Conway. The very thought makes me feel queer. However, I expect I shall get on better now than I did last time. What an ass I was, to be sure, on that voyage!"

"Well, I do think your four months with the regiment have done you a world of good, Stapleton. You certainly were a stuck-up sort of personage when you came on board in the Thames. I think it is an awful mistake for a fellow to be educated at home, instead of being sent to school; they are sure to have to suffer for it afterward."

"Well, I have suffered for it to some extent," Stapleton said. "The lessons I got at first were sharp ones; but they certainly did me good."

"There is no doubt about that," Ralph agreed; "and I think there is a good deal of credit due to you, Stapleton, for having taken things in the right way. I wonder where we shall be stationed in America, and whether we shall have any fighting? Upon the whole we have no very great reason to be proud of our feats of arms in America; but I hope we shall do better next time. You see, in the last struggle we knew nothing of their tactics, and were at a great disadvantage; but after fighting its way through the Peninsular, I don't think there is any fear of the regiment not giving a good account of itself, if it is called upon to do so, out there."

The next day an orderly came into the room just after mess-dinner had commenced. He whispered to the adjutant, who at once rose.

"Mr. President," he said to the major who was at the head of the table, "I must ask you to excuse me leaving

the table. The colonel wishes to see me immediately at
his quarters."

"What can be the matter now?" one of the officers
said. "It must be something of importance or the colonel would never have called Hallowes out in that way."

"Heard of some still away among the hills, I suppose.
That means a night's tramp for some of us. Too bad to
be put to this sort of work within a week of sailing on
foreign service," grumbled another.

Various guesses were made as to the nature of the
business, and several wagers were laid on the subject. In
ten minutes the adjutant returned. He was evidently
excited, and all listened with great interest as, instead of
resuming his seat, he remained standing.

"Gentlemen," he said, "I have great news for you.
A vessel has just come in from Plymouth with dispatches.
Napoleon has escaped from Elba. He has landed in
France, and been received with enthusiasm. The troops
have joined him, and he is already close to Paris, which
he is expected to enter without opposition. The King
of France has fled."

For a moment there was silence, then the major leaped
to his feet.

"Three cheers, gentlemen!" and all of those present
joined in a hearty cheer.

Then a sudden silence fell upon them. The first idea
that had struck each man was that the news meant their
again taking the field for another stirring campaign.
Then the dismal thought occurred to them that the regiment was under orders for America. It soon found expression in words.

"Why, major, they surely won't be sending us across
the Atlantic now this news has arrived. The Powers
will never permit all their work to be undone, and Napo-

leon to mount the throne of France again. Why, in a short time all Europe will be in a blaze, and how is England to take the field again? The greater portion of Wellington's army are scattered over the world—in America, India, and the Colonies. I don't believe there are half a dozen of the old fighting regiments available, and even their ranks are half-filled with raw recruits. Almost all the regiments at home are mere skeletons. Surely they will never be sending us away at such a moment?"

"That I can say nothing about," the adjutant replied. "Certainly no counter orders have reached the colonel this evening. I don't suppose anything will be decided upon for some time. The Powers will all exchange notes and hold councils and spend weeks in talk before they make up their mind whether anything is to be done, and if so what; and long before they come to any decision on the subject we shall be on the other side of the Atlantic, and then, possibly, after all the trials and monotony of perhaps a two months' voyage, we may land there only to be fetched back again. I quite agree with you that England can put nothing worth calling an army in the field, and that it would be madness to send a fine regiment out of the country at the present moment. But everyone knows the lack of wisdom with which we are governed, and the miserable slowness of our military authorities. It is not likely even to occur to any one to countermand our orders, but it will certainly be disgusting in the extreme to have to start just at the present moment."

"Beside," another officer said, "it will be maddening to be two months at sea without news, and to know that perhaps all Europe is in arms and tremendous events going on and we out of it altogether."

"I should think nothing will be done just at present," the major said. "Every country in Europe has been disbanding its armies just as we have since peace was proclaimed, and it will be a long time before any of them are ready to take the field in anything like force. Even Napoleon himself, great organizer as he is, will take some time to put all France under arms again. An army is a machine that cannot be created in a day. The soldiers have to clothed, arms to be manufactured, the cavalry to be mounted, the artillery to be organized, and a field train got together. No, I should say that at least four months must elapse before fighting begins in earnest. With anything like a favorable wind we should be across in America in a month. If orders are sent out a month after we start we may be back in time for the opening ball. Judging from the past, it is likely to be a long business unseating Napoleon again, and if we are not in for the first of it we may be in plenty of time for a fair share of the fighting, always supposing that the authorities are sufficiently awake to the merits of the regiment to recall us."

"How is the wind this evening?" one of the officers asked.

"It was westerly when we came in," Lieutenant Desmond said. "Why do you ask?"

"Why, as long as it blows from the west there is not much chance of the transports getting in here."

"That is so," the major agreed. "The question for us to consider is whether we ought to pray for a fair wind or a foul. A fair wind will take us quickly across the Atlantic and will give us a chance of getting back in time. A foul wind may possibly give them time to make up their minds at the Horse Guards, and to stop us before we start. It is a nice question."

"There is no hope whatever, major, that our government will make up their minds before the wind changes; not if it blew in one quarter longer than it has ever been known to do since the beginning of the world. Especially, as not only they, but all the governments of Europe have to come to a decision."

"Oh, if we had to wait for that it would be hopeless; but at the same time, as it must be evident to any individual of the meanest capacity that something or other for which troops will be required will have to be done, surely a month ought to be sufficient for the idea to occur to some one in authority that it would be as well not to be sending soldiers abroad until matters are finally settled."

"I agree with you," the adjutant said. "Therefore I think we had best decide that our hopes and wishes shall be unanimous in favor of a continuance of westerly winds."

Never were the weathercocks watched more anxiously than they were by the officers and men of the Twenty-eighth for the next fortnight. The elements certainly appeared favorable to their wishes, and the wind blew steadily from the desired quarter, so that it was not until ten days after they were expected that the two transports which were to convey the Twenty-eighth to America dropped anchor in Cork harbor.

Captain O'Connor rejoined the regiment on the evening before the transports arrived. He walked with two sticks, but this was a measure of precaution rather than of necessity.

"I feel like an impostor," he said, laughing, as he replied to the welcome of his comrades. "I believe I could safely throw away these sticks and dance a jig; but the doctor has laid his commands on me, and my man, who has been ruling me with a rod of iron, will not permit the slightest infringement of them. He seems to consider that he is responsible for me in all respects, and if he had been master and I man he could not have behaved with grosser despotism."

"I am glad to see you looking so well, O'Connor," Ralph said, shaking his captain warmly by the hand.

"I don't know whether I do right in shaking hands with you, Conway," O'Connor said. "I have been thinking it over while I have been lying there, and I have come to the conclusion that it's you I have to thank for this affair altogether."

There was a general laugh. "How do you make that out?" Ralph asked.

"It's clear enough, now my eyes are opened. It was you who discovered that passage, and when you did so you said at once to yourself, now, I will get O'Connor and Desmond to go down this place, they are safe to break their necks, and then I shall get all the honor and glory of the affair. And so it came about. There were Desmond and I lying on the top of each other with the breath knocked clean out of our bodies, while you were doing all the fighting and getting the credit of the affair. I appeal to all friends here if it is not a most suspicious affair."

There was a chorus of agreement. "We did not think it of you, Conway;" "A most disgraceful trick;" "Ought to be sent to Coventry;" "Ought to be drummed out of the regiment;" mingled with shouts of laughter.

"By the way, the trial of those fellows comes on next week," one of the officers said when the laughter subsided; "so if the transports don't come in you will be able to see the last of them, O'Connor."

"I shall have no objection to see that red rascal hung;

but as to the other poor devils, I should be glad enough
for them to get off. An Irish peasant sees no harm in
making whisky, and it's only human nature to resist
when you are attacked; beside it was the Red Captain's
gang that set them to fighting, no doubt. If it hadn't
been for them I don't suppose there would have been a
shot fired. I hope that's the view the authorities will
take of it."

As it turned out this was the view taken by the prose-
cuting counsel at the trial. The Red Captain was tried
for the murder of his officer and for the shooting of two
constables in Galway, was found guilty, and hung. The
others were put on trial together for armed resistance
to his majesty's forces, and for killing and slaying three
soldiers. Their counsel pleaded that they were acting
under the compulsion of the gang of desperadoes with
them, that it was these and these only who had fired
upon the soldiers as they ascended the rocks, and that
the peasants themselves had no firearms; indeed, it was
proved that only five guns were found in the cave. He
admitted that in their desperation at the last moment the
men had defended themselves with pikes and bludgeons;
but this he urged was but an effort of despair, and not
with any premeditated idea of resisting the troops. He
pointed out that as all the soldiers had fallen by gunshot
wounds, none of the prisoners at the bar had any hand in
their death. The counsel for the crown did not press for
capital sentences. Two of the men, who had before
suffered terms of imprisonment for being concerned in
running illicit stills, were sentenced to transportation.
The others escaped with terms of imprisonment.

CHAPTER XIV.

THE NEW HOUSEMAID.

"WHAT do you think of the new housemaid, Charlotte?"

"As she has only been here twenty-four hours," Miss Penfold replied, "I don't think I can say anything about it, Eleanor. All servants behave decently for the first week or two, then their faults begin to come out. However, she seems quiet in her way of going about, and that is something. My room was carefully dusted this morning. These are the only two points on which I can at present say anything."

"I met her in the passage this morning," Eleanor Penfold said, "and it seemed to me that her face reminded me of some one. Did that strike you?"

"Not at all," the elder sister replied decidedly. "I am not given to fancies about such things. I saw no likeness to any one, and if I had done so I should not gave given it a second thought. The one point with us is whether the woman is clean, quiet, steady, and thoroughly up to her work. Her reference said she was all these things, and I hope she will prove so. She is older than I like servants to be, that is, when they first come to us. A young girl is teachable, but when a servant has once got into certain ways there is never any altering them. However, if she knows her work it does not matter; and there's one comfort, at her age she is less likely to be coming to us one day or other soon and saying that she wants to leave us to get married."

The new servant, Anna, as she was called in the house soon settled down to her duty. Miss Penfold allowed that she knew her work and did it carefully. The servants did not quite understand the newcomer. She was pleasant and friendly, but somehow "she was not," as one of them said, "of their sort." This they put down partly to the fact that she had been in service in London, and was not accustomed to country ways. However, she was evidently obliging and quiet, and smoothed away any slight feeling of hostility with which the under housemaid was at first disposed to feel against her for coming in as a stranger over her head, by saying that as she had no acquaintances in the village she had no desire to go out, and that whenever her turn came to do so the other might take her place. As Jane was keeping company with the blacksmith's son, this concession greatly pleased her; and although at first she had been disappointed that she had not on Martha's leaving succeeded to her place, the fact that she was but twenty-one, while the newcomer was a good many years her senior, went far to reconcile her to being passed over.

Mrs. Conway had not been twenty-four hours in the house before she discovered there was an obstacle in the way of her search that she had not foreseen. She had dusted the drawing-room and dining-room, and then went to the door of the room which she supposed to be the library. She found it locked. At dinner she asked the other housemaid what the room opposite the dining-room was, and where was the key.

"That was master's library," the girl said. "Miss Penfold always keeps it locked, and no one is allowed to go in. It's just as he left it; at least Martha said so, for I have never been inside since. On the first day of each month it is opened and dusted. Miss Penfold always

used to go in with Martha and stay there while she did
the work. She said it was to see that nothing was
moved, but Martha used to think there was another
reason."

"What is that?" Mrs. Conway asked.

Jane shook her head and glanced at the butler, as
much as to say she did not care about speaking before
him; but presently when she had an opportunity of talking alone with the newcomer she said: "I didn't want
to say anything before James, he holds with the Miss
Penfolds. He only came a month or two before master's
death and did not know much about him, and he will
have it they have been ill treated, and that the lawyer
and all of them ought to be punished for going on as if
the Miss Penfolds had done something wrong about the
will. Cook, she doesn't give no opinion; but Martha
and me both thought they knew something about it, and
were keeping Miss Withers and young Conway out of
their rights. But I forgot that you were a stranger, and
didn't know nothing about the will."

Then she told Mrs. Conway all about the will being
missing, and how Mr. Tallboys, who had made it for Mr.
Penfold, said that all the property had been left to Mabel
Withers, who was the daughter of the clergyman and a
great pet of the master's, and to a boy who had been
staying there some months before, and whose name was
Conway.

"Well, Martha and me believed that they," and she
nodded toward the drawing-room, "must know something about it; for Mr. Tallboys would have it that it
was stowed away in some secret hiding place, and has
been looking for it here and pulling down the wainscotting and all sorts. And, of course, if there was a secret
hiding-place the Miss Penfolds would know of it as well

as their brother. Martha used to think that the reason why the Miss Penfolds had the room shut up, and would never let her go into it without one of them being there to look after her, was that the hiding-place was somewhere in the library, and that they were afraid that when she was dusting and doing up she might come upon the will.''

The same conclusion had flashed across Mrs. Conway's mind as soon as she heard that the room was kept locked.

"If the will is really hidden away,'' she said, "it's likely enough to be as you say; but I shouldn't think two ladies would do such a thing as that.''

"Oh, you don't know them,'' Jane said sharply. "They are two regular old cats they are, and hunt one about all over the house as if they thought one was going to steal something. They was fond of their brother in their way, but, bless you, they treated him like a child, and he das'ent call his soul his own; and you may be sure they didn't like the thought that he had left his money away from them, and that some one else would become master and missis of the Hall while they were living. Martha and me was both of one mind that the old women were likely enough to do it if they had a chance. I would give a good deal if I could find the will myself just to see their faces; interfering old things. It was only two Sundays ago they told me after I came out of church that they didn't approve of the ribbons in my bonnet; just as if a girl was to go about as if she was a convict.''

"But you say there were men searching here, Jane. How was it they didn't find it if it's in the library, and how was it the Miss Penfolds allowed them to search?''

"They couldn't help it,'' Jane replied. "There was an order from the court in London, or a judge or some

one, and they couldn't stop it. They went away when
the men came and didn't come back till it was all over.
I don't know how it was that they didn't find it in the
library, for they searched it regular. I was in there two
or three times while they were at work, and they took
out all the books from the shelves and pulled down a lot
of the wood-work and turned it all upside down, but
they couldn't find anything. Still, you see, it ain't a
likely tale of theirs as they keeps the door locked because
they want it to be just as he left it, when it's all been
turned topsy-turvy and everything put out of its place.

"That's what Martha and me couldn't get over, though
Martha told me they done their best to have it put just
as it was; and there's paper and pens on the table, just
to pretend it is exactly as it used to be and that no one
hadn't been in. As if they cared so much about him. I
call it sickening, that's what I calls it. The Withers
don't come here now. They used to be often here in
the master's time, but they are not friends with them
now. Last Sunday the parson he made it hot for them,
and preached a sermon about secrets being known and
undiscovered things coming to light. Of course he didn't
say nothing special about wills, but they felt it, I could
see. Our pew's on the opposite side of the church, and
I could see their faces. Miss Penfold she got white, and
pinched up her lips, and if she could have given a piece
of her mind to the parson she would have done so; and
Eleanor she got red and looked as if she was going to
cry.

"She is a lot better than her sister, she is; and if any
wrong's been done it's the old one that's done it, I am
sure, and Martha always said so too. I could put up
with the younger one very well, but I can't abide Miss
Penfold."

"I am quite anxious to see the room, Jane, after what you have been telling me about it."

"Well, you will see it in about a week. It's always on the first of the month that it is done up; and you will see the old woman will go in with you, and watch you all the time like a cat watches a mouse. Martha used to say so. But there—as you are not from this part of the country, and she won't think as you know nothing about the will or care nothing about it, she won't keep such a sharp lookout after you as she did with Martha."

Upon the following Sunday Mrs. Withers, on the way home from church, asked her husband with some anxiety whether he was not well. "I noticed you were quite pale in church, James, and you lost your place once or twice, and seemed as if you really weren't attending to what you were doing?"

"Then I am afraid, my dear, I seemed what I was, for I was tremendously surprised; and though I tried hard to keep my thoughts from wandering I am afraid I succeeded very badly."

"Surprised, James! What was it?"

"I will tell you, my dear. You know that letter we had a fortnight ago from Mrs. Conway, and that we puzzled over it a good deal. After talking as usual about her being determined to find the will and set matters straight, she said that we might possibly see her before long, and begged us not to show any surprise or to seem to recognize her. Well, you know, we talked it over, and could make nothing of it. Now I know what she means."

"What! Did you see her in church to-day, James?"

"I did, Amy; and where do you think she was?"

"I can't guess, James. Why, where could she be, and where can she be staying if not with us? I didn't see her. Are you sure you are not mistaken?"

"She was sitting behind you, Amy, which will account for your not seeing her. She was sitting in the Penfolds servants' pew, in a plain straw bonnet and quiet clothes like the others."

"Among the Penfolds' servants, James! Are you dreaming?"

"Not at all, my dear; there she was, sure enough. I could not possibly be mistaken."

Mrs. Withers was silent for some time with surprise.

"But what can she be doing there, James? Do you mean to say that you think that she has really gone to service at the Hall?"

"That is what I do think," the clergyman replied. "You know how she said over and over again that she was determined somehow to find the will. Well, I believe that she has in some way in pursuance of that purpose gone as a servant to the Penfolds. Now, my dear, you will not be surprised that I found it somewhat difficult to keep my thoughts from wandering."

"No, indeed, James. I am sure if I had been in your place I should have stopped altogether. Well, if that is so, it explains what she said in her letter about our not recognizing her; but how could she do such a thing, and what will come of it?"

"I have no idea how she managed to get there, Amy; but certainly she must have managed very cleverly somehow. What she is there to do is clear enough. She is going to search herself for the will. Whether she will ever find it or not is another matter; but I can hardly believe she can succeed after the thorough search Tallboys said he made of the house. Still that is what she means, I have not a shadow of doubt about it."

"I should never have thought for a moment she was the sort of woman to undertake such a thing," Mrs.

Withers said. "Why, she will have to do servant's work, and to run all sorts of risks of being found out, and then I don't know what they mightn't do to her!"

"I don't see that they could do much, my dear, unless perhaps they prosecuted her for obtaining the place with a false character, which I suppose she must have done. Still it required no ordinary pluck for a woman to undertake such a scheme, and it will require patience and nerve to carry it through; but I don't know that I agree with you that she is not the sort of woman I should have thought capable of undertaking such a business. She was quiet enough when we met her in the town; but I believe from what I have heard that she was a high-spirited girl, and when we saw her, you know, she was on the eve of parting with her son. As she was evidently wrapped up in him, that would of course make her more quiet and silent than usual. I thought she bore up remarkably well, and admired the effort she made to prevent any display of her feeling marring the pleasant time we were having in London."

"But how about Mabel, James? Had we better tell her about this? You see, if she happens to meet Mrs. Conway she might betray her secret—might run up and address her by her name."

"That is certainly a difficulty, my dear; and I don't quite know what to do about it. What do you think yourself?"

"I think we had better postpone the matter, James, by sending Mabel away for a bit. You know my sister has asked her several times to go and stay with her on a visit at Bath. We have never cared to let her go away from us; but I do think now that it will be a good thing for me to write to Harriet, and tell her that if it will be convenient for her to take Mabel, we shall be glad to send her to her for a few months in order that she may take lessons in French and music. There are, of course, plenty of good masters there. In that way we shall get rid of the necessity for speaking to Mabel about it at all, and I should think it likely that Mrs. Conway would have left the Hall long before she returns."

"Perhaps she will, my dear, though I would not count upon that too much. I imagine that as Mrs. Conway has had nerve and courage enough to propose and so far carry out this singular plan of hers, she will have resolution enough to continue to play her part till she either finds the will, or becomes thoroughly convinced that it is absolutely not to be found."

And so Mrs. Withers wrote to her sister, and ten days later Mr. Withers started with Mabel for Bath.

Mrs. Conway had some difficulty in restraining all show of excitement, and in assuming a passive and indifferent air as upon the first of the month Miss Penfold unlocked the door of the library and led the way into the room.

"This was my brother's library. You will understand, Anna, that I wish everything to remain exactly as it is. You will therefore be careful to place everything as you find it—each article of furniture, and the books and papers on the table. You will just sweep the floor and dust everything. Beyond that we wish nothing done to the room."

Mrs. Conway began her work quietly. Miss Penfold watched her for some little time, and then said:

"You will leave the door open, Anna; it is better to let the air circulate as much as possible. When the weather gets warmer you will also leave the windows open while you are at work; but the air is too damp at present."

"Would you like me to light a fire to air the room, Miss Penfold?"

"Certainly not," Miss Penfold said decidedly, "there is no occasion whatever for it. If I have not returned by the time you have finished the room, come and tell me when you have done. I always make a point of locking the door myself."

So saying Miss Penfold went out, leaving the door wide open behind her.

"Have you left her alone there?" Eleanor asked her sister as she entered the sitting-room.

"Certainly I have," Miss Penfold said coldly. "I do wish you would not be so nervous, Eleanor. The woman can have no interest in this matter. She may have heard of it from the other servants, but it can be nothing to her. You know as well as I do that there is no chance of her stumbling upon it by accident. It was different with the last girl. Of course they were always talking about the will, and she might have tried, as a matter of curiosity, to find it, or she might have been bribed by those Withers or by that man Tallboys; but it is different now. This woman can have no interest in it, and will only want to get her work done as soon as possible. My being always in the room with her as I was with Martha might excite comment. I should never have done it in Martha's case if you had not been so absurdly nervous; for you know very well there was no real danger of her ever finding the place however closely she looked for it. But now there's a change it is quite time to drop it, or a rumor will be getting about that we are afraid of any of our servants remaining for a moment alone in the library."

"I wish we had never done it. I do wish we had never done it," Eleanor murmured pitifully.

"I am ashamed of you, Eleanor," Miss Penfold said coldly. "You are worse than a child with your laments and complainings. What have we done? Nothing. We have no certainty that there is a will in existence; and if we had, it's not our business to assist to carry out a monstrous wrong against ourselves, and to put that woman's son as master here. How many times have we talked this over, and it's always the same. You keep on trembling at shadows."

"I should not care if it was not for the night, Charlotte. I am always dreaming that Herbert is coming to my bedside and looking so stern and angry, and saying, 'Let justice be done.'"

"Bah!" Miss Penfold said contemptuously. "You must eat less supper, Eleanor. If you were not such a coward you would not dream such things. I have no patience with your folly."

"I know it is foolish, Charlotte, but I can't help it; my nerves were never as strong as yours. I quite agreed with you from the first about it. I think it was infamous that Herbert should have passed us over, and that it is not to be expected we should aid in the discovery of such a wicked will. Still I can't help being unhappy about it, and lying awake at night and dreaming. No one can help their dreams."

"Your dreams are a mere repetition of your thoughts," Miss Penfold said scornfully. "If you worry while you are awake, you will worry while you are asleep. We have done nothing criminal. We have meddled with no will, nor hidden one. We simply refuse to aid in the discovery of an unjust document, and by so doing prevent a great wrong being done to ourselves. To my mind the thing is perfectly simple, and my conscience wholly acquits me of any wrong-doing."

Left to herself, Mrs. Conway took an earnest look round the room. Somewhere no doubt within its limits lay the key of the secret that would give wealth to Ralph. Where was it? The walls were completely covered by bookshelves. These were handsomely carved, and dark with age. One of the Penfolds had evidently been a bookworm, and had spared no pains and expense in carrying out his hobby. The housemaid had said that all the books had been removed, and that nothing had been found behind them. Still there might well be some spring that had escaped their notice. At any rate the ground must be gone over again.

Then the spring might lie among the carved work of the bookcases themselves. This must be gone over inch by inch. That was evidently the first work to be done. The mantel and its supports were of richly carved woodwork. These, too, must be searched. In the first place, however, she had to carry out her work; and laying aside determinately all thought of the missing will, she began to dust and sweep. At the end of an hour, when she happened to turn round, she saw Miss Penfold standing in the doorway. She had not heard her footstep, and at once decided in her mind that it would be necessary to be extremely careful in her search, as at any moment Miss Penfold might look in upon her without warning.

"Have you nearly finished, Anna?" Miss Penfold asked.

"It will take me another hour at least to dust the woodwork properly, Miss Penfold. I have done the carpet and furniture."

Miss Penfold made no remark but went away again.

"She is not likely to come back for a few minutes," Mrs. Conway said to herself. "I think I can safely carry out one of my plans."

She took from her pocket a ball of thin string, one end of which was attached to a tiny brad awl. Going into one corner of the room she fixed the brad awl into the woodwork; then, unwinding the ball, proceeded to the other end of the room, straining the string tightly, and tied a knot to mark the length. Then she went back and crossed the room, and again make a knot to mark the width. Then she hastily gathered up the string, pulled the brad awl from the woodwork, and put them in her pocket. While she had been carrying this out she retained a duster in one hand, and dusted the wood work as she moved along, trusting that if Miss Penfold should look in, the string, which was of a dark color, would be unnoticed by her. However she gave a sigh of relief when the operation was complete, and the string and brad awl hidden away. She then continued her work until in about three-quarters of an hour Miss Penfold again appeared.

"I think that will do very well, Anna; it is quite impossible to get all the dust out of the carving. It would take you all day to go over it, and you would need steps for the upper part. That need only be done occasionally." She gave an approving glance round as she noticed that the new housemaid had carefully placed every article in the exact place in which she had found it. Mrs. Conway gathered up the brooms and dusters and left the room, Miss Penfold carefully locking the door after her.

"That is something done," Mrs. Conway said to herself; "and will, I think, save me an immense deal of trouble. To-morrow I will measure the rooms next to it. The passage runs along the side and it is hardly possible that there can be any receptacle there; the wall is not thick enough for a place of any size. It must be at one end or the other, or else under the floor."

The following morning she measured the dining-room, and what was now known as the housekepeer's room, but which in years gone by had been called the still room; and the following day slipped out of doors as soon as she came downstairs and took the outside measurement of the side of the house, marking on the string the position and width of each window. She had only now to make a plan and compare the figures. She found that between the back of the bookcase—for she had taken out a few books to ascertain its depth—and the panel of the dining-room there was a thickness of two feet; but between the library and the housekeeper's room there were fully five feet unaccounted for.

In both were deep old-fashioned fireplaces back to back; and even allowing but six inches between these, the depth there would be accounted for, but on either side of the fireplaces there would be a wide space. There were certainly no cupboards visible in the library, for the bookcases extended from the fireplace to the wall on each side. In the housekeeper's room there were cupboards on each side of the chimney-piece, but these were shallow, not being above nine inches in depth; therefore behind these there was a considerable space unaccounted for. It was evident to Mrs. Conway that her first search must lie in this direction. Here might lie two chambers each three feet wide by eight feet long.

Mrs. Conway's spirits rose at this discovery, and she sighed impatiently at the thought that another month must elapse before she could even commence the search. Brooding over the matter continually, there was one point that did not escape her. These old hiding-places were made either to conceal proscribed priests or hunted fugitives, and were constructed with the greatest care. As she had so easily discovered the spot where a hidden room might be situated, it would be discovered with the same ease by those who were on the search for fugitives, and who would naturally be well acquainted with the positions where hiding-places would be likely to be situated. The moment they looked into the cupboard, its shallowness would suggest to them that there must be a wide empty space behind it, and by setting to work with axes, picks, and crowbars, they would soon discover by force the secret she was trying to penetrate by stratgem.

This reflection considerably damped her hopes; but she thought that possibly from this easily-discoverable hiding-place there might be some access, much more difficult to trace, to another lying below. At any rate she determined that if she did find the secret entrance to these little rooms, and found that they were empty she would not be disheartened, but would search further until she found either some secret closet where the will might be placed, or an entrance to some perhaps larger hiding-place below. Her subsequent search outside showed her that there existed several small iron gratings about six inches long and three deep, close down to the soil of the border. No doubt these were intended to give ventilation underneath the floors, which were some two feet above the outside level, but one of them might also afford ventilation to an underground chamber.

Three months passed, and on the occasion of each of her visits to the room she devoted some time to the examination of the carved woodwork round the fireplace and that of the bookcases, but without making any discovery whatever; and it became evident to her that a far closer search would be needed than the short and hasty examination that was all she dared to make, with the possibility that at any moment Miss Penfold might appear at the door. Accordingly she wrote to Mr. Tallboys, and told

him that it would be necessary for her to obtain a cake
of very soft wax, four inches long and two inches wide,
and asked him to procure it for her, and to send it in a
wooden box to her by the carrier's cart that once a week
journeyed from Weymouth to the villages in the neighborhood of the Hall.

Ten days later she received the wax, and the next time
the day for cleaning the library arrived she quietly with-
drew the key from the door as soon as Miss Penfold had
left her, laid it on the wax, and pressed it steadily until
a deep impression was made upon its surface. Then she
carefully examined the key to see that no particle of wax
had stuck between the wards, replaced it in the door,
closed the lid of the little box in which the wax lay, and
put it in her pocket, and then set to at her work of
cleaning.

Upon this occasion she spent no time in trying to find
the spring. There was danger now as always of Miss
Penfold's coming, and as she would soon have the means
of entering the room at her will she would run no risk.
A few days later she asked for a day to go to Weymouth
to purchase some things of which she had need, and
when there she called upon Mr. Tallboys.

"How are you, Mrs. Conway?" the lawyer said when
the door had closed behind her. "Have you come to
tell me that you give up the search as hopeless?"

"Not at all," she replied with decision. "I told you
in my letter that I had discovered the probable position
of the hiding-place, and told you of the difficulties there
were in making a thorough search for it owing to the
room being always kept locked. I have come now to
ask you to get a key made from this," and she produced
the wax. "It would be suspicious if I were to go to a
locksmith here and ask for such a thing; he would think

at once that I was a servant who wanted to rob my mistress. But of course it will be different with you. Beside, I thought that if you did not like to get it done here, you might send the wax up to London and get the key made there."

"This is becoming more and more serious, Mrs. Conway," Mr. Tallboys said gravely. "Nothing very terrible could happen to you beyond being turned out of the house even were it discovered who you really are; but if you were found at night, and I suppose your intention is to work at night, in the library, with a false key in your possession, you might be arrested for an attempt at theft, and could only clear yourself by explaining before the magistrates who you were, and with what motive you were acting, which would give rise to much unpleasant talk, would render any pursuance of your plan impossible, and might not improbably induce these women to destroy the will, if they have not already done so."

"I am quite convinced they have not done that, Mr. Tallboys. The anxiety they have about any one entering the room, and the manner in which Miss Penfold pops in occasionally to see what I am doing, is quite proof in my mind that the will is still in existence; for if they had destroyed it, they would have no further anxiety on the subject. No, I have thought it all over, and must run the risk. There is no other way of making a complete search; and in one night there by myself I could do far more than in a twelvemonths' visits as at present. There are two or three more things I wish you would procure for me. I want a man's coat and cap, rough ones, such as a burglar might wear. You see, if by any chance I am met by those women going downstairs, or returning to my room, I must give them a start. Dressed up like that, and with a piece of crape over my face, I should be taken for a burglar. I don't think Miss Penfold is very easily frightened; but at the same time I fancy I might alarm her into returning to her room, and should be able to get back to mine before the house was roused. I shall always unfasten a window on the ground floor and lift it a little, so that it would be supposed that the intruder entered and escaped that way."

Mr. Tallboys smiled a little, but said, "It is a very risky business, Mrs. Conway. Miss Penfold is just the sort of woman to keep pistols in her bedroom."

"One must risk something when one is fighting for a fortune," Mrs. Conway said quietly. "I hope that I shall not be heard. There are always creakings and noises in an old house like that. The doors are thick and well fitting, and there is little chance of my footsteps being heard. It is only by an accident, such as one of them being unable to sleep and getting up and walking over the house, that they are likely to run against me, and it is not probable she would have a pistol in her hand then. No, I do not think there is the least fear of anything of that sort. The only fear I have is of being detected in some other way before I have done what I have to do, and the risk of that grows less and less every day.

"I have been there over four months now, and am perfectly at home. I was at first afraid of a sudden meeting with Mr. Withers, or his wife, or Mabel; but that has passed away now. I saw he recognized me the first Sunday in church, and I wrote to him; of course sending the letter to Dover to be sent back from there. He answered me praying me to give up what he called my mad-brained attempt, and saying it made him and his wife quite unhappy to think of my being at the Hall. He told me that at present they had not told Mabel that

I was there, but had sent her away to school at Bath. She is with an aunt, and will not be home again for some months; so I am safe from her. No, I am not in the least anxious about myself. I cannot say as much about Ralph. His regiment has just gone out to Belgium, and I suppose there will be fighting presently. I think of that more now than I do of this will, Mr. Tallboys. If I had known what was coming, I would not have begun this search until it was all over. What use would it be for me to find the will if anything happened to him."

"It is clearly of no use my trying to dissuade you from carrying out your plans, Mrs. Conway; and although I cannot altogether approve of them, I will do my best to help you as far as lies in my power, and you shall have the key down very shortly. How shall I send it over?"

"I have ordered a dress and some other things at Wilson's in the High Street. The dress has to be made up, and will not be ready for a week. I have told them there will be three or four other parcels, which they are to put in the box and send it on by the carrier. I have ordered a pair of boots to be made for me and one or two other things, and told them not to close the box until this day fortnight, by which time all the other things I have ordered will be sent in to them. I hope you will have got the key before that."

"Oh, yes, I should think it would be done in a week at latest. You certainly deserve success, Mrs. Conway, for you seem to provide for every contingency."

CHAPTER XV.

IN BELGIUM.

THERE was a general feeling of depression in the regiment when it was known that the transports had arrived in harbor. As a rule regiments embarking for service abroad start in high spirits, and whatever private regrets are felt at parting from friends, the troops march gayly down to the point of embarkation. But this was not the case as the Twenty-eighth with the band at its head playing "The girl I left behind me," passed through the streets of Cork on its march down to the spot ten miles away where the transports were lying. There was not one from the colonel down to the youngest drummer-boy but felt that he had been deprived of the chance of taking part in a stirring campaign, and that he was going into a sort of exile. The baggage had been sent on the previous day, and the regiment on arriving at the harbor was speedily transferred in large lighters to the two transports.

"They are two fine ships, anyhow," Captain O'Connor said to Ralph as the barge carrying his company approached the side of one of them. "Rather different craft to that in which we made our last voyage together. We shall have comfortable quarters on board her, and ought to make a pleasant passage if we have but decent weather."

"Yes, if anything could make our voyage pleasant under the circumstances," Ralph replied dismally.

"Oh, it's no use thinking any more about that," O'Connor said cheerfully. "We must make the best of matters, and hope that we shall soon be on our way back again; if not, I dare say we shall have a pleasant time in Canada. With your knowledge of French, Conway, you will make a great hit among the fair Canadians."

"I didn't think of that," Ralph laughed. "Yes, the prospect is a cheering one. I promise you, O'Connor, that I will do the best I can for you. Well, here we are alongside."

"Good afternoon, captain. When are we going to sail?" O'Connor asked the master of the vessel as he stepped on deck.

"You must ask the clerk of the weather," the skipper replied. "At present there is not a breath of wind stirring, and from the look of the sky I see no chance of a change at present."

Day after day passed, and still the vessels remained at anchor. Not a breath of wind stirred the water, and the troops had nothing to do but to lounge idly about the decks and whistle for a breeze. Whenever a vessel came in from England boats were lowered and rowed alongside to get the latest news. This was little enough. It was, however, known that all the powers had determined to refuse to recognize Napoleon as Emperor of France, and that a great coalition against him was being arranged. There were rumors that Belgium was likely to be the scene of operations.

Already, by the terms of the late treaty, several English regiments were stationed on the Belgian frontier, and three or four more were already under orders to embark for that country. It was reported that Russia, Austria, and Prussia were taking steps to arm. The militia had been called out at home, and high bounties

were offered for volunteers from these regiments into
the line. Recruiting was going on vigorously all over
the country. Horses were being bought up, and efforts
made to place the attenuated regiments on a war footing.
All this was tantalizing news to the Twenty-eighth. The
colonel was known to have written to influential friends
in London, begging them to urge upon the authorities
the folly of allowing a fine regiment like his to leave the
country at such a moment. But little was hoped from
this, for at any moment a change in the weather might
place them beyond the possibility of a recall.

Three weeks passed and then the barometer fell, and
there were signs of a change. There was bustle and
movement on board the ships, and even the soldiers were
glad that the monotony of their imprisonment on board
was about to come to an end, and their voyage to commence. The sails were loosed from their gaskets, and
the sounds of the drum and fifes struck up as the cap-
stans were manned, the soldiers lending a hand at the
bars, and the chains came clanking in at the hawse-holes.

"There is a vessel coming in round the point," O'Connor said. "But we shall hardly get the last news; we
shall be under way before she anchors "

"She is signaling to the fort on the hill," Ralph said,
as he watched the flags run up on the signal-staff on the
summit of Spike Island; "and they are answering down
below there at the station in front of the commandant's
house."

A moment later a gun was fired.

"That's to call our attention, I think," the skipper
said, taking up his glass and directing it to the shore.
"Yes, there is our number flying. Get the signal-book,
boy. Mr. Smith, run up the answering pennant."

As soon as this ascended the flags on shore were lowered, and a fresh set run up—3. 5. 0. 4.

"Give me the book. 'The vessels are not to sail until further orders,' " he read aloud.

"Hooray, lads!" Captain O'Connor shouted at the top of his voice. "We are stopped until further orders."

A loud cheer broke from the troops, which was echoed by a roar from the other vessel; and for a few minutes the greatest excitement reigned. The men threw their caps into the air, and shouted until they were hoarse. The officers shook each other by the hand, and all were frantic with delight at the narrow escape they had had.

As soon as the brig had dropped anchor boats rowed off to her, but nothing further was learned. Just as she was leaving Plymouth an officer had come on board with dispatches, and instructions to the captain to signal immediately he arrived at Cork that if the Twenty-eighth had not already sailed they were to be stopped. Owing to the lightness of the wind the brig had been eight days on her passage from Plymouth.

For another fortnight the regiment remained on board ship. The imprisonment was borne more patiently, now they felt sure that they were not at any rate to be sent across the Atlantic. Then a vessel arrived with orders that the Twenty-eighth were at once to proceed to Ostend, and two hours afterward the transports set sail.

Belgium was hardly the spot which the troops in general would have approved of as the scene of operations, for the disastrous expedition to Walcheren was still fresh in mens' minds. They would, moreover, have preferred a campaign in which they would have fought without being compelled to act with a foreign army, and would have had all the honor and glory to themselves. Still Belgium recalled the triumphs of Marlborough, and although every mail brought news of the tremendous efforts Napoleon was making to reorganize the fighting power of

France, and of the manner in which the veterans of his former wars had responded to the call, there was not a doubt of success in the minds of the Twenty-eighth, from the colonel down to the youngest drummer-boy.

Ralph was sorry that he had not been able to pay a flying visit to his mother before his departure on active and dangerous service.

He had been somewhat puzzled by her letters ever since he had been away. They had been almost entirely devoted to his doings, and had said very little about herself beyond the fact that she was in excellent health. She had answered his questions as to his various friends and acquaintances in Dover; but these references had been short, and she had said nothing about the details of her daily life, the visits she paid, and the coming in of old friends to see her. She had evidently been staying a good deal, he thought, with the Withers, and she kept him fully informed about them, although she did not mention when she went there or when she had returned.

She frequently spoke about the missing will, and of her hopes it would some day be recovered; and had mentioned that the search for it was still being maintained, and that she felt confident that sooner or later it would come to light. But even as to this she gave him no specific details; and he felt that, even apart from his desire to see his mother, he should greatly enjoy a long talk with her, to find out about everything that had been going on during his absence.

Mrs. Conway had indeed abstained from giving her son the slightest inkling of the work upon which she was engaged; for she was sure he would be altogether opposed to her plan, and would be greatly disturbed and grieved at the thought of her being in any menial position. Whether if, when he returned, and she had not attained the object of her search she would let him know what she was doing she had not decided; but she was determined that at any rate until he came home on leave he should know nothing about it.

"So we are going to fight Bony at last, Mister Conway," Ralph's servant said to him. "We've never had that luck before. He has always sent his generals against us, but, by jabbers, he will find that he has not got Roosians and Proosians this time."

"It will be hot work, Denis; for we shall have the best troops of France against us, and Napoleon himself in command."

"It's little we care for the French, your honor. Didn't we meet them in Spain and bate them? Sure, they are are hardly worth counting."

"You will find them fight very much better now they have their emperor with them. You know, Wellington had all his work to beat them."

"Yes, but he did bate them, your honor."

"That's true enough, Denis; but his troops now are old soldiers, most of whom have been fighting for years, while a great part of our force will be no better than militia."

"They won't fight any the worse for that, your honor," Denis said confidently. "We will bate them whenever we meet them. You see if we don't."

"We will try anyhow, Denis; and if all the regiments were as good as our own I should feel very sure about it. I wish, though, we were going to fight by ourselves; we know what we can do, but we do not know how the Belgians and Dutch and Germans who will be with us can be depended upon."

"If I were the duke I wouldn't dipend on them at all, at all, your honor. I would just put them all in the rare, and lave our fellows to do the work. They are miserable, half-starved cratures all them foreigners, they tells me; and if a man is not fed, sure you can't expect him to fight. I couldn't do it myself. And I hope the duke ain't going to put us on short rations, because it would be murther entirely on the boys to make them fight with impty stomachs."

"I fancy we shall be all right as to that, Denis. I expect that we shall wait quiet till the French attack us, and waiting quiet means getting plenty of food."

"And dacent food, I hope, your honor; not the sort of thing they say them foreigners lives on. Denis Mulligan could live on frogs and snails as well as another, no doubt; but it would go sorely against me, your honor."

"I don't think there's much chance of your having to live on that Denis. You will get rations there just the same as you did in Spain."

"What! beef and mutton, your honor? I suppose they will bring them across from England?"

"They may bring some across, Denis; but I suppose they will be able to buy plenty for the supply of the army out there."

"What! have they got cattle and sheep there, your honor?" Denis asked incredulously.

"Of course they have, Denis; just the same as we have."

"The hathens!" Denis exclaimed. "To think that men who can get beef and mutton should feed upon such cratures as snails and such like. It's downright flying in the face of Providence, your honor."

"Nonsense, Denis; they eat beef and mutton just the same as we do. As to the frogs and snails, these are expensive luxuries, just as game is with us. There is nothing more nasty about snails after all than there is about oysters; and as to frogs they were regarded as great dainties by the Romans, who certainly knew what good eating was."

"Sure, I am a Roman myself, your honor—so are most of the men of the regiment—but I never heard tell of sich a thing."

"Not that sort of Roman, Denis," Ralph laughed. "The old Romans—people who lived long before there were any popes—a people who could fight as well as any that ever lived, and who were as fond of good living as they were of fighting."

"Well, your honor, there is no accounting for tastes. There was Bridget Maloney, whom I courted before I entered the regiment. Well, your honor, if you would believe it, she threw over a dacent boy like myself, and married a little omadoun of a man about five feet high, and with one shoulder higher than the other. That was why I took to soldiering, your honor. No, there is no accounting for tastes anyhow. There's the mess-bugle, your honor. Next time we hear it, it will be at say, and maybe there won't be many ready to attind to it."

Denis' prediction was verified. The vessel sailed at two o'clock in the afternoon, and by six was rolling heavily, and a brisk wind was blowing. The Twenty-eighth had not long before made the voyage from the south of France, but they had been favored by exceptionally fine weather, and had experienced nothing like the tossing they were now undergoing. The consequence was that only about half a dozen officers obeyed the bugle call to mess.

There was a general feeling of satisfaction when the low coast round Ostend was sighted, for the voyage throughout had been a rough one. Under certain circumstances a sea voyage is delightful, but confinement in a crowded transport in rough weather is the reverse of a pleasant experience. The space below decks was too small to accommodate the whole of the troops, and a third of their number had to be constantly on deck; and this for a ten days' voyage in a heavy sea, with occasional rain-showers, is not, under ordinary circumstances, calculated to raise the spirits of troops. But men bound on active and dangerous service are always in the highest spirits, and make light of disagreeables and hardships of all kinds.

They had expected to find Ostend full of troops, for several regiments had landed before them; but they soon found they were to be marched inland. As soon as the regiment had landed they marched to a spot where a standing camp had been erected for the use of troops on their passage through. Their baggage was at once sent forward, and the men had therefore nothing to do but to clean up their arms and accoutrements, and to wander as they pleased through the town. They started early next morning, and after two days' marching arrived at Ghent, where several regiments were quartered, either in the town itself or in the villages round it. Ralph's company had billets allotted to them in a village a mile from the town, a cottage being placed at the disposal of the captain and his two subalterns. The next morning, after the parade of the regiment was over, most of the officers and many of the men paid a visit to the town, where the fugitive King of France had now established his court.

Ralph, who years before had read the history of Ghent, was greatly interested in the quaint old town; though it was difficult to imagine from the appearance of its quiet streets that its inhabitants had once been the most turbulent in Europe. Here Von Artevelde was killed, and the streets often ran with the blood of contending factions.

Was it possible that the fathers of these quiet workmen in blouses, armed with axes and pikes, had defeated the chivalry of France, and all but annihilated the force of the Duke of Anjou? What a number of convents there were! The monks seemed a full third of the population, and it was curious to hear everyone talking in French when the French were the enemy they were going to meet. The populace were quite as interested in their English visitors as the latter were with them. The English scarlet was altogether strange to them, and the dress of the men of the Highland regiment, who were encamped next to the Twenty-eighth, filled them with astonishment.

For a fortnight the regiment remained at Ghent, then they with some others of the same division marched to Brussels, and took up their quarters in villages round the town. The Twenty-eighth belonged to Picton's division, which formed part of the reserve concentrated round Brussels. The first army corps, consisting of the second and third divisions of Dutch and Belgians, and the first and third of the British, extended from Enghien on the right to Quatre Bras on the left. The first British division were at the former town, the third between Soignies and Rœulx, while the Belgians and Dutch lay between Nivelles and Quatre Bras.

The second army corps held the ground on the right of the first, and extended to Oudenarde on the Scheldt. The cavalry, with the exception of the Brunswick brigade, were posted at Grammont, Mons, and Rœulx, their outposts being thrown forward as far as Maubeuge and Beaumont. The Prussians were on the left of Wellington's force, and extended from Ligny through Namur toward Liege, their advanced posts being at Charleroi, where Zieten's division had their headquarters. But although the allied armies thus formed together the arc

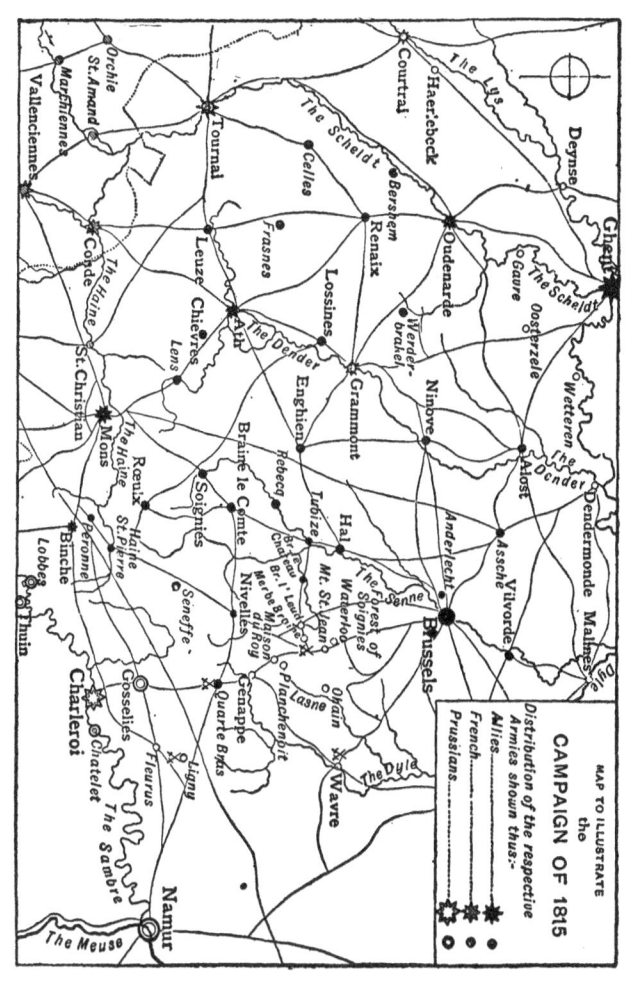

MAP TO ILLUSTRATE
the
CAMPAIGN OF 1815

Distribution of the respective
Armies shown thus:-
Allies ....
French ....
Prussians ....

of a large circle covering Brussels, they were entirely distinct. The British drew their supplies from Ostend, on the right of their position, while Liege on the extreme left was the base of the Prussians.

Napoleon's movements were uncertain. He might either advance upon Namur and cut off the Prussians from their base, or between Grammont and Oudenarde, by which measure he would similarly cut the British off from Ostend; or he might advance from Charleroi direct upon Brussels, breaking through at the point where Wellington's left joined the Prussian right. The Duke of Wellington believed that he would attempt the second of these alternatives, as in that case he would fall upon the British before the Prussians could come up to their assistance, and if successful would not only cut them off from the base of supplies, but would be able to march straight upon Brussels. It was to defeat this plan that the duke posted the largest proportion of his British troops along the frontier, holding, however, two British divisions and the Brunswick and Nassau troops in and round Brussels, where they were nearly equidistant from any point that could be attacked, and could be moved forward as soon as the enemy's intentions became manifest.

By the time that the whole of the forces were assembled Wellington had ninety thousand men under his orders; Blucher, the Prussian general, had one hundred and sixteen thousand; while Napoleon had one hundred and twenty-five thousand with which to encounter this vastly superior force. Upon the other hand, Napoleon's were all veteran troops, and the French had for a long time been accustomed to victory over the Prussians. Of Wellington's force fully a half were of mixed nationalities: Belgians, Dutch, Brunswickers, and Hessians;

while his British division consisted chiefly of young troops, so hastily raised that a great number of them absolutely fought at Waterloo in the uniforms of the militia regiments from which they had been drafted.

It seemed, however, a well-nigh desperate enterprise for Napoleon to attack so greatly superior a force. But he had, in fact, no choice but to do so; for Russia and Austria were arming, and their forces would soon be advancing upon France, and it was therefore necessary if possible to defeat the British and Prussians before they could arrive. Could he succeed in doing this the enthusiasm that would be excited in France would enable him vastly to increase his army. In the meantime his confidence in his own military genius was unbounded, and the history of his past wars contained many triumphs won under circumstances far less favorable than the present.

During the weeks that elapsed while the three great armies were assembling and taking up their positions, the troops stationed round Brussels had a pleasant time of it. The city itself was crowded with visitors. Here were a number of the wives and friends of the officers of the various armies. Here were many of the French nobility, who had abandoned France upon the landing of Napoleon. Here were numbers of people attracted by curiosity, or the desire of being present at the theater of great events, together with a crowd of simple pleasure-seekers; for Europe had for many years been closed to Englishmen, and as soon as peace had been proclaimed great numbers had crossed the Channel to visit Paris, and had traveled in Germany, Italy, and Switzerland.

The news of Napoleon's return to France had occasioned a great scare among the tourists. A very few days sufficed for the desertion of Paris and other French towns, and so great was the crowd that the packet-boats between Calais and Dover were insufficient to carry them. Many of the visitors to Paris instead of leaving for England made for Belgium, and were joined there by travelers hurrying back from Austria, Germany, and other parts of Europe; for none could say what course the events that would follow Napoleon's return from Elba might take. At Brussels, however, they felt safe; the distance to England was short, and they could, if necessary, leave at any time. Beside, between Belgium and France twelve thousand British troops had been stationed in the strong places, in accordance with the terms of the treaty of Fontainebleau and an agreement made with her allies after the fall of Napoleon.

The streets of Brussels were ablaze with bright colors. Staff-officers in the uniforms of a number of nationalities dashed through the streets, followed by their orderlies. Now and then two or three general officers, riding at a slower pace and engaged in earnest talk, passed along, while the pavements were occupied by crowds of men and officers in all the varieties of British, Dutch, Belgian, Brunswick, Hanoverian, Hessian, and Prussian uniforms. Although Belgium had cast in her lot with the allies the people were by no means unanimous in their sympathies; and, indeed, the majority, from their similarity both in religion and tongue to the French, sympathized with them rather than with the allies, who were for the most part both Protestant and foreigners.

Those who entertained these sentiments, however, kept them to themselves, while the rest fraternized to the best of their power with the troops, many of whom were quartered in the town. As for amusements, there were for the officers the theaters and an opera, while many of the ladies staying in Brussels kept almost open houses;

races and athletic sports were got up for the men. The weather at the latter end of May and during the early days of June was delightful; and although all knew that the storm might at any moment burst, it was difficult to believe while so enjoying themselves that to-morrow they might be called upon to meet the enemy in deadly conflict. Even Denis Mulligan had nothing to complain about in his rations, and allowed to Ralph that the Belgians were much more decent people than he had expected to find them.

The months of April and May had passed quietly on the frontier. The cavalry of the allied army on one side, and the French mounted gendarmerie on the other, maintained a vigilant watch over each others' movements, and each endeavored to prevent the passing out of persons who might carry news of the intentions and position of their armies. But the line was far too long to be strictly watched, and French loyalists on the one side and Belgian sympathizers with France on the other, managed to pass with sufficient regularity to keep the generals informed of the movements of their opponents.

Wellington, then, was perfectly aware of the gathering of Napoleon's forces upon the other side of the frontier; but they, like his own troops were scattered over a long front, and yet there was no indication whatever as to the point where Napoleon was likely to break through. During the past three months large bodies of men had labored to restore the ruined fortifications of the frontier towns. The moats had been cleared out and deepened, the walls repaired, and the sluices restored, so that in case of necessity a wide tract of country could be laid under water.

These precautions had been specially taken on the right of the British position where Wellington expected

Napoleon's attack, and the general calculated that with the aid of the obstacles so interposed to Napoleon's advance, the troops stationed there would be able to check the tide of invasion until the whole army arrived to their assistance. The country between Brussels and the frontier was reconnoitered, and engineer officers were employed in making sketches of all the positions that appeared likely to offer special advantages as battlefields for an army standing on the defense.

Among others the fields lying in front of the village of Waterloo were mapped, and the spot was specially marked by the duke as one to be occupied in case the enemy forced a way between the British and Prussian armies. On the 12th of June the Duke of Wellington learned that Napoleon and the guards had left Paris for the North, and the next day the officer in command of the cavalry outposts reported that the pickets of French cavalry which had so long faced him had disappeared, and that he had learned from some French custom-house officers that hostilities were about to commence.

On the 15th of June, Ralph Conway had gone with Stapleton into Brussels as usual. Everything was going on with its accustomed regularity. A military band was playing in the park. Numbers of well-appointed carriages, filled with well-dressed ladies, drove to and fro, and crowds of officers and civilians strolled under the trees, greeting their acquaintances and discussing the latest gossip of the town. As to the coming of the French, the topic was so threadbare that no one alluded to it; and no stranger could have imagined from the aspect of the scene that three great armies were lying thirty or forty miles away in readiness to engage at any moment in a desperate struggle. The great subject of talk was the ball that was to be given that evening by the Duchess of Richmond; this was expected altogether to outshine any of the other festivities that had taken place in Brussels during that gay season. It was about half-past four in the afternoon tnat the young men saw Captain O'Connor approaching.

"Can you young fellows keep a secret?" he asked.

"I think so," Ralph laughed.

"I suppose you are both going to the ball?"

"Of course we are. We are both off duty, and Stapleton here is quite absorbed in the thought of the conquests he intends to make."

"Well, the secret is this. It is quite probable you will not go to the ball at all."

"Why! How it that?" the young officers exclaimed simultaneously. "Is the regiment ordered away?"

"Not yet, lads; but it may be. I have just seen the colonel. He dined with the duke at three o'clock. There were a lot of officers there, and the Prince of Orange, who had just come in from the outposts for the ball, told him that the Prussians at Thuin were attacked this morning, and that a heavy cannonade was going on when he left. Orders were issued half an hour ago for the whole of the troops to be in readiness to march at a moment's notice. There's no saying yet which way the French may come, and this attack upon the Prussians may be only a feint; so not a soldier can be moved till more is known. The first division is ordered to collect at Ath to-night, the third at Braine-le-Comte, and the fourth at Grammont. The fifth—that is ours—with the Eighty-first and the Hanoverian brigade, and the sixth division, of course collect here. All are to be in readiness to march at a moment's notice. The Prince of Orange is to gather the second and third Dutch divisions at Nivelles. Of course this first skirmish may only be intended to feel our force and positions; but at any rate, it is a sign that the game is going to begin."

"But if the orders are issued, and the troops are to collect to-night, the secret cannot be kept long."

"No; by this time the divisional orders will be published, and everyone will know it in an hour or two. There is really no secret about it, lads. If there had been the colonel wouldn't have told me, and I shouldn't have told you. See, the news is circulating already."

A change was indeed taking place in the position of the scene. The loungers were gathering in little groups, talking eagerly and excitedly. The orders for the concentration of the divisions had become known, though as yet all were in ignorance as to the reason for their issue. The three officers joined some of the groups and listened to the talk. The general idea was that the duke had heard that the French were gathering for an attack, and these measures were merely precautionary. It might be days yet before the affair really began. Still it was important news; and there were pale faces among the ladies at this sudden reminder that the assembly at Brussels was not a mere holiday gathering, but that war, grim, earnest, and terrible, was impending.

"We had better be getting back to our quarters," Captain O'Connor said. "Everything will have to be packed up this evening."

"But does this mean that the troops are to be under arms all night?" Stapleton asked.

"That it does, Stapleton. Of course they won't be kept standing in line; but when troops are ordered to be in readiness to march at a moment's notice, on such a business as this, it means that they will all be assembled. Then probably they will be allowed to lie down, and perhaps will light bivouac fires. But it means business, I can tell you."

"Then I for one shan't go to the ball," Ralph said. "No doubt it will be a pretty sight; but there have been lots of balls, and this bivouac will be a new experience altogether."

"I don't know that you are wrong, Conway," Captain O'Connor said. "Beside, you will probably find the colonel will issue orders that only a certain number of officers may go. I shall look in for an hour or two just to see the scene. But I don't know many people, and with a room full of generals and colonels, and three or four men to each lady, there won't be much chance of getting partners."

When they reached the village Stapleton said good-by to them, as his company lay half a mile further on; and Captain O'Connor and Ralph entered their quarters. They found their servants busy packing up the baggage.

"What is this all about, O'Connor?" Lieutenant Desmond asked.

"It is in orders that the whole division is to assemble to-night in readiness to march at a moment's notice. News has come that the French have attacked the Prussian outposts, and the duke is not to be caught napping. Of course it may be nothing but an outpost skirmish; still it may be the beginning of operations on a grand scale."

"And there is an order," Desmond said dolefully, "that only one officer in each company is to go to the ball."

"You want to go—eh, Desmond?"

"Well, of course I should like to go, and so would everyone. I suppose, however, it can't be helped; for of course you will go yourself."

"Well, I have made up my mind to look in for an hour or two. Conway doesn't wish to go. I'll tell you how we will arrange, Desmond. What the order means is that two officers must stop with their company. It doesn't matter in the least who they are; so that there are two out of the three with the men. Dancing will begin about eight o'clock. I will look in there at nine. An hour will be enough for me; so I will come back to the company, and you can slip away and stop there till it's over.''

"Thank you very much," Desmond said gratefully.

"And look here, Desmond. You had better arrange with your man to leave your undress uniform out; so that when you get back from the ball you can slip into it and have the other packed up. That's what I am going to do. I can't afford to have my best uniform spoiled by having to sleep in it in the mud. A captain's pay doesn't run to such extravagance as that.''

"What will be done with the baggage if we have to march?''

"Oh, I don't suppose we shall march to-night. But if we do, the quartermaster will detail a party to collect all the baggage left behind and put it in store. We needn't bother about that; especially when, for aught we know, we may never come back to claim it.''

But although O'Connor did not know it, the duke had by this time received news indicating that the attack upon the Prussian outpost was the beginning of a great movement, and that the whole French army were pressing forward by the road where the Prussian and British army joined hands.

At daybreak the French had advanced in three columns —the right upon Chatelet, five miles below Charleroi, on the Sambre; the center on Charleroi itself; the left on Marchienne. Zieten, who was in command of the Prussian corps d'armée, defended the bridges at these three

points stoutly, and then contested every foot of the
ground, his cavalry making frequent charges; so that at
the end of the day the French had only advanced five
miles. This stout resistance enabled Blucher to bring
up two out of his other three corps, Bulow, whose corps
was at Liege, forty miles away, receiving his orders too
late to march that day. The rest of the Prussian army
concentrated round the villages of Fleurs and Ligny.

Accordingly at ten o'clock in the evening orders were
issued by Wellington for the third division to march at
once from Braine-le-Comte to Nivelles, for the first to
move from Enghien to Braine-le-Comte, and for the
second and fourth divisions to march from Ath and
Grammont on Enghien. No fresh orders were issued to
the troops round Brussels; and although it was known at
the ball that the troops were in readiness to march at a
moment's notice, there were none except the generals
and a few members of the staff who had an idea that the
moment was so near at hand. The regiments stationed
at a distance from Brussels were assembled in the park
by ten o'clock in the evening; then arms were piled, and
the men permitted to fall out.

Only a few lighted fires, for the night was warm. The
artillery, however, who had all along been bivouacked in
the park, had their fires going as usual, and round these
many of the troops gathered, but the greater part
wrapped themselves in their cloaks and went quietly to
sleep. Ralph strolled about for an hour or two, chatting
with other officers and looking at the groups of sleepers,
and listening to the talk of the soldiers gathered round
the fires. Among them were many old Peninsular men,
whose experience now rendered them authorities among
the younger soldiers, who listened eagerly to the details
of the desperate struggle at Albuera, the terrible storm-

ing of the fortresses, and lighter tales of life and adventure in Spain. Many of the men whose quarters lay near the scene of assembly had been permitted to return to them, with strict orders to be ready to join the ranks should the bugle sound.

CHAPTER XVI.

FOUND AT LAST.

As soon as Mrs. Conway received the box she set to work in earnest. Directly the house was still and a sufficient time had elapsed for the Miss Penfolds to have fallen asleep, she rose from the bed on which she had lain down without undressing, put on the coat and hat, and made her way noiselessly down to the library. As she kept the lock well oiled she entered noiselessly, and then locking the door behind her lighted a candle and commenced her search. On the fifth night she was rewarded by finding that the center of what looked like a solidly carved flower in the ornamentation of the mantelpiece gave way under the pressure of her finger, and at the same moment she heard a slight click. Beyond this nothing was apparent; and after trying everything within reach she came to the conclusion that it needed a second spring to be touched to reveal the entrance.

It took her another three weeks before she found this. It was a slight projection, about as large as a button, in the inside of the chimney behind the mantel. Pressing this and the other spring simultaneously, the bookcase on the left of the fireplace suddenly swung open three or four inches. For a moment she stood breathless with excitement, hesitating before she entered; then she swung the bookcase open. There, as she had expected, was a little room seven feet long by four deep; but, to her bitter disappointment, it was bare and empty. A

few scraps of paper lay on the ground, but there was no
furniture, chest, or boxes in the room. The revulsion
was so great that Mrs. Conway returned into the library,
, threw herself into a chair, and had a long cry. Then
she went back into the room and carefully examined the
pieces of paper lying on the ground. One of them was a
portion of a letter, and she recognized at once the handwriting of Mr. Tallboys.

It contained only the words: "My dear Mr. Penfold—
In accordance with your request I send you the—"
But above was the date, which was ten days only anterior
to Mr. Penfold's death. Mrs. Conway had no doubt that
the word that should have followed the fragment was
"will," and that this was the letter that Mr. Tallboys
had sent over with that document. It was important
evidence, as it showed that Mr. Penfold had been in the
habit of using this place during his lifetime, and that he
had entered it after he had received the will from his
solicitor a few days before his death. Why should he
have entered it except to put the will in a place of security? Where that place was she did not know, but she
felt certain that it was somewhere within reach of her
hand.

"If it is here it must be found," she said resolutely;
"but I won't begin to look for it to-night. It must be
three o'clock already, and I will think the matter over
thoroughly before I begin again. It is something to
have found out as much as I have. I ought to be encouraged instead of being disappointed."

That day she wrote to Mr. Tallboys, giving him a full
account of the discovery which she had made, and in-
closing the fragment of his letter. She did not renew
her search for the next two nights; for her long watch-
fulness and excitement had told upon her, and she felt

that she needed rest before she set about the second part of the search.   She received a letter from Mr. Tallboys in reply to that she had sent him:

"MY DEAR MRS. CONWAY: I congratulate you most heartily upon the great success you have met with.   I own that I have never been very hopeful, for after the thorough search we made of the room I hardly thought it likely that you would succeed when we had failed; however, you have done so, and I cannot doubt that a similar success will attend your further efforts.   In a small bare room such as you describe the difficulties in the way of finding the hidden receptacle cannot be so great as those you have already overcome.   You are perfectly correct in your supposition that the fragment you sent me was part of the letter that I sent over with the will to Mr. Penfold by my clerk.   I have compared it with the copy in my letter book, and find that it is the same.   As you say, this letter proves conclusively that Mr. Penfold was in this secret room after he received the will, and one can assign no reason for his going there unless to put the will away in what he considered a secure hiding-place.   That it is still somewhere there I have no doubt whatever, and I shall await with much anxiety news as to your further progress."

Thinking the matter over, Mrs. Conway had come to the conclusion that the hiding-place could only be under one of the stone flags of the floor or in the wall against the fireplace, or rather in that part of it above the fireplace.   There would not be thickness enough in the walls separating the secret chamber from the passage or the rooms on either side of it; but the chimney would not be of the same width as the open fireplace below, and there might well be a space there sufficient for a good-sized closet.   It was here, therefore, that she determined to begin her search.   The next night, then, after touch-

ing the springs and entering the secret chamber, she began carefully to examine each stone in the wall next the
fireplace at a distance about four feet above the ground.

In five minutes she uttered an exclamation of satisfaction. One of the stones, above eighteen inches square,
although like the rest fitting closely to those adjoining
it, was not, like the others, bedded in cement. So close
was the join that it needed a close inspection to see that
it was different from those around it. Still, upon close
examination, it was evident that it was not cemented in.
Taking out a penknife from her pocket, she found that
the joint was too close even to allow this to be inserted
for any distance. There was no keyhole or any other
visible means of opening it, and she searched the walls
in vain for any hidden spring.

For a whole week she continued the search, but without the slightest success, and at last began almost to
despair; for at the end of that time she was convinced
that she had passed her fingers again and again over
every square inch of the floor and walls within her reach.
Completely worn out with her sleepless nights, she determined to take a little rest, and to abstain altogether
for a few nights from the search. On the third night,
however, an idea suddenly occurred to her. She rose at
once, dressed herself, and was about to go downstairs,
when she thought that she heard a noise below. She
returned at once to her room, hid away her hat and coat,
and again went to the top of the stairs and listened.

Yes, she had not been mistaken; she distinctly heard
sounds below, and, she thought, the murmur of men's
voices. After a moment's thought she returned again to
her room, took off her dress and threw a shawl round her
shoulders, and then stole quietly down the stairs to the
next floor and knocked gently at Miss Penfold's door.

She repeated the knock two or three times, and then heard Miss Penfold's voice asking who was there. She did not speak, but knocked again. This time the voice came from the other side of the door.

"It is me, Miss Penfold—Anna Sibthorpe."

The door was unlocked and opened.

"What is it, Anna?"

"There is some one in the house, ma'am; I can hear them moving about down below, and I think I can hear men's voices."

Miss Penfold came out and listened.

"Yes, there is some one there," she said. "Go and call the butler and the others. I shall be ready by the time you come down."

In two or three minutes the servants, headed by the butler, who had armed himself with a blunderbuss that always hung in his room ready for action, came downstairs. Miss Penfold came out to meet them half-dressed. She had a pistol in her hand. The maids had armed themselves with pokers and brooms.

"Have you looked to the priming of your blunderbuss?" Miss Penfold asked quietly.

"No, ma'am."

"Well, then, look now," she said sharply. "What's the use of having a weapon if you don't see that it's in order?"

"It's all right, ma'am," the butler said, examining the priming.

"Well, then, come along and don't make a noise."

They went downstairs noiselessly, and paused when they reached the hall. The sounds came from the drawing-room. Miss Penfold led the way to the door, turned the handle, and flung it open. Three men were seen in the act of packing up some of the valuables. They

started up with an exclamation. Miss Penfold fired, and
there was a cry of pain. A moment later there was a
roar as the blunderbuss went off, the contents lodging in
the ceiling. Without hesitating for a moment the three
men made a rush to the open window, and were gone.

"John Wilton," Miss Penfold said sternly, "you are a
fool! I give you a month's notice from to-day. Fasten
up the shutters again and all go off to bed." And without another word she turned and went upstairs. As she
reached the landing her sister ran out of her room in
great alarm.

"What is the matter, Charlotte? I heard two explo-
sions."

"It is nothing, Eleanor. Some men broke into the
house, and we have gone down and frightened them
away. I did not think it was worth while disturbing
you, as you are so easily alarmed; but it is all over now,
and the servants are shutting up the house again. I will
tell you all about it in the morning. Go to bed again at
once, or you will catch cold. Good-night."

Directly Miss Penfold had gone upstairs a hubbub of
talk burst out from the female servants.

"It's disgraceful, John! With that great gun you
ought to have shot them all dead."

"It went off by itself," John said, "just as I was going
to level it."

"Went off by itself!" the cook said scornfully. "It
never went off of itself when it was hanging above your
bed. Guns never go off by themselves, no more than
girls do. I am surprised at you, John. Why, I have
heard you talk a score of times of what you would do if
burglars came; and now here you have been and knocked
a big hole in the ceiling. Why missus has twenty times
as much courage as you have. She shot straight, she

did, for I heard one of the men give a squalk. Oh, you
men are pitiful creatures, after all!"

"You wouldn't have been so mighty brave, cook, if
Miss Penfold and me hadn't been in front of you."

"A lot of use you were!" the cook retorted. "Six feet
one of flesh, and no heart in it! Why, I would have
knocked him down with a broom if I had been within
reach of him."

"Yes, that we would, cook," the under-housemaid
said. "I had got my poker ready, and I would have
given it them nicely if I could have got within reach.
Miss Penfold was just as cool as if she had been eating
her breakfast, and so was we all except John."

John had by this time fastened up the shutter again,
and feeling that his persecutors were too many for him
he slunk off at once to his room; and the others, beginning to feel that their garments were scarcely fitted for
the cold night air, postponed their discussion of the
affair until the following morning. The next morning
after breakfast the servants were called into the dining-
room, and Miss Penfold interrogated them closely as to
whether any of them had seen strange men about, or had
been questioned by any one they knew as to valuables at
the Hall.

"If it had not been for Anna," she said, when she had
finished without eliciting any information, "the house
would have been robbed, and not any of us would have
been any the wiser. It was most fortunate that, as she
says, she happened to be awake and heard the sounds;
and she acted very properly in coming quietly down to
wake me. If the one man in the house," and she looked
scornfully at the unfortunate butler, "had been possessed
of the courage of a man the whole of them would have
been shot; for they were standing close together, and
he could hardly have missed them if he had tried.

"If that weapon had been in the hands of Anna, instead of those of John Wilton, the results would have been very different. However, John Wilton, you have been a good servant generally, and I suppose it is not your fault if you have not the courage of a mouse, therefore I shall withdraw my notice for you to leave. I shall make arrangements for the gardener to sleep in the house in future, and you will hand that blunderbuss over to him. I shall write to-day to the ironmonger at Weymouth to come over and fix bells to all the shutters, and to arrange wires for a bell from my room to that which the gardener will occupy."

At breakfast Miss Penfold informed her sister of what had taken place the night before.

"I shall write, of course, to the head constable at Weymouth to send over to inquire about it, but I have very little hope that he will discover anything, Eleanor."

"Why do you think that, Charlotte? You said that you were convinced you had wounded one of the men; so they ought to be able to trace him." ·

"I dare say they would if this had been an ordinarytheft; but I am convinced that it was not."

"Not an ordinary theft! What do you mean?"

"I have no doubt in my mind, Eleanor, that it was another attempt to discover the will."

"Do you think so?" Eleanor said in an awed voice. "That is terrible. But you said the men were engaged in packing up the candlesticks and ornaments."

"Oh, I believe that was a mere blind. Of course they would wish us to believe they were simply burglars, and therefore they acted as such to begin with. But there has never been any attempt on the house during the forty years we have lived here. Why should there be so now? If Anna had not fortunately heard those men I believe that when they had packed up a few things to give the idea that they were burglars, they would have gone to the library and set to to ransack it and find the will.''

"But they would never have found it, Charlotte. It is too well hidden for that.''

"There is no knowing,'' Miss Penfold said gloomily. So long as it is in existence we shall never feel comfortable. It will be much better to destroy it.''

"No, no!'' Eleanor exclaimed. "We agreed, Charlotte, that there was no reason why we should assist them to find it; but that is altogether a different thing from destroying it. I should never feel happy again if we did.''

"As for that,'' Miss Penfold said somewhat scornfully, "you don't seem very happy now. You are always fretting and fidgeting over it.''

"It is not I who am fancying that these burglars came after the will,'' Eleanor answered in an aggrieved voice.

"No; that is the way with timid people,'' Miss Penfold said. "They are often afraid of shadows, and see no danger where danger really exists. At any rate, I am determined to see whether the will really is where we suppose it to be. If it is I shall take it out and hide it in the mattress of my bed. We know that it will be safe there at any rate as long as I live, though I think it wiser to destroy it.''

"No, no,'' Eleanor exclaimed; "anything but that. I sleep badly enough now, and am always dreaming that Herbert is standing by my bedside with a reproachful look upon his face. I should never dare sleep at all if we were to destroy it.''

"I have no patience with such childish fancies, as I have told you over and over again,'' Miss Penfold said sharply. "If I am ready to take the risk of doing it, I do not see that you need fret about it. However, I am ready to give in to your prejudices, and indeed would rather not destroy it myself if it can be safely kept elsewhere. At any rate I shall move it from its hiding-place. We know that it is there and nowhere else that it will be searched for, and with it in my room we need have no more uneasiness. I can unsew the straw *pailliasse* at the bottom of my bed, and when it is safely in there I shall have no fear whatever."

"Of course you can do as you like, Charlotte," Eleanor said feebly; "but for my part I would much rather go on as we are. We don't know now that the will really exists, and I would much rather go on thinking that there is a doubt about it."

"Very well, then; go on so, Eleanor. You need ask no questions of me, and I shall tell you nothing. Only remember, if I die before you don't part with the *pailliasse* on my bed."

Mrs. Conway thought a good deal during the day about the events of the night before, and determined to be more cautious than ever in her operations; for she thought it probable that Miss Penfold would be even more wakeful and suspicious than before. She would have left the search alone for a few days had it not been for the idea that had taken her from her bed the night before. It had struck her then as possible that the spring opening the secret closet might be in the chimney behind it, and that it was necessary to touch this from the outside before opening the door of the secret room.

She was convinced that had there been a spring in the room itself she must have discovered it, but it never before struck her that it might be at the back of the closet.

She felt that she must satisfy herself on this point whatever the risk of discovery. Accordingly at the usual hour
she made her way downstairs. She had put the key in
the door, and was in the act of turning it when she heard
a noise upstairs. She opened the door and stood looking up the stairs. In a moment she saw a light, and
directly afterward Miss Penfold appeared at the top holding a candle in her hand. Knowing she was as yet un-
seen, Mrs. Conway entered the library and closed the
door behind her. Then she hurried to the fireplace,
touched the two springs, pulled the bookcase open and
entered the secret chamber, and closed the bookcase
behind her.

She had often examined the lock, thinking that the
secret spring of the closet might be concealed here. It
was a large old-fashioned one, and moved two bolts, one
at the top of the door and one at the bottom. These she
had already discovered could be easily opened from the
inside. She imagined that Miss Penfold was merely
going round the house to see that all was secure, and she
had, contrary to her practice, taken the key from the
door of the library in order that Miss Penfold might
enter it if she chose. But the thought now flashed across
her that possibly she might intend to open the secret
room; and to prevent this she now thrust the barrel of
the pistol she carried in between the back of the bolt and
the piece of iron against which it shot, so that the action
of the springs could not throw it out of its place.

Breathlessly she listened. Presently she heard a sharp
click in the wall behind her. She had scarcely time
to wonder what this meant when she heard a sound
in the lock close to her. It was repeated again and
again. Then she felt a slight tremor of the door as if
somebody was trying to shake it. Her heart almost

One 28th.   MRS. CONWAY DISCOVERS THE WILL.—Page 311.

stood still. Miss Penfold was evidently trying to open
the chamber; and, though she knew the lock could not
open so long as she held the pistol in the place, she felt
her breath coming fast and her heart beating. For five
minutes the attempts to open the door continued. Then
all was still again.

For half an hour she remained without moving; then,
as all continued quiet, she guessed that Miss Penfold,
finding the springs did not act, had returned to her
room. She now rose to her feet, drew out her dark lantern, and turned to the wall by her side. She gave an
exclamation of joy—the stone that she had so long vainly
endeavored to move was swung open. Miss Penfold who
of course had the secret, had touched the spring outside
before attempting to open the chamber, and the stone,
which was set in iron, had swung open on a hinge. In
a moment Mrs. Conway explored the contents. The
closet was about two feet square by nine inches in depth,
and contained two shelves. There were several papers
in it, and the very first upon which she placed her hand
was marked "The Last Will and Testament of Herbert
Penfold."

So overwhelmed was Mrs. Conway at this termination
to her long search that she sank on the ground, and it ＼
was some time before she could collect herself sufficiently
to consider what was her best course. It was evident
that for some reason Miss Penfold had been about to
visit the secret room to see that the will was still in
safety. The failure of the springs to act had, of course,
disconcerted her; but she might try again in the morning, and would then be able to enter the room, and would
discover that the will was missing.

It was clearly the best course to make off at once. She
remembered now that she had noticed a tiny hole no big-

ger than a nail-hole in the door, and had found that upon the other side it was just above a row of books in the shelves somewhat lower in height than the rest, and was evidently intended to enable the occupant of the chamber to obtain a view of the library, and see whether that room was occupied. She applied her eye to it at once, and saw that all was dark. Concealing the lantern again beneath her coat, she drew back the bolts gently and stepped out. Then she went to one of the windows, took down the bell, carefully unbarred the shutters, threw up the window and stepped out.

She sped cross the garden, down the drive, and through the gate, and then hurried at the top of her speed toward the village. She had gone about half the distance when she heard a horse's footsteps approaching. The road ran between two high hedges and there was no place for concealment. She therefore walked along by the edge of the road close to the hedge, hoping that the horseman would pass without noticing her. His eyes, however, were too much accustomed to the darkness. He reined in his horse when he came to her, and a moment later the light of a small lantern fell on her face.

"Who are you?" a voice asked, "and where are you going?"

"I am going to the vicarage," she said, "to see Mr. Withers."

"A likely story that," he said. "What is this? A woman with a man's hat and coat! There is something wrong here," and leaning down he caught her by the collar. She saw by the light of his lantern that he was a mounted patrol.

"It is quite true, constable," she said. "I have put these things on in a hurry, but I am going to see Mr. Withers on a question of life and death. Take me to the vicarage, and if when you get there you find my story is not true you can lock me up if you like."

The constable was puzzled. The voice was apparently that of a lady, and yet her attire, and her presence abroad at two o'clock in the morning, was suspicious in the extreme. He paused irresolute.

"I don't like to disturb the vicar at this time of night," he said. "I will take you to the village lockup and go up to him in the morning."

"Please don't do that," she said. "I am a lady, and have a very good reason for what I am doing. I can promise you that Mr. Withers will not be angry at being called up; indeed he will be greatly pleased. Come, constable," she went on, seeing that he hesitated, "I will give you a couple of guineas to take me direct to the vicarage."

"Well, ma'am," the constable said, "if you are sure Mr. Withers will not be angry at being called up at such an hour I will take you; but you know he is a magistrate, and it would never do to play tricks upon him."

"There are no tricks, constable. He knows me very well, and will be pleased to see me even at this hour."

Greatly puzzled over the whole proceeding the constable turned, and still keeping a firm hold of her collar walked his horse back toward the village.

"You really need not hold me so tightly," Mrs. Conway said. "If I wanted to get away I could have done so in a moment; for I have a pistol in my pocket, and could have shot you the moment you turned your lantern away from me."

Somewhat startled at this information the constable released his hold, satisfied that his prisoner could not escape by speed. As a measure of precaution he made her walk a pace or two ahead, and kept the light of his lantern upon her while he held his pistol ready for action in his hand in case she should suddenly turn upon him. They went through the village, and five minutes afterward entered the gate of the vicarage. On reaching the door Mrs. Conway rang the bell. A moment later a window above opened.

"What is it?" a man's voice asked. "Am I wanted anywhere?"

"I am the mounted patrol, sir," the constable said, "and I have met a suspicious sort of person in the road. She said she was coming to you, and you knew her; and though it didn't seem a likely sort of story, I thought it better to run the risk of disturbing you instead of taking her to the lockup."

"It is I, Mr. Withers," Mrs. Conway said, taking off her hat and stepping out so that the light of the policeman's lantern fell upon her. "Please let me in, I have got it."

"Good heavens!" Mr. Withers exclaimed, startled out of his usual tranquillity. "It is all right, constable, I will be down in a minute."

"There, constable, you see I spoke truly," Mrs. Conway said, and taking her purse from her pocket she extracted by the light of the lantern two guineas and handed them to the man.

"Oh, I don't want to take your money, ma'am," he said apologetically. "You must excuse my not believing you, but it did seem a rum start."

"You are quite right, constable," she replied. "The circumstances were suspicious, and you only did your duty. However, you might have made it very unpleasant for me if you had chosen to take me to the lockup instead of bringing me here, and I am very willing to give you what I promised you. I can afford it **very** well," she said cheerfully, as he still hesitated, "and I dare say it will be useful to you."

The man took the money and touched his hat, and sat quiet until the door opened, and Mr. Withers in a dressing-gown and holding a candle appeared.

"You have done quite right in bringing the lady up here," Mr. Withers said; "but you need not go talking about it in the village."

"Very well, sir; I will say nothing about it. Good-night, sir. Good-night ma'am."

"My dear Mrs. Conway, what has happened to bring you here at this hour of the night?" Mr. Withers asked as he closed the door behind. "Did I understand you to say that you have got it? Is it possible that you have found the will?"

"Quite possible, Mr. Withers. Here it is in its envelope, with the seals unbroken."

"You astound me!" Mr. Withers exclaimed. At this moment Mrs. Withers made her appearance at the top of the stairs, her husband having briefly said as he hurried out of the room that it was Mrs. Conway.

"Amy," he said, "here is Mrs. Conway. And, what do you think? she has brought the missing will with her."

With an exclamation Mrs. Withers ran downstairs and threw her arms round Mrs. Conway. "You dear brave creature," she said, "I have been longing to speak to you for the last six months. It seems so unnatural your being close to us, and my not being able to see you. And you have really found the will? I can hardly believe it. How has it all come about?"

"Don't bother her, Amy," Mr. Withers said; for now that the excitement was past Mrs. Conway was trembling all over, and was scarcely able to keep her feet. "She is

overtired and overexcited. Take her straight up to the
spare room and get her to bed. I will make her a tumbler of hot port wine and water. The water is sure to
be warm in the kitchen, and a stick or two will make it
boil by the time she is ready for it. We will hear all
about it in the morning. We have got the will safe, and
we have got her; that is quite enough for us for to night,
all the rest will keep very well until to-morrow. '

In a few minutes Mrs. Conway was in bed, and after
drinking the tumbler of hot negus Mr. Withers had prepared for her she soon fell asleep.

Mrs. Withers came into the room early in the morning. "My husband says you are not to think of getting
up unless you feel quite equal to it, and I agree with
him; so if you like I will bring breakfast up to you, and
then you can go off to sleep again for a bit."

"Oh, no, thank you," Mrs. Conway replied. "Now
that I am fairly awake and realize where I am, I am perfectly ready to get up. I could not think the first
moment I opened my eyes where I had got to, and
fancied I had overslept myself and should get a nice
scolding."

"You must wear one of my dresses, my dear," the
vicar's wife said. "You have done with that servant's
gown for good. I will bring you one in a few minutes."

In half an hour Mrs. Conway came down in a pretty
morning dress of Mrs. Withers'. Mabel had that moment made her appearance in the breakfast-room. She
had returned only a week before from her stay at Bath,
having positively mutinied against the proposal that she
should stay there for another six months. She started at
the entry of a stranger.

"Don't you know me, Mabel?" Mrs. Conway said,
holding out her hand.

"Why—why—" Mabel exclaimed, "it's Mrs. Conway. When did you come, and what have you been doing to yourself? Why, your hair is quite a different color! What does it all mean, mamma?" she asked in bewilderment.

"Mrs. Conway came last night, Mabel, after you were in bed."

"But you didn't tell me she was coming, mamma."

"We didn't know ourselves, dear; she arrived quite unexpectedly."

"And—" and Mabel stopped.

"And I have got on one of your mamma's dresses," Mrs. Conway laughed, interpreting Mabel's look of surprise. "Yes, dear, and as you say, I have dyed my hair."

"But why, Mrs. Conway? It was such a pretty color before."

"And it will be again some day, I hope, for I am not going to dye it any more."

"I am glad of that," Mabel said frankly; "for you look quite different somehow. But why did you do it? and why— Is there anything the matter, Mrs. Conway," she broke off suddenly, "that you come here without being expected, and are wearing one of mamma's dresses, and have dyed your hair, and look so different altogether? Have you heard anything about Ralph?"

"You will hear all about it presently, Mabel," Mr. Withers, who had just come into the room, said. "You owe a great debt of gratitude to Mrs. Conway, as you will hear presently; for she has for six months been working in the interest of Ralph and you. Now, don't open your eyes so wide, but sit down to the table. After we have had breakfast Mrs. Conway will tell us all about it."

"By the way, Mrs. Conway, have you heard the news?"

"What news, Mrs. Withers?"

"In the newspaper I got yesterday evening it was said that a despatch had just been received from the Duke of Wellington saying he had news that Bonaparte was advancing, and that he had just issued orders for the troops to march forward to support the Prussians, who were likely to be first attacked."

"No, I had heard nothing about it," Mrs. Conway said, turning pale. "Then there is going to be a battle, and Ralph will be engaged."

"You must not alarm yourself," the vicar said. "You know the troops are very widely scattered, and his regiment may not be up in time; beside, you see, the Prussians are likely to be first attacked, and they may beat the French before the English get up to join in the battle."

"Now, Mrs. Conway," Mr. Withers said when they had finished breakfast, "please take pity on us and tell us all about it."

"Is Mabel to go away, or is she to hear it all, James?" Mrs. Withers asked.

"What do you think, Mrs. Conway?"

"I see no reason whatever against her hearing. Mabel is fast growing up. You are past fifteen now, are you not, Mabel?"

"Yes, Mrs. Conway."

"Then I think she has a right to hear all about it. She is, after all, the party most interested."

"Thank you, Mrs. Conway," the girl said. "Please let us go out into the garden and sit in the chairs under the shade of that tree. I can see it is going to be a long story, and it will be delightful out there; and then papa can smoke his after-breakfast cigar."

"Very well, Mabel; if your mamma has no objection, I am quite willing."

The chairs were taken out into the shade of the tree and the party sat down, Mabel all excitement, for as yet she knew nothing whatever of what had happened, and was puzzling herself in vain as to how Mrs. Conway could have been working in her interest.

"In the first place, Mabel," Mrs. Conway began, "I suppose you have no idea why you were sent away to Bath?"

Mabel opened her eyes in surprise.

"I thought I went there to get lessons in music and French and dancing."

"Well, you did go for that purpose, but for something else also. You were sent away in order that you might not see me."

"Not see you, Mrs. Conway! Why, you must be joking. Why, papa, what reason could there possibly be why I should not see Mrs. Conway? And beside, you never told me in your letter that she had been here."

"I have not been here—at least not in this house; but I was in the church every Sunday. I was there before you went away, although you did not see me. I was sitting in the pew with the Hall servants."

"With the Hall servants!" Mabel repeated in astonishment. "What did you sit with them for? and where were you staying? and why did you come to the church every Sunday and not come here?"

"That's just the story you are going to hear, Mabel. You heard of course, that it was Mr. Penfold's intention to leave you half his estates?"

"Yes, I heard that; and then there was no will found so of course I didn't get it."

"No, my dear; but as we all believed that there was such a will, we were naturally unwilling to let the matter rest. Still, the chance of finding it seemed very remote.

You remember we spoke to you about it when they offered you that hundred a year."

"Yes, papa, you told me then that you thought they were keeping me out of my rights, and that was why I ought to refuse to take it. Yes, you did say they were keeping Ralph out too, and that was partly why you thought I ought not to agree to take the money; and of course I thought so too, because that would seem as if we had deserted Ralph."

"Well, Mabel, at that time the chance of our ever hearing anything of the will was so remote that I think both your mother and myself had entirely given up hope, and I am sure we should never have taken any more steps in the matter. Fortunately Mrs. Conway possesses a great deal more energy and perseverance than we have, and when she found that we gave it up, and that Mr. Tallboys gave it up, she determined to take the matter in her own hands. Now she will tell us how she has succeeded, and you must listen quietly and not ask more questions than you can help till she has finished."

"Well, my dear," Mrs. Conway went on, "Mr. Tallboys, Mr. Penfold's lawyer, did everything he possibly could to find the will, but he could not do so; and as my son was with you the person that had been robbed, I thought it was my duty to undertake the search myself."

Mrs. Conway then related step by step the measures she had taken to obtain a situation as servant at the Hall, and then went on to tell the manner in which she had carried on the search, and how success had finally crowned her efforts, her story being frequently interrupted by exclamations and questions from her hearers.

"What do you mean to do next?" Mr. Withers asked when she concluded.

"I will ask you to drive me over at once to Weymouth,

I shall not feel comfortable until I have placed the will in Mr. Tallboys' hands; and directly I have done that I shall go over to Brussels. I may perhaps get there before any great battle is fought; and I should like to see Ralph before that, if possible, and at any rate be there to nurse him if he was wounded. I shall ask Mr. Tallboys if he can spare time to go across with me to Brussels. I should not want him to stop there, but only to take me over. I should think there would be no difficulty in hiring a small vessel at Weymouth to take me to Ostend, especially as money is no object now. If Mr. Tallboys cannot spare time himself, he can send a clerk with me or get somebody who will take me in charge; but at any rate I intend to go by myself if necessary. I do not suppose it will cause any delay about the will, Mr. Withers; for of course there must be some trouble in having it proved."

"It can make no difference, Mrs. Conway. I do not give that the least thought. I will go round at once and tell William to put in the horses."

"Mabel and I will go over too, James," Mrs. Withers said; "we cannot sit quiet all day after this excitement. Beside, I want to hear what Mr. Tallboys says."

Mr. Withers returned in a few minutes, looking grave.

"William has just come up from the village, and says that half an hour ago a man rode up from the Hall with word that the doctor was to go over at once, for that Eleanor Penfold had just had a stroke or fit of some sort and was terribly bad. I am sorry this new trouble has befallen them; but they have brought it entirely upon themselves, poor ladies. However, justice must be done; but I am sure you will agree with me, Mrs. Conway, that if the matter can possibly be arranged without exposure and publicity it shall be done so."

CHAPTER XVII.

QUATRE BRAS.

At ten o'clock Captain O'Connor returned and Lieutenant Desmond hurried off.

"Were you sorry to leave, O'Connor?" Ralph asked that officer.

"No; I was glad to get away," he replied. "Knowing as I do that in another twenty-four hours we may be engaged, and that in forty-eight the greatest battle of the age may take place, it was horribly sad to look on at the scene and wonder how many of the men laughing and flirting and dancing so gayly there would be so soon lying stark and cold, how many broken hearts there would be among the women. I felt heartily glad that I had neither wife nor sweetheart there. It is not often I feel in low spirits, but for once one could not help thinking. Here it is a different thing; we are all soldiers, and whatever comes we must do our duty and take our chance. But the gayety of that scene jarred upon me, and I could see there were many, especially the older men, who were thinking as I did. I dare say if I had found any partners and gone in for dancing I should have thought but little about it; but standing looking on the thoughts came. I think you were right, Conway, not to go."

"Have you heard any news of what has taken place to-day?"

"Yes. I was standing by the colonel when Picton came up to him and said:

" 'There's been sharp fighting on the frontier. Zieten gave the French a deal of trouble, and only fell back about six miles. The other corps, except Bulow's, will all join them to-night.

" 'It is a thousand pities that Zieten did not send off a mounted messenger to us directly he became engaged. If he had done so we might have started at one o'clock to-day, and should have been in line with the Prussians to-morrow. I suppose he thought Blucher would send, and Blucher thought he had sent; and so between them nothing was done, and we only got the news at seven o'clock this evening. Nine precious hours thrown away. It is just a blunder of this sort that makes all the difference between failure and success in war. Had the message been sent, we and the Dutch divisions and the troops from Braine le-Comte might all have been up by the morning. As it is, Blucher, with only three out of his four army corps, has the whole of the French army facing him, and must either fall back without fighting or fight against superior numbers—that is, if Napoleon throws his whole force upon him, as I suppose he will. It is enough to provoke a saint.'

" 'Which will Blucher do, do you think, general?' the colonel asked.

" 'He sends word that he shall fight where he is; and in that case, if Napoleon throws his whole force on him, he is nearly certain to be beaten, and then we shall have Napoleon on us the next day.'

"And now, Conway, I think it better to get a few hours' sleep if we can; for to-morrow will be a heavy day for us, unless I am mistaken."

It was some time before Ralph slept, but when he did

so he slept soundly, waking up with a start as the sound of a bugle rang out in the night air. It was taken up by the bugles of the whole division, and Brussels, which had but an hour before echoed with the sound of the carriages returning from the ball, woke with a start.

With the sound of the bugle was mingled that of the Highland pipes, and in a few minutes the streets swarmed with the soldiers; for there was scarce a house but had either officers or men quartered in it. The upper windows were thrown up and the inhabitants inquired the cause of the uproar, and soon the whole population were in the streets. There was no delay. The soldiers had packed their knapsacks before lying down to sleep, and in a quarter of an hour from the sound of a bugle the regiments were forming up in the park. They were surrounded by an anxious crowd. Weeping women were embracing their husbands and lovers; the inhabitants looked pale and scared, and the wildest rumors were already circulating among them; mounted officers dashed to and fro, bugles kept on sounding the assembly; and the heavy rumble of guns was heard as the artillery came up and took up their appointed position.

In half an hour from the sound of the first warning bugle the head of the column began to move, just as daylight was breaking. Comparatively few of the officers of Ralph's regiment were married men, and there were therefore fewer of those agonizing partings that wrung the hearts of many belonging to regiments that had been quartered for some time at home; but Ralph saw enough to convince him that the soldier should remain a single man at any rate during such times as he is likely to be called upon for serious service in the field. It was a relief when the bands of the regiment struck up, and

with a light step the troops marched away from the city where they had spent so many pleasant weeks.

As the troops marched on their spirits rose—and indeed the British soldier is always at his gayest when there is a prospect of fighting—the hum of voices rose along the column, jokes were exchanged, and there was laughter and merriment. The pace was not rapid, and there were frequent stoppages, for a long column cannot march at the same pace as a single regiment; and it was ten o'clock when they halted at Mount St. Jean, fourteen miles from Brussels. Here the men sat down by the roadside, opened their haversacks, and partook of a hasty meal. Suddenly there was a cheer from the rear of the column. Nearer and nearer it grew, and the regiment leaped to their feet and joined in the shout, as the Duke of Wellington, with a brilliant staff, rode forward on his way to the front.

Already a booming of guns in the distance told that the troops were engaged, and there was another cheer when the order ran along the line to fall in again.

Fighting had indeed begun soon after daylight. Prince Bernhard who commanded the division of Dutch troops at Quatre Bras, had commenced hostilities as soon as it was light by attacking the French in front of him; and the Prince of Orange, who had ridden to Nivelles, directly the ball was over, brought on the Dutch troops from that town, and joining Prince Bernhard drove back the French to within a mile of Frasnes.

The Duke of Wellington reached Quatre Bras soon after eleven, and finding that there was no immediate danger there, galloped away to communicate with Blucher.

He found that the latter had gathered three of his corps, and occupied a chain of low hills extending from

Bry to Tongres. The rivulet of Ligny wound in front of it, and the villages of St. Armand and Ligny at the foot of the slope were occupied as outposts. These villages were some distance in front of the hills, and were too far off for the troops there to be readily reinforced from the army on the heights. The Duke of Wellington was of opinion that the position was not a good one, and he is said to have remarked to Blucher: "Every man knows his own people best, but I can only say that with a British army I should not occupy this ground as you do."

Had the duke been able to concentrate his force round Quatre Bras in time, he intended to aid the Prussians by taking the offensive; but the unfortunate delay that had taken place in sending the news of the French advance on the previous morning rendered it now impossible that he should do so, and he therefore rode back to Quatre Bras to arrange for its defence against the French corps that was evidently gathering to attack it.

It was well for the allies that Napoleon was not in a position to attack in force at daybreak. His troops, instead of being concentrated the night before at Fleurus, were scattered over a considerable extent of country, and many of them were still beyond the Sambre. Marshal Ney, who had been appointed to the command of the corps, intended to push through Quatre Bras and march straight on Brussels, had only arrived the evening before, and was ignorant of the position of the various divisions under his command. Therefore it was not until two o'clock in the afternoon that Napoleon advanced with sixty thousand men to attack the Prussians at Ligny, while at about the same hour the column under Ney advanced from Frasnes against Quatre Bras. The delay was fatal to Napoleon's plans.

Had the battles commenced at daybreak, Ney could have brushed aside the defenders of Quatre Bras, and would have been at Mount St. Jean by the time the English came up. The Prussians would have been beaten by noon instead of at dusk, and before nightfall their retreat would have been converted into a rout, and on the following day Napoleon's whole army would have been in a position to have fallen upon the only British divisions that Wellington could by that time have collected to oppose him, and would probably have been in possession of Brussels before night.

Thus, while the delay in sending news to Wellington prevented the allies combining against the French on the 16th of June, the delay of Napoleon in attacking that morning more than counterbalanced the error. There was the less excuse for that delay, inasmuch as he had himself chosen his time for fighting, and should not have advanced until he had his whole force well up and ready for action; and as the advance during the first day's fighting had been so slow, the whole army might well have been gathered at nightfall round Fleurus ready to give battle at the first dawn of day.

Fighting as he did against vastly superior forces, Napoleon's one hope of success lay in crushing the Prussians before the English—who, as he well knew, were scattered over a large extent of country—could come up, and his failure to do this cost him his empire.

The artillery fire ceased in front before the column continued its march for Mount St. Jean. The Prince of Orange had paused in his advance when he saw how strong was the French force round Frasnes, and Ney was not yet ready to attack. Therefore from eleven until two there was a cessation of operations, and the ardor of the troops flagged somewhat as they tramped along the dusty road between Mount St. Jean and Genappe.

The Prince of Orange was having an anxious time
while the British column was pressing forward to his
assistance. As the hours went by he saw the enemy's
forces in front of him accumulating, while he knew that
his own supports must be still some distance away.
Nevertheless, he prepared to defend Quatre Bras to the
last. He had with him six thousand eight hundred and
thirty-two infantry and sixteen cannon, while Ney had
gathered seventeen thousand men and thirty-eight guns
to attack him. The latter should have had with him
D'Erlon's corps of twenty thousand men, and forty-six
guns, but these were suddenly withdrawn by Napoleon
when the latter found that the Prussian force was
stronger than he had expected. They had just reached
the field of Ligny when an order from Ney again caused
them to retrace their steps to Quatre Bras, where they
arrived just after the fighting there had come to an end.
Thus twenty thousand men with forty-six guns were absolutely thrown away, while their presence with either
Napoleon or Ney would have been invaluable.

Soon after two o'clock Picton's division, which headed
the column, heard several cannon shots fired in rapid
succession, and in another minute a perfect roar of artillery broke out. The battle had evidently begun; and
the weary men, who had already marched over twenty
miles, straightened themselves up, the pace quickened,
and the division pressed eagerly forward. A few minutes
later an even heavier and more continuous roar of cannon
broke out away to the left. Napoleon was attacking the
Prussians. The talking and laughing ceased now. Even
the oldest soldiers were awed by that roar of fire, and the
younger ones glanced in each others, faces to see whether
others felt the same vague feeling of discomfort they
themselves experienced; and yet terrible as was evidently

the conflict raging in front, each man longed to take his part in it.

The officers' orders to the men to step out briskly were given in cheerful and confident voices, and the men themselves—with their fingers tightening on their muskets, and their eyes looking intently forward as if they could pierce the distance and realize the scene enacting there—pressed on doggedly and determinedly. Messenger after messenger rode up to General Picton, who was marching at the head of the column, begging him to hurry on, for that the Prince of Orange was step by step being driven back. But the troops were already doing their best.

The Dutch and Belgian troops had fought with considerable bravery, and had held the village of Piermont and a farm near it for some time before they fell back to the wood of Bossu. Here they make a stout stand again, but were at length driven out and were beginning to lose heart, and in a few minutes would have given way when they saw on the long straight road behind them the red line of Picton's column. The glad news that help was at hand ran quickly through the wood, and the Belgians met their foes with fresh courage.

Picton's force consisted of the Eighth and Ninth British Brigades, the former under General Sir James Kempt, the latter under Sir Denis Pack. With them were the Fourth Brigade of Hanoverians, with two batteries of artillery—the one Hanoverian, the other British. The excitement of the troops increased as they neared Quatre Bras, and a loud cheer ran along the line as they neared the wood, and took their place by the side of the hardly pressed Dutch and Belgians. Pack's brigade consisted of the first battalion Forty-second,

second Forty-fourth, first Ninety-second, and first Ninety-
fifth, while Kempt had under him the first Twenty-
eighth, first Thirty-second, first Seventy-ninth, and Third
Royals.

The aspect of the fight was speedily changed now.
The French, who had been advancing with shouts of
triumph, were at once hurled back, and the defenders a
few minutes later were strengthened by the arrival of the
greater part of the Duke of Brunswick's corps. In point
of numbers the combatants were now nearly equal, as the
allies had eighteen thousand infantry, two thousand cavalry, and twenty-eight guns on the field. Of these, however, but eight thousand at most were British. Picton
at once sent forward the first battalion of the Ninety-
fifth, and these cleared a little wood in the front of
Piermont of the French light troops, and restored the
communication between Quatre Bras and Ligny.

Ney, however, was preparing to advance again in force.
His front was covered with a double hedgerow, which
afforded admirable shelter to his skirmishers, while his
artillery were so placed on rising ground in the rear of
his position as to sweep the whole country over which
his column would advance to the attack. At this moment the duke returned from his conference with
Blucher. He at once saw that the enemy had gathered a
heavy column behind the wood of Bossu, and directed
the Prince of Orange to withdraw the guns that were too
far advanced, and to gather the Dutch and Belgian troops
to oppose the advance, at the same time he sent forward
the Twenty-eighth to their assistance.

They arrived, however, too late; for the French swept
the Belgians before them and advanced steadily, while
their artillery from the high ground opened a furious
cannonade upon Picton's division. One of the Brunswick

One 28th. A TARGET FOR THE ENEMY.—Page 331.

regiments now joined the Belgians, but in spite of this reinforcement the latter were driven from the wood of Bossu, which they had occupied when the British first came up. The British troops were suffering heavily from the artillery fire to which their own guns could make no effectual reply.

"Pretty hot this, Conway," Captain O'Connor said to Ralph. "It's not pleasant standing here being made a target of."

"That it's not," Ralph said heartily. "I call it horribly unpleasant. I shouldn't mind it so much if we were doing something."

It was indeed trying for young soldiers under fire for the first time. The French had got the range accurately, and every moment gaps were made in the line as the round shot plowed through them. The officers walked backward and forward in front of their men with exhortations to stand steady.

"It will be our turn presently, lads," Captain O'Connor said assuringly. "We will turn the tables on them by and by, never fear."

There was not long to wait. Clouds of French skirmishers were seen advancing through the hedgerows, and stealing behind the thickets and woods that skirted the road, and a moment later the orders came for the light companies of all the regiments of Picton's division to advance.

"Forward, lads!" Captain O'Connor said. "It's our turn now. Keep cool and don't waste your ammunition."

With a cheer his company followed him. Every hedge, bank, and tree that could afford shelter was seized upon, and a sharp crackling fire at once replied to that of the French skirmishers. The light companies were then armed with far better weapons than those in use by the

rest of the troops, and a soldier could have told at once
by the sharp crackling sound along the front of the
British line that it was the light companies that were
engaged. But now a heavy column of troops was seen
advancing from the village held by the French; and this,
as it approached the part of the line held by the Brunswickers, broke up into several columns. The Germans
were falling back, when the duke sent Picton's two brigades to meet the enemy halfway. The Ninety-second
were left behind in reserve on the road, the light companies were called in, Picton placed himself in front of
the long line, and with a tremendous cheer this advanced
to meet the heavy French columns.

It was thus through the wars of the period that the
English and French always fought: the French in massive
column, the English in long line. Once again, as at
Albuera and in many a stricken field, the line proved
the conqueror. Overlapping the columns opposed to it,
pouring scathing volleys upon each flank, and then
charging on the shaken mass with the bayonet, the
British regiments drove the enemy back beyond the
hedgerows, and were with difficulty restrained from
following them up the face of the opposite hill.

On the right, however, the Brunswickers were suffering
heavily from the cannonade of the French, and were
only prevented from breaking by the coolness of their
chief. The Duke of Brunswick rode backward and forward in front of them, smoking his pipe and chatting
cheerfully with his officers, seemingly unconscious of
the storm of fire: and even the most nervous of his young
troops felt ashamed to show signs of faltering when their
commander and chief set them such an example. Four
guns, which at his request Wellington had sent to him,
came up and opened fire; but so completely were they

overmatched that in five minutes two were disabled and the other two silenced.

As soon as this was done two French columns of infantry, preceded by a battalion in line, advanced along the edge of the wood, while a heavy mass of cavalry advanced along the Ghent road, and threatened the Brunswickers with destruction. The Brunswick, Dutch, and Belgian skirmishers fell back before those of the French. The Duke of Brunswick placed himself before a regiment of lancers and charged the French infantry; but these stood steady, and received the lancers with so heavy a fire that they retreated in confusion on Quatre Bras. The duke now ordered the infantry to fall back in good order, but by this time they were too shaken to do so. The French artillery smote them with terrible effect; the infantry swept them with bullets; the cavalry were preparing to charge. No wonder then that the young troops lost their self-possession, broke, and fled in utter confusion, some through Quatre Bras others through the English regiments on the left of the village.

At this moment the gallant Duke of Brunswick, while striving to rally one of his regiments, received a mortal wound. He died a few minutes later, as his father had died on the field of Jena. The Brunswick hussars were now ordered to advance and cover the retreat of the infantry; but as they moved toward the enemy they lost heart, turned, and fled from the field, the French lancers charging hotly among them. So closely were the two bodies mixed together that the Forty-second and Forty-fourth which were posted on the left of the road, could not distinguish friend from foe.

Before the former regiment had time to form square the French were upon them, and for two or three minutes a desperate hand-to-hand conflict took place between

bayonet and lance. The Forty-fourth did not attempt to
form a square. Its colonel faced the rear rank about, and
these poured so tremendous a volley into the French
cavalry that they reeled back in confusion. Two companies of the Forty-second which had been cut off from
the rest were almost annihilated; but the rest of the
square closed in around French cavalry who had pierced
them and destroyed them to a man. The Twenty-eighth
also repulsed the enemy.

"What do you think of it now, Conway?" Captain
O'Connor asked as the French retreated.

"I feel all right now," Ralph said; "though I thought
just now that it was all over with me. A big Frenchman
was just dealing a sweeping cut at me when a musket
shot struck him. Still this is a thousand times better
than standing still and being pounded by their artillery.
I confess I felt horribly uncomfortable while that was
going on."

"I dare say you did, lad."

The Duke of Wellington had, upon the fall of their
commander, in vain endeavored to rally the flying Brunswickers. As he was so engaged the cavalry column
swept down upon him. He put spurs to his horse and
galloped to the spot where the Ninety-second were lying
behind a ditch bordering the road. The French were
close to his heels. He shouted to the men of the Ninety-
second in front of him to throw themselves down, and
setting spurs to his horse leaped the ditch and the men
behind it, and instantly the Highlanders poured so terrible a volley into the French cavalry that a hundred sad-
dles were emptied.

The cavalry recoiled for a moment in confusion, but
then reformed and retired in good order. Some of the
leading squadrons, however, had galloped on into the

village, and cut down some stragglers there; but the Highlanders closed round them, and, being pent up in a farmyard from which there was but one outlet, scarce a man who had entered escaped.

The French had now received heavy reinforcement—Kellermann's heavy horse having come upon the field—and as neither the Dutch nor Belgian cavalry would face the French troopers they were free to employ their whole cavalry force against the British infantry.

Again and again they charged down upon the Twenty-eighth, Forty-second, Forty-fourth, and First Royals. The Twenty-eighth and the Royals did not indeed wait to be attacked, but led by Picton and Kempt in person resolutely advanced to charge the French cavalry. This feat, seldom exampled in military history, was rendered necessary in order to cover the flank of the Forty-second and Forty-fourth, now, by the flight of the Brunswickers, Dutch, and Belgians, open to the attacks of the French cavalry. The fields here were covered with a growth of tall rye, that concealed the approach of the French cavalry till they were within a few yards of the infantry, and it was only by the tramp of the horses as they rushed through the corn that the British square knew when their foes would be upon them.

Picton in the center of the Twenty-eighth encouraged them by his presence, and they stood firm, although the cavalry again and again charged down until their horse's chests touched the close line of bayonets. They were every time repulsed with heavy loss. The Thirty-second, Seventy-ninth, and Ninety-fifth were also exposed to similar attacks; but everywhere the British soldiers stood firmly shoulder to shoulder, and nowhere did the French succeed in breaking their ranks.

At five o'clock fresh guns and cavalry reinforced Ney,

and his infantry again advanced in great force through the wood of Bossu. The British squares were decimated by the fire of the artillery, and several batteries were advanced to comparatively short range, and opened with destructive effect.

Stoutly as the eight thousand British had fought— deserted though they were by their allies—against Ney's overpowering numbers, they could not much longer have stood their ground, when at the critical moment General Alten's division came up by the Nivelles road to their aid. Halket's British brigade advanced between the wood of Bossu and the Charleroi road; while the Hanoverian brigade took up ground to the left, and gave their support to the hardly-pressed British.

Ney now pushed forward every man at his disposal. His masses of cavalry charged down, and falling upon the Sixty-ninth, one of the regiments just arrived, cut it up terribly, and carried off one of its colors. The Thirty-second, however, belonging to the same brigade, repulsed a similar attempt with terrible slaughter. The French infantry, supported by a column of cuirassiers, advanced against the Hanoverians, and driving them back approached the spot where the Ninety-second were lying. Major-General Barnes rode up to the Highlanders taking off his hat, and shouted: "Now, Ninety-second, follow me!"

The Highlanders sprang from the ditch in which they were lying, the bagpipes struck up the slogan of the regiment, and with leveled bayonets they threw themselves upon the French column. In vain its leading companies attempted to make a stand. The Highlanders drove them back in confusion, and they broke and fled to the shelter of the hedgerows, where they tried to resist the advance, but the Highlanders burst through without a pause. Their colonel, John Cameron, fell dead; but his men, more furious than before, flung themselves on the French, and drove them back in confusion into the wood.

Ney still thought of renewing the attack; but D'Erlon's corps had not yet arrived, while at this moment two light battalions of Brunswickers, with two batteries of artillery, came up, and almost immediately afterward General Cooke's division, comprising two brigades of the guards, reached the spot. The latter at once advanced against the French skirmishers, just as they were issuing afresh from the wood of Bossu. The guards had undergone a tremendous march; but all thought of fatigue was lost in their excitement, and they swept the French before them and pressed forward. As they did so the whole British line advanced, Halket's brigade on the one flank the guards on the other.

In vain the French cavalry charged again and again. In vain the French infantry strove to stem the tide. One after another the positions they had so hardly won were wrested from them. Picton's division retook the village; Piermont was carried by the Ninty-fifth and the German legion; while the guards drove the enemy entirely out of the wood of Bossu. Night was now falling, and Ney fell back under cover of darkness to his original position in Frasnes; while the British lighted their fires, and bivouacked on the ground they had so bravely held.

As soon as the order came for the troops to bivouac where they were standing, arms were piled and the men set to work. Parties chopped down hedges and broke up fences, and fires were soon blazing. Owing to the late hour at which the fight terminated, and the confusion among the baggage wagons that were now beginning to arrive from the rear, no regular distribution of rations could be made. Most of the men, however, had filled their haversacks before leaving their quarters on the previous evening, and a party sent down the road obtained a sufficient supply of bread for the rest from a commissariat wagon. While the fires were being lighted the light company were ordered to aid in the work of collecting the wounded. The other regiments had also sent out parties, and for hours the work went on. Owing to the frequent movements of the troops, and the darkness of the night, it was difficult to discover the wounded, and there were no materials at hand from which torches could be made.

No distinction was made between friend and foe. The bodies found to be cold and stiff were left where they lay; the rest were lifted and carried to one or other of the spots where the surgeons of the force were hard at work giving a first dressing to the wounds, or, where absolutely necessary, performing amputations. After an hour's work the light company was relieved by the grenadiers, and these in turn by the other companies, so that all might have a chance of obtaining as much sleep as possible.

The troops were indeed terribly fatigued, for they had had a thirty miles' march, and nearly six hours continuous fighting; but they were in high spirits at their success, although suffering severely from want of water. They had started in the morning with full canteens, but the dusty march had produced such thirst that most of these were emptied long before they reached the field of battle; and no water was to be found near the spot where the Twenty-eighth were bivouacked, and indeed with the exception of the regiments in the village, who obtained water from the wells, the whole army lay down without a drink. Water had, however, been fetched for

the wounded, whose first cry as their comrades reached
them had always been for it; and even when the search
had ceased for the night, there were numbers still lying
in agony scattered over the field. Ralph had before
starting filled a canteen with brandy and water at the
suggestion of Captain O'Connor.

"The less you drink, lad, while on the march the better; but the chances are you will find by night that every
drop is worth its weight in gold. If you have the bad
luck to be wounded yourself, the contents of the canteen
may save your life; and if you don't want it yourself,
you may be sure that there will be scores of poor fellows
to whom a mouthful will be a blessing indeed."

So Ralph had found it. He had drunk very sparingly
on the way, scarcely permitting himself to do more than
to wet his lips; but when he set about the work of collecting the wounded, he felt more than amply rewarded
for his little self-sacrifice by the grateful thanks of the
poor fellows to whom he was able to give a mouthful of
his hoarded store. It was not until his return to the
bivouac, after his hour's turn of duty, that he learned
the extent of the loss of the regiment. He knew by the
smallness of the number who mustered for the search how
much his own company had suffered, and in the brief
intervals in the struggle he had heard something of what
was doing elsewhere. Lieutenant Desmond had fallen
early in the fight, shot through the heart as the light
companies went out to oppose the French skirmishers.
Captain O'Connor had received a lance wound through
his arm; but had made a sling of his sash, and had kept
his place at the head of his company.

The officers were all gathered round a fire when Ralph
returned to the bivouac.

"I see you have your arm in a sling, O'Connor," he
said. "Nothing serious, I hope?"

"No, I think not; but it's confoundedly painful. It was a French lancer did it. Fortunately one of the men bayoneted him at the very instant he struck me, and it was only the head of the lance that went through my arm. Still, it made a hole big enough to be uncommonly painful; the more so because it gave it a frightful wrench as the man dropped the lance. However, there is nothing to grumble at; and I may consider myself lucky indeed to have got off with a flesh wound when so many good fellows have fallen."

"Yes, considering the number engaged, the losses have been terribly heavy," the major said. "It looked very bad for a time."

"That it did," O'Connor agreed. "That's what comes of fighting with little mongrels by the side of you. It's always been the case when we get mixed up with other nationalities. Look at Fontenoy, look at Talavera. If I were a general I would simply fight my battles in my own way with my own men. If any allies I had liked to come up and fight on their own account, all the better; but I wouldn't rely upon them in the very slightest."

"The Belgians and Dutch fought very fairly at the beginning, O'Connor."

"Yes, I will admit that. But what's the good of fighting at the beginning if you are going to bolt in the middle of a battle? If we had had two or three regiments of our own cavalry, it would have made all the difference in the world; but when they went off, horse and foot and left our division alone to face the whole force of the enemy, I hardly even hoped we should hold our ground till Alten came up."

"Yes, he was just in the nick of time; but even with him we should have had to fall back if Cooke had not arrived with the guards. By the way, has any one heard what has taken place on our left?"

"We have heard nothing; but I think there is no doubt the Prussians must have been thrashed. One could hear the roar of fire over there occasionally, and I am sure it got farther off at the end of the day; beside, if Blucher had beaten Napoleon, our friends over there would be falling back, and you can see by their long lines of fire they have not done so. I dare say we shall hear all about it to-morrow. Anyhow, I think we had better lie down and get as much sleep as we can, we may have another hard day's work before us."

CHAPTER XVIII.

WATERLOO.

THE Prussians indeed had been beaten at Ligny.
Their three corps, numbering eighty thousand men, with
two hundred and twenty-four guns, had been attacked by
Napoleon with sixty thousand men, with two hundred
and four guns. The battle was contested with extraordi-
nary obstinacy on both sides. The villages of Ligny and
St. Armand were taken and retaken over and over again,
and for hours the desperate strife in and around them
continued without cessation. Both parties continued to
send down reinforcements to these points, but neither
could succeed in obtaining entire possession of them.

The faults which Wellington had perceived in the
Prussian position told against Blucher. The villages
were too far in advance of the heights on which the army
was posted, and his reinforcements were therefore a long
time in reaching the spot where they were required to
act. They were, too, as they descended the hill, under
the observation of Napoleon, who was able to anticipate
their arrival by moving up supports on his side, and who
noted the time when Blucher's last reserves behind Ligny
had come into action. At this critical moment General
Lobau arrived from Charleroi with twelve thousand fresh
men and thirty-eight guns, and at seven o'clock in the
evening Napoleon launched this force with his division
of guards, twenty thousand strong, who had hitherto
been kept in reserve, against the enemy.

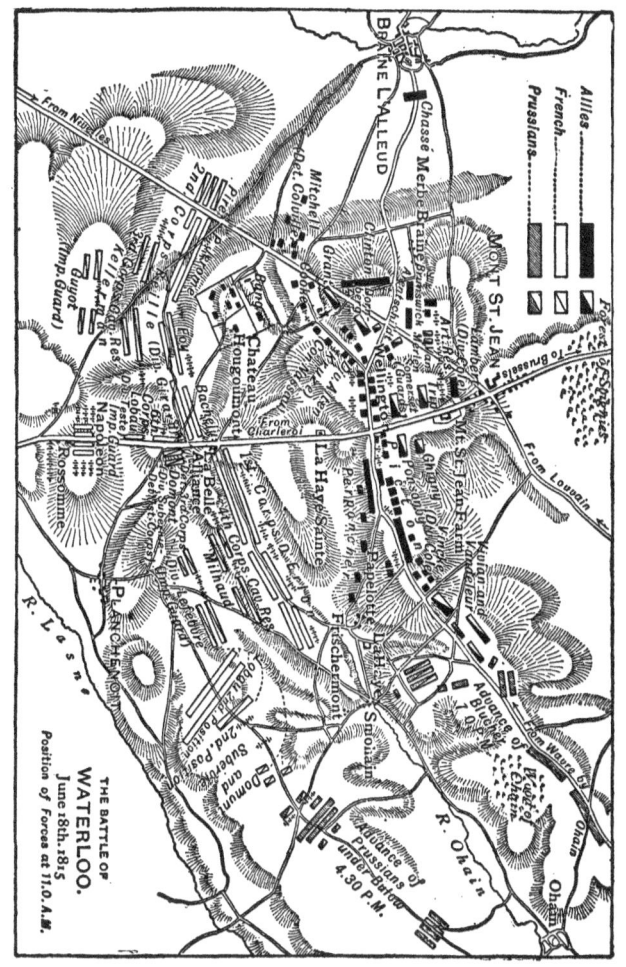

THE BATTLE OF
WATERLOO.
June 18th. 1815.
Position of Forces at 11.0. A.M.

Ligny was captured and the victory won. The Prussians throughout the day had fought with great bravery. They had a long score to wipe out against the French, and were inspired as much by national hatred as by military ardor; and they owed their defeat rather to the disadvantages of the position they held than to the superior fighting qualities of the French. Their cavalry had several times made desperate charges; sometimes against the French horse, at others upon columns of infantry. In one of these Blucher himself was with them; and as they were in turn driven back by a charge of the French cuirassiers his horse was shot, bringing him to the ground. His aid-de-camp leaped off and threw his cloak over him as the cuirassiers came thundering past, intent upon overtaking the Prussian cavalry. They paid no attention to the solitary dismounted man, and a few minutes later again passed the spot, this time in retreat, a fresh party of Prussian cavalry having met them. Again they passed by the fallen general, little dreaming· that one of their most formidable and determined enemies lay there at their mercy. As soon as the Prussians came up the dead horse was moved, and Blucher, who was insensible, carried to the rear, when he soon recovered and · resumed the command.

But though beaten the Prussians were by no means routed. They had lost the key of their position; but night came on before the combat terminated, and under cover of the darkness they fell back quietly and in good order. General Thielmann's corps on the extreme Prussian left had taken but little part in the fighting; and as the center and right of the Prussian army retreated he advanced, fell upon the French in the darkness, and for some time forced them back, thus giving time to the rest of the army to reform its ranks and recover its discipline.

After having rendered great service by thus occupying the enemy Thielmann took up a position on the heights, and remained facing the French, while the other *corps d'armé* took post in his rear.

The French were too weary to follow up the advantage they had gained; the night passed without any attack being made, and at daybreak the Prussians started on their march to Wavre, the cavalry remaining behind to cover the movement, check pursuit, and conceal if possible from the French the line by which the army was falling back. Had the pursuit been taken up at daybreak by the French, they would soon have driven in the cavalry and ascertained the route taken by the infantry; but it was not until many hours had elapsed that the French got into motion, and by that time the Prussian cavalry had disappeared from their front, and nothing remained to inform them of the line by which the enemy had retreated.

There was a general feeling of disappointment among the gallant defenders of Quatre Bras when on the following morning orders were issued for them to abandon the ground they had so stoutly held. They had been astir at daylight, firearms were cleaned, fresh ammunition served out from the reserve wagons, and the men fell into the ranks, expecting that in a short time they would again be engaged; but no movement could be seen on the part of the enemy, and arms were again piled. The commissariat wagons had come up in the night, and rations were served out to the troops and breakfast prepared. As soon as this was over strong parties were again sent over the battlefield to collect any wounded who had escaped the search of the night before. As soon as these were collected the whole of the wounded were placed in ambulance wagons and country carts, and despatched to Brussels.

Presently a general movement of the great baggage trains was observed by the troops to be taking place, and the long column moved along the road to the north. The duke had sent off a staff-officer at daybreak to ascertain the state of things at Ligny; he returned with the report that the Prussians had left the field. He then sent out a small party of cavalry under Lieutenant-Colonel Sir Alexander Gordon. This officer pushed forward until he encountered General Zieten, who was still at Sombreuf, but a mile distant from the battlefield. The general informed him of the whole events of the preceding day, and gave him the important intelligence that Blucher had retreated to Wavre, and would join hands with Wellington at Mount St. Jean, which the English general had previously fixed upon as the scene of the battle for the defense of Brussels.

The news relieved Wellington of all anxiety. It had been before arranged that Blucher if defeated, should if possible fall back to Wavre; but it was by no means certain that he would be able to do this, and had he been compelled by the events of the conflict to retire upon his base at Namur he would have been unable to effect a junction for some days with Wellington, and the latter would have been obliged single-handed to bear the whole brunt of Napoleon's attack. The latter's plans had indeed been entirely based on the supposition that Blucher would retreat upon Namur; and in order to force him to do so he had abstained from all attack upon the Prussian left, and employed his whole strength against the right and center, so as to swing him round, and force him to retire by way of Namur.

As soon as Wellington learned that Blucher had carried out the arrangement agreed upon his mind was at ease. Orders were sent off at once to the troops advan-

ing from various directions that they should move upon
Mount St. Jean. All the baggage was sent back to Brussels, while provisions for the troops were to be left at
Mount St. Jean, where also the whole of the ammunition
wagons were to be concentrated. Horsemen were sent
along the road to keep the baggage train moving, and
they had orders that if the troops at Quatre Bras fell
back upon them they were at once to clear the road of all
vehicles.

Having issued all these orders, and seen that everything was in train, Wellington allowed the troops at
Quatre Bras to rest themselves, and ordered their dinners, to be cooked. No movement was yet to be seen on
the part of the French; there was, therefore, no occasion
to hurry. Those, therefore, of the men who were not
out on patrol stretched themselves on the ground and
rested till noon. Dinner over the infantry marched off
in two columns, the cavalry remaining until four o'clock
in the afternoon, when upon the advance of Ney in front
and Napoleon on the left they fell back, and after some
sharp skirmishes with the enemy's light cavalry joined
the infantry before nightfall in their position near Mount
St. Jean and Waterloo. Rain had fallen for a time during the afternoon of the battle, and now at four o'clock
it again began to come down heavily, soaking the troops
to the skin.

"This is miserable, Stapleton," Ralph said to his
friend, after the regiment had piled arms on the ground
pointed out to them by the officers of the quartermaster's
department.

"I am rather glad to hear you say it is miserable,
Ralph. I was certainly thinking so myself; but you
always accuse me of being a grumbler, so I thought I
would hold my tongue."

Ralph laughed. "I don't think any one could deny that it is miserable, Stapleton; but some people keep up their spirits under miserable circumstances and others don't. This is one of the occasions on which it is really very hard to feel cheerful. There is not a dry thing in the regiment; the rain is coming down steadily and looks as if it meant to keep it up all night. The ground is fast turning into soft mud, and we have got to sleep upon it, or rather in it; for by the time we are ready to lie down it will be soft enough to let us sink right in. I think the best plan will be to try to get hold of a small bundle of rushes or straw, or something of that sort, to keep our heads above it, otherwise we shall risk suffocation."

"It is beastly," Stapleton said emphatically. "Look at the men; what a change in them since we marched along this road yesterday. Then they were full of fun and spirits, now they look washed out and miserable. Were the French to attack us now you wouldn't see our men fight as you did yesterday."

"But you must remember, Stapleton, the French are just as wet as we are. This is not a little private rain of our own, you know, got up for our special annoyance; but it extends right over the country."

"What nonsense you talk, Conway; as if I didn't know that."

"Well, you spoke as if you didn't, Stapleton; but you will see the fellows will fight when they are called upon. Just at present they are not only wet but they are disgusted. And I own it is disgusting after fighting as hard as we did yesterday to find it's all been of no use, and that instead of marching against the enemy we are marching away from them. Of course it can't be helped; and if we had waited another half-hour we should have had all the French army on us, and yesterday's work would have been mere child's play to it. Still I can quite enter into the soldier's feelings. Of course they do not understand the position, and regard it as simply a retreat instead of a mere shifting of ground to take up a better position and fight again to-morrow.

Still this is a nice position, isn't it? You see there's room enough along on the top of this slope for our whole army, and our guns will sweep the dip between us and the opposite rise, and if they attack they will have to experience the same sensations we did yesterday, of being pounded and pounded without the satisfaction of being able to return their fire.

"They must cross that dip to get at us—at least if they attack, which I suppose they will, as they will be the strongest party—and our artillery will be able to play upon them splendidly from this road. Then, too, there are two or three farmhouses nearer our side than theirs, and I suppose they will be held in force.

"That looks rather a nice old place among the trees there on our right. It has a wall and inclosure, and they will have hard work to turn us out of it. Yes, I call this a fine place for a battle; and we shall have the advantage here of being able to see all over the field and of knowing what is going on in other places, while yesterday one couldn't see three yards before one. During the whole time one was fighting, one felt that it might be of no use after all, for we might be getting smashed up in some other part of the field."

"I never thought anything about it," Stapleton said. "My only idea was that I must look as if I wasn't afraid, and must set a good example to the men, and that it was all very unpleasant, and that probably my turn might come next, and that I would give a good deal for something like a gallon of beer. As far as I can remember those were my leading ideas yesterday."

"Well, Denis, what is it?" Ralph asked his servant, who approached with a long face.

"Have you any dry tinder about you, your honor? I have been trying to strike a light for the last half-hour till the tinder box is full of water, and I have knocked all the skin off my knuckles."

"That's bad, Denis; but I don't think you will get a fire anyhow. The wood must be all too soaked to burn."

"I think it will go, sor, if I can once get it to light. I have pulled up some pea-sticks from an old woman's garden; and the ould witch came out and began at me as if I was robbing her of her eldest daughter. It was lucky I had a shilling about me, or be jabbers she would have brought down the provost's guard upon me, and then maybe I would have had my back warmed the least taste in the world more than was pleasant. I hid the sticks under a wagon to keep them dry, and Mike Doolan is standing sentry over them. I promised him a stick or two for his own kindling. The weather is too bad entirely, your honor, and the boys are well-nigh broken-hearted at turning their backs to the Frenchmen."

"Ah, well, they will turn their faces to-morrow, Denis; and as for the weather, I guess you have got wet before now digging praties in the old country."

"I have that, your honor, many and many a time; and it's little I cared for it. But then there was a place to go into, and dry clothes to put on, and a warm male to look forward to, with perhaps a drop of the crater afterward; and that makes all the difference in the world. What we are going to do to-night, sorra of me knows."

"You will have to lie down in the mud, Denis."

"Is it lie down, your honor? And when shall I get

the mud off my uniform? and what will the duke say in
the morning if he comes round and sees me look like a
hog that has been rowling in his sty?''

"You won't be worse than any one else, Denis; you see
we shall all be in the same boat. Well, here's the tinder. I should recommend you to break up a cartridge,
and sprinkle the powder in among the leaves that you
light your fire with.''

"That's the difficulty, your honor; I have got some
wood, but divil a dry leaf can I find.''

"Look here, Denis. Open your knapsack under the
wagon, and take out a shirt and tear it into strips. You
will soon get a fire with that, and we can easily replace
the shirt afterward.''

"That's a grand idea, your honor. That will do it,
sure enough. Faith, and when the boys see how I do it,
there will be many a shirt burned this evening.''

"But how about wood, Denis?''

"There's plenty of wood, your honor. The commis-
saries have had two or three score of woodcutters at work
on the edge of the forest all day, and there's timber felled
and split enough for all of us and to spare. The pioneers
of all the regiments have gone off with their axes to help,
and I will warrant there will be a blaze all along the line
presently. Now I will be off, your honor; for the cooks
are ready to boil the kettles as soon as we can get a fire.''

Great masses of the enemy could now be seen arriving
on the crest of the opposite rise. Presently, these broke
up into regiments, and then moved along the crest,
halted, and fell out. It was evident that nothing would
be done till next morning, for it was already beginning
to get dusk.

In a few minutes smoke rose in the rear of the regiment, and ere long half a dozen great fires were blazing.

Men came from the regiments near to borrow brands.
The news soon spread along the line of the means by
which the Twenty-eighth had kindled their fires and, as
Denis had foretold, the number of shirts sacrificed for
this purpose was large. Strong parties from each regiment were told off to go to the woodpiles and bring up
logs, and in spite of the continued downfall of rain the
men's spirits rose, and merry laughs were heard among
the groups gathered round the fires. The officers had
one to themselves; and a kettle was soon boiling, and tin
cups of strong grog handed round. Of food, however,
there was little beyond what scraps remained in the
haversacks; for the commissariat wagons had retired
from Quatre Bras to leave room for those carrying the
ammunition, and were now so far in the rear that it was
impossible to get at their contents, and distribute them
among the troops. For an hour or two they chatted
round the fire, and discussed the probabilities of the
struggle that would begin in the morning.

Just as night fell there was a sharp artillery fight between two batteries of Picton's division and the same
number of the French. The latter commenced the fight
by opening fire upon the infantry position, but were too
far away to do much harm. Picton's guns got the range
of a column of infantry, and created great havoc among
them. Darkness put a stop to the fight, but until late at
night skirmishes took place between the outposts. A
troop of the Seventh Hussars charged and drove back
a body of light cavalry, who kept on disturbing the
videttes; and the Second Light Dragoons of the king's
German legion, posted in front of Hougoumont, charged
and drove back a column of the enemy's cavalry that
approached too close.

Gradually the fires burned low—the incessant downpour of rain so drenching the logs that it was impossible to keep them alight—and the troops lay down, with their knapsacks under their heads, turned the capes of the greatcoats over their faces, and in spite of the deep soft mud below them, and the pouring rain above, soon sank to sleep. All night long a deep sound filled the air, telling of the heavy trains of artillery and ammunition wagons arriving from the rear to both armies. But nothing short of a heavy cannonade would have aroused the weary soldiers from their deep sleep.

At twelve o'clock Ralph was called up, as his company had to relieve that which furnished the posts in front of the position of the regiment. The orders were not to fire unless fired upon. A third of the men were thrown out as sentries; the others lay upon the ground, fifty yards in rear, ready to move forward to their support if necessary. Captain O'Connor left Ralph with the reserve, and himself paced up and down along the line of sentries, who were relieved every hour until morning broke, when the company rejoined the regiment.

The troops could now obtain a view of the ground upon which they were to fight. Their line extended some two miles in length, along the brow of a gradually sloping rise, the two extremities of which projected somewhat beyond the center. The ground was open, without woods or hedgerows. About halfway down the slope lay four farms. On the right was Hougoumont; a chateau with farm buildings attached to it and a chapel. In front of this lay a thick wood with a close hedge, and the house and farm buildings were surrounded by a strong wall. In front of the center of the line lay the farm and inclosures of La Haye Sainte, abutting on the main Charleroi road, which, as it passed the farm, ran between two deep banks. In front of the left of the line were the hamlets of Papelotte and La Haye. At the top of the ridge the ground sloped backward, and the infantry were posted a little in rear of the crest, which hid them from the sight of the enemy, and protected them from artillery fire. The whole of the slope, and the valley beyond it was covered with waving corn or high grass, now ready for cutting.

Upon the opposite side of the valley there was a similar rise, and on this was the French position. Nearly in the center of this - stood the farm called La Belle·Alliance, close to which Napoleon took up his stand during the battle. Behind the British position the ground fell away and then rose again gently to a crest, on which stood the villages of Waterloo and Mount St. Jean. The great forest of Soignies extended to this point, so that if obliged to fall back Wellington had in his rear a position as defensible as that which he now occupied.

The allies were arranged in the following order: On the extreme left were Vandeleur's and Vivian's light cavalry brigades. Then came Picton's division, the first line being composed of Hanoverians, Dutch, and Belgians, with Pack's British brigade, which had suffered so severely in Quatre Bras, in its rear, and Kempt's brigade extending to the Charleroi road. Alten's division was on the right of Picton's. Its second brigade, close to the road, consisted of the First and Second light battalions of the German legion, and the Sixth and Eighth battalions of the line. The Second German battalion was stationed in the farm of La Haye Sainte. Next to these came a Hanoverian brigade, on the right of whom were Halket's British brigade. On the extreme right was Cooke's division, consisting of two brigades of the guards, having with them a Nassau regiment, and two companies of Hanoverian riflemen.

Behind the infantry line lay the cavalry. In reserve were a brigade of the fourth division, the whole of the second division, and the Brunswickers, Dutch, and Belgians. The artillery were placed at intervals between the infantry, and on various commanding points along the ridge.

The duke had expected to be attacked early, as it was of the utmost importance to Napoleon to crush the British before the Prussians could come up; but the rain, which began to hold up as daylight appeared, had so soddened the deep soil that Napoleon thought that his cavalry, upon whom he greatly depended, would not be able to act, and he therefore lost many precious hours before he set his troops in motion.

From the British position the heavy masses of French troops could be seen moving on the opposite heights to get into the position assigned to them; for it was scarcely a mile from the crest of one slope to that of the other.

In point of numbers the armies were not ill-matched. Wellington had forty-nine thousand six hundred and eight infantry, twelve thousand four hundred and two cavalry, five thousand six hundred and forty-five artillerymen, and one hundred and fifty-six guns. Napoleon, who had detached Grouchy with his division in pursuit of the Prussians, had with him forty-eight thousand nine hundred and fifty infantry, fifteen thousand seven hundred and sixty-five cavalry, seven thousand two hundred and thirty-two artillerymen, and two hundred and forty-six guns. He had, therefore, four thousand three hundred men and ninety guns more than Wellington. But this does not represent the full disparity of strength, for Wellington had but eighteen thousand five hundred British infantry including the German legion—who having fought through the Peninsular were excellent troops—

seven thousand eight hundred cavalry and three thousand five hundred artillery. The remainder of his force consisted of troops of Hanover, Brunswick, Nassau, Holland, and Belgium, upon whom comparatively little reliance could be placed. The British infantry consisted almost entirely of young soldiers; while the whole of Napoleon's force were veterans.

As early as six o'clock in the morning both armies had taken up the positions in which they were intended to fight. The British infantry were lying down, the cavalry dismounted in their rear, and so completely were they hidden from the sight of the French that Napoleon believed they had retreated, and was greatly enraged at their having, as he supposed, escaped him. While he was expressing his annoyance, General Foy, who had served against the duke in the Peninsula, rode up and said:

"Your majesty is distressing yourself without just reason. Wellington never shows his troops until they are needed. A patrol of horse will soon find out whether he is before us or not, and if he be I warn your majesty that the British infantry are the very devil to fight."

The emperor soon discovered that the British were still in front of him; for the English regiments were directed to clean their arms by firing them off, and the heavy fusillade reached Napoleon's ears. At eight o'clock Wellington, who was anxiously looking over in the direction from which he expected the Prussians to appear, saw a body of mounted men in the distance, and soon afterward a Prussian orderly rode in and informed him that they were on the march to his assistance, and would soon be on the field.

Grouchy had, in fact, altogether failed to intercept them. Napoleon had made up his mind that after Ligny the Prussians would retreat toward Namur, and sent

Grouchy in pursuit of them along that road. That officer had gone many miles before he discovered the route they had really taken, and only came up with the rear of their colunm at Wavre on the morning of Waterloo. Blucher left one division to oppose him, and marched with the other three to join Wellington.

It was not until nearly ten o'clock that the French attack began; then a column moved down from the heights of La Belle Alliance against the wood of Hougoumont, and as it approached the leading companies broke up into skirmishing order. As these arrived within musketry range a scattering fire broke out from the hedges in front of the wood, and the battle of Waterloo had begun.

Soon from the high ground behind Hougoumont the batteries of artillery opened fire on the French column. Its skirmishers advanced bravely, and constantly reinforced, drove back the Hanoverian and Nassau riflemen in front of the wood. Then Bull's battery of howitzers opened with shell upon them; and so well were these served that the French skirmishers fell back, hotly pressed by the First and Second brigade of guards issuing from the chateau. The roar of cannon speedily extended along both crests; the British aiming at the French columns, the French, who could see no foes with the exception of the lines of skirmishers, firing upon the British batteries. The French therefore suffered severely, while the allies, sheltered behind the crest, were only exposed to the fire of the shot which grazed the ground in front, and then came plunging in among them.

Prince Jerome, who commanded on Napoleon's left, sent strong columns of support to his skirmishers acting against the right of the wood of Hougoumont, while

Foy's division moved to attack it in front. In spite of a terrific fire of artillery poured upon them these brave troops moved on, supported by the concentrated fire of their powerful artillery against the British position. The light companies of the guards, after an obstinate resistance, were forced back through the wood. The French pushed on through the trees until they reached the hedge, which seemed to them to be the only defense of the buildings. But thirty yards in the rear was the orchard wall, flanked on the right by the low brick terraces of the garden. The whole of these had been carefully loopholed, and so terrible a storm of fire opened upon the French that they recoiled and sought shelter among the trees and ditches in the rear.

Jerome, seeing that his skirmishers had won the wood, and knowing nothing of the formidable defenses that arrested their advance, poured fresh masses of men down to their assistance. Although they suffered terribly from the British artillery fire, they gathered in the wood in such numbers that they gradually drove back the defenders into the buildings and yard, and completely surrounded the chateau. The defenders had not even time properly to barricade the gate. This was burst open and dense masses rushed in. The guards met them with the bayonet, and after fierce fighting drove them out and closed the gate again, and with their musketry fire compelled them to fall back from the buildings. Some of the French, however, advanced higher up the slope, and opened fire upon one of the batteries with such effect that it had to withdraw. Four fresh companies of the guards advanced against them, cleared them away, and reinforced the defenders of the chateau.

A desperate fight raged round the buildings, and one of the enemy's shells falling upon the chateau set it on fire. But the defense still continued, until Lord Saltoun, repulsing a desperate attack, and reinforced by two companies which came down the hill to his assistance, drove the enemy back and recaptured the orchard. This desperate conflict had lasted for three hours.

While it was going on Ney led twenty thousand men against the center and left of the British position, advancing as usual in heavy column. Just as they were setting out at one o'clock Napoleon discovered the Prussians advancing.

He sent off a despatch to Grouchy ordering him to move straight upon the field of battle; but that general did not receive it until seven in the evening, when the fight was nearly over. It was just two when the columns poured down the hill, their attack heralded by a terrific fire upon the British line opposed to them. The slaughter among Picton's division was great; but although the Dutch and Hanoverians were shaken by the iron hail, they stood their ground. When the columns reached the dip of the valley and began to ascend the slopes toward the British division they threw out clouds of skirmishers and between these and the light troops of the allies firing at once began, and increased in volume as the French neared the advanced posts of La Haye Sainte, Papelotte, and La Haye.

The division of Durette drove out the Nassau troops from Papelotte; but reinforcements arrived from the British line, and the French in turn were expelled. The other three French columns advanced steadily, with thirty light guns in the intervals between them. Donzelat's brigade attacked La Haye Sainte, and, in spite of a gallant resistance by the Germans, made its way into the orchard and surrounded the inclosures. Another brigade, pushing along on the other side of the Charleroi

road, were met by the fire of two companies of the rifle
brigade who occupied a sandpit there, and by their
heavy and accurate fire checked the French advance.
The other two divisions moved straight against that part
of the crest held by Picton's division.

The men of the Dutch-Belgian brigade, as soon as fire
was opened upon them, lost all order and took to their
heels, amid the yells and execrations of the brigades of
Kempt and Pack behind them, and it was with difficulty
that the British soldiers were kept from firing into the
fugitives. The Dutch artillery behind them tried to
arrest the mob; but nothing could stop them—they
fairly ran over guns, men, and horses, rushed down the
valley and through the village of Mount St. Jean, and
were not seen again in the field during the rest of the
day. Picton's division was now left alone to bear the
brunt of the French attack. The battle at Quatre Bras
had terribly thinned its ranks, and the two brigades together did not muster more than three thousand men.
Picton formed the whole in line, and prepared to resist
the charge of thirteen thousand infantry, beside heavy
masses of cavalry, who were pressing forward, having in
spite of a stout resistance driven in the riflemen from
the sandpit and the road above it. As the columns
neared the British line the fire from the French batteries
suddenly ceased, their own troops now serving as a
screen to the British. The heads of the columns halted
and began to deploy into line; Picton seized the moment,
and shouted "A volley, and then charge!"

The French were but thirty yards away. A tremendous volley was poured into them, and then the British
with a shout rushed forward, scrambled through a double
hedgerow that separated them from the French, and fell
upon them with the bayonet. The charge was irresisti-

ble. Taken in the act of deploying, the very numbers of
the French told against them, and they were borne down
the slope in confusion. Picton, struck by a musket ball
in the head, fell dead, and Kempt assumed the command,
and his brigade followed up the attack and continued to
drive the enemy down the hill. In the meantime the
French cavalry were approaching. The cuirassiers had
passed La Haye Sainte, and almost cut to pieces a Hanoverian battalion which was advancing to reinforce the
defenders.

At this moment Lord Edward Somerset led the house-
hold brigade of cavalry against the cuirassiers, and the
élite of the cavalry of the two nations met with a tremendous shock; but the weight and impetus of the heavy
British horsemen, aided by the fact that they were descending the hill, while their opponents had hardly recovered their formation after cutting up the Hanoverians,
proved irresistible, and the cuirassiers were driven down
the hill. A desperate hand-to-hand conflict took place;
and it was here that Shaw, who had been a prize-fighter
before he enlisted in the Second Life Guards, killed no
less than seven Frenchmen with his own hand, receiving,
however, so many wounds, that on the return of the
regiment from its charge he could no longer sit his
horse, and crawling behind a house died there from loss
of blood.

While the Second Life Guards and First Dragoon
Guards pursued the cuirassiers down the slope, the
Royals, Scots Greys, and Inniskillens rode to the assist-
ance of Pack's brigade, which had been assailed by four
strong brigades of the enemy. Pack rode along at the
front of his line calling upon his men to stand steady
The enemy crossed a hedge within forty yards of the
Ninety-second, and delivered their fire. The Highlanders

waited till they approached within half the distance, and then pouring in a volley, charged with leveled bayonets. The French stood firm, and the Ninety-second, numbering less than two hundred and fifty men, burst in among them; a mere handful among their foes. But just at this moment Ponsonby's heavy cavalry came up, and passing through the intervals of the companies and battalions, fell upon the French infantry. In vain the enemy endeavored to keep their formation; their front was burst in, their center penetrated, and their rear dispersed, and in five minutes the great column was a mass of fugitives. Great numbers were killed, and two thousand prisoners taken.

CHAPTER XIX.

THE ROUT.

WHILE Pack's brigade secured the prisoners taken by
the cavalry and sent them to the rear, the cavalry themselves continued their charge. In vain Ponsonby
ordered the trumpeters to sound the halt. Carried away
by the excitement of their success—an excitement in
which the horses shared—the three regiments galloped
on. The Royals on the right fell upon two French regiments advancing in column, broke them, and cut them
up terribly. The Inniskillens also fell on two French
line regiments, shattered them with their charge, and
took great numbers of prisoners, whole companies running up the hill and surrendering to the infantry in
order to escape from the terrible horsemen.

The cavalry were now terribly scattered; the three
regiments of Ponsonby's brigade were far down in the
valley, as were the Second Life Guards and First
Dragoon Guards. The First Life Guards and the Blues
were still engaged with the cuirassiers opposed to them;
for these, although driven back, were fighting doggedly.
The Greys, who should have been in reserve, galloped
ahead and joined Ponsonby's squadrons, and the two
brigades of heavy cavalry were far away from all support. When they reached the bottom of the hill a tremendous fire was poured from a compact corps of infantry and some pieces of cannon on the right into the
Royals, Inniskillens, and Second Life Guards, and a fresh

column of cuirassiers advanced against them. They wheeled about and fell back in great confusion and with heavy loss, their horses being completely blown with their long gallop across the heavy ground.

These regiments had fared, however, better than the Greys, Royals, and Inniskillens on the left, for they, having encountered no infantry fire, had charged up the hill until level with the French guns, when, turning sharp to the left, they swept along the line cutting up the artillerymen, until suddenly they were charged by a brigade of lancers, while a large body of infantry threatened their line of retreat. Fortunately at this moment the light cavalry came up to their assistance.

Riding right through the infantry column the light cavalry fell upon the French lancers and rolled them over with the fury of their charge, and then charged another regiment of lancers and checked their advance. Light and heavy horse were now mixed up together, and a fresh body of French cavalry coming up, drove them down the hill with great loss—they being saved, indeed, from total destruction by the Eleventh Hussars, who, coming up last, had kept their formation. Covered by these the remnants of the cavalry regained their own crest on the hill, and reformed under cover of the infantry. General Ponsonby was killed, and his brother, the colonel of the Twelfth, severely wounded and left on the field.

While this desperate fight had been raging on the center and left, fresh columns had advanced from Jerome's and Foy's divisions against Hougoumont, and had again, after obstinate fighting, captured the orchard and surrounded the chateau, but were once more repulsed by a fresh battalion of guards who moved down the slope to the assistance of their hardly-pressed comrades. Then for a while the fighting slackened, but the artillery duel raged as fiercely as ever. The gunners on both sides had now got the exact range, and the carnage was terrible. The French shells again set Hougoumont on fire, and all the badly wounded who had been carried inside perished in the flames.

At the end of an hour fresh columns of attack moved against the chateau, while at the same moment forty squadrons of cavalry advanced across the valley toward thre English position.

The English batteries played upon them with round shot, and, as they came near, with grape and canister; but the horsemen rode on, and at a steady trot arrived within forty yards of the English squares, when with a shout they galloped forward, and in a moment the whole of the advanced batteries of the allies were in their possession; for Wellington's orders had been that the artillerymen should stand to their guns till the last moment, and then run for shelter behind the squares. The French cavalry paused for a moment in astonishment at the sight that met their eyes. They had believed that the British were broken and disorganized, but no sooner had they passed over the slope than they saw the British and German squares bristling with bayonets and standing calm and immovable.

The artillery on both sides had ceased their fire, and a dead silence had succeeded the terrible din that had raged but a moment before. Then with a shout the cavalry again charged, but in no case did they dash against the hedges of bayonets, from which a storm of fire was now pouring. Breaking into squadrons they rode through the intervals between the squares and completely enveloped them; but Lord Uxbridge gathered the remains of the British cavalry together, charged them, and drove them back through the squares and down the hill. Receiving reinforcements the French again advanced, again enveloped the squares, and were again hurled back.

While this was going on the battle was still raging round Hougoumont and La Haye Sainte, against which a portion of Reille's division had advanced; but the Germans resisted as obstinately as did the guards, and as the French cavalry retired for the second time the infantry fell back, and for a time the slope of the English position was again clear of the enemy.

For a time the battle languished, and then Napoleon brought up thirty-seven fresh squadrons of cavalry, and these, with the remains of those who had before charged, rode up the slope. But although they swept on and passed the British squares, they could not succeed in shaking them. A body of horse, however, sweeping down toward the Dutch and Belgians at the end of the line, these at once marched off the field without firing a musket, and the brigade of cavalry with them galloped away at full speed.

The position was a singular one; and had Napoleon ordered his infantry to advance in the rear of the cavalry, the issue of the day might have been changed. In appearance the French were masters of the position. Their masses of cavalry hid the British squares from sight. The British cavalry were too weak to charge, and most of the guns were in the possession of the French; but the latter's infantry were far away, and after sustaining the fire of the squares for a long time, the cavalry began to draw off. Lord Uxbridge now endeavored to persuade the Cumberland Hanoverian Hussars, who had not so far been engaged, to charge; but instead of obeying orders they turned and rode off, and never drew bridle until they reached Brussels, where they reported that the British army had been destroyed.

Adams' brigade were now brought up from the reserve, and drove back the French infantry and cavalry who had come up to the top of the crest beyond Hougoumont. On the other side Ney·sent a column against La Haye Sainte. The Germans made a gallant stand; but they were cut off from all assistance, outnumbered, and were altogether without ammunition; and although they defended themselves with their bayonets to the end, they were slain almost to a man, and La Haye Sainte was captured at last. But beyond this the French could not advance; and though column after column moved forward to the attack on the crest, they were each and all beaten back.

It was now nearly seven o'clock in the evening, and the Prussians were engaged at St. Lambert, Napoleon having detached Lobau's corps to arrest their progress. Their march had been a terrible one. They had to traverse country roads softened by the rain; the men were up to their ankles in mud, guns and carriages stuck fast, and it was not until after tremendous efforts that the leading squadron of their cavalry passed through the wood of Wavre and came in view of the battle that was raging. It was then past four o'clock, and another hour passed before any considerable number of infantry arrived. It was at this time Napoleon sent Lobau against them. He was able for a time to resist their advance; but as fresh troops came up from the rear the Prussians began to win their way forward, and Napoleon was obliged to send two more divisions of the Young Guard to check them.

He now saw that all was lost unless he could, before the whole of the Prussian army arrived, break down the resistance of the British. He therefore prepared for a final effort. Ney was to collect all his infantry, and, ad-

vancing past La Haye Sainte, to fall upon the center of
the British line. The guard, who had hitherto been
held in reserve, was to pass Hougoumont and attack the
left center. The cavalry were to follow in support.

A cannonade even more heavy and terrible than before,
for the guns of the reserve had been brought up, opened
upon the British, and the squares were now melting away
fast. But no reinforcements could be sent to them, for
the whole of the British troops were now in action, and
their allies had for the most part long before left the field.

Every gun was brought to the front, the remains of
the cavalry gathered together as a reserve; and some of
the Prussians now approaching the left, the cavalry
there were brought to the center to aid in the defense of
the threatened point. Just as these arrangements were
completed the enemy advanced in tremendous force from
the inclosure of La Haye Sainte, and with their fire so
completely mastered that of the remnants of the infantry,
that their light guns were brought up to within a hundred yards of the British line and opened with grape
upon the squares. Two Hanoverian battalions were almost
annihilated, the brigade of the German legion almost
ceased to exist.

A Brunswick cavalry regiment that had hitherto fought
gallantly lost heart and would have fled had not the British cavalry behind them prevented them from doing so.

In the meantime the Imperial Guard in two heavy
columns, led by Ney himself, were advancing, the guards
being followed by every available man of the infantry
and cavalry. One of these columns skirted the inclosure
of the Hougoumont, the other moved against the center.
They pressed forward until they reached the top of the
slope, and a hundred cannon were brought up and un-
limbered, while the artillery on the opposite slope rained

round shot and shell upon the British squares and artillery. The English guns tried in vain to answer them: they were wholly overmatched. Gun after gun was dismounted, horses and men destroyed; but as soon as the leading column of the guards reached the point when their own guns had to cease fire, the English artillery opened again, and terrible was the havoc they made in the dense columns. Still the guard pressed on until they reached the top of the crest; and then the British guards leaped to their feet and poured in a tremendous volley at close quarters, fell on the flank of the column, broke it, and hurled it down the hill.

The guards were recalled and prepared to oppose the second column, but their aid was not needed; the Fifty-second threw themselves upon its flank, the Seventy-first and Ninety-fifth swept its head with their volleys, and as the column broke and retired the Duke of Wellington gave the orders the men had been longing for since the fight began. The squares broke into lines, and the British, cheering wildly, descended the crest. The French retreat became a rout, cavalry and infantry fell upon them, the artillery plied them with their fire, the Prussians poured down upon their flank. By eight o'clock the splendid army of Napoleon was a mass of disorganized fugitives.

For ten hours the battle had raged. To the men in the squares it seemed a lifetime. "When shall we get at them? when shall we get at them?" was their constant cry as the round shot swept their ranks, although from their position behind the crest they could see nothing of their enemies. Nothing is harder than to suffer in inactivity, and the efforts of the officers were principally directed to appeasing the impatience of their men. "Our turn will come presently, lads." "Yes, but who

will be alive when it does come?'' a query which was
very hard to answer, as hour by hour the. ranks melted
away. Although they kept a cheerful countenance and
spoke hopefully to the men, it seemed to the officers
themselves that the prospect was well-nigh hopeless.
Picton's brigade mustered scarce half their strength
when the battle began. They were to have fought in the
second line this day; but the defection of their allies in
front of them had placed them in the front, and upon
them and upon the defenders of Hougoumont the brunt
of the battle had fallen, and as the squares grew smaller
and smaller it seemed even to the officers that the end
must come before long.

"This cannot last," Captain O'Connor said to Ralph
when the day was but half over. "They will never beat
us, but by the time they get here there will be nobody
left to beat. I don't think we are more than two hundred strong now, and every minute the force is diminish-
ing. I don't wonder the men are impatient. We bar-
gained for fighting, but I never reckoned on standing for
hours to be shot at without even a chance to reply."

It was just after this that the French cavalry burst
upon the squares; but this cheered rather than depressed
the spirits of the men. For a time they were free from
the artillery fire, and now had a chance of active work.
Thus as the fire flashed from the faces of the square the
men laughed and joked, and it was with regret that they
saw the cuirassiers fall back before the charge of Lord
Uxbridge's cavalry, for they knew that the moment this
screen was removed the French artillery would open
again.

Ralph's chief sensation was that of wonder that he was
alive; so overwhelming was the din, so incessant the rain
of shot, it seemed to him a marvel how any one could
remain alive within its range.

Almost mechanically he repeated the orders, "Close up, close up!" as the square dwindled and dwindled. He longed as impatiently as the men for the advance, and would have gladly charged against impossible odds rather than remain immovable under fire. When the order at length came he did not hear it. Just after the storm of fire that heralded the advance of the guards broke out, a round shot struck him high up on the left arm. He was conscious only of a dull, numbing sensation, and after that knew no more of what was taking place.

It was pitch dark before he became conscious. Fires were burning at various points along the ridge; for when the victory was complete the British retired to the position they had held so long, and the Prussian cavalry took up the pursuit. Fires had been lighted with broken gun carriages and shattered artillery wagons, and parties with torches were collecting the wounded. Ralph found that his head was being supported, and that a hand was pouring spirits and water down his throat. The hand was a shaky one, and its owner was crying loudly. As he opened his eyes the man broke into a torrent of thankful exclamations.

"The Lord be praised, Mr. Conway. Sure, I thought you were dead and kilt entirely."

"Is that you, Denis?"

"Sure and it's no one else, your honor."

"Is the battle over?"

"It is that. The French are miles away, and the Proosians at their heels."

"What has happened to me, Denis?"

"Well, your honor's hurt a bit in the arm, but it will all come right presently."

It was well for Ralph that he had been struck before

One 28th.   AT THE MOMENT OF VICTORY.—Page 370.

the order came for the advance, for as he fell the one surviving surgeon of the regiment had at once attended to him, had fixed a tourniquet on the stump of his arm, tied the arteries, and roughly bandaged it. Had he not been instantly seen to he would have bled to death in a few minutes.

Denis now called to one of the parties who were moving about with stretchers. Ralph was lifted on to it and carried to the village of Waterloo where he was placed in an ambulance wagon which, as soon as it was full, started for Brussels.

The fighting was now over, and Denis asked leave to accompany his master. The rout of the enemy had been so thorough and complete that it was not thought probable any serious resistance could be offered to the advance of the allied armies to Paris, and he therefore obtained leave without difficulty to remain with his master. Ralph suffered from exhaustion rather than pain on the journey to Brussels, and several times became almost unconscious. At four o'clock in the morning the ambulance stopped at a handsome house that its owner had placed at the disposal of the authorities for the use of wounded officers. He was carried upstairs and placed in bed in a room on the second story. Denis at once proceeded to install himself there. He brought down a mattress from a room above, laid it in the corner, throwing his greatcoat over it, then as soon as he thought the shops were open he hurried out and bought a kettle and saucepan, two cups and tumblers, a small basin, and several other articles.

"There, your honor," he said as he returned. "Now we have got iverything we need, and I can make soups and drinks for your honor, and boil myself a tater widout having to go hunting all over the house for the things to do it with."

A few minutes later two surgeons entered the room and examined Ralph's arm. They agreed at once that it was necessary to amputate it three inches higher up. Ralph winced when he heard the news.

"It won't hurt you very much," one of the surgeons said. "The nerves are all numbed with the shock they have had, but it is absolutely necessary in order that a neat stump may be made of it. The bone is all projecting now; and even if the wound healed over, which I don't think it would, you would have trouble with it all your life."

"Of course if it must be done, it must," Ralph said. "There isn't much left of it now."

"There is not enough to be of much use," the surgeon agreed; "but even a shorter stump that you can fit appliances on to will be a great deal more handy than one with which nothing can be done."

The operation was performed at once, and although Ralph had to press his lips hard together to prevent himself from crying out, he did find it less painful than he had expected.

"There, you will do now," the surgeon said. "Here, my man, take that basin and a tumbler and run downstairs to the kitchen. They will give you some broth there and some weak spirits and water. Bring them up at once."

Ralph took a spoonful or two of the broth, and a sip of the spirits, and then lay back and presently dozed off to sleep. Denis had followed the surgeons out of the room.

"What instructions is there, your honor?"

"Your master is just to be kept quiet. If he is thirsty give him some lemonade. You can obtain that or anything else you require below."

"And about myself, sir. I wouldn't speak about it but I have had nothing to eat since yesterday morning, and I don't like leaving Mr. Conway alone even to buy myself a mouthful."

"You will not have regular rations, but all officers' servants and orderlies will obtain food below. Meals will be served out at eight in the morning, one, and six. You take down your pannikin, and can either eat your food there or bring it up here as you choose. Breakfast will not be ready for two hours yet; but there are several others in the same plight as yourself, and you will find plenty to eat below."

Denis took his place by his master's bedside until he saw that he was sound asleep, then taking the pannikin from the top of the knapsack he stole noiselessly out, and in two or three minutes later he returned with the pannikin full of soup, a small loaf, and a ration of wine.

"By jabers," he said to himself as he sat down to eat them, "these are good quarters entirely. I should wish for nothing better if it wasn't for the master lying there. Lashings to eat and drink, and a room fit for a king. Nothing to do but to wait upon his honor. I suppose after to-day I shall be able to stale out for a few minutes sometimes for a draw of me pipe. It would never do to be smoking here. The master wouldn't mind it; but I expect them doctors would be for sending me back to my regiment if they were to come in and smell it."

After he had finished his meal, Denis took his seat by Ralph's bedside; but he was thoroughly exhausted. He had not slept a wink since the night before the battle, and after the fatigue of the day had been tramping all night by the side of the ambulance, which was constantly stopped by the numerous vehicles that had broken down or been overturned by the way. After waking up suddenly with a jerk once or twice, he muttered to himself, "I will just take five minutes on the bed, then I shall be all right again," and threw himself down on his mattress with his greatcoat for a pillow, and slept for several hours. So heavy was his slumber that he was not even roused when the surgeons came round at ten o'clock to see how Ralph was. He had just woke.

"How do you feel, Mr. Conway?"

"I feel quite comfortable," Ralph said, "but shall be glad of a drink. Where is my man?"

"He is asleep there in the corner," the surgeon said. "I will give you a drink of lemonade. The poor fellow is worn out, no doubt."

"Oh, yes; please don't wake him," Ralph said. "I am glad he is asleep; for he had all that terrible day yesterday, and was on his feet all night. I shan't want anything but this lemonade; and I have no doubt I shall go straight off to sleep again as soon as you have gone."

It was not until just one o'clock that Denis woke. He at once got up and went to Ralph's side. The latter opened his eyes.

"How do you feel now, your honor?"

"Oh, I am getting on very well, Denis. My arm hardly hurts me at all at present. I expect it will ache worse presently."

"I have been having a few minutes' sleep your honor. And now, if you don't want me for a minute, I will run down and see about breakfast. I should think it must be nearly ready."

"See about dinner, you mean, Denis. Why, it's just one o'clock."

"One o'clock! Your honor must be draming."

"I don't think so, Denis. There is my watch on the table."

"Why, your honor does not mean to say," Denis said
in great astonishment, "that I have been sleeping for five
hours? The watch must have gone wrong."

"The watch is right enough, Denis. I heard it strike
twelve by the church clocks before I dozed off last time.
Why, the surgeons came in at ten o'clock and gave me
some lemonade."

"And me to know nothing about it! Denis Mulligan,
you ought to be ashamed of yourself—slaping like a pig
in a stye, with your master laying wounded there beside
you, and no one to look after him. I just laid down for
five minutes' nap, your honor, seeing that you had gone
off into a beautiful sleep, and never dreamed of more
than that."

"It was the best thing you could do, Denis. You had
been twenty-four hours on your feet, and you would have
been fit for nothing if you hadn't had a good rest. Now
go downstairs and get your dinner, and when you come
back again you can bring me up a basin of broth and a
piece of bread. I begin to feel hungry; and that's a
capital sign, I believe."

When Ralph had finished his broth he said to Denis,
"I shan't want anything now for some time, Denis. You
can put a glass of lemonade within reach of my hand,
and then I shall do very well for an hour or two. I am
quite sure you must be dying for a pipe; so go out and
take a turn. It will freshen you up; and you can bring
me back what news you can gather as to the losses yesterday, and whether the army started in pursuit of the
French."

It was some time before Denis would consent to leave
the room; but at last, seeing that Ralph really wished it,
he went out for an hour, and returned full of the rumors
he had picked up of the terrible losses of the British,

and the utter rout of the French army. The next morning Ralph had a great surprise; for just as he had finished his breakfast there was a tap at the door, and a lady entered. Ralph could hardly believe his eyes as his mother ran forward to the bed. But the pressure of her arms and her kisses soon showed him that it was a reality.

"Why, mother darling!" he exclaimed, "how on earth did you get here?"

"I came across in a smack to Ostend, Ralph, and then came on by carriage. I got here last night, and learned at the quartermaster-general's office that you were wounded and were somewhere in Brussels, at least they believed you were here somewhere, but they could not say where. They let me have a copy of the list of the houses that had been allotted for the use of wounded officers. It was too late to begin the search last night, but I have been three hours going round this morning. I saw the surgeon downstairs and he told me—" and her lips quivered and her eyes filled with tears.

"That I had lost my left arm, mother. Well, that is nothing to fret about when thousands have been killed. One can do very well without a left arm; and I think, on the whole, that I have been wonderfully lucky. Denis!" But Denis was not in the room, having, as soon as he had discovered who Ralph's visitor was, gone out to leave them alone. "And have you made this journey all by yourself, mother?"

"No, my dear. Mr. Tallboys was good enough to come over to take care of me by the way."

"Mr. Tallboys, mother! How did he know that you were coming?"

"Well, I told him, Ralph. But that is a long story, and you shall hear it another day. The doctor said you

had better not do much talking now. Mr. Tallboys will
stay here a day or two and then go home. I intend to
take a room somewhere close by and install myself here
as your head nurse."

"I shan't want much nursing, mother; but I shall be
delighted to have you with me. I have a capital servant.
The man I told you about in my letters. He is a most
amusing fellow and very much attached to me. Do you
know, he got leave directly the battle was over, and was
all night walking by the side of the ambulance wagon.
He is a capital fellow. By the way, mother, I suppose
the will has not turned up yet? You said in your last
letter you had great hopes of its being found."

"It has been found, Ralph; and it is all just as we
supposed. But how it was found, or anything about it,
you mustn't ask at present. It is a long story, and I
must insist now that you lie quiet and go to sleep."

"Well, I will try, mother. Will you just look outside
the door and see if Denis is there? Denis, this is my
mother," he said as the soldier came in. "She has come
over to help nurse me; and as she will be principally
with me in the daytime, you will be at liberty to be out
whenever you like."

"Sure, and I am glad the lady has come, Mr. Conway;
though I would have done the best I could for you.
Still, a man is but a poor crater in a sick-room. Can I
get you anything ma'am?"

"Well, I have had nothing this morning, Denis; and
if you could get me a cup of tea and some bread and
butter, if it is not against the rules, I should be very
glad."

"Sure, I will do that, ma'am, with the greatest pleasure in life," Denis said; and presently returned bring
up a tray with tea, bread and butter, and a plate of cold
meat.

"Is there anything else, ma'am?"

"Well, Denis, I should be very much obliged if you will take a note from me to a gentleman named Tallboys, whom you will find at the Hotel de L'Europe. Give it to him yourself if you can. He will be glad to hear from you about my son, how he is going on and so on."

For the next few days Ralph's arm was exceedingly painful, attended by a certain amount of fever. At the end of that time he began to improve, and his wound made steady progress toward recovery. After staying for four days at Brussels, Mr. Tallboys had returned home. Mrs. Conway and Denis divided the nursing between them, sitting up on alternate nights.

A fortnight after Mrs. Conway's arrival Ralph said, "Now, mother, I shall be up to-morrow and can therefore be considered as fairly convalescent, so there can be no reason now why you should not tell the story about the finding of the will. You told me in one of your letters before Christmas that Mr. Tallboys had failed altogether. So how did it come to be found?"

Mrs. Conway thereupon told the story. When she came to the point where she had gone as a servant to the Hall, Ralph interrupted her with a loud protest. "I don't like that, mother; I don't like the idea of your having gone as a servant, whatever the stake was. If I had been at home and had known it, I certainly would not have let you go, not if there had been ten fortunes to be gained by it. The idea of your having to go and live as a servant, and work for people like that is horrid!"

"There was nothing very unpleasant about it, Ralph. I had plenty to do and to think about, and the time passed a great deal more rapidly than it would have done if I had been staying at home all by myself. It would have been very lonely and dull then; and I can assure you that I considered it no hardship at all being at the Hall. But you must not interrupt me in my story. If you do I shall tell you nothing more about it until you get home to England."

This threat effectually sealed Ralph's lips, and beyond occasional exclamations he said nothing until the story was ended.

"Well, it's all very wonderful, mother," he said; "and I should never have thought for a moment that you were so brave, and could have put things together like that, and could have carried out such a scheme. But I am awfully glad you have succeeded; because you had set your mind on it, and the money will I hope make you quite comfortable. How much was it after all mother? You never told me that."

"It is half of Mr. Penfold's estates, and of the money he had invested, which is a very large sum, Ralph; although I do not know how much."

"Half the estate! Why, it will make me quite a rich man. I never dreamed it was anything like that. I thought most likely it was enough to continue the allowance that he said he should make me. Why, mother, it is tremendous! And what becomes of the other half?"

"That is left to Mabel Withers, Ralph. You two divide everything that he left."

"Well, that certainly is rather hard upon his sisters," Ralph said; "and I don't blame them for being against it. Though, of course, it was not right to keep the will hidden."

"Mr. Penfold did not leave anything to them, because they are both very well provided for. Their father left them a handsome sum at his death; and as they have been living at the Hall ever since, and can have spent nothing, they must be very amply provided for. Their brother, therefore, naturally considered he was perfectly at liberty to leave his property as he chose. I do not think the Miss Penfolds have the slightest reason to grumble, after living as they have done for the last twenty years at their brother's expense."

"Of course that makes a difference," Ralph agreed; "it certainly didn't seem nice that Mabel and I, who are no relation by blood to Mr. Penfold, should come into the property that his sisters expected would be theirs. But, of course, now you explain it, it is different."

"I do not think in any case, Ralph, Mr. Penfold would have left his fortune to his sisters. He was a man very averse to exerting his own will, and I am sure that he submitted to, rather than liked, his sisters' residence at the Hall. I know that he considered, and justly, that they had once committed a cruel wrong upon him, and had in a way spoiled his life. I question whether he really ever forgave them."

"I see, mother," Ralph said. "Well, now, about myself; I should think there can be no occasion for me to continue in the army unless I like?"

"I hope you won't like, Ralph. In the first place I want to have you with me; and in the second, you will be a large landowner, and property has its duties."

"Well, there is no necessity to decide about that at present. The doctor said yesterday I should certainly get three months' sick leave before I rejoined. By all we hear the fighting is at an end, and there is no fear whatever that Napoleon will have it in his power to cause trouble in the future. They will take care of that, whatever they do with him. If there is going to be peace everywhere, I do not know that I should care very much about staying in the army; but, as I said, we need not decide at present."

Ten days later, Ralph was so far recovered that he was able to return home with his mother. As soon as she informed him of her arrival at Dover, Mr. Tallboys wrote to tell her that he had had an interview in London with the Miss Penfolds' lawyer, who informed him that he had instructions from his clients to examine the will, and if satisfied of its genuineness, to offer no opposition whatever to its being proved. Mr. Tallboys had thereupon shown him the will, and had no difficulty in convincing him that it was the document he himself had drawn up, and Mr. Penfold had signed in his presence.

The lawyer has placed all the deeds and documents relating to Mr. Penfold's property in my hands, and, as I was of course before well aware, my late client died worth a very considerable property in addition to his large estates in this country. For the last twenty years his income has exceeded his expenditure by an average of three thousand a year, and as the surpluses have been judiciously invested, and as the prices of all funds and stocks now stand vastly higher than they did during the course of the long war, their total value now amounts to something over a hundred and thirty thousand pounds.

"The property in this country was valued, at the time Mr. Penfold drew up his will, at eighty thousand pounds; these estates he left to your son, and the sum of eighty thousand pounds, in various investments, to Miss Withers, and directed that the residue, whatever it might be at his death, should be equally divided between them. Your son's share, therefore, will amount to about twenty-five thousand pounds. I may say that the outlying farms, which were settled by deed as a security for the four hundred pounds annually paid to you, are not included in the above valuation, but are ordered to revert to the main estate upon your decease.

"The formalities will all be completed in the course of a short time. I may say that from the totals to be divided must be deduted the legacy duties, which, as your son and Miss Withers are strangers by blood to the testator, will be heavy." Mr. Tallboys added that he heard the younger Miss Penfold was now recovering from her serious illness, but it was not probable she would ever be again herself. He had received, he said, a letter that morning from their solicitor, saying that as soon as Miss Eleanor Penfold could be moved, which it was hoped would be in the course of another week, the ladies would vacate possession of the Hall.

A fortnight later Mrs. Conway and Ralph left Dover for London, leaving orders with an agent to sell the furniture of their house. All Ralph's old friends on the shore had been made happy with handsome presents. After a short stay in London they went down, and Ralph took possession of the Hall. He soon found there was abundance of occupation for his time on the estate, and that this would be increased when, as would doubtless be the case, he was placed on the Commission of Peace for the county, as Herbert Penfold had been before him.

As soon as Ralph had completely recovered his health and strength he told his mother that she must spare him for a week, as he had promised that he would on the first opportunity go over to Dunkirk to see his friend Jacques.

He crossed by the packet from Dover to Calais, and thence by coach to Dunkirk. Here he inquired among the fishermen for Jacques, and found that he had returned before Napoleon broke out from Elba, and that he was owner of a fishing smack which was now at sea. The next day Jacques returned, and his delight at meeting Ralph was unbounded. He took him home to his neat cottage where his pretty young wife was already installed. Ralph remained two days with him, and obtained a promise from him that he would once a year sail over to Weymouth and pay him a visit.

"I am a rich man, Jacques, now. At present I see you want nothing, but should any accident befall your fishing boat, or you have need for money for any other cause, write to me, and the money for a new boat or for any other purpose shall be yours at once. I could afford to give you a hundred boats without hurting myself, so do not hesitate for a moment in letting me know if I can help you. It will be a real pleasure to me to do so."

Jacques kept his promise, and never missed coming over once year to pay Ralph a visit, and as his five sons one after another grew up to be able to manage boats for themselves, they were each presented one by Ralph. Jacques himself prospered as a fisherman, and never required the assistance Ralph would have been glad to give him.

Neither Ralph nor Mabel Withers was informed of the expression of Mr. Penfold's hopes in his will that they would some day be married, the two mothers agreeing cordially that nothing was so likely to defeat the carrying out of Mr. Penfold's wishes as for the young people to have any suspicions of them. They were still but boy and girl, and were now perfectly happy in their unrestrained intercourse, for not a day passed that the two families did not see something of each other; but had they had a suspicion of the truth it would have rendered them shy and awkward with each other, and have thrown them much more widely apart.

"We both hope that it will come about, Mrs. Conway," Mrs. Withers said one day; "and I certainly think there is every prospect of it. Let us leave well alone, and allow it to come about naturally and without interference."

As soon as Ralph left the army he purchased Denis Mulligan's discharge, and the Irishman was installed as butler and Ralph's special servant at the Hall, and remained in his service to the end of his life.   In due time the natural change in the relations between the two young people came about, and their youthful friendship ripened into love.   When Ralph was twenty-three, and Mabel had just come of age, she changed her name and took up her place at the Hall, Mrs. Conway gladly handing over the reins of government to her.   She herself lived with her children, for she was almost as fond of Mabel as of Ralph, to the end of a long life; and deep was the regret among her children and grandchildren when she was at last laid in Bilston Church, close to the resting-place of Herbert Penfold.

THE END.